Eddy's Story

by Caroline Smith

Table of Contents

Eddy's Story is a biography of my father. The names of himself and his family are true but parts of the story as to friends and events have been fictionalized and the names of those people with whom he lived and interacted are fictional.

Dedication:

To My brother Brian who began the research and follow-up that led to Eddy's story
And to my husband Tony who spent countless hours reading, reviewing and critiquing my story.

Acknowledgements:

From the time that my father revealed his background as a British Home Child to my brother Brian to the writing of this story, there are so many people to thank. My brother was able to contact our brothers in Asheville whom we did not know existed until after my father's death. He found my father's siblings still alive in England. And subsequent visits and continued correspondence and phone calls with my cousin Roderick have opened up so much of my father's story.

I wish to thank my sister Noeline for her ongoing encouragement throughout the writing of this story. And I must mention my husband Tony again for his insight, his knowledge especially of London dialogue and cockney rhyming slang and his work in reviewing each chapter, formatting my story and being there every step of the way.

I am indebted to Shawnee Sue Steeves and Ethel Bellevue, my writing partners who have been with me throughout most of my writing for their invaluable suggestions, critiques and help. I am indebted also to the AX Writing group in Sussex and to Choice Cuts where I shared various chapters of my story.

In addition, I wish to thank Bruce and Susan Armstrong and Gary Denniss for their help and hospitality in introducing me to the people and the places where my father lived and played as a boy.

I wish to thank the Dr. Barnardo Homes, still in operation, for the information package sent to me in which I found valuable information of my father's early years, both when he first arrived at the home and throughout his stay in Bracebridge, Ontario.

Preface

Eddy's Story began when my father gathered us around a roaring fire and with ample cups of tea or hot cocoa told us the tales of the Land of Plenty. His land was the great Muskoka woods where he lived as a child from 1910 to 1919. We met and loved the characters he created. There was Minnie the Owl, Great Claws and Swiftfoot, the eagles, John Squirrel and Harry the hare and many others. Every story which he made up on the spot was filled with adventure and every time he began, he would say, "Now remember the last time when Minnie was searching for John Squirrel, well"..and a new story would begin and the plot would become more tangled and suspenseful.

Dad was resourceful, imaginative and a fine spinner of yarns. He had a twinkle in his eye and he could reduce us to spasms of laughter with his imitations of people. He worked at being a house painter. He had been a merchant marine for many years but now that he had his own hundred acres, he bought an old truck when he could finally afford it and he managed to get a tractor. After so much heart ache as a little boy working for a harsh task master, he finally had what he had always wanted; a place of his own, freedom to do as he pleased and time to play at the fiddle, write letters to the editor and be at peace.

We had recently immigrated as a family to a rural place on the Bay of Fundy called Mispec in Saint John County. We arrived from Wales on the SS Acquitania at the port of Halifax in October 1947. I was 9. There was our mother, Lena and my 2 brothers, Brian and Warren. My name is Caroline. My sister Noeline was the only child born in Canada.

We lived in the home my father built from 1947. My father lived there until his death in July 1983. Between the time that my father was sent to Canada in 1910 and the time when he returned to Canada with a family in tow in 1947, much had happened. Eddy's story, the one you are about to read, is Dad's early story which really begins in London in 1902 and after this, there is another vital circuitous story of what happens after he gets on a ship in Montreal and returns to England in 1919.

But that would be another book.

Chapter One: Confused

It was a cold damp morning in London. The day was January 3, 1910. Edward George held his mother's hand as they boarded the tram to Stepney Causeway to the Dr. Thomas Barnardo Home for boys.

They called him Eddy. He was a clever boy, a little mischievous, handsome at seven years of age with dark curly hair and piercing dark brown eyes. Some said he was a "bit of a handful."

Eddy watched with fascination as the wires guiding the tram along seemed to make a whirring sound like the wind. It was like a magic show. He had never been in a tram before.

His mother didn't say much and Eddy was too busy looking out the window watching the Tower of London and St. Paul's Cathedral whizz by. Before long, they came to a stop and Eddy followed his mother as she stepped down. They climbed down the steps to the pavement and began walking up the street alive with horses, trams, an occasional motor car and people. Everywhere there were people, young and old, commoner and aristocrat, street beggar and priest. It seemed like a circus but still everyone went about their daily business without a thought for the other. It was a busy city, the largest in the world, and people were coming in droves to find work, to go to school or just to watch the puppet shows in the square. The vendors yelled out their wares and Eddy wanted more than anything one of those bright red lollipops at the costermongers. His mother took his hand and hurried him along.

"Where are we going, Mum?"

She didn't answer but she squeezed his hand a little tighter while holding her feathered hat down to stop it from flying off. The wind had come up whipping the flags that draped the poles along the busy street. She pulled her skirt and petticoat tight against her body. They had an appointment at one o'clock and they could not be late. Eddy pulled his hand out from his mother's tight grasp and yanked at her skirt.

"I'm cold."

"Just walk a bit faster, Eddy. That will warm you up."

"But, but, where are we going?"

"Hush up, Eddy."

They rounded the corner, near the railway tracks and there, taking up a whole block was a large imposing building. It was grey and stark like its surroundings.

It looked a bit like a factory but a bit like a palace too with its turret, on top of which flew the Union Jack, the pride of the Empire.

They walked up to the door on the far left end of the building and rang the doorbell. After a few minutes a kindly old man beckoned them in. Bowing like a footman, he ushered them into a large reception room with heavy drapery and overstuffed chairs. In the corner, there was another seating arrangement for children. The chairs were smaller and made of wood. Eddy was told to sit there. A prim woman probably in her mid fifty's beckoned Eddy's mother to her desk in the foyer.

"You are late, Miss Tompkins. We were expecting you at one o'clock sharp. We run this place like clockwork."

Eddy's mother shuddered a little at the calling out of "Miss" but no matter.

"Is everything alright?"

"Yes, Miss Tompkins. It's all arranged."

"Thank you."

She stepped back for a moment and then walked over to her little boy. She tried to smile but her lips quivered a little. "I'll be back, Eddy, with some nice sweets for you. It won't be long. Be a good boy."

 (Eddy had just been admitted to the Dr. Barnardo's Home for Boys at 18 Stepney Causeway in the Ratcliff area of east London.)

"Come along, boy," said the matron, "We're going upstairs to take your picture."

"Where's my Mum? I want to go home."

 He didn't cry. He knew that crying only made things worse."Big boys don't cry." his father said.

He missed his Dad but something had happened. He knew that. There was a new baby brother and that was the last straw. At least that's what he thought he heard when he thought about it.

Eddy walked in silence up three flights of dark stairs. Another boy, a bit older than him, was in front of him and the matron pushed them along. Finally, they reached the top of the building and were ushered into a dark room that contained an oak chair with sturdy arms and a large camera on a tripod.

Eddy stood in the doorway while the older boy sat in the chair.

"The photographer will be here shortly. Joseph, you will be first because you are older."

Just as matron stepped out, Joseph jumped up and pushed Eddy to the floor. "What are you doing here? You stupid kid! Did they catch you under the arches? They found me in the warehouse. I'm tough and I'm going to watch you closely. You rotten ugly orphan!"

"I'm not an orphan. I've got a Mum and Dad. And I've got a brother, James, a sister, Beatrice and a baby brother, Arthur. Me Mum's gone to get me sweets. She'll be back shortly. You won't be able to touch me. You'll see."

A tear started down Eddy's cheek. He pulled himself to his feet just as the photographer arrived.

Chapter 2: A difficult time

It was two o'clock and the sun had broken through the tiny window in the studio. Eddy loved the sun and there had been too much rain lately. He had no idea what was happening to him but the man had given him a wink when he passed him in the hall. He was tall and he sported a beard and mustache. He could be a magician or a photographer, Eddy thought.

Eddy watched through the open door as the man arranged the camera on the tripod. It looked like a large wooden box. Next to it was a tall light fixture and on the table were a number of items organized for the sitting.

Eddy remembered a man on his street with a similar box. He had taken a picture of Eddy and his friends playing marbles near Westminster Bridge. He seemed businesslike but he had stopped to talk to the children even if he might have been in a hurry to some important event.

The cameraman moved a large armchair a few feet in front of the camera and he marked the floor with an X.

The matron whose name was Miss Perkins kept a close watch of the two boys, particularly Joseph who had been fidgeting in his chair. It was the first day in this strange place for both boys. And they were the first of the children to be admitted that day. It was the custom for all boys to be photographed immediately after the necessary papers had been drawn up downstairs. Joseph was wearing shabby clothes and he probably had neither washed nor eaten for a while. Eddy was wearing a neat boys' outfit which his mother had probably sewn. Eddy continued to watch what he could of the photographer as he set the stage for taking pictures.

"Joseph, you are first, remember. Before you go in, here is an outfit to put on. Go into that room with the wash basin and wash your face and hands. Then take off what you are wearing and put them in that box in the corner. You can't have your picture taken with those rags."

"Ah don't want to change. Ah just want to go back where I came from before they rescued me. I didn't want to be rescued. I liked it the way it was."

"You will do as you're told."

Eddy listened but paid no mind. He was too interested in the photographer and the adventure. He might be a cameraman, some day, or maybe a magician which he liked even more.

Joseph stepped into the studio looking like a little gentleman. He was a handsome lad really once he was cleaned up. He glanced at Eddy and by the way he cocked his head Eddy could see that the boy rather liked the way he looked with his blond hair and striking blue eyes and nice new trousers, shirt and cardigan. For a moment at least, he was special.

Joseph took his seat in front of the camera man and the picture taking began. Eddy had turned away by then because Miss Perkins insisted on wiping off the tears that had dried on his face. She straightened his Eaton collar and told him to pull up his socks.

It was now Eddy's turn. Miss Perkins guided him into the studio and the camera man beckoned him to sit on the chair. It was so tall that Eddy's feet did not reach the floor.

"Rest your right hand on the chair arm, Eddy. That's your name, isn't it?"

"Yep."

The camera man smiled. He couldn't help but wonder about the child, all alone in this institution and only seven years old. Such a pretty boy with dark wavy hair and dark eyes. He could not allow his emotions to get in the way. He was the official photographer of the Dr. Barnardo Home at Stepney Causeway and this was the Stepney Causeway Studio.

Eddy watched as the camera man took out the frosted plate and inserted the camera plate in preparation. The lens was focused on the little boy.

"Look at the camera, Eddy."

"Snap."

The man squeezed Eddy's hand as he passed him a lollipop whispering, "Don't say anything. Put it in your pocket for later."

The picture taking over, the boys were ushered down the stairs to a waiting room. Then they were escorted to the dormitory in the building next door. A smiling chamber maid met them at the door.

"Good morning, Miss Perkins. The beds are ready for the new boys."

"I'll show you your beds just for a minute. You are meeting with the head matron and some of the boys that will share the dormitory with you."

"What!" Joseph shouted." I want to go home."

"You have no home to go to." glared Miss Perkins her face rigid, pulled tight by the grey knot at the back of her head.

"But I do." said Eddy. "Please, miss, may I see my mother?"

Joseph was about to shove him but he stopped.

"When ar' ya gonna feed us?"

"Right after you meet the governor and don't be rude 'cause they'll knock that out of you very quickly."

"Na, they won't."

Eddy started to cry.

"Where's my Mum? Where's my little sister?"

Joseph moved over beside Eddy and even though he could be mean and cruel, he felt a twinge of pity for the little boy.

"Ah, com wiv me mate. A'll show you what's what."

They looked about at the large room filled to the brim with metal frame beds, all made up exactly with the same with a sheet and coarse blanket.

"Come along now. We're going downstairs."

The first day in this huge place was frightening for a little boy. He was confused and very, very tired. All he could think of was home and he missed his little sister Beatrice. She was always smiling and he loved being her big brother especially when they went to the park to play. Actually the park was a bit of grass across the railway tracks beside his home but they could sit there near the river and watch the ships come in and out. He would take her by the hand and walk there. His mother was too busy with her sewing to even look up to see if they were still in the small parlour sitting on the floor after their breakfast of cold porridge. So they could just slip away.

Now, he was surrounded by quick marching boys, yelling matrons and surly older boys who seemed to be in charge.

By now, Joseph was fuming. He stamped his feet and clenched his fists.

"Ah'm goin' to bolt this place. You'll see."

The tall fat boy who was marching the children down the hall stopped and stamped his feet. Sharply turning around, he stood in front of the new boy and bellowed.

"You shape up or I'll send you to the master for discipline and it won't be funny."

Eddy just kept walking through another long hall on which hung dour pictures of clergymen and the doctor himself. What was happening? Where was he? Where was his mother? She had said she was coming back with some sweets but it was already night and she was afraid to venture out.

"I miss Beatrice", he said.

" Don' ya worry none. 'Ya'll see her soon. A'll see to that." said Joseph.

Gone was the mean boy he had met earlier by the cameraman's studio. Joseph had taken Eddy under his wing. He would make sure Eddy was safe.

Eddy had never walked so much nor climbed up and down so many stairs. His legs could hardly reach from one to the other and he was fed up with this walking. The matron pushed him into another hall and as he travelled down what seemed like an endless tunnel, he finally thought he smelled food. "Maybe, its mashed potatoes and gravy." he thought. Joseph, only a few steps ahead, picked up his feet in an effort to run.

"Slow down, boy." shouted the matron, but by this time his feet had a mind of their own.

"Tha're gonna give us sum grub, Eddy. Hurry up."

They rounded the corner and came into a large room filled with tables and boys. Matron sat them at the table close to the front. "You will sit here for every meal from now on. Now mind your manners." She turned away and returned to the lobby.

Everything was set, even a placemat on which their numbers was written. Eddy's was Tompkins 104 . He was given a coarsely woven napkin and told to sit quietly. The overseer, a short man wearing a clerical corner, rose up. "All stand! And repeat after me, for what we are about to receive, make us truly thankful!"

The hall echoed with the noise of many boys, all of different sizes, all rising from their chairs. In gaudy unison, their voices spoke the lines. "For what we are about to receive, make us truly thankful."

"I wanna know what a'm eatin' first." said Joseph.

Eddy shuddered. He knew what could happen if you dared to be that bold. James, his elder brother had sassed his father just once and he got the back end of his hand right across his face. Joseph sensing Eddy's discomfort said no more. Luckily the noise of the boys' movements in rising and shuffling must have drowned out his words because no adult looked his way.

"You may sit down."

The thunder of the seating quieted to a whisper as the maids brought the food plates to the table.

The Boys' Home Time Table was strict. Breakfast at 7 AM sharp, Dinner at 12 and afternoon Tea at 5 o'clock.

This must have been the 5 o'clock sitting. Eddie had not eaten since his mother had served him a bowl of porridge at their Lambeth flat before she dressed him in his best suit for the journey.

The plate was sparsely covered with mashed potatoes with a bit of gravy, a thin slice of beef and some turnips and carrots. On the side were a slice of white bread with drippings, a cup of tea and a small bowl of pudding.

Eddy picked up his fork and began to pick at the food. Joseph was almost finished before Eddy had even started. There was very little chatter except for the sounds of over 400 hungry boys having the last meal of the day. Eddy just went through the motions. He felt so very much alone.

"Get moving you lot. It's vesper time in the chapel."

"Yes, sirs" they chanted like an ill trained choir and they rose in unison too. All except Eddy and Joseph that is. Eddy was asleep in his hard wooden chair. Joseph sat still beside him not getting up like the rest.

"We'll have none of that." The head boy yanked Eddy's hands and pulled him up.

"Hey, can't ya see the boy's tired. Leave 'im alone."

"How dare you speak to me like that".

Joseph protested but there was no stopping the march and into the chapel they were herded.

The hymns were sung and prayers were monotonously said and Eddy fell asleep again. He awoke with a start with a smack on his back and he sleep walked up the stairs to the dormitory which would be his sleeping quarters for the next several months.

Over the dormitory door was the label, 'Aberdeen House' and at the doorway was an older boy. Eddy learned later that he was the Head prefect for this house. His name was Harris. Eddy couldn't know but this was set up like a poor man's version of Eton or Harrow, with their system of headmasters, masters, head boys and prefects. This was all much too confusing. Eddy stared to sob. He was inconsolable and the prefect was having none of it.

"Chin up, 'ol boy. We'll teach ya the ropes but right now, you're going to bed."

Eddy stumbled as he made his way through the maize. A hundred boys slept in this room. There was hardly space between beds and he was lost among all the chatter and confusion. He couldn't stop crying. "Mum, Mum."

The prefect just wanted to get this over. "Here's your bed, Tompkins, It's yours while you're here. Step up sharply boy."

The beds were high off the floor and Eddy had to climb up the two steps on the side. Someone brought a warm blanket to spread over him and a little boy about his own age came over to his side and whispered, "It will be okay. It's not all that bad. You'll see."

Eddy looked around for Joseph but Joseph being older was in another room. He had been afraid of Joseph at first. But, he knew that Joseph had a good heart because he had kept him close in those first few hours. He missed him.

The room was long and narrow. The wall was white, the sheets were white and the lights were white. But Eddy had fallen fast asleep and mercifully he could dream in colour. He didn't know if he was asleep or awake. The day just passed had been a whirlwind of commands. It all came to him as though in a dream.

Chapter 3: Remembering

Day Two dawned. The boys were awakened by the sharp ringing of a bell. It echoed through the huge and sparse room full of boys. There was hardly any room between the beds. Eddy woke with a start. He had been dreaming and he didn't want to leave his bed in the flat.

He shared the bed with his big brother James and his little sister Beatrice. In the corner was his new baby brother, Arthur. His mother slept next to the cradle. They were cozy together and, in the winter especially, they cuddled together for warmth. There was a coal fireplace and when they could afford it, the fire was kept alight all night and the flickering flames were like a moving picture book. Eddy loved to watch it and it soothed him to sleep. There had been a time when the coal man came every week to deliver the precious fuel. There was a time when the milkman came every day and life was good. His father Teddy, after whom he was named, stayed with them and at night he told them stories of giants and dragons. He would make them come to life as he took on each character.

"Once upon a time, in a land of mirrors, there lived a fairy queen. She loved to look at herself in the mirror so much that she decided to have mirrors placed all over the city and even out in the country but, one day, a wicked giant came to the palace and demanded that all the mirrors be taken away. He was a hideous creature with only one eye, a long nose and ears the size of boots. He hated to look at himself."

Teddy was a ticket agent at Euston Station but secretly he was a busker and often he would entertain folks at the park. It was a secret that the children kept. If his boss knew, he would be fired. So they kept the secret and Eddy never breathed a word.

His mother, Ellen, worked from dawn to dusk. She designed and created dresses for elegant ladies who lived in the fine homes of London. Her fingers were red with sewing and sometimes she was short tempered. She and Teddy lived together but were not married. There used to be laughter in their home but now with the birth of the new baby, Teddy had moved out and they had to manage on their own.

"Where is Daddy?"

"He'll be back soon. He is away on holiday, Eddy. You don't need to worry none."

Suddenly a bell jarred the silence. It was louder than Big Ben that tolled the time every hour near where Eddy had lived with his parents.

"Eddy. Get up and get dressed. It's time to go for breakfast."

He rubbed his eyes and looked around. He stumbled about looking for his clothes forgetting that he had on a night shirt and then he remembered that the chamber maid had taken off his street clothes and he had no idea where they were.

Lucy, the maid who was busy helping one of the boys, could see that Eddy was searching for something so she turned her back on the child and moved over to Eddy's side of the bed.

"What's up matey? Are you lost?"

"I don't know what to wear. My street clothes are gone."

"Dan't worry. I got your new clothes ready in a box under the bed. We'll get you dressed. Cours', you'll all look the same. Navy blue trousers, light blue shirt and navy cardigan. And navy blue socks."

"Mum's comin' to get me so give me my old clothes back."

"Sorry, Eddy, you are one of us now. Your Mum's not comin' back."

Eddy climbed back on the bed and curled up like a hedgehog and sobbed.

The head prefect was having none of this. He shoved Lucy aside and forced Eddy to get dressed. "I'll have none of this sobbing. You will get dressed. Now!" and after pulling on his clothes, he grabbed Eddy's arm and marched him down to breakfast.

Sobbing did him no good and he was hungry He was used to porridge at home. But at least he had a slice of bread with butter and a cup of tea.

Chores were next. It would be the same every day from now on. Even the little boys had work assigned.

The overseer was the head of the kitchen staff and his most hated job was teaching the new boys how to keep the dining and kitchen area clean. In his estimation, the new recruits, as he called them, were completely useless so instruction had to be swift and sharp. Beckoning Eddy towards him, he called out. "Hey you boy. Come here. We've all got jobs and yours is scrubbing down the tables."

Eddy stumbled towards him. Trembling, he said," What do I have to do?"

"Work for your keep boy. That's what ya got to do. "Here" he said as he shoved the scrubbing brush in Eddy's hand. "You're going to scrub every one of these tables."

He put his burly hand over Eddy's tiny one and pressed down so hard that Eddy yelped like a puppy in pain" Keep the brush moving like this, do ya hear?" He didn't let up until Eddy could do it on his own. Eddy squirmed and winced but he knew he had to do it or he would have this brute's hand on his again.

"I hate him." he whispered but he did not cry. This was to be his job every morning after breakfast and he was learning that he had to do what he was told. He would have to get used to order. Everything was controlled by the bell. A bell to wake up. A bell for breakfast.

At 9 o'clock, the boys were marched to the playground or drill field as they came to call it. Morning drill was designed to keep the boys fit.

"A healthy mind in a healthy body." was Dr. Barnardo's motto.

The head prefect of Aberdeen House herded his boys into his circle. The other houses took their place as well. The prefect was tall. His hair was blond but the handsome boy with the voice of a sergeant upset Eddy. His eyes could pierce a target like a spear. Eddy had already seen him bossing a small boy with such ferocity that the child put his head down and squashed himself into the floor. He was the one who terrified the younger boys as they were getting prepared for bed the night before. And he was the one who pushed him about before breakfast. Discipline and order was everything. It had to be with that many boys to handle.

"One, two, One, two!"

They marched first in a circle then all around the compound. Then feet together and feet apart, they jumped in unison clapping their hands with each movement. Eddy was out of step but so were all the new boys. He stumbled but caught his balance.

"Tompkins, straighten up!"

Eddy wasn't having any of this. He had to stand up to bullies on the street even if they were bigger than he. He summoned the courage to say, "Don't wanna. I ain't in prison."

"You will be boy, if I hear any sass from you."

Eddy felt his chest tighten and his fists clench.

"Wher's me mum? I wanna go home."

"You ain't got a home to go to. Yar mum ain't comin' back. Never."

"What did this punk know about his mother?" he said to himself.

He looked for Joseph. He wanted to yell. He wanted to run. He wanted to yell obscenities. He knew the street words for "Get away from me" but he straightened up like a soldier.

"Get back in line, boy. March. Math class next!"

Eddy joined the rest and marched around the field. He had no choice. Inside his head he knew he would have to learn the hard way. He had lived by his wits on the street. Now, he would have to follow rules and toe the line.

Chapter 4: Getting used to classes and routine

The second day had started with breakfast and Morning Prayer. It would be followed every day by the routine of chores, drill and school. The younger boys would have some classes and story time in the Library. The older boys would be sent to the shops at the back of the building where they would learn a trade. There was a need for tailors, carpenters, brush makers and shoemakers as well as bakers and printers. It was the rule of the land for boys to go to school half time so the morning was spent learning the 3 R's, Reading, Writing and 'Rithmatic. The other half was spent in the shop.

At 10 o'clock sharp on Eddy's third day the bell sounded even louder than the day before. The boys were ushered into a large classroom. There were books on the shelves, a blackboard at the front and slates on every table. The master, a kindly older man stood at the front of the room behind what seemed like a pulpit, the kind he had seen in church. He was dressed formally and he held a pointer in his hand. Eddy had never been in a classroom before but the idea fascinated him. He wanted to learn to read. His father read when he wasn't telling stories and Eddy loved the look of a special picture book his father had read with stories like Jack and the Bean Stalk. He loved the pictures mostly.

The master put down his pointer and announced that they would begin their studies in subtraction. And then he winked. "I've had a change of heart. We'll do Maths tomorrow." He picked up a leather bound book labeled 'Greek Myths for Children' and laid it on the pulpit in front of him and began to read. The story he chose was 'Ulysses' and his voyage home from Troy. The teacher's voice was smooth and pitched just right for the children. He was old but he made the story come alive. Eddy followed every word and every dialogue. He could picture Ulysses in his boat sailing the green blue sea watching for sea serpents as they sailed towards their island home of Ithaca. The boys sat still as the master came to the end of the chapter and closed the big book. "Tomorrow" he said, "we will learn about the Cyclops with one eye but that will be after learning how to subtract numbers."

Eddy spent his third afternoon learning to make his bed. Lucy, the kind chamber maid taught him how. She was sweet and pretty with golden curls, rosy cheeks and a pleasant smile.

Eddy stood at his bed along with Arthur, his next over bed mate with the same name as Eddy's baby brother, and Gordon, Arthur's older brother, who was next in the line. "Take this white sheet and stretch it over the bed. You can work together you three. Your hands are too small on your own."

They pulled the sheet down over the mattress on all four sides and tucked it in as Lucy instructed. "Now, take the second sheet and do the same, leaving room for your noggin (head) of course."

The boys snickered but Lucy only smiled.

"Last is the blanket. Don't tuck that in. Smooth it so there's no wrinkles at all." Eddy, Arthur and Gordon worked together to make all three beds and that took a long time. "You'll learn to be much faster than that. After all, this is your first time trying."

Lucy didn't call them by name. They would only be known by their surnames, Tompkins and Evans but she didn't like that rule. "Good afternoon, boys. I will see you tomorrow. After that, you are on your own. Inspection is on Friday, 8 o'clock after the first bell sounds. You'll have to be quick!"

The routine was always the same. The boys would find a way to play, Eddy was sure of that. They had to have some fun. After bed making chores, they went to the library. The old cleric who had ushered Eddy and his mother into the lobby on the first day was there to greet them. "Good afternoon. We are reading the story of David and Goliath today. Take your seats please."

Eddy was overjoyed. The Math master who was also a Classics teacher had read the story of an ancient hero in the class before and now he was going to be treated to another hero from the Bible.

The book was illustrated. On the cover was a picture of the giant Goliath, towering over the young boy, David. He had a huge sword in his hand and David had only his sling shot. "In the ancient times, there was a boy whose name was David. He was brave and daring......"

"Imagine David killing that mean giant Goliath with just one shot. He hit him right between the eyes." he said to himself. "And, next week we will find out about the one eyed monster in Math class. Maybe it's a counting game."

As he got up from his seat to leave along with the other boys, the old cleric smiled and whispered, "How are you doing, boy? Hope they're treating you okay."

Eddy smiled.

After Reading time, the boys went outside for supervised play but thankfully, they could devise their own games and not be drilled as they were every morning after breakfast. Eddy and his new mates Arthur and Gordon ran madly around the playground playing tag and then when they were thoroughly winded, they sat down to a game of marbles. Only the bell sounding Tea time stopped their play and they were lined up to go to the Dining Room. The days went by in the same way except on Sunday when it was church, bible reading, choir practice, and vespers all day but he did look forward to Sunday dinner of roast mutton or pork.

Chapter 5: Chosen for Canada

Eddy was settling in as best he could. The routine provided a kind of comfort. He could be sure of what was to happen every hour of the day. He could remember when he was not sure if he would get a bite to eat between his mother's frantic sewing. It was what kept them going. She would say, "You will have to understand that I have to do this. I have to finish this dress tonight. Dinner will have to wait. And, Eddy, go down to the pub and see if you can run some errands and maybe they will give you a bite to eat. Bring back the extras for Beatie."

At the home, the bell would ring for three square meals a day and, in between, they were kept busy. Arthur and Gordon were his work buddies and they had fun together. He was learning a bit about them as each day went on. It wasn't all work. When the maids snuck out to catch a bit of fresh air and maybe a smoke, they could sneak into a corner and play marbles. Gordon always kept some in his pockets, the shinier the better. He learned that they were brothers. They didn't look much like each other except they both had red hair and freckles but Gordon had a mole in the middle of his forehead.

Eddy was drawn to the mole for some reason and he said, "Gee, matey, what's that mole doing on yer face. Have you always 'ad it?"

"Yeah and it gives me grief but I can't do a thing about it. My Gran tried to burn it off once with her cigarette. I screamed and she pulled back but she couldn't stand it and said it was the devil's mark."

"Rotten luck, Gord. And anyways how did you get to come here with your brother?"

"We came here together with our Gram. After our mum died, someone took us to the country to Gram's. First time, we met her, she was none too pleased to see us."

"What was it like in the country?"

"Oh, there were chickens and a pig but the house was small. We had to sleep in the back room which had been a coal shed even if it had two cots and a box to put our things in."

"You must have got all covered with coal?"

"Yea, a bit 'cause there was still coal in the corner of the room but we were okay with that as long as she fed us and let us play in the field. All she did was moan. 'You boys are too much for me. Your Mum chose to go to the big city. I was against it. Now she's dead and you're here. I can't have it.' And anyway, she had told the man who brought us that she wasn't keeping us. Didn't take her long to bring us to the home. She knew that over the door of Stepney House was the sign 'No destitute Child ever refused.' The vicar had told her this. She didn't want us and she couldn't look after us. So here we are."

Gordon was a bit taller than Arthur but he didn't push him around. They were best mates. And now Eddy was becoming almost a brother too. They would stick together no matter what. Eddy didn't feel alone now. He didn't wait every day for his Mum to come to get him as he used to. He didn't cry himself to sleep now.

He missed Joseph a lot though. Joseph, being older, went to the shop to learn a trade. They could not even share meals together like they had. He had to learn that there was a big difference between a boy of 7 and a boy of 12. They had to live apart.

It was good that Eddy had playmates because he could have fun with them even in this institution that ran by bells, matrons, clerics, prefects and the Governor.

Eddy turned 8 on May 10, 1910. He had been at the home since January, 5 long months away. There was no cake and no Happy Birthday greeting. Of course, he hadn't ever had a cake or presents. Maybe he should tell his mates but then he didn't want to be a cry baby.

"Tompkins, please report to the Master's office." said the prefect, Harris.

It was 3 o'clock and the beds had been made and he was just entering the library for the afternoon story. Today, they would learn about Daniel in the Lion's den. He could hardly wait.

"Oh, well, I'll ask to borrow it so I can catch up with the rest." Eddy had learned to read a bit by now and there were lots of pictures and the cleric was kind.

He walked right up to the Head Master's door and waited to be called.

"Tompkins. Please enter now."

Eddy walked in head up, chin tucked in. He stood at attention before the Governor's desk. Eddy had grown a bit taller. He could stand up for himself.

"I wonder what the Governor wants." He thought.

"Sit down, boy. You are 8 years old today. The masters tell me you are a good boy, a good worker and an excellent student. They say that geography is your favourite subject. Is that so?"

"Yes, sir."

"Have you learned about Canada, boy?"

"A little bit, sir."

"Would you like to go to Canada?"

"I'm not sure. But maybe it would be nice."

"Eddy, for the next month, you are going to study all about Canada. You will take some exams and we will prepare you for your big adventure. They say it is The Land of Plenty. We only send the best to Canada. You will be hearing a lot more. But for now, you are dismissed."

"Thank you, sir."

As Eddy was leaving, he thought he saw his old mate, Joseph, walking down the hall. He missed him and he wondered what had become of him.

"Joseph! Joseph!"

The boy disappeared around the corner. Eddy was sure it was him even if he looked like a new boy with his new cadet style uniform.

Eddy wasn't sure whether to jump in excitement or worry what would become of him. But it didn't matter. Eddy's head was full of stories. Jack and the Beanstalk was his favourite, even if the story of Daniel and the Lion's den had been interrupted by the call to the governor's office. He imagined himself climbing the beanstalk to a special and fantastic adventure. But now, he had a special place to go. The Governor had put him on The Canada List and he was going to Canada.

He had glanced at a book about lumberjacks in the library and he wondered if he might meet one of them. With lessons in the afternoon, he wondered if he could muster up the courage to ask his teacher if he could see a map. As he walked down the hall towards the classroom, Arthur and Gordon caught up with him, brimming with excitement.

"We are on the Canada List, Eddy. We are going to Canada."

"Come on. Are you sure?'

"I'll be happy to leave this place." said Arthur

"Me too." repeated Gordon.

They had become close mates in the last few months. Gordon was already 9 and Arthur was 8 like Eddy. Suddenly, Eddy grabbed Arthur's hand and shook it the way he had seen his father do. Men shook hands especially when they had something important to say.

"I'm on the list too."

"When did you find out?" Gordon asked

"Just a few minutes ago, I was frightened when they called me to the Governor's office. What have I done? I thought."

"And…?" said Arthur

"Well", I said to myself shivering as though a strong wind had hit me," I'm 8 years old today. What did I do? Did they know that I had snuck out of the dining room the other day because I hated the same old porridge? I hid in the broom closet so no one could see me. But, no one said anything so I figured I was okay. Then, I wondered because I had just turned 8 if I would get a present the way children in books do. Then, just like that, he told me I was going to Canada."

The boys put their arms around each other and when the bell rang, they walked tall and entered the classroom. As they walked in, their teacher summoned them to sit in the front. He said nothing but they sort of knew that they were special.

They had heard that only the smartest, healthiest boys were chosen.

This was Dr. Barnardo's doing. The boys had been told that 4 shiploads of boys were sent to Canada every year. It was safe to cross the ocean in the summer months and it was already late May.

They would be lumberjacks in the wilderness. They would be dressed in red plaid shirts and overalls and they would carry big axes and saws. It was all so thrilling. Eddy dreamed of the beanstalk but now it was a ship and he was on it.

The first lesson of the day was geography. Mr. Roberts called the boys to sit in a semicircle in front of a large map of the world. Today, there were 16 boys, less than the usual number of 44.

The minute Eddy saw the map, he smiled. "Mr. Roberts must have known what I was thinking."

The map was mostly blue and white except for the bold colonies of the British Empire coloured in red. Mr. Roberts with his pointer spelled out each colony, Canada, South Africa, Australia, New Zealand, and India.

"This continent is North America, " he said. It used to be all red but this one broke away and it is now The United States of America. The one above is The Dominion of Canada. Across this large blue ocean, also marked in red, is New Zealand and Australia, loyal colonies of Great Britain. The sun never sets on a country that isn't British."

Gordon put his hand up. "Why are we going to Canada?

One of my mates said he is going to Aus."

"I am not teaching you why, Gordon, just where. Now sit up and listen."

Eddy stiffened. His legs felt like slates. His mouth was dry. He didn't like it when the masters corrected the boys. It made the boys feel even smaller than they were and that wasn't right. Eddy almost spoke out but he caught himself before he said anything.

Mr. Roberts spent a moment on the Continent of Africa and pointed out South Africa. We will look at that another day. "Our concentration is Canada. All of you lot are going there."

Eddy could imagine himself on a ship with tall masts. Maybe he would be Sinbad the sailor. That was another book he had seen in the library. The words were big and he hadn't mastered reading yet but he was improving every day.

"Now", said Mr. Roberts, "It is time for dinner. Tomorrow, you will begin to learn about this big country you are going to. Dismissed!"

Chapter 6: So much to do

There was so much to do now. The excitement of getting on a ship was fading. It might not be like a story book after all. The maid had told him that her cousin went out to Canada two years ago as a domestic servant and she hadn't heard from her since. Eddy was tired of being pushed this way and that and he wanted to be back home. He especially missed little Beatrice.

Gordon said we were in a whirlwind and he was getting confused. There were medicals to be endured and vaccinations, whatever that was. And more stuff to learn about the big country across the sea.

"What's a whirlwind?"

"It's just a saying really."

This was medical day. They had been marched from the dining room after breakfast. Eddy, Arthur and Gordon stayed together. And even though Gordon was older, he didn't know what to expect. They sat down on the floor outside the doctor's office. Nodding off, Eddy began to drift into sleep. It wasn't the first time Eddy had fallen asleep in transit. It seemed he could disappear inside a crowd anywhere at any time.

He dreamed of whirlwinds. Eddy didn't know anything about whirlwinds except that one time, the wind came up over the Thames near his home and knocked his little sister over. Suddenly there were crowds around her and he didn't know which way to turn. And then the rain came down in buckets. He was shivering and cold as ice and being pushed further and further away by the crowd. A policeman picked Beatrice up and carried her to the police carriage at the side of the road.

He ran breathless to her side "Is she all right, sir?"

"Yes, boy, she is soaking though. She needs to get these clothes off and get in a warm bath. We'll take her to your home. Where is it, boy?"

He could barely find his way. He had walked this way a few times but never in a storm. Somehow, his instincts led him along and the policeman holding little Beatrice' hand, walked behind. They reached the brick building where they lived and proceeded up the stairs to their flat. The bobby knocked three times each time louder than the first.

"No answer."

He tried the door knocker and the door opened. An older woman came to the door.

"What do you want?"

"Are you the mother?"

"No, no, I am looking after the baby while the mother is out."

"Eddy. Beatrice. Look at you! Come in this instant. Your mother will be very cross when she sees you."

"You take your clothes off. Eddy, you deserve a hiding. Go into the bedroom at once."

"Eddy, wake up. We were talking about what we have to do and you were somewhere else- were you dreaming or something."

"I was just remembering about the wind storm and home." He said.

The matron, the one in charge of the dining room, had force marched each boy up the stairs to a large white washed room. The door was slightly ajar and when Arthur peered inside, the nurse yelled, "Close that door immediately."

Being tired, they had decided to sit down and wait for the others to arrive. For some reason, they had been sent up earlier than the other boys. When the matron arrived and saw Eddy fast asleep, she gathered her skirts about her and almost flung herself at him. Gordon and Arthur had heard her coming and ducked away in time.

"Get up at once you lazy creature." yelled Miss Perkins raising her hand. "Tompkins, I've told you countless times about sitting down when you're supposed to be standing. There won't be a next time. I'll have you caned."

At the entrance of the white room was a dark oak desk. Beside it stood a tall man with a beard; he was wearing a long white coat. Two nurses stood beside him. One had grey hair and glasses and the other was young with dark hair pulled back in a bun. They were both dressed in white and on their heads was a crisp starched white hat.

It all looked clean, efficient and frightening. The doctor had a large black bag which he was opening as the boys marched in. The grey haired nurse spoke sharply. "Take off your clothes and put them down beside you."

"With everybody looking?" said Arthur.

"What did you say, boy? "The older nurse shouted.

"Nothing." Arthur murmured.

By now, there were too many boys and too much to do for her to do anything about it so miraculously, she let it pass.

Some boys snickered at seeing so many bare behinds. And Eddy heard a few jokes about "Bare Bums". But no matter, the doctor had work to do. Finally Eddy was called to the table. He looked at the tag on his coat. It read Dr. Mason.

Dr. Mason took out his note book, noted the number and name, and called "Tompkins". Eddy tiptoed to the table and stood at attention. The doctor took out his stethoscope and listened to his chest. "Put your hands up over your head; now let me examine your hands and fingers; now stick out your tongue." Then using a flat wooden stick about the size of a small ruler and pressing it sharply on the boy's tongue, he said say "Agh". When the examination was complete, he sent him to the nurses' station.

Eddy was already dreading this because some boys had cried out after getting something stuck in their upper left arm. He heard one little fellow yell. "I ain't doing this. I hate you. Let me go."

"Tompkins. Your turn."

He tried to be brave but his lower lip quivered and he fought to keep from crying. But when the nurse took out a large needle, he screamed, "No."

It took her two seconds to hold his arm, swab it with alcohol, and jab him. "Now, go along. Tomorrow, you'll get the small pox vaccination and this will seem easy."

Later that night in bed, he dreamt of being taken by monsters and put in a cave.

Sure enough, the next day was vaccination day. The medical and inoculations were completed but that was just the beginning. Canada would not accept any child who had not been vaccinated for small pox and Eddy had heard that it was painful. He tried to imagine finding a way to avoid it.

Arthur and Gordon were waiting to be called and they were determined to go through with it. "It's gotta be done, Eddy, unless you want to stay here forever," said Gordon who as the oldest of the three of them was wiser and more sensible.

"I'm scared and I don't want them to stick needles into me like that."

"Just come along with us and let's get jabbed together. It won't be so bad then."

"Arthur, you're next!'" said the younger black haired nurse. Arthur was relieved to have her lead him in. He didn't like the old grey haired one. She was mean.

Once Eddy entered the room, he realized that there was a long line up of boys. Dressed all the same, they were like choir boys out of place here in this drab white room. There was scarcely a sound as the boys silently snaked their way to the nurse's station. He had to wait his turn.

Eddy and Gordon were right behind him waiting to be jabbed. . Eddy tried to back up and sneak out but Gordon put his arm around him and pulled him back. "You gotta be a man. That's all there is to it. How you gonna get on in Canada if you're not?"

Eddy could see the grey haired nurse by the desk and he shivered. He had to drum up courage like Gordon said. "I'll have to imagine the forest and imagine myself holding an axe in front of a big tree."

The geography master had shown them the pictures of lumberjacks in northern Ontario. He had already taught them the geography of Canada particularly this part because that's where most of the boys were going. Eddy had memorized the place names of the bigger cities like Toronto and Kingston and he knew the names of the great lakes and the great river, the St. Lawrence.

"Eddy stop your dreaming. Move up. It's time." said Gordon who was next to get the needle after Arthur.

The nurse drew out a large needle with an instrument to scratch the skin. She handled it like a hammer ready to pound nails but she was quick and before Arthur could look away, the task was done and a large red mark covered the upper part of his arm. He didn't even whimper. Gordon smiled at his brave little brother.

When Gordon's turn came, he marched with his chin out straight up to the nurse and said,"I'm ready. Here's my arm. Give me a jab."

Watching Gordon, Eddy had to muster his courage. He could not let his friends down. He put his imagination glasses on and bit his lip. He watched the nurse pull out the needle and the scraper.

He looked away and held himself together. "I can do this. I can do this," he said over and over-just under his breath. "Scrape, scrape some more and then jab. That was quick and it didn't hurt as much as I thought" he said to himself. At this, he hustled out the door to join his friends.

"Let's hold hands and swear to be brave at all times. Forever!"

"That's over", said Gordon. "They can't do much more to us, can they."

Now, they had to wait for their final call to the Governor's office. They had passed the school exams; they had proved that they were good upright boys with strong moral characters, at least that's what they had been told, and they were physically fit according to the games master.

Dr. Barnardo wanted only the best to go to Canada. "They're the pride of England," he said. He even allowed for a little playfulness in their character. They had to be strong and resilient when they faced the challenges of the New World.

The boys walked back to the library. The story today was 'Treasure Island'. As they entered the room, the old cleric had started the third chapter. "Sit down boys. I'll fill you in on what has happened so far." And so he did. The adventure of the vaccination was over and they could rest in peace.

It was now June 3 and they had heard that the second sailing was to be on the 10th.

Eddy wondered what happened to Joseph. He wondered if Joseph would sail with him to Canada. He thought how jolly that would be. He was sure he had seen him a few days ago walking down the hall in his new cadet uniform but he hadn't seen him since. In fact, after the first few days at the home, he hadn't seen Joseph at all.

He remembered the first day they had met and Joseph had been so horrible to him but, then, he remembered Joseph's kindness in the dining room and before he went to his dorm.

Joseph had no parents who cared for him. When he was found, he was living in a filthy warehouse, stealing scraps of food and living by his wits but he had a lot of good in him and Eddy knew that.

"I must find out where he is?" thought Eddy. "Who can I ask?"

He knew that Joseph would have been sent to the shops to learn a trade. He wondered what trade he preferred if preferences were allowed in this place. He would have to wait on these things but he somehow believed that the answers would come.

Chapter 7: Only a few days left before Sailing

Everybody was busy. The geography master had given his last lecture on Canada. This time, he showed pictures of farms with cows and sheep and hogs and happy boys on wagons with pitch forks in their hands. Everyone was smiling. The fields were yellow with newly mown hay and the harvest had begun.

No one asked questions on this day. There was an uneasy tension in the room and the boys were unusually quiet. Eddy was deep in thought especially as he remembered Beatrice, his little sister. His mother's face was fading from him. She hadn't returned. She had not sent him a birthday card. It was as though she had vanished from the earth.

Arthur came over to him as they got up to leave the room. "What's up, matie. Ya sure look glum."

"Am okay."

It was PT break and they could go outside. Suddenly, there was a rush to the door and a burst into the fresh air and green of the playground. In the distance, some boys were playing cricket. Eddy just ran and ran around the field. The master had said, "Go!" It didn't matter; he just ran until the sweat poured from his forehead and he was still running when Arthur and Gordon stopped in front of him and said, "Eddy, what's up?"

He stopped. And then the tears came. He sat down on the grass and cried.

"What's wrong, mate?"

Eddy didn't know what was wrong. He was just plain scared.

The bell rang again and the boys were marched inside to the dining room where the tables were stacked on one side and the chairs were arranged in rows.

The older boys in charge gave out numbers to each assembled boy.

"Hold those numbers close to you. Ya're goin' to need it upstairs.

It's picture taking day."

"The last time we had ar' pictures taken was when we come te' this place", said Gordon. "It was me an' Arthur. Our grandmother had left us dahn' stairs."

Eddy remembered the man who took the picture. He had snuck a lollipop in his pocket. He remembered Joseph too and he could almost laugh to himself now that Joseph wasn't a bully any more. It seemed so long ago. But it was only 5 months at the Home. Time didn't mean anything at all.

The boys were called out in groups of 10. They called them by numbers. Eddy had Number 22. He was herded into a smaller room where the chamber maids were lined up to help the boys try on their new travelling outfits. He looked around for Arthur and Gordon but they were not there. He knew the other boys by sight but he had not formed any friendships with them except, maybe, to say "Hi or how's it goin"?

"Cheer up. It's gonna be alright. They're not gonna' kill ya." said the very same maid who had taken them to their dorm on the first day there. She was slightly plump, red cheeked and ever so nice. He remembered her name. It was Lucy and she had been a friend to him, taking care to notice him and to take him aside and give him a sweet.

On racks along the far wall hung coats, breeches and shirts. There were numbers on each set to match the numbers the boys held in their hands. "Stand straight, Eddy." said Lucy. "I need to measure your height and your width round the waist and across the shoulders."

Eddy couldn't remember ever being measured but then he recalled his mother measuring him for clothes that she made for him from old material left over from her dressmaking. After the measurements were taken and matched with an outfit which had been sewn by dressmakers and young lady apprentices at the Home, Lucy found a set of clothing that corresponded to Eddy's measurements. She pinned the Number 22 to them. All the outfits would be taken upstairs, where the dressing was about to begin. Everything at Dr. Barnardo's was done like clockwork. Everything.

After the boys had their outfits numbered, they stood up and one by one they were marched into a second room much larger than the costume one. Here, there were 4 barber chairs complete with barbers. They wore white coats with the barber's pole embroidered on their right arm.

"Number 22. Come ahead. Put your package down. The outfit, I mean. Sit here."

The barber was a man slightly older than most of the masters. He had a kind face, a mustache and his head was bald.

Eddy looked around and hair was falling everywhere. His dark brown curls, slightly longer than when he first arrived in January, were about to come off. The barber picked up his cutting shears and within minutes, Eddy's curls were gone. He could feel the hair at the back of his neck yank a bit and it hurt. The last was a razor cut and when the barber was through, Eddy was almost as bald as the barber himself. He couldn't see himself but he knew that his head was bear. All he could feel when he touched his head was rough skin.

Almost as fast as he had come in, he was marched out of the room. The boys looked at each other. They were like soldiers ready for battle. Gone were the heads of blond or red or black. Now, they were like newly shorn sheep ready to bolt.

"Gor' blimey. You look like a dodo."

"You too."

What a day! Another march. This time up the stairs for picture taking. They were going back to the same rooms at the top of the building where they had had their pictures taken when they first arrived. What a hubbub it was but, as usual, it was all done with precision. And no explanations.

Boxes of the travel outfits carried by the older boys, 20 at a time, and maids to help dress the younger ones, made it up the three flights of stairs followed by a stampede of children. Somewhere among them was Eddy. Arthur and Gordon must have been in another group because Eddy kept looking for them, even daring to call their names whilst being ferried in military fashion towards his destiny.

He couldn't even feel his legs. He was being lifted up and away by the pushing and shoving of so many determined boys. No one knew what to expect but they all remembered their first days here and the picture taking that had to happen before they knew what was happening to them. They had to be catalogued and photographed before they could become Barnardo children.

Now that they had spent some months in this strict institution, they felt a kind of kinship with everyone else. They had been wrenched from their homes, their alleyways, their work houses or sometimes from the funeral parlours where their mothers were laid out. They had been disciplined, marched, pushed and created into the mould Dr. Barnardo had in mind for boys travelling to the colonies. They had to be upright, polite, willing English boys.

Eddy was finally on the top floor. He was lined up along the wall and told to stand still and wait for his number to be called. He had Number 22 in his pocket and he waited.

The head boy of his dorm worked the line checking every boy to make sure they were present. The maids sat in the large room opposite the photography studio. The outfits were laid out carefully in neat piles. They waited for the boys to be ushered in 5 at a time.

The photographer arrived with his black cloak. The camera was set up and ready for the onslaught. This was going to be an arduous task. Altogether, over the next 3 days, 178 boys were going to have their final pictures taken. These were the pictures, along with the first ones taken when the boys first arrived, that were to be kept for safe keeping and for the archives.

Eddy remembered his first day here and he remembered the camera man. It fascinated him then and he was just as curious on this day. "I'd like to have my own camera," he thought, "but I'd be taking pictures of horses and carriages, swans and trains."

It was good that Eddy could wonder off in his mind whenever he had to do what everyone was doing, especially when he didn't understand anything. It had been that way ever since he arrived. He had to learn to be regimented and controlled but he didn't like it. It had been much better at home even if he rarely saw his father and even though his mother worked from dawn to dusk sewing. Her fingers were always raw and covered with pinholes from all the times that the needle punctured her skin. Just the same, he could come and go as he pleased and he could play with his little sister and go to the sweet shop where the confectionary lady would give him a toffee or two.

"Tompkins, Number 22"

He jumped out of his reverie, and stood at attention. "Yes, sir!"

"Proceed to that room opposite."

Eddy walked in with his head down. He was going to be pushed and made to get dressed in front of the maids. He hated being stripped down to his underwear.

"My name is Hilda. I'm going to get your dress outfit and you're going to put it on."

She first brought the black britches, a white shirt and black stockings and told Eddy to start dressing. He pulled on the coarsely woven pants and then tried to put on the woolen stockings which felt like leggings. Eddy struggled to pull one up to his left knee with Hilda using the full force of her arms to wrench it into shape. The right leg was easier once Hilda had shamed him into doing it himself. Afterwards, she brought a black woolen sweater. It fitted tight around his neck and itched a little. He hated it already.

After his britches, shirt, tie and socks were secure, Hilda brought a navy coat just like the coats that the mariners wear when they come on shore. It was a smart looking coat. He wondered why he was being fitted out like a merchant marine officer cadet. It had two rows of four brass buttons down the front and two brass buttons on the sleeve. It was heavy so Hilda lifted it up and put Eddy into it. She pulled the sleeves over his arms. Eddy slouched. He felt like a sardine in a can, all squashed up.

"Stand up tall, boy. Be proud. You are going to Canada."

What a difference from the day he first came to the Home. On that day, he was wearing a little boys' dress up outfit with an Eton collar. Around his waist was a belt with a shiny buckle. His mother had dressed him especially well that day. His hair was shiny and well combed.

Now, he stood tall but his face was sombre. His brow was wrinkled, his eyes wide open and his mouth tightly closed. Later, when people saw his picture, they would say that Eddy looked puzzled. Some said he looked angry. Others saw a bewildered little boy.

"Now go outside and join the line for your picture." said Hilda smiling from the corner of her mouth.

The photographer peeked outside to check on the numbers in the hall. He caught a glimpse of Eddy and gave him a wink. Eddy wondered if there would be a lollipop in his pocket after he left the studio.

"Number 22, Tompkins! Come forward. It's your turn."

One by one the boys had gone into the studio, all looking alike in their naval uniforms. All had newly shaved heads and everyone was quiet. No one understood what was happening. They were just going through the motions and they had to behave. Perhaps, they could have a jolly pillow fight later in the dorm.

Eddy walked in and sat down on the same chair he sat in when he had his picture taken the first time. He saw the same camera and equipment. Everything was the same and everything was different. Eddy was confused and scared. Snap!

What the camera saw was a little boy of eight, all alone, away from his family. Five months ago, it snapped a sweet little boy, innocent and curious. Now, Eddy wore a frown and his chin was defiant.

"You can get up now and here's a lollipop for you."

"Thank you, sir."

Eddy left the studio and joined the others. It was time for tea.

Chapter 8: The day of Leaving.

It was May 24. There was a buzz in the air and a sense of excitement but only when they made the announcement did it all become real. The boys on the Canada List were called to go to chapel. They had had their breakfast a bit earlier that day. They were to report at sharp 6 AM and the boys were told to wear their night shirts.

"Why night shirts?" thought Eddy. "We always have to dress in our school clothes to be downstairs in the dining room for 7."

"Hurry up. Move. Move. There's no time to dawdle." said the dorm prefect. "They'll tell you when you get down there."

Eddy looked over at the next bed where Arthur was still sleeping but he didn't see Gordon. He must have got up before the bell. Before he could utter a sound, prefect Harris pushed him towards the stairs. "We haven't got all day. Hurry."

"Gor' blimey, what's the rush?" said Eddy.

"Hey, you got some cheek. You're getting too saucy for your own good, Tompkins. Get goin' or A'll cane ya!"

At that, Eddy picked up his heels and joined the rest.

When they got to the dining room, there was quite a stir. The governor paraded in and in his most Public School-master voice, he said, "At ease, boys. Sit down and breakfast will be served promptly. This is the biggest day of your life. You are leaving for Canada."

A huge "Whoopee!" rose from the mass of nightshirt clad boys.

"Please stand for grace."

He repeated the words the boys knew well, and then they were told to sit down. Eddy looked around for Gordon and he worried that Arthur was still in bed. He couldn't see him and he couldn't understand why Gordon wasn't sitting in his usual place.

Immediately after breakfast, the boys were hurried upstairs again. The crowded room was transformed. Beside each bed was a trunk, and on the bed was the outfit they had been fitted with a few days ago plus a travel bag for the journey.

Eddy stared at the trunk next to his bed and realizing that it actually belonged to him, he gasped, "That's mine, all mine, 'cause my name's on it." There it was, Edward George Tompkins, printed in bold dark lettering and taking up most of the front side.

The chamber maids stood at attention at the door and the headmaster stuck his head in to say, "Cheerio, lads, I'll see you in the chapel in a half hour sharp. No dawdling and no talk. Just get on with it."

There must have been a lot of planning and activity to make all this happen but there was no mistaking this. They meant business when they said they were going to be shipped to Canada. The trunks seemed to have minds of their own and each one seemed especially chosen for each boy. Each trunk was made of wood and covered with something that looked like alligator skin. It would have been made by the boys in the shop. It would have taken hours of training before they could master the carpentry needed to construct a solid and sturdy box that could withstand a train journey and a ship's crossing. It would have to withstand being tossed in the baggage cars of trains and thrown on board ships by stevedores. It would have to tolerate indifference and rough treatment. These trunks were not the property of the rich. They would simply have to survive the voyage.

"Joseph probably had a hand in this." said Eddy as he reached down and slowly lifted the lid. He wasn't supposed to. He was sure of that but Eddy was a curious child and he wanted to know what was inside. As it turned out, there were no toys or fun books, just the Bible, a Sankey hymn book, a Traveler's Guide and Pilgrim's Progress and new outfits to be worn in Canada. He wasn't much interested in the new clothing which included a cap, an overcoat, muffler and gloves, a Sunday suit, a second best suit, a working suit and 2 pairs of overalls. It took up most of the space but he did notice two pairs of boots, running shoes and a pair of rubbers and there was even a sewing kit, called housewife's kit, underwear, 2 pairs of braces, 3 shirts, 4 collars and 2 ties plus handkerchiefs, 1 jersey and 2 pairs of knee high stockings.

He knew that there had to be clothes but the boots especially intrigued him. It meant that he would be a cowboy after all. Whenever they talked about Canada, he imagined cowboys and Indians and ice cream. "They say Canadians like ice cream and there's ice cream parlours everywhere."

In the sea of activity, Eddy finally got dressed. He put on black britches, dark knee socks, a crisp white shirt and a high necked sweater. Everyone was doing the same but he was too busy to notice. He didn't hear the buzz and the clatter and he couldn't see through the beds, the maids, the trunks and the confusion.

"I say," said Harris, "you look smart Tompkins, Here's your tag with your name and number A2410. You'll wear it around your neck. Wear it everywhere from now on. They need to know who you are. Chin up and step sharply. We 're going to chapel."

The trunk stayed by the bed but Eddy was sure that it would eventually go with him. He rather liked the trunk. It was new and it was his. He couldn't remember ever having anything that was new that belonged to him and even though there was no Robinson Crusoe, he was satisfied.

It seemed they were always being herded somewhere but this time there was a note of finality about it. All the boys seemed to sense this and they walked sharply like cadets to the chapel they had spent every morning and evening in for all the time they were at the home. There were always prayers and hymns and a lecture.

The boys filed in two by two and sat on the hard benches. By the time, they were seated, the chapel was full. Eddy could not remember that many boys in one place.

"All stand." said the Governor. "Repeat after me the Apostles Creed. 'I believe in the father almighty, etc'. Now sit down."

Eddy kept looking for Gordon and Arthur and didn't really concentrate on the Apostles' Creed.

The Governor, stern faced and in his best vicar's spoke loud and clear,

"You are gathered together ready to leave on a great adventure. You have been chosen because you are the best British boys and you will be an honour to your country. Always remember, to be polite and to be a shining example in your new country. Good luck and God bless."

The room went quiet while the Governor shifted his feet from side to side and then in a much subdued tone, he said, "Now together, let's repeat the Lord's Prayer. 'Our father who art in heaven, Hallowed be thy name'. Amen."

"Please stand for the National anthem, 'God save our gracious king……'"

The governor, usually dour and unsmiling brushed a tear from his eye as he thought about the days at the home with the boys now bound for Canada. He had grown fond of them and was sad to see them go.

"Dismissed."

As they filed out in their cadet coats and brass buttons, they looked like a marching column off to war. Boys and masters and maids waving handkerchiefs, they marched to the beat of the Barnardo band. With trumpets and drums and cornets in perfect unison, they strutted out of their home at Stepney Causeway and on to the train, which was called by the locals, The Bernardo Express. They were bound for Liverpool and the docks where the SS Sicilian was waiting for them to board.

Eddy looked around one more time.

"Where are my mates?" he cried.

Chapter 9: On the Train and to the ship.

The boys boarded the Barnardo express after marching in step from the home they had known since being unceremoniously dropped off in ones and twos and threes, months ago.

For Eddy it was 5 months since his mother had brought him with a promise to return with his favourite sweets. She never returned and Eddy could hardly bring her face into view now. He thought about her from time to time and, sometimes, he would whimper a little when he remembered that cold, damp day in January. But today, he was taken up with the music, the marching and the fun of it all.

Every boy was dressed the same but each boy was still himself even with an identifying number beside his name on the tag slung around his neck. Eddy would be A2410 for the duration of the long trip to Liverpool and on to Canada until he reached his destination, whatever that might be.

Every boy had his story. Some had been brought by mothers in desperation; others had been picked up on the streets. Some came from the numerous workhouses and homes of industry. Some had quieted their anger; others had become silent; but some were just kids on an adventure. Eddy was excited and maybe even happy.

Onlookers were waving handkerchiefs and every once in a while, a woman dressed in black would walk along. She was looking for someone but she seemed hesitant and would stop here and there. Eddy glanced at her and thought he saw tears running down her cheek.

"No, it couldn't be her. She is not wearing a hat. Mum always did." he thought. Quickly brushing away the image, he turned and kept marching.

Soon, they reached the platform. The steam engine towered over them as it moved slowly into the station. Behind it were the passenger cars going back as far as the eyes could see. The engine hissed like a giant tea kettle as it came to a stop.

On the platform a multitude of children stood, boys in cadet uniform and girls with bonnets, plain grey skirts and green capes. Beneath the hats, no pretty curls tapered over their shoulders. Like the boys, they had been shaved to prevent a lice epidemic. How those little girls must have cried when barbers reached for scissors to cut their shiny locks of platinum, brown, red and pitch black.

Eddy had never seen such an array of girls. If only Beatrice were among them but he couldn't see through the throngs. He did see some small girls in the group but he could not make out their faces and, in any case, he wasn't sure he remembered what she looked like.

Walking in and around them were the overseers, men and women, speaking to a child here, reprimanding someone there and looking very busy. One by one, the children were pushed toward the platform of each carriage, sometimes being hoisted because their legs were too short for the height of the steel step.

Slowly and methodically, everyone went inside and found their way to the compartment assigned.

It had been painstakingly planned and the masters and matrons used every inch of energy they could muster to seat each boy and each girl in the right compartment with the right prefect to watch over them. The ages were mixed deliberately so that there was at least one older child and one younger child in the mix. Boys and girls were strictly segregated. It was the way things were done.

Eddy was placed in Compartment Ten. He had hoped that Gordon or Arthur would be one of his companions but there was no one he knew well although he recognized everyone. The little room was functional and just right for the job of transport. There were two seats facing each other in each compartment. They were made of wood covered with brown upholstery cloth but, in spite of some stuffing, they were hard and unforgiving and ahead of them lay a journey of several hours. Above the seats was a storage area. The one window in the crowded space looked out at the town and the door opened up to the corridor along the train.

This train was organized especially for the Dr. Barnardo Homes to carry these little children to the docks. Only the first two carriages had any pretence of elegance and they contained a dining car and a comfortable car with plush seats, a table and an ash tray. The third car was the galley and already, big pots of soup were boiling on the stoves.

The adults could sit in the special carriage when they had their break from monitoring the children. There were strict orders about this. No one was to be caught 'off guard'.

Eddy put his travel bag up in the storage area and sat down. His feet could barely touch the floor. He wriggled into position and looked around. "Where are my friends?" he thought. "I wanted to sit beside them today. Drats! Gor' Blimey."

Eddy looked out the window and he could see the boys' trunks being loaded on. There were miles of them. It was taking longer for them to be put on board than the loading of the children. When this task was completed, the station master yelled, "All doors secured." Raising the whistle to his lips, he sounded the parting.

Suddenly there was a lurch and the train jumped forward. Then the Chug, chug faster and faster and they were out of the station and moving along the tracks through the grimy back streets of London. They moved past Piccadilly Square and past Westminster Bridge where Eddy had lived with his family. Eddy could hardly see any buildings. It was becoming a blur. Faster and faster. Louder and louder until they were outside London and crossing the green fields of Bedfordshire.

The talking became just noise that made his eyes close and soon he was nodding off to sleep. Suddenly the high pitch of "Tea time. Tea time", jolted him into the waking world. The steward opened the door with one hand, balancing the tray with the other. Steam wafted from the tin cups and there were sandwiches for everyone and biscuits too.

The boys began to chat since the prefect encouraged them to share any stories they might want to tell as they sipped their tea and managed the sandwiches on their laps. They had all been reluctant to speak before this. There were 8 of them crammed into the carriage and it was a long journey.

"It's gone 10 AM," said the prefect who had a watch. No one asked him about that but a watch was rare especially among this group of boys.

"Where did he get it? Who was he?" they thought.

But no matter. Eddy certainly wasn't going to ask him. Eddy had learned 'to keep his powder dry'. It was an expression that really meant, "Don't give away everything at once." You had to be cool, calm and collected.

"We won't get to Liverpool until at least 6 0'clock. Then we have to board the ship. Eat up mates. You might not get any more grub 'till then."

"Can I have another cuppa?"

"What about another sandwich?"

"That's it. No more".

They sighed.

"Just grin and bear it."

"Another grown up saying, I guess", thought Eddy.

Now that the boys had loosened up, they began to share their experiences.

"I was brought to the home a year ago" said the oldest boy.

"I am 12 and my name is Robert. I was living rough down by London Bridge. Ever 'ear of 'Boiled Beef and Carrots'? We got wha'ver we could when we went to the open market. Wanna 'ear it?"

No one said anything but Robert proceeded with the song anyway.

> Boiled beef and carrots,
> Boiled beef and carrots,
> That's the stuff for your "Derby Kell",
> Makes you fit and keeps you well.
> Don't live like vegetarians
> On food they give to parrots,
> Blow out your kite, from morn 'til night,
> On boiled beef and carrots.

"There's always grub there if you're fast enough. Anyhow, they picked me up, the Barnardo's, I mean. It's better now and they taught me a trade. I can mend shoes so s 'all be a shoemaker in Canada and make lots 'o money."

"Oh, yea, I had it rough too but am okay now". The boy in the corner closest to the window whispered. At that, he turned his back to them and stared out the window.

"My name is Earl", said the prefect. "I don't know how long I've been at Barnardo's but it's a long time. They made me prefect last year.

'An if you're wondering about the watch, my father gave that to me before he died. He was a school teacher but he got sick. Mother died of a broken heart and my aunt brought us, me and my two brothers, to the home. They took my sisters somewhere else. I'm going with you to Canada. You can bet on that."

"My name is Eddy. My Mum brought me to the home awhile ago. She never came back. I miss my little sister though."

As the train whizzed through the open country of field and farm, the boys began to nod off. The constant rhythm was like a cradle and soon every eye was closed. Only Earl stayed awake with his book, 'Pilgrims Progress' which he had been told to read. All the head boys were given the book after chapel and they were expected to complete it before they embarked on Canada's shores.

"Let it be your guiding light!" said the chaplain.

At 4 o'clock, Earl put the book away. He could hear the stewards moving down the passageway.

"I was joking with you about the food earlier There's more. The steward told me that when I stepped out to walk down the corridor across to the next car to go to the bog' It's goin' to be served soon."

Sure enough, no sooner had he spoken, when the steward came to the door, held it, as before, with one hand, while balancing a tray of soup and slices of bread on a tray. Even with the moving train, he could balance and hold the try upright so that nothing would spill. He put the tray down on the floor and picked up each bowl in turn and gave it to the boys. He passed the bread to Earl who distributed it fairly to everybody.

The boys were hungry. They gulped down the chicken vegetable soup and devoured the bread as though they had not eaten in a week.

"Mmm! Good," said the boy in the corner. "It's better than Barnardo's."

After they had eaten, they passed their bowls to Earl and he, in turn, rang for the steward who had forgotten to leave the tray. They sure could do with a table in this car.

The train lurched ahead and slowed down. They were coming to a tall bridge somewhere in the west. The whistle blew three times and then the engine speeded up and continued on its way through countryside as green as emeralds. Eddy could see the blossoms on the apple trees that they passed and in the distance were cattle and sheep.

It was now 4.30.

The movement of the train lulled the occupants to sleep once again and the room was quiet except for some snoring in the corner. Minutes buzzed by and soon they were coming in to the big seaport of Liverpool.

"Wake up, boys."

They shook the sleep from their eyes and sat up and bent their heads to the window.

In the distance they could see the docks and the ships waiting to sail. "There so many of them in every size and colour." Earl said, "See if you can see our ship. The Sicilian. It's got one red funnel. It's docked down there somewhere."

There were cargo ships bound for the Orient and large passenger ships ready to embark with emigrants bound for New York, Boston and Quebec. Some had two funnels and others still had the sailing masts of yesteryear.

The train which had slowed down considerably in the last half hour was moving no faster than a boy on a bike and then it suddenly came to a stop.

"Liverpool" Get ready to embark."

They were close to the docks. The train platform was right across from the loading dock and, through the window, there was their ship.

Eddy scrambled to get a look but he was overwhelmed by everyone else pushing to see the ship that would take them to Canada.

Chapter 10: On board sailing to Canada

What a scramble! Everyone was pushing and shoving and getting nowhere until a loud voice bellowed "Stop, Wait and Listen." "Stay where you are in your compartments until the roll call. Masters, Matrons, Line up your charges and proceed slowly down the corridor to the platform. There is to be silence."

Earl ordered the boys to get their travel bags down from storage and line up in front of the door. Eddy and his new found companions did what they were told, lining up like soldiers waiting for the next command. They had, after all, been used to regimentation and orders at the Home. The only difference was, they were on a grand adventure and they wanted to get on that ship. What boy hadn't dreamed of sailing on the high seas?

Eddy was first in line and he stepped out into the corridor walking deliberately one step in front of the other until he reached the platform, the boys behind him with Earl at the rear. The boys filed out from one end of the train while the girls filed out from the other. Masses of children were ferried into rows until the gathering was complete. Then the roll call began.

"Alan."

"'Ere."

"Aiken."

"'Ere."

Finally, Eddy heard his name.

"Tompkins."

"'Ere, sir."

It continued until the last name, "Vickers" was called.

All accounted for.

"Proceed."

Each child was ushered up the gangplank of the SS Sicilian, one of the main ships of the Allan Line that ferried the home children across to Canada. Altogether there were 201 children from the Dr. Barnardo Homes of 18-26 Stepney Causeway and the Girls Home and 1203 passengers, 80 of whom would be coming aboard in Le Havre. The crew consisted of Captain William Wallace, his first officers, and 40 crewmen, plus the ship's doctor and nurse. The ship was sturdy and large enough to accommodate all the passengers both first class, second class and steerage.

The SS Sicilian was an imposing vessel, not as massive as the giant passenger steamers that plied the Atlantic from Liverpool to New York carrying the masses of voyagers on their way to a better life, but big enough to carry the boys and girls being sent across the ocean to people they did not know far from families who had put them in the holding home. It had been built in Belfast and first launched in 1899. The Sicilian had a single funnel and mast unlike many of the steamships going to New York that had up to 4 funnels and one main mast.

Now, when the children were assembled on deck, the call went out, "Prefects gather your charges. It's time for pictures to be taken. Report to the Main Deck immediately." This would be the final pictorial record of the children before leaving for Canada.

The children were assembled on deck and organized into the ideal camera position to be photographed. The boys had berets on their heads now and the girls' bonnets had been set just right on their heads. The younger boys sat cross legged on the deck while the older boys stood behind them. The girls were on one end and the boys on the other. The photographer joked with the children moving back and forth to get exactly the right wide angle shots.

"Smile. Let's 'ave it, your biggest smile."

"Don't break the camera boy." He said to the boy in the back who was sticking out his tongue. "Smile."

The smallest girl in the front began to sob. More girls joined in until there was too much confusion to carry on. The girls' matron came to the front and tried to soothe the little ones.

"Silence!" roared the headmaster clapping his hands. "We will have silence. Now!"

The camera man knew that the only way he would get a good picture was to relax the children. Yelling by the adults in charge would only mean sulky faces and anguished expressions. He had a bag of tricks up his sleeve. As the children watched, the camera man took out his Punch and Judy arsenal and before Punch had even started to speak, the children started to laugh.

"Alright. Now, let's see your smile. By golly!"

Eddy, always fascinated by cameras watched intently as the photographer manoeuvered his giant camera with the photographic plates, walking effortlessly back and forth to catch the right expression. Eddy looked around to see if Gordon and Arthur were in the group and he hoped Joseph would be on board.

"They got to be here. It ain't fair if they're not. I don' wanna be alone without ma mates," he thought.

"Chin up. Smile for one last shot. Thank you, boys and girls. Good day."

The children started to fidget but the master in charge of all of them, said,

"Stay in your places. We have a lot to do. You can look around and talk a bit but don't move out of where you are."

"Eddy, hey Eddy." a voice whispered.

Eddy thought he could make it out.

"Eddy, old mate, it's me, Gordon!"

Overjoyed, Eddy looked behind him. It was Gordon. He was on board after all. Eddy edged his way back to get beside his friend. They kept their voices low.

"Gor' blimey, Gord. Wher 'ya 'bin. I been lookin' fo' ya everywhere."

"I was late." said Gordon,"getting down to the dinin' 'all. They wouldn't let Arthur come wiv me and I ran to the Governor's office before they could stop me. 'Why, why can't ma little brother com wiv me. He's all I got. It's me and 'im. That's it.' I says. And the Governor pipes and says, 'Sorry, Evans. Arthur has poor eyesight. He didn't pass the test. He can't come with you'. " But when I pleaded almost getting down on my knees and thinking nothing I said would make any difference, he said, 'We'll make sure he gets to Canada in due time and then you will be together.' I got to believe 'im. He musta felt sorry for me 'cause he took me by the arm, made me get a sandwich from the maid, urged the maid, Lucy, to go upstairs with me to help me get dressed and packed and join you lot but I must have been the last on the train in the last car. He made sure my trunk got on the train too."

"Too bad about this but we'll be mates on the ship and when we get to Canada, we'll wait together until Arthur arrives on the next boat." said Eddy.

"It ain't fair; just ain't fair. Arthur will be so lonely without me. He depends on me fo' everyfing."

"He'll get through it, Gordon." said Eddy. "It will be all right. We'll all be together soon."

Suddenly the words, "All Stand and Listen", blasted the air.

The children stopped their chatter and looked up.

The day was closing down and there was the smell of something tasty coming up from below. The children realized they were hungry and they were tired of being shuffled about. But there was a lot more organizing to be done and dinner would have to wait.

They first learned that they would be in the same groups as they were on the train. Each group of 10 boys was assigned the same prefect and, in turn, each group of 10 was part of a group of 30 with a master in charge. The head master in charge of everyone was Rev Philip Thomas, a man of 55 who was heading to Toronto to be a minister in the new Anglican Church on Yonge Street. He was known as a strict master who had taught in a boarding school before deciding to return to his first profession and take up the ministry again. He had no sense of humour and he was known as a disciplinarian. Dr. Barnardo had to be absolutely certain that the man in charge be of impeccable morals and high standards and capable of supervising a large number of boys who had to be watched not only because of their possible high jinks but also to protect them from falling overboard.

The young man in charge of Eddy's group of 30 had volunteered to take this position in return for a free passage to Canada. He was a novice, only 20 years of age, and he had been chosen because of his impeccable manners and excellent breeding as the son of a renowned Anglo Irish clergyman. His name was David Ryan. He had his work cut out for him and there would not be much time for a leisurely stroll on the deck or time to play cards with the crew.

Suddenly there sounded a loud whistle and a call over the loud speaker:

"Prefects, line up your boys. We are going down below to check your berths. Watch your step and move quickly. Go."

Earl, the prefect, had lined up his boys to go below deck when Eddy grabbed his arm to get his attention.

"Earl, I've got to speak to you. My mate, Gordon, just got here in time for the pictures. He was the last on the train. Can you please put him in our group? His brother, Arthur, was left behind and we want to be together in the sleeping quarters."

"Eddy, this is not the time to ask me anything. Ask me when we get downstairs."

"Please, Earl, I've got to know now so I can fetch him. He's still up on the main deck. I think they've forgotten about him and figured he stayed back."

"Alright, alright. I'll sort it. Our master is a nice fellow. I'll talk to him when we get to the bunks."

Eddy leaped in the air and with a "Whoopee!" He started up the stairs.

"Hey, not so fast, Eddy. I'll go and get Gordon after I get you all arranged."

Feeling a lot better knowing that Gordon would join his group, Eddy smiled and proceeded down the steps with the rest and just when they reached their berths, he spied his old friend, Joseph, at the back of the line.

"My ol' mate." He said to himself. "Hurray. It's a good day, after all."

Chapter 11: Settling on Board

The gathering was hurried and a bit chaotic because all the boys and girls had to be ushered to their berths which would be their sleeping quarters for the duration of the trip across the Atlantic. The children were tired after the long train journey and they were simply part of some long human chain shuffled hither and yon. They still had their land legs and had no idea what lay ahead.

"Step up and Move Ahead." shouted the masters. "Down the steps and turn left."

The children proceeded down three flights of stairs to a large holding room with bunk beds from one end to the other. The girls had already moved to the right to their sleeping area well away from the boys. Eddy strained under the weight of his travel bag and was shoved and pushed to the other side of the deck. With the stampeding horde of boys pushing against him, Eddy was taken to his sleeping quarters and ushered to his bunk which would be bed and refuge for the voyage.

"We'll not stop here now." said the master. "We are going to the dining room first. You must be hungry."

Eddy wasn't sure what to do.

"Don't dawdle, Tompkins. " Earl yelled

It was the first time on board that he had been called by his surname. Earl must not be too pleased with him.

"Pick up your feet and move!"

The dining area was a large room not far from where they would spend their nights and that was just fine with Eddy. The tables were as long as London milk carts and there were 12 chairs at each. There must have been 20 tables in a room that should have contained 10. They had just enough room between them to allow passage through. The tables were made of wood and each boasted a serviceable white tablecloth. Carefully laid out were 12 tin plates, a fork and knife along with a roughly sewn cloth napkin to the left of the plate. To the right was a tin cup for each boy.

Eddy sat down with his new mates from the train and to his surprise Gordon had joined them. Earl was true to his word. He had kept his promise. When they were all seated, Earl joined them. Next to him was a table of older boys with Joseph right in the centre. Eddy couldn't believe his good luck. He looked across the table to catch his eye. Joseph gave him a wink and beckoned him to come over to sit beside him. Eddy knew there were strict rules of behaviour at table. He looked at Earl who had noticed the exchange of glances and hoped Earl would understand.

"It's all right matey. He can come over and sit with you tonight. I know him from the shop where we both studied carpentry. He's a good lad."

Joseph shuffled his way over and sat between Eddy and Gordon.

"Bin a long time, mate. Whacha been doin' since we last talked. I missed ya."

Eddy was a bit shy and barely got out the words, "Missed ya too."

They chatted a bit but when the head master in charge of all the children on board walked in, everyone went quiet. "Good evening lads. You have had a long journey and now you are embarking on a whole new adventure. You have been trained well and I expect you to do as you did at Dr. Barnardo's Home. You will sit up straight, listen to orders, mind your manners and be good English boys. Do you hear?"

"Yes, sir." the boys echoed in unison.

"Now, it's time for dinner."

This was answered by a thundering applause and hand clapping so loud that it echoed all along the deck.

White clad stewards walked in and set down the plates in front of what seemed like thousands of boys. The plates were steaming with hot food, roast beef, vegetables, mashed potatoes and gravy. Along the table they set bowls of white bread and loads of butter such as they had never seen in all their lives. This food had come from Canada and there was lots of it. The boys could hardly wait to start but they knew from practice that grace came first.

"Abide with us and bless this food. In the name of the Father, the son and the Holy Ghost." said the master. "Now you can begin."

Eddy, Gordon and Joseph dug in and savoured every bite.

For Joseph who had spent so much time living out in the street or hiding in a warehouse before he was picked up and taken to Barnardo's this meal was the best meal ever. Eddy could remember good meals when he lived with his mother and father but that was a long time ago.

When the meal was over, the boys were directed to stay for a short chapel service. They knew what this would be and they sat through the prayers, the creed and the talk but most were nodding off and Eddy could barely keep his eyes open.

When the droning ceased, they moved back to their bunks, got out their night shirts and climbed into their new beds. Each would have to find his way to sleep in this huge room painted in ship's grey filled with beds with barely a space between each one. And since each was a bunk bed, it was more crowded than they could remember from their sleeping quarters back at the home. Each bed was covered with a charcoal coloured blanket tucked tightly so that no evidence of sheets could be seen.

Eddy got in the bottom bunk.

Joseph was over in the bunks closest to the washing facilities but Gordon's bed was just above Eddy's.

"That's a bit o' luck." said Eddy. "Night, Gordon."

"Night Eddy. See ya in the morning."

Eddy dreamed of cowboys. He was riding the range with a rifle in one hand and the reins in the other. This was too fantastic. He didn't want to wake when he heard the call.

"Wake up, get washed and dressed. It's breakfast time."

After a breakfast of eggs and bacon, toast, butter and jam, the boys were manoeuvred up to the main deck. What a hustle and bustle. The one funnel spouted steam and the engines roared below. The captain was on the bridge; the crew stood at their stations. The anchor was raised and secured and the ship was loosed from its moorings.

On the platform below, a crowd had gathered. Some were waving Union Jacks. Others had white handkerchiefs. Most of the people were families of first and second class passengers and some were the wives or mothers of the crew. The captain's wife stood out among them arrayed in a flowery hat and clothes of the latest fashion, probably bought at one of the great department stores, perhaps Selfridge's of London.

No family of the children would have been there since they had either relinquished their rights by signing those cumbersome papers when they brought their children to the home or the parents had died leaving their children, orphans. Life had been impossible for those countless mothers who neither had the means or the ability to raise their children. The children were bound to carry out the plans of the countless homes that had sprung up in the England of Queen Victoria and now her heir, King Edward. Poverty was rife while merchants and the wealthy grew rich. The only hope came from people like Dr. Barnardo who saw the suffering and strove to make things better. The plans devised by these philanthropists seemed simple enough as an answer to the plight of the poor. England had too many desperate people and Canada as a young nation needed people to work the farms. And it was thought that children being young and eager to learn would make the best labourers. The hope and the belief was that they would prosper in their new country. And so, the children aboard the SS Sicilian on this fine day in late May, 1910, were called "the flower of the flock and they were to make England proud".

A woman dressed in black moved back and forth along the dock as though to get a glimpse of someone on the ship but the sun in her eyes blinded her so that she could not pick out individual passengers. It was strange but Eddy was sure she was the same woman who had watched them as they lined up to get the train on the day before.

The SS Sicilian moved away from its berth and moved slowly out of the harbour toward the open sea. The whistle blew and a cheer went up.

The passengers, mostly immigrants heading for the unknown, and the ones left behind on the shore, cheered and waved their last goodbyes to each other.

Many would never see England again.

Eddy and his friends clung to the side of the ship and waved too. They had no idea of what lay before them but they were excited just the same, except for Gordon who kept thinking about his little brother Arthur who had been left behind. Even though they had promised Gordon, Arthur would join him soon, he couldn't be sure. He had been disappointed ever since his grandmother had taken him to the home and left him. Nevertheless, he would use all his wits to make sure Arthur would join him and join him soon.

They would not be leaving Europe yet, they learned, because there were passengers to pick up at Le Havre, France. They were bound for Quebec and a new life working land of their own deeded to them by the Province of Quebec This meant a day in the English Channel before heading out past Ireland and the open sea. It also meant another language on board to join with several dialects from different parts of Europe including Germany, the Netherlands and Norway.

Captain Wallace steadied the Sicilian into the vast north Atlantic.

That first day at sea was frightening not because of the waves and the ships movement down into the waves and up but scary because of all the tummy aches. Most of the passengers were sea sick.

Sea gulls followed them like a flotilla waiting for the debris tossed overboard from the stern. They dove in to catch the fish heads, beef bones and acres of torn bread now skimming the water. Nothing was wasted and scavengers as they were, they served the ship well.

"It will take a day or two to get your sea legs." a sailor told Eddy, Gordon and Joseph who were gathered in a group on deck.

"What's that mean?" said Joseph.

"You'll see. Just don't eat too much, matey's. You'll get used to it and you'll be a sailor like me before you reach land again."

Nobody could eat and the food was so appetizing. They would have to wait it out. They huddled together and sat down on the deck. They didn't talk much either.

Chapter 12: Learning how to be a sailor

The first day on board their ship, the SS Sicilian, had been rough but not because of the sea. The old sailor told the boys sitting by the life boat that it was smooth sailing. "The sea's like glass." he said.

"So, why we feelin' this way? Been belching all day and every time I got to run down those hairy steps to the toilet, I feel worse." yelled Joseph.

"Y' ain't got your sea legs yet but ya will. It'll take a day of two." Joseph looked at the old boy and questioned him more. "Got this head ache and me gut feels like its explodin'. I thought we're supposed to have fun."

The old sailor simply smiled and walked away. Night was coming on and the children were rounded up to go below deck to their bunks. Eddy could smell the food coming from the kitchen. He wanted to eat but he'd have to wait until tomorrow. He got to his bunk, threw off his clothes and fell asleep. He'd drift off into dream land and imagine himself on a horse on the prairie. Sometimes he preferred to sleep because he was always on an adventure that he could control. Lately, life seemed to just happen and the whirlwind sometimes frightened him. He was safe now in his reverie.

All around him were boys, some restless, some fast asleep. They were all traveling westward towards the setting sun. The wake up gong made him jump. He could tell it was morning by the light outside the porthole and the knot in his stomach had gone. He was hungry.

The boys scrambled out of their beds and walked to the wash house. There were hand basins all along the wall and urinals along the other. The few towel racks were by the door. Earl, with his group of 10, lined them up at the wash basins and each boy took the wash cloth on the side of each sink to wipe away his night face and make it bright and rosy. It woke them from their dreamy state and made them ready for their second day at sea. Gordon was next to Eddy and all they could think of was going up on deck but they knew they had to wash first.

Those who could eat gobbled down their breakfast served by the stewards in white and then they pushed their way to the stairs. Most of the masters were still in bed because they were so violently ill from the motion of the ship. This suited the older boys in particular because they knew that without the masters, they could do as they liked.

When the boys got on deck, all their pent up energy was unleashed. Suddenly bedlam was the rule. Joseph let out a yelp and he went running across the deck. The sun was up and the sea was calm. Following him was almost everyone who'd been downstairs in the bunks. Only a few were still sea sick. The old sailor was right, "You'll feel a lot better when you get your sea legs."

Eddy and Gordon lagged behind. The older boys were taller, stronger and their legs were longer and they could run. On the other end of the ship, the girls were up to a bit of high jinks too but it was manifested in skipping ropes which another crew member had salvaged.

Their skirts swung around their waists and for a moment Joseph and Earl stopped to take a look.

"Gosh, they're pretty good looking." Joseph said.

He was heading over to their side when old Rev. Thomas stopped him. "Whoa boy, this is the line you won't cross. Get back to your side. Now!"

Earl knew he had to show some leadership and he pushed Joseph to the corner. "Come on, matey. You know better. Go over by the life boats and wait for me." Joseph reluctantly obeyed but he was angry.

Eddy and Gordon got out their marbles and sitting on the deck, they started to play. Other boys were tossing a ball and some were getting awfully close to the mast which they wanted to climb. In fact, the boy who had sat in the corner of the train compartment who had said hardly anything was already part way up. "Get down, you fool!" yelled the old sailor who had talked to them yesterday. "Get down immediately!"

"Nah!"

"Gutter snipe. Git down or a'll flail ya good."

The boy whose name was John climbed down but he was none too happy about it. He liked the idea of going to the top to reach the flag and to peer across the ocean. He might sight a whale or a shark. He had read about them and they were awesome.

John, the quiet one so called had a mean side and he and Robert, the boy who had lived rough on the street and who loved to sing, "Boiled Beef and Carrots" could be bullies when they got together. Today was the day to strike out. The boys had a fleeting acquaintance before they ended up at Barnardo's. They had been raised in the slums of the east End and they were sick and tired of being cooped up, yelled at and pushed around. They were sick of being good little English boys at the Dr. Barnardo home. They wanted some fun.

Strutting around the deck gathering some like minded boys, they pushed their way past the boys playing ball and spied Eddy and Gordon on the deck floor with their marbles. Robert walked up to Gordon and kicked the marble out of his hand.

"Give me back my marble."

"Naw, you ain't getting nuffin' back."

"Give Gordon his marble. It ain't yours" said Eddy.

"Finders, Keepers." piped up John with a smirk that could scare a copper.

"It ain't yours. Give it back."

John pounced on Eddy and pushed his face into the wooden deck. Eddy screamed and Gordon yelled. "Help!"

"You say that again and 'am heavin' you over the side. You'd make good food for sharks." bellowed the bullies.

Hearing the commotion, Joseph came running, summoning Earl to help him.

He grabbed Robert by the scruff of the neck and heaved him across to the life boat. Earl grabbed John by both arms and the others scrambled and ran. They knew they were in big trouble.

Joseph took both Eddy and Gordon to the side by the funnel and after they had stopped crying, he said, "Now, boys, you're goin' to have to learn how to stand up for yourselves. I am going to teach you. It's called prize fightin' and it's the right way to fight. It's fair and when you learn how, no bully will ever try to hurt you again."

"But, they're bigger than us." said Gordon and Eddy in unison

"After tea, we'll meet down below where no one's around and I'll show you the ropes."

Meanwhile, while the boys were getting over their ordeal, the girls were enjoying themselves skipping and playing catch. Their matron was a pretty girl of about 20. She had chestnut coloured hair tied in a bow. She wore high heels, a blue serge dress and a Scottish tartan cape. She laughed as she watched her charges enjoying themselves on their second day at sea.

From a distance she was being admired by a handsome young man with his charges on the other side. David, the master in charge of the boys in Eddy's group, was trying to figure a way to meet her without breaking the rules or neglecting his duties.

The bell rang out for tea and everyone headed for the dining room. Romance would have to wait.

Eddy finally put away his tears and feelings of unworthiness and almost devoured the meal served as usual by the crew dressed in their best whites even on a voyage with few high paying passengers but that was their duty and the boys appreciated the attention.

Joseph, ever questioning everything and everybody, nodded his head in a thank you after the meal was complete. He was anxious to take Eddy and Gordon below deck to teach them about the martial arts. He was a born leader and he even knew the Marquis of Queensbury rules which governed prize fights now that it had become more accepted and legitimate. At Barnardo's, he had learned to read and one of the masters had told him about these rules because secretly he went to matches and even fancied himself a prize fighter.

Joseph eyed Eddy and with a small hand gesture beckoned him over. "Meet me downstairs on the next landing; then follow me to the cargo hold. No one will be around then because the crew will still be in the dining bay."

Eddy and Gordon did exactly as they were told and quietly snuck down the stairs making sure they were alone. They met up with Joseph and wove their way stealthily to the appointed gathering place.

Eddy was nervous but curious as well. Gordon simply pushed forward not even bothering to look behind him.

"Now, boys, "am goin' to teach ya the basics. 'Am just learnin' meself. But, no mine, I know enuf. Ya jest gotta know how to defend yerself. Thar's lots of bullies waitin"roun every corner"

Eddy shivered and Gordon straightened up to the biggest height he knew.

"Okay, boys, Git yar left hand up to yar' chin. Stand wiv yar feet apart. And bounce on em. Ya, that's it Gord'

"Here Eddy, let me lift up yar left hand. Gor' blimy, Eddy, it ain't 'ard. Keep tryin. ' Keep bouncing. Keep yar belly in. Git yar south paw up to yer chin. Good, Gord, ya getting' it Now put up ya right hand up to ya jaw. Punch and pretend ya hittin' a wall. Jes look at 'is eyes and shoot yer fist straight 'at it."

Eddy kept bouncing and Gordon got swinging. Joseph kept circling them and then after a few tries, he put them in a ring he had created with rope on the ground. "Okay boys, ya' gonna prize fight. Pretend like, of course."

Eddy took his place opposite his mate. Both boys moved their left hands to their chin. Bouncing on both feet as though in a dance, Gordon let out his right fist and punched Eddy hard enough to knock him down. But, Eddy jumped up fast, and circled Gordon, this time giving him a punch of his own. It was all in fun. Joseph never let it go beyond four rounds and the boys were getting the hang of it.

"Okay, mates, that's it for today. We'll have a go at it tomorrow."

Tired, they snuck back upstairs and joined the rest of the children in the dining room for evening prayers and song. Nobody seemed to have missed them and David, their master, was dreaming about the pretty girl with the sparkling eyes and chestnut brown hair.

"Time for kip. Off to your bunks. Sleep tight. More adventure tomorrow."

Chapter 13: Iceberg ahead

It was June 8 and they had been at sea for 15 days. There had been a storm and everyone was battened down below deck. Tempers flared and the masters and matrons were kept busy running from deck to deck trying to keep up with the bedlam and chaos of boys whimpering in corners, boys fighting and running everywhere and girls crying for home. Eddy was terrified but Earl and David were too busy to pay attention. All he could think of was home by London Bridge, the market sellers, the pub where he could catch a bit of grub and his sister, Beatrice. Bee, he called her.

A voice shattered the silence and everyone was summoned to the dining bay. Captain Wallace, a tall and imposing man, stood at the front and summoned everyone to stand at ease.

"The storm has subsided and by tomorrow, we will be sailing close to Newfoundland along the Grand Banks. You may catch an iceberg and know that you are not far from land. The journey is almost over. We'll signal you when it's safe to go back on deck."

"Glad that's over." said David.

Then the bell sounded with an announcement, "All crew report to the main deck."

Ever curious, Gordon jumped up and climbed the stairs too, hiding as best he could from everyone in charge. He peered around and hurried over to the place where the mast stood and hid behind some ropes and boxes.

The crew with brooms and buckets in hand began to clean the deck and make it ready for passengers. There was nothing to fear and as soon as he saw there was a clearing, Gordon hopped from one step to another until he got next to Eddy.

"Dan' worry nun'. All good up there. Tha' just cleanin' and makin it ready for us."

" Wern't ya scared Gordon? A bin shakin' in ma boots. When the boat heaved and the water rushed from side to side, I thought for sure, we were goin' down and the sea monsters- remember, Sinbad- would eat us. "

"Na, never. Eddy don't be daft. Come on. Joseph is waiting in the cargo hold for us.

Let's hav' a good fight. We know how."

Up on deck, now that the masters and matrons could go up by ones and twos, David moved over ever so slightly to the pretty young woman in charge of her group of girls and dared to ask her name.

"Molly" she said. "What's yours?"

"David" he said shyly.

They sat as close as they could and exchanged a few words but David was sure he had met the girl of his dreams. Night was closing over the ship. The stars had come out. The sea quieted and a sense of purpose rose in both young people but they would wait for now.

The children in their bunks waited for a new day and a new beginning. Perhaps, it was the talk the head cleric had given at chapel. Perhaps, it was the captain assuring them that the worst was over and that they would have a free day on deck in the morning.

The last two days at sea had been miserable because the captain assumed total control over everyone and everything. He had to have absolute authority of the ship, his crew and his precious cargo of children destined for the new world.

It had been a summer storm but that could spell disaster and his eyes were on this port of call, the destination of all these children. He had been stern and determined and no one questioned his seamanship. It was going to be smooth sailing from now on.

The next day was the best day of the entire voyage. The SS Sicilian with its one funnel, two masts and a single screw moved at a speed of 13 knots. She was slow but steady. Compared to the grander vessels, she was solid and steadfast but not pretty. But, she had proved herself on this voyage and the captain was proud to say that she was the most magnificent ship he had ever sailed. You could hear her swell up with pride.

After breakfast and roll call, masters and boys, matron and girls went up to the top and found their places on deck. The sun shone brightly and the sky was ablaze in blue and mauve. It was June 9, 16 days at sea.

After the initial quiet, the children began to find their friends. David and Molly exchanged glances across the masts but today was going to be far too busy to catch some time together and, anyway, it was strictly forbidden to fraternize with female passengers.

Eddy stood by the funnel with his friends Gordon and Earl and Joseph stood by the mast with his arms folded and his eyes fixed on the horizon. Suddenly, he yelled, "What's that over there?"

As they got closer, he and a few others yelled, "Gor blimey, it's a mountain of ice. Can't be."

If an ice mountain can be beautiful even if dangerous, this was magnificent. Eddy was mesmerized. He gasped and barely uttered, "I'd like to climb that."

It looked inviting with it blue and white walls. The sunlight bounced off it creating tiny rainbows and Eddy was sure that inside lived a snow princess and her maidens. It seemed so close and yet so far.

The ship slowed as the captain frantically steered to the right to avoid a collision. He knew too well the fury of icebergs and this seemed far too close and there had been no warning, This time luck was on their side. As they had weathered the storm, they had passed the berg and they could see land.

"Everyone ran to the side of the ship peering into the horizon. Yes, it was land and the captain announced. "We are just off the coast of Newfoundland founded by John Cabot and we're sailing through the Cabot Straight. Soon, we'll be in the Gulf of St. Lawrence and, tomorrow, we reach our destination. Canada."

Some of the geography lessons that Eddy had absorbed at the Barnardo Home were coming true. There really was a place called Canada. The gulls from this side of the ocean welcomed them even it was the grub they were after.

All the sea life seemed to welcome them. A large sea turtle swam alongside and they had seen a pod of whales. It seemed perfectly natural to Eddy and this was shortly after the old cleric had read them the story of Jonah in the Whale.

He could imagine himself a friend of the hump back but he would swim on his back and not be lured inside and he would dive with him to the sea palaces below.

Eddy told Gordon that he had seen a mermaid too. Gordon just smiled because he knew Eddy had a big imagination.

The ship seemed to slow down as it made its way through the Cabot Strait and into the Gulf of St. Lawrence. The masters and matrons gathered their charges and unceremoniously marched them to the dining area. They couldn't take any chances with the children who were excited enough. The last thing they needed was the call, 'Child overboard.'

Word had come, that it happened on another ship last year. Boys were playing too close to the barrier and one bold and foolish lad had leaned over too far to see an iceberg and had lost his balance and fell. His body was never recovered. It had been drilled into them that they could never take their eyes off the children, not for a moment.

The head master brought all the children together this time- the boys on one side and the girls on the other.

"After our tea, you are to come directly here for chapel and then you will be dismissed for bed time. Tomorrow, we will reach the end of our journey and you will need to be alert and ready for the train trip to follow. Tomorrow morning, bright and early, I will show you where we are on the map so that you can follow our journey down the mighty river, the St. Lawrence that will take you into this great land."

They were dismissed to their own dining area. Tonight, it was whispered, they would have the best meal of the voyage. Eddy, Earl and Gordon were almost too excited to eat. The meals on board had been the best in their lives.

"If this is what we can expect in Canada", said David, the young master, "we should dine very well indeed."

This wasn't high tea. This was dinner. They had roast beef, roast potatoes, cabbage, turnip and peas. The stewards served extra helpings of bread and butter and heaping glasses of milk.

Eddy who had such excitement this day seeing his very first ice mountain was almost shaking with anticipation.

"Gordon, are ya happy?"

"Ya, kind of but I still don't what's in store and I miss Arthur more today than ever. When I come into port, he'll be sitting in his bed alone wondering where I am. First thing I am doin' when I get to Canada, is to ask about my brother. I want him on the next boat and I am not leaving the ship until they tell me, he'll be joining me soon."

David overheard him and said, "I'll do all I can to help you. It's not fair that your brother was kept behind."

After dinner, the gong rang, and as requested the children filed into the main dining area which had stood for the chapel for this voyage. The head master called them all to prayer.

"Guide us, great redeemer, to the Promised Land. As you lead your people out of Egypt, so now lead us to this new country. God be with you all."

Prayers over and a pep talk about being good children and the pride of England and all, they were sent to their beds.

Joseph who had been noticeably absent came over to Eddy and Gordon and whispered.

"Well, matey's we'll sneak one more prize fight in downstairs in the morning just after dawn. You'll have to dress quickly and tiptoe down the hall to meet me outside the cargo hold. Ya gotta be ready for anythin' now. Ya know the ropes! See ya in the morning."

Chapter 14: Sailing down the St. Lawrence to Quebec City

Dense fog shrouded the sun as the ship's bow ploughed steadily ahead. Gulls wailed and the waves crashed.

The children having been well served by a hearty breakfast had gathered for their last geography lesson. The master stood near a large map of Eastern Canada which he had spread out on the dining room table. He could only summon about 20 boys at a time for the lesson. The rest sat quietly to wait their turn. Eddy had squeezed to the front because he wanted to learn everything he could this morning. Joseph was on the opposite side of the map and all eyes were on the master, the map and his big pointer.

"See here. This is Newfoundland which you passed yesterday. Over here is the Isle de Madeleine. When the fog lifts as I hope it will, you might be able to see the houses on the island. Imagine that. There are settlers on these little islands, mostly fishermen farmers. They are a hardy lot. After we leave these islands, we will steer between Ile d'Anticosti and the Gaspe Peninsula. These lands were discovered by John Cabot."

Eddy desperate to be heard, belted out, "Gor" Blimey I remember him. He was Italian wasn't he?"

"Yes, Eddy, that's right. You have a good memory."

Eddy blushed but sat a little further up on his seat, his shoulders pressed hard against the back of the chair.

"Remember" continued the Master, "that he was working for the King of England and so he declared this land the property of King James. Quebec belonged to the French. They got into a battle later on but the English won at the Battle of the Plains of Abraham. Some day, you might read this story and you can say, 'we've been there and we have seen the battle ground.' Once round the corner of the Gaspe, we will head down the river St. Lawrence to Quebec City. Now boys, move back so another group of boys can gather around the map. Wait here though until everyone has had a chance to learn the geography of this place. Once the fog has lifted you can go up on deck."

Just as the Master said, "Once the fog has lifted", Gordon, ever anxious, had already gone up stairs to look for himself. He yelled down, "It's all clear, we can go on deck and have a look."

Now with the sun shining bright, the children rushed to the side of the ship to see the land up close. They screamed in delight. So long they had been at sea watching the waves hit the sides of the ship and sometimes they had been afraid. Like a dream, they could see the houses appear out of the fog, fishing boats at work bringing in the catch and icebergs hugging the tiny harbours as the ship wound its way through the shipping lane well established from years of sailing these waters.

In the distance they could see a ship similar to theirs. There had been an exchange of funnel charges and their ships flags blew in the ocean breeze. It was the SS Corinthian and on board like the SS Sicilian would have been boys and girls from the orphan homes of England bound for lives in this unknown land. The Corinthian would have had passengers bound for settlement and some bound for the emerging cities of Montreal and Toronto. Some would be continuing west to the prairies. Everyone seemed on the move.

Strangely, even though there were so many people on board, the children hardly came across them during the voyage because there had been strict separation of these street children as they were called and the paying passengers. They never sat down together for meals and 7 o'clock, night time, meant bedtime and strict orders to behave.

The ship slowed down to 8 knots as it moved into the St. Lawrence. To their right, were the Laurentian Mountains, the tops still covered with snow. To the left were the green fields of the farms stretched out in long strips from the shore to the woodlands beyond. It was the way of French settlement.

The children who would go on to the English speaking provinces would find the layout of farms closer to that of their homeland and they would see that forests had to be cut first before settlement could begin. But this would be discovered later and most of them were too young and too accustomed to city life to even think about it.

As they continued on, a small vessel pulled alongside and two men were hoisted aboard. The slight man was the pilot and it was his duty to guide the ocean craft to port. The older man, too well dressed for this task, turned out to be the doctor and his task was monumental. He was brought on board to examine every single passenger for the Government of Canada. His name was Dr. LeBlanc, a French citizen, now employed by Canada. He had to stamp each paper with a clean bill of health. If they didn't pass, they would have to remain on board to be shipped back on the return voyage. He would recruit the ships' physician and nurse to help him.

By bringing Dr. LeBlanc on board, the Government eliminated the need to dock at the Quarantine Station at Grosse Isle. Years ago, back about 50 years, there had been outbreaks of cholera and typhus and the only way to protect Canadians was to quarantine every passenger until the scourge passed. Many would die and their graves are scattered among the rock and flowering shrubs of this isolated island.

The minute he was on board he began his job in earnest. Dr. Phillip and Nurse O'Hara, the ship's physician and nurse, helped him. There were 1404 passengers and crew members to examine and he had only 12 hours to complete his job.

First he examined the first class passengers in the upper region of the ship. Theirs had been a voyage of luxury not up to the standards of the Cunard liners but special for them on this ship and most were bound for Montreal, the financial hub of Quebec.

As he moved down to the steerage area with its passengers bound for whatever job they could find or eventually get a grant of land to settle and farm, he came first to the children's area. He was stunned at the number of boys and girls some as young as 5 and others barely 14. They looked in remarkably good health considering what he had read about them. He knew that many had been rescued from the slums of London and that they were often called street Arabs, unruly street urchins and thieves. To his astonishment, they were clean, well dressed and well spoken even if they still had broad cockney accents.

Second in the examination line was a handsome boy with black hair and piercing dark eyes.

"What's your name, boy?"

"Eddy".

"How are you feeling after your long voyage?"

"Vew'y good, sir."

"Let me listen to your chest. Breathe in and breathe out. That's good. Let me check your eyes and ears? Open your eyes wide. That's right."

He put an instrument in Eddy's ear. "Looks good. Where are you going, Eddy?"

"I dunno, sir."

"Well good luck just the same. Next!"

He continued until everyone had been examined.

Fortunately, there had been no illness on board except for sea sickness. Most passengers were young and healthy and two of the young women married only a year or so, had given birth on the high seas. The babies were thriving in the ocean air.

The SS Sicilian plied its way up the river and with sleepy passengers now with their medical cards stamped, 'Passed medical. All clear', they came to port. The citadel of Quebec and the rock that Wolfe and his invading army had climbed to The Plains of Abraham to take Quebec, welcomed them to Canada.

Now the task of Immigration and the giving of Papers of Naturalization lay ahead. It would have to wait. Everyone was sleeping save the crew. It was 5.30 AM.

Chapter 15: In the new world

Eddy woke up with a start. He was used to the soft cradle-like movement of his ship. It lulled him to sleep in the evening and it kept him dreaming before the screaming bell announcing 'Wake up' sounded. Only once on the voyage had the ship been harsh moving erratically up and down and side to side and that was during the summer storm which they had all survived to talk about.

He must have been dreaming because when he jumped up with the bell, he was surrounded by boys jumping up and down on their bunks yelling "Canada, Canada, Canada!" There was no stopping them and no stopping the excitement. Yawning, he exclaimed, "I am dreaming of ice cream and horses. Where are we?"

"You're in Canada, Eddy." said the young master, David. "You've slept in. Get washed and dressed and hurry to the dining room. It's going to be a long day."

He got dressed in his Sunday best as he was told and sat down to his last breakfast on board. All the boys and girls had been instructed to take their best outfit from their carrying bag. It was important to be at their spiffiest for the Immigration Officers who could reject them even on their first day in the country and they had to look their best when they arrived at the receiving home in Toronto.

Everyone was lined up to go up on deck where the captain was to say a few words before they departed. They marched up the stairs in two's and resumed their cadet like marching as they had been taught. It had been 17 days at sea- a lifetime for children so young.

"It has been a pleasure having you all on board. God speed and God bless every one of you." said the captain looking down at the children especially.

The old sailor who had taught them a bit about seafaring came up to Eddy and his companions and shook their hand. Winking at Eddy, he said "You earned your sea legs alright boys. Now, you're gonna learn to be farmers. Ha! Ha! Good luck. Maybe we'll meet again if ever you go back to the old country."

After hugs and kisses and teary farewells, the passengers moved carefully down the gang plank to a large throng of well wishers and dignitaries. The children were hustled into a large shed where immigration officials sat in front of barriers designed to stop any one from rushing beyond the gates. As was the custom with the children from the sending Homes, the children were separated from the main passengers who were processed in a larger more comfortable building.

David gathered his group, Earl helping to guide the boys along. Eddy was looking for Joseph but he couldn't see him and Gordon was being ushered into another room. He suddenly felt alone. His eyes filled with tears and he felt cold. His world, kept comfortable by his dreams, was slowly collapsing and he wasn't sure what was happening to him. It had been fun on the ship. He was becoming a good little fighter and felt sure that he could handle himself with any bully now.

Joseph had reminded him just last night with, "You're goin' to be a good fighter, Eddy. Keep your wits about you and don't back down."

Eddy looked around again and smiled as he spied Joseph up front with some of the older boys. He seemed to have grown tall on the trip over. He was worried about Gordon, though. Why was he taken into a room by himself?

Earl, sensing Eddy's concerns, came over and snuck a sweet into his pocket. "That should make you feel better. Chin up, Eddy, it's goin' to be alright."

By now, he was getting close to the official who was stamping something and pushing them through.

"Step up. Boy."

Eddy was summoned to the desk of a man who looked like a policeman and that made Eddy shiver. He had seen them in London and they could drag you off to the working house or jail. He had some papers before him. "Name?"

"Eddy."

"Full name?"

"Edward George Tompkins, sir."

"Who is with you, boy?"

"I am with the Dr. Barnardo party, sir."

"How old are you?"

"Seven years old."

Eddy had forgotten that he had had a birthday and that he was now 8.

"Excuse me, sir, I'm 8 years old. I had a birthday at the home before I left."

"Never mind. Your paper is stamped. You're 7."

Eddy's document was stamped with the official government stamp. It read:

"Edward George Tompkins, seven years old, travelling alone!

Destination: Toronto, Ontario, Landed immigrant.

June 10, 1910."

That stamp, Landed Immigrant, was the lodestone everyone wanted and this little boy from London, all alone in this new world, had a ticket that could sustain him always. He was a British subject and a Landed Immigrant in Canada. What a feat!

No sooner had his papers been stamped, he was hustled to a waiting train of the Grand Trunk Railway, the train destined to bring him and many of the boys to Toronto to wait for placement in a Canadian home. Some children had already been assigned to families and would be dropped off in stations and halts along the track and the girls were destined for a large home in Peterborough.

The train seemed so big compared to what he remembered of trains going by his flat near Westminster Bridge and the train that took him to Liverpool. He could see the massive wheels and it seemed so high off the ground. Already, the engine was warming up and the stokers were hard at work filling the engine box with coal in preparation for the long journey of about 500 miles to the metropolitan city, Toronto. He tried to look along its length and he lost sight of it. There seemed to be no end.

It had been raining but now the sun had come out and he found himself strangely warm. He wanted to take off his naval style coat and pull his socks and shoes off. He wanted to talk to Gordon and share his excitement about the train and the journey ahead with him but he and Joseph were nowhere to be seen.

"Where are my mates? Where are they?"

Eddy started shivering again. He shivered when he was nervous even if it was very warm. It wasn't the same without his special mates.

"Get moving, boy," said the porter. "We haven't got all day. No time to dawdle."

When he reached the platform, he tried to climb up but his legs were too short. A boost from behind hoisted him up and then Eddy was on the connecting ramp between the coaches.

He was roasting by now. The summer heat was intense. He had never known heat like this in London.

"Where is the snow?" he thought.

He had been told that winter was the main season and, except for pictures of wheat fields, farm hands and cowboys, most of the pictures were of snow piled as high as houses and sleighs ploughing through with horses adorned with bells and smoke coming out of their nostrils.

Once inside the train, he could see that it was a large coach, not like the small compartment he had been in on his way from the home to the docks at Liverpool.

It took him a while to realize that the coaches which were called cars were connected like a huge centipede with a hundred legs and that you could go from coach to coach stepping across the connecting barrier if you wanted to go to the dining car or go to the 'bog'. There were strict rules about this on the English trains and the coaches didn't stretch out into the distance like these.

As Eddy stood by the window waiting for his seat assignment, he looked out at the ship now with all its passengers on dry land. He watched the dock crew at work unloading the hundreds of trunks and sea bags full of the belongings of French, English, German, Irish and those from other lands who had had a varied voyage from luxury to steerage on ship but on dry land, all had a song in their heart because this land offered hope and dreams fulfilled.

Eddy looked at the young men, taller than the men at home, and stronger, carrying the loads without effort and to his surprise, he could see Dr. Barnardo trunks with their emblem of the home. These alligator skin covered trunks carried clothes deemed suitable for young men in their new station and bibles and hymn books to keep them on the right side of God. The trunks were moved toward the train and he could hear the porters loading them aboard.

Soon, Eddy was joined by Earl and David Ryan, the kind young master who had accompanied them on their voyage.

"Where should I sit, sir?" asked Eddy.

"Anywhere you want." winked David.

That was a change. On the last train, 10 boys were assigned to each compartment regardless of the wishes of the boys. They wanted to be with their mates, to sit beside them, play card games and joke about.

"I'd like to sit with Gordon and Joseph," said Eddy.

"Sorry, Eddy. Gordon won't be coming with us. I shouldn't tell you but I will because I know how close you both were."

Eddy felt a cold chill and his lower lip quivered. "Why can't he be with us?"

"Do you remember that you told me that you saw a lady in black when we left the home and then you saw her later at the docks in Liverpool? You thought that it might be your mother come to see you off but then you realized that it wasn't her. Well, it turned out to be Gordon and Arthur's great aunt. She is their grandmother's sister and she has come into money through a well placed marriage to a rich merchant. When she learned about Gordon and Arthur being taken to Dr. Barnardo's by her sister, she was appalled. She had been very fond of their mother and was shocked to think that her very own sister would send them away."

Eddy sensing a change in Master Ryan's tone said, "Will she come out with Arthur on the next ship to join him."

"No, Eddy. Gordon is being sent back when the ship sails in two more days. He and his brother Arthur who was kept back, remember, will be taken to their great aunt's estate and raised as young gentlemen. Gordon hesitated because he didn't want to leave you, Eddy, but he had no choice. Life will be better for him and it is best this way." David said rubbing Eddy gently on his forehead.

Eddy put his head down and sobbed. He and Gordon were such great mates; they were like brothers and they were planning to become cowboys on the open range. "No fair! I don' want to go anywhere without him."

David and Earl tried to make him laugh by making funny faces and pretending to be Punch and Judy but Eddy was inconsolable. They had to let him cry until he could cry no more. "No fair; no fair."

Oblivious to Eddy's sobs, the train lurched forward bound for Toronto and the home there. The wheels throbbed and the whistle gave three loud shrieks and the "All aboard" call was lost in the clamour and the noise. It was 9 o'clock in the morning, June 10, the first day in Canada.

Chapter 16: On the train to Toronto

The train, now fully loaded with passengers from the ship and a few locals who were travelling to Montreal, began to move. The huge wheels of the locomotive began to grind forward with a 'Chug, Chug a Chug' motion picking up speed as it moved out of the station.

Eddy strained at the window catching sight of his ship still in port but already loading up with goods and far fewer passengers for the trip back to Liverpool. He wondered where Gordon would be while he waited for his passage back to England. His great aunt, the lady in black, would be waiting for him on the other side and Arthur would be there too.

Not once did Gordon come into his sight so all he could do was cry out to himself, "We won't be cowboys together. I miss you matey. Hope it will be alright."

David was looking too but not at ships. He was thinking about Molly and wondering what car she was in. He knew that they were heading for the Girls Receiving home called Hazel Brae in a town called Peterborough and he hoped that he could be spared from his duties to try to find her but, right now, the boys were hungry. After all, they had been up early and had gone through so much with immigration and all.

"Gather up boys. We are going to the dining car. You must be very careful as you move through the train especially when you step across from one car to the other. You are a nimble footed lot so you should be alright. Step up sharply."

Eddy followed right behind his master with the other boys behind him. The train rumbled forward with its continuous 'chug, chug a chug' rhythm. It kept the beat as the locomotive picked up speed, then slowed down around the curves of the great river, the St. Lawrence, picking up speed again as it sped through the farmlands of Quebec.

They arrived at the dining car about 11.00 a.m. and sat down at checker tablecloths and plain dishes and cutlery. "Not as fancy as the ship." thought Eddy but food was uttermost in his mind.

Before David sat down with them, though, he leaned towards the table of girls at the other end of the diner to see if Molly was with them, and there she was prettier and more enchanting than ever.

Eddy was curious but he knew he would have to sit still until the waiter took their order and since his master was preoccupied, he had to wait. When David turned back to the table, he summoned the waiter and whispered in his ear. The waiter nodded in reply and David announced, "Boys, I have an errand at the next table, so be patient and wait until your food arrives."

David moved over to Molly's table and asked if he could take a seat beside her. She reddened in the face just a little and the girls stifled their giggles at seeing such a handsome young man and a master at that.

Eddy strained his ears towards the table to overhear David say, "May I write to you when I get to Toronto?"

"Yes." she said.

"Perhaps, we can meet for a coffee later after the children settle down for a sleep. We'll be getting into Toronto by about 3 in the morning."

"We expect to arrive in Peterborough by 12 tonight." Molly answered.

"How about meeting here at 9 this evening?"

"If I can get leave, I will."

At that, David returned to his table of boys and Molly attended to the little girl by the window. She looked so forlorn in her uniform dress of grey with a white collar. All the girls were dressed the same but she was the youngest, and barely 5. Molly put her arm around the child and before long, a smile spread across her sweet face.

The sandwiches were delicious and the tea warm. The boys didn't talk much and David wore a grin as wide as a full moon. Now with their bellies full, they moved back across the barriers to their own car and settled in for the rest of the journey.

By 4 in the afternoon, the train slowed down and came to a stop in Montreal. Everyone got off for a break and some fresh air. They stood on the platform and some of the children ran about skipping and jumping and getting their exercise as the mentors had instructed them to do.

"All Aboard!"

Eddy had enjoyed his few minutes in the big city. He thought of London and his father. He could barely make him out but he thought he could remember his dark hair and mustache and he remembered his voice.

"Eddy, you been a good boy today? Want to go for a walk?"

Eddy was remembering his Dad as a busker, telling stories and singing a ballad about a sailor at the pub. "Don't tell your mother about this," he had whispered as they headed back to the flat.

"All aboard! Last call for Toronto."

"Hurry up, Eddy. You're day dreaming again. Wake up boy and get movin'," said Earl as he pushed him up the steps. "Next time, I'm caning you. Do you understand?"

They settled in and this time, David went to the dining car alone ordering more sandwiches and tea for the boys to eat at their seats. He was anxious to get them ready for the few hours of sleep they could grab before they would have to get out at their destination early in the morning. He wanted to save time in the dining car for his hoped for meeting with Molly at 9.

As the train moved beyond Montreal, it picked up speed passing villages and fields only the outline of which could be made out in the dark. Every few towns, the train would stop and boys would depart. Eddy watched as buggies drove up to rural stations to pick up these English boys now bound to them by contract. Four sets of boys got off at Kingston and he jumped when he saw Joseph. He had looked for him when they first arrived in Quebec. He was hard to find being older and with another group of boys who needed less supervision.

Frantically waving, Eddy tried knocking on the train window but Joseph didn't see him. Eddy wiping a tear from his eye watched Joseph climb into the buggy as the train pulled out of the station. "Joseph. Joseph!" He screamed but it was no use. Eddy collapsed in tears and there was no consoling him.

His best mates, Gordon and Joseph were gone and he felt a huge lump in his throat and sadness such as he had never known before; even the sadness of his mother leaving him all alone at Dr. Barnardo's Home was not as bad.

"Want my sandwich," said the boy sitting opposite.

"Oh, alright."

As night fell, the Grand Trunk locomotive kept its relentless rhythm and the engineer blew his whistle in his distinctive style, 3 short whistles and one long piercing one as they approached each stop. Eddy was getting used to it and he could anticipate the stops as the train slowed and the whistle blew to signify another halt. More boys got off, sometimes only one at a time. It was hard to imagine what it was like for them after travelling so far to be at a small Canadian station at night all alone waiting for a buggy of a family they didn't know.

The girls stayed together. It wasn't safe for a girl alone at night in a strange place in a strange country. The boys dosed off one by one and Eddy fell asleep. Earl had given them each a blanket so that they could curl up on the seat and make themselves comfortable.

Rich passengers were in the Pullman cars with their own bed and toiletries and stewards to look after them. They would have eaten in a first class carriage and wine would have been their sleeping potion.

Lights were dimmed and this pleased David who by now was sitting in the dining car with Molly. They sat close together and made plans for their future. They wouldn't be going back to England when this land welcomed them with such open arms.

The boys and girls in their separate cars had mostly all nodded off to sleep although they were often jolted awake as the train came into a station to let passengers off. Molly and David were back with their charges even if both dreamed of a cabin on the open plain with a garden and some sheep and goats. They were planning to buy some books on farming if and when they could get away from their respective employers in Peterborough and Toronto. In the meantime, they had pledged to exchange letters and try to get a weekend pass so they could meet.

It was close to 12 o'clock. Molly and the other matrons gathered the girls, checked their carrying bags, and sat each girl down for a last minute hair brush and a fresh face cloth to brighten their sleepy faces.

"Peterborough. Next stop. Proceed to the exit."

They barely picked up their feet as they pushed their way to the door. The train had slowed to a halt, the wheels screeched to a stop, and the whistle blew. The girls, dressed in their school girl uniform with their bonnets secured, climbed down the steps to the platform. Molly walked among them and the head matron counted each girl to make sure they were all there ready for their next journey.

Three horse drawn buggies were waiting and after their Barnardo trunks were loaded, the girls climbed on. The young matrons followed picking up their long skirts and balancing on their high boots. The driver picked up his riding whip and the horses started up. They were going to Hazel Brae, a mansion on the outskirts of the town, bought by the Barnardo charity to house girls arriving from England. It would be their home until they were chosen by a Canadian family.

David looked out the window and hoped he would see Molly to wave her goodbye. Eddy looked out too but not seeing anything except buggies, he sat down again and fell asleep.

After not much more than ten minutes, the engines engaged, and the wheels started moving, and the train left the station. In the night, it whisked along through dark country and open fields, past waterfalls and across rivers until it came to its destination, Toronto. It was 3.35 in the morning, June 11.

"Last stop!"

Chapter 17: Toronto

It was dark except for the lights in the railway cars and the lights at Union Station. "Wake up boys. This is where we get off." said David.

It took a few minutes for the boys to get accustomed to the lights, which had been dimmed for the journey from Peterborough to the last station and their arrival in the big city. They donned their cadet jackets, put on their berets and reached for their carrying cases.

"Follow me," David called.

Eddy got in line and stumbled forward, almost plunging onto the platform below. There were porters to guide them as they were marched into the towering station, with its massive ceilings and white pillars. Eddy thought he was in a palace but for the scores of long seats and weary passengers either lying on the benches or sitting on their luggage on the floor.

Outside, Eddy had his first glance at the city at night with its gas lamps aglow. It was eerie and cold even if it was June. David looked at his pocket watch and watched for the carriages that would take them to their temporary home in Toronto. The boys leaned against the wall as sleep wanted to overtake them again.

Suddenly five carriages pulled up, the horses stomping and the drivers, yelling "Ho, Ho there. Ho!" It was pandemonium and yet the drivers sorted things out quite quickly. A young man jumped down and moved immediately to David who was obviously in charge."My name is Stephen. You must be Master Ryan. Pleased to meet ya."

"Nice to meet you as well."

"Load up!" He yelled and the other drivers followed suit.

There were still 67 remaining boys after so many had left the train this long night. Most would already be in bed in their new homes. Eddy was boosted up first onto a stool and then into the open cart. It was more like a milk cart than a carriage. He was soon pushed into place between Earl and Robert, the boy who had bullied him on the ship. No matter, it was dark and all the boys were past being tired. They were too tired to know how exhausted they really were.

When everyone was on board, the horses snorted, the drivers raised their whips and they moved out to the waiting street. They went at a fairly fast clip, moving from one street to another until they reached 538 Jarvis Street.

There in the dark stood the Canadian headquarters of Dr. Barnardo in Canada. Even in the faded light, it was an imposing Victorian structure built of grey stone. It had been the city dwelling of a wealthy merchant and now, with a large extension added to the back, it could certainly house a large number of migrant boys. Its huge windows in the bay front looked ready to swallow the children and the night only added to the terror Eddy felt.

The horses pulled up in front of the stone wall with its large iron gates open to receive them and then proceeded to the front of the house. They knew the way because they had been here many times before. The oak doors, even though open, seemed ready to shut at any moment. The porter stood at attention and beckoned the drivers to stop. The horses stopped on cue and the prefects yelled, "We're here. Get moving, boys. "

The boys picked up their weary legs and, wiping the tired from their eyes, they slowly descended from the carriages and found their feet on the hard surface of the pavement. Eddy was in a daze. Only the prefect Earl was wide awake and David, the young master, was in the carriage ahead of them. He, along with the other young masters, who had accompanied the boys from the time they left Stepney Causeway on May 28, had an onerous task ahead. How could they get all these boys into the home and into bed with a minimum of disruption at 4 in the morning?

"Come on boys. Grab your bags and line up so we can count heads."

"Where are we?" said Robert, scowling in the early morning dew. "What's next?"

Mr. Ryan, the name they had to call their master even if they had become familiar with him on board ship, didn't answer except to say.

"Stand still and answer when called." "Robert Merithew."

'Ere"

"Sir." said Mr. Ryan.

"Yes, sir." Robert shot out.

"Edward G Tompkins"

"Present sir."

After they were all accounted for, they proceeded by following the lantern carried by Earl. They climbed the steps and entered a large gas lit hall. The maids stood around the edge looking tired and a little annoyed at being up this time of night. The matron sat in a large chair at the centre and beckoned them in. "We will dispense with niceties, this time of night, 'er, morning. Girls, escort these charges to their dormitory. The trunks will be delivered shortly but you can put the boys to bed right away."

It didn't take long for everyone to be settled in for the rest of the night, come morning. Eddy was the first to fall asleep. But before Eddy was in dreamland, a bell sounded and everyone was up and scrambling.

"What's this place? Not more bloody orders. Not more school?"

First thing was the WC and washing off all the dirt of travel.

"You clean behind your ears and brush your teeth. Down to breakfast by 7.00 sharp."

Eddy found himself bewildered. After all that, he was in a home again and in a city. He thought he'd be on the wide open range. They sat together and after prayers, busily dove into the food. The helpings were smaller than what they had on board the Sicilian and there were no eggs and bacon. They were back to institutional porridge, dry toast and luke warm tea.

Breakfast past, they received their marching orders. They were going to have to do chores again, cleaning the plates, washing the tables, scrubbing the floors, making the beds, and everything else the matron ordered.

The building seemed like a large hollow cave with dark wallpaper, heavy furnishings and massive stairs. The dormitories were in an extension on the back. The dining room was on the main floor beyond the parlour and reception room. This was going to be a hard place to clean and they already had their tasks assigned.

Outside was a tree lined garden with oak and maple and summer flowers. Eddy hoped he would get a chance to play. It was going to be a waiting game until every boy was placed in a home. The process began the following day. Already, there were stacks of requests for children.

One read, "Looking for a boy over 12, strong and intelligent, to help us with farm chores. His schooling is guaranteed."

Another said, "Wanted 2 boys around 14. Must have training in carpentry; be intelligent and willing to take instructions." Each letter was accompanied by two letters of reference from a clergyman and either a banker, lawyer or school teacher.

People came from the countryside outside the Toronto home, eager to pick out a boy who could help with the heavy duties of farm work. A few lived in the city and were looking to eventually adopt a boy who had intellectual promise. All wanted a pure Anglo Saxon child preferably blond and blue eyed.

As they gathered in the large hall, they chatted with one another. In these early days of the Dominion, farmers knew almost everyone from their various agricultural circles and county fairs set up to display their livestock and their wares each summer. And all of them went to the auctions where livestock was bought and sold.

After breakfast, Eddy was summoned to a classroom where tables were set up and papers prepared. Eddy fumbled with his hands and scratched behind his ears as he waited to be called. He stood in one corner with some of the boys he had come to know. The would be foster parents were brought in by the matron and seated in 2 rows, as they waited for their names to be called.

Eddy could hear them talking amongst themselves. "They have funny accents and they don't look very able."

But then someone would follow with, "My neighbour Bob is overjoyed with his new boy. A real worker and a good kid too."

Others remarked, "Not sure, if I would want that one."

While someone said, "Give him a chance, Roy."

One by one, boys and foster parents were matched and after several days, most boys had been placed with a family. There were forms to be filled and guarantees that the child would be treated as one of the family, provided with food, board and clothing and assured an education.

It was now day 4 and no one had looked at Eddy. Maybe his dark curly hair and piercing brown eyes were the wrong colour or maybe he was too small. He couldn't get used to this institution and he wanted to have a place of his own like the others.

He looked for Earl and David Ryan but it wasn't to be because Earl had already been placed with a rich family in Toronto. A well dressed and impeccably mannered couple had inquired about the possibility of adoption since they had no children of their own. They had thought of a small boy of perhaps 6 or 7 but they were impressed by the young prefect. He stood tall and bright among the others. His early breeding as a child of a school master was evident in the way he moved and in the way he spoke. "We would like to meet with the young man over there," they said to the matron.

"It can be arranged immediately. Please come to this room over here."

In no time, papers were signed, and the necessary arrangements were made for Earl to go with this family.

Eddy looked around. There were still 16 children here. They could have some fun together. "Wanna go out and play? We can get some balls from one of the maids and go out to the garden."

"We can't do that!"

"Why not? Let's go."

The younger of the maids caught Eddy's eye and winked. She had the footballs ready and she had checked with matron, who gave her permission to get the boys outside for a game of football. It was hot outside, a hotter heat than they knew in London but they felt free and that was all that mattered.

The next morning after breakfast, a farmer and his wife came with a request. They had thought to adopt but they weren't sure. They needed help on the farm, a newly settled homestead and there was work to do. All the older boys had been placed so they decided on Edward. Soon he was ushered in and examined from head to toe. Mrs. Lynch was impressed. She liked Eddy's open face, his broad smile and his black curly hair, which although short had grown from the stubble of the shaving a few weeks ago. Mr. Lynch, a dour man in his early forties, took some persuading.

"I like him. He seems like a nice boy." said his wife.

"He is awful small. What's he going to do with our bullock? The kid would run at the first sight of him."

"Let's take him home and try him out."

"Come here, boy." said Mr. Lynch," Let me see you up close. Stand up and jump up as far as you can. Good. Now keep jumping moving your arms as well."

"Why are you doing this John? The boy is young and he is frightened."

"Keep jumping until I tell you to stop."

Eddy jumped and jumped until the farmer yelled, "Stop."

"He'll never make it. He's a runt. I don't want him."

At that, they walked out the door, Mrs. Lynch muttering something to herself and Mr. Lynch stomping out, saying, "None of these street-Arabs for me."

Chapter 18: Waiting

Before the Lynch's left the home on Jarvis Street, Eddie had decided that he wanted none of them. Even Mrs. Lynch who had said nice things about him was not to his liking. She was too much under her husband's dominance to be of any use to a young boy and Eddy remembered too well what his own parents were like. Certainly his mother cowered under the influence of her common law husband.

He was only eight but he had seen a lot of life and he just wanted to be free. He felt hemmed in within the city limits. He could hear the rattle of the daily carriages as they hurried through the streets at all times of the day and well into the night. There was a garden and he had been able to play with his new mates but so much had happened.

He had taken the train from the London home to the docks and there he had met prefect, Earl and Master Ryan and he had been introduced to Robert who had been such a bully on the ship. His best mate, Gordon, was heading back to England to be with his brother Arthur and their great aunt who had vowed to give them a much better life in her big country home. His pal and helpmate, Joseph, had left the train for some farm somewhere. He missed all of them. It was so lonely without them.

On the train to Toronto, he had witnessed the blooming romance between Mistress Molly and Master Ryan. He could only hope that they would find each other soon as they had promised. And now Prefect Earl who had befriended him was going off with a rich couple. He was sure he would never see him again and that was upsetting too. He was sad at the thought that he was alone without true friends. Now, there wasn't even school to attend or routines he had learned to accept. There was comfort in the familiar.

Everything in this receiving home was new and frightening. It was a dark mansion given to the Barnardo Charity as a place for boys to stay while they waited for a placement with a family. During the day, light filtered through dark draperies but at night, it seemed to creak and whisper things and he was frightened.

If only he was back with his mother, his baby brother, his sister and James the oldest boy. It was coming back to him. They shared only two rooms but his mother made it cozy and in the good times, there was always a fire in the hearth even in summer. It kept the cold out and the warmth in.

Now, here he was, far away and in a strange land with people with strange accents and unfamiliar ways. They were quieter and more subdued. Eddy liked the sound of the vendors at the market at home. Their voices were loud, a bit cocky and cheery. "Any ol' bottles and bones? 'Ere lady have some of the 'ere cockles. Fry 'em up tonight."

But nothing was the same really. His mother never came back and there was no letter from her. Other boys had received letters and even packages from home. He didn't know what had happened but in his files at the Dr. Bernardo Institute it was written that James was on the farm with his grandparents; Beatrice was being boarded out and his mother was in a home for the destitute with her new baby. Her common law husband had beaten her and left her broken when the authorities found her and removed her to a safe place.

A bell rang and tea was served in the dining area. Eddy was startled but it broke him out of his reverie. There was lots of noise coming from the room and Eddy joined them for tea and biscuits.

"Where was ya, Eddy?" Said one of his new found mates. "We thought you were going to leave us. You spent a long time with that family who came to see you."

"They didn't want me and anyway, I didn't like them so it's just as well."

Later that afternoon, well after the Lynch's had left the building without a word to the governor, Eddy was summoned to the office.

"Tompkins, you didn't impress this family and they had travelled all the way from Guelph, a city of considerable distance away from Toronto, to take you home with them."

"A didn' do anything. Just jumped up and down like he told me. He said I was a runt and not any use to him on the farm."

"What's a 'street Arab' sir? That's what he called me when he was leaving."

The governor snorted and whisked Eddy away. "Go to your room, boy."

There had been a growing outcry against these child immigrants. Some members of parliament said that it was a mistake to bring these children from the streets of England's slums.

"They will contaminate our pure stock. We must put a stop to this."

Members of the press wrote stories of children who were caught stealing or of children running away from their Canadian homes. There were articles describing them as street urchins, gutter rats and street Arabs and saying that they were of low intelligence and untrustworthy. Instead of writing about the children and how they must have felt being taken away from England and dumped into homes of people they didn't know who only wanted them as workers on their farms, they said that Canada would be better off without them.

There were, of course, those who believed that these children would blossom in their new homes and become productive members of society. They believed that with the right environment and upbringing, they could achieve great things.

Eddy went to his dormitory, lay down on his hard bed, and sobbed. "It ain't fair. It ain't fair. I wanna go home."

But he was a tough kid underneath all this and soon he got up and went down stairs to join the others for a game of ball in the garden.

Every day for the next several weeks, men travelling alone, couples waiting for an interview and older spinsters looking for an able helper, came to Jarvis Street and slowly, the boys were matched and sent off to farms all over southern Ontario. Some were sent to the new settlements further north.

It was July 2. Eddy had been in this home since he arrived on June 11 exhausted from the long train trip from Port Levis. He had become friendly with the maids and the chief matron had taken a liking to him. She felt sorry for the little boy with the curly brown hair and the twinkling eyes. At least now he had hair on his head and not a shaven space.

"The only thing keeping Eddy from finding a home of his own is his age and his height." Matron said to the governor. "He can't help that."

"He may be in luck." the governor said. "I have a letter here from a childless couple in Bracebridge". They are an older couple, farmers in a new township, and they wish to adopt a boy from the home. They are well thought of as these letters attest. They have a nice home and look forward to a child to make it complete."

Letters were exchanged, a contract signed, and guarantees given as to the welfare of the child. After the papers were checked and checked again, Eddy was summoned to the office. "I have good news, Eddy. You are going to a home in a northern settlement called Bracebridge. You will travel by train and Mr. Mitchell will meet you at the station. You will leave tomorrow morning, precisely on July 7. Be up sharply, washed and ready when I call you."

Preparations were made. Eddy's trunk, packed with his belongings, some new shirts and trousers for summer wear plus a new pair of shoes, had become his special friend. He even talked to it when he was sitting up in bed and all the boys were asleep. They had been together since England and Eddy was proud to be its owner. There was a familiarity that comforted. It smelled of the shop where it was made and he liked its fake alligator skin. The Bible, hymn book and Pilgrim's Progress had been put in last. Finally his trunk was firmly closed and stamped for shipping. His name Edward George Tompkins was written in bold letters on the top. His carry bag which was by now scuffed from the rough treatment it had received as it was heaved from one compartment to the next in the train and on the ship lay beside the trunk.

"Eddy, stand still while I wash your face again and comb your hair", said the young maid he adored. She was the one who brought him footballs to play in the garden and she was the one who would bring him an extra bun before bedtime. "Be a good boy, Eddy", she said as she brushed him a kiss. "I'll miss you."

"A'll miss you too." At that, Eddy walked downstairs. The governor accompanied him to the waiting carriage and bid him farewell.

It was 8 AM. The train would be leaving in an hour. It was called The Great Northern. The driver heaved the trunk into the carriage with Eddy right behind. He waved goodbye and off he was on his most memorable journey of all. He wouldn't know a soul but he went through the paces like a marionette. He felt like a character in a Punch and Judy Show.

Waiting for Eddy in the kitchen of their brick farmhouse, Mrs. Mitchell mused. "Wonder what our little boy will be like? I hope he likes us."

"Not so soon, Mary", said her husband who was more interested in a helper than a son. He needed help with the chores, help with the livestock and he didn't want another mouth to feed, if the boy couldn't meet his standards. "We didn't say we're adopting him. This is a trial period. Remember."

As the carriage reached the Station, Eddy remembered the white pillars and the shops selling sweets. His little maid had given him 1 shilling for chocolates.

The driver stopped and entered the massive Train Station. He walked, as instructed, to the ticket booth and bought a one way ticket to Bracebridge. After this, he returned and taking Eddy by the hand, he led him to a booth that said "Traveler's Aid". After some brief words about the boy and the fact that he was travelling alone, arrangements were made to escort Eddy to the platform and help him aboard. The conductor, a good looking young man new at the job himself but anxious to please was told about Eddy and he assured the lady from the Traveler's Aid that he would make sure that Eddy got off at the right station.

"Don't you worry none. I'll see to it that the lad knows when to get off and all that."

"Thank you. Now Eddy, make sure you listen well."

With a bounce followed by clicking his shiny shoes together, the conductor said, "Come along young man. You're in for an adventure."

Chapter 19: Arriving in Bracebridge

Eddy was becoming accustomed to trains. He loved the big steam engine which puffed and huffed as it entered the station. It was in control and had a mind of its own. The station masters, the porters, the conductors all paid homage to it but the engineer was the only one who had the authority to move the train to its destination. Eddy wanted to be in charge and sit up in the engineer's box and take the controls. "Some day, I am going to put on the railway hat, climb up to the top of the engine, hoot the whistle and make her go!"

For now, he was on the train to the north. He was going to the Muskoka where Red Indians hunted and lived off the land. He was happiest when he dreamed of these things. He didn't want to think about the merry go round he was on with so much happening. He was safe in his stories and when he day-dreamed he could be anywhere and he could be anyone. Lately, after seeing the vast forests out of the window, he imagined himself living in a lodge sitting by a big log fire, not quite like the fires his mother used to make in their few rooms in London but warm and cheery just the same.

There were some other boys on the train and some he recognized from the Dr. Barnardo Home which seemed so far away. But it had only been a few weeks. They travelled alone like him now and the only thing that distinguished them from the other passengers were the name tags that hung around their necks and their identical clothing. Their trunks would have been in the cargo bay.

The cars were full of families, some speaking foreign languages and all looking both excited and bewildered. Most were heading to surveyed lots that had been granted and a number would be met by relatives from the old country. It was all new but for a small boy like Eddy, it was becoming scary.

He had no idea where he was going and what he would find when he got there but, maybe, because he was so young, his mind was a blank slate and could not think beyond the present. Perhaps, this was a blessing. The trip would take the best part of the day and he was expected to arrive at his destination by 5 o'clock.

Back on the farm, Mary Mitchell was making chocolate covered cookies. She was humming a tune she sang when she was in the kitchen. Charles Mitchell, her husband, was out in the fields checking on his corn plants. The cows had been milked and they grazed in the upper pasture. At the bottom of the hill was the railway, the very one that would bring Eddy here today. The buggy waited outside for the dappled mare.

Eddy sat very still. He wanted to spend a bit of the money that the nicest girl in the world, the young maid in the Toronto home, had slipped into his hand. He looked around to see if there was a canteen or someplace where he could get a sweet or maybe an ice-cream. No one paid any attention to him. They were too busy in their own lives. "I'll find it myself." He thought. He looked around to see if there was anyone he knew but they seemed to have vanished into thin air. "I can ask the conductor. He'll know."

By now, he was well on his way to Bracebridge, the town where the family to whom he would be indentured lived. Papers had been signed guaranteeing that Eddy would work on the farm until the age of 21. A small sum of money was to be set aside every year and put in a special fund held by the Imperial Bank of Commerce until he reached the age of maturity. Then if he held up his end of the contract, he would receive the money on his departure.

Sometimes, the children were adopted taking on the family name of the 'owners'; sometimes, they inherited the farm.

Eddy knew none of this. All he could do was travel toward his destination and dream of being the engineer in charge of a train like this. There were two engines hauling a long string of passenger cars. There were steep inclines and many twists in the track going north through rugged forest, swamp and lake country. The spruce trees towered over the countryside and the boreal forest of the Canadian Shield was hardly welcoming. It was a place for bear and moose and lynx. Suddenly, they were passing a lake the size of an ocean to their right and Eddy could see large boats hauling logs.

"Gor' Blimey, Are we back at sea. Are we going home?"

The other boys scrambled to look and suddenly the car was loud like a playground with boys jumping down from their seats and pushing their way to the window. "Woa, hear, hear, ther'll be none of this. Get back to your seats you lot or I'll put you off right here."

The whistle blew as they came to a halt. The name Orillia was blazoned in bright blue over the station. After boarding a few passengers, it continued on its way up to Washago and through Gravenhurst.

Only the seasoned travelers could know that they were in God's country. Only recently had the land been opened up for new comers. The forest was primeval. No axe or saw had ever touched the spruce and the pine, wide and tall except when men forged a way through to build a railway.

To the left if they could have seen that far, lay Georgian Bay and beyond Lake Huron was the great Superior as big as any ocean. The steam engine struggled as it climbed a steep grade and then the engineer blew the whistle again. The wheels seemed to squeal as it came to a halt at the station. It looked like a large house made of wood and boasting a gable in the centre. Eddy didn't think it could be a station after the huge one he had seen in London and Liverpool and the imposing one just built in Toronto.

"BRACEBRIDGE" called out the conductor in a loud almost shrilling voice.

Eddy was jolted almost out of his seat when the train stopped.

"ALL PASSENGERS FOR BRACEBRIDGE, this is your destination!"

Mothers and fathers gathered their children and their belongings and moved toward the steps. Pushing and shoving, they forced their way to the waiting room mostly to rearrange themselves after the day's ride. Women fixed their hats or tidied their little girls' hair. For many it was their first stop in what was to be their home. Women gathered up their skirts; the little girls clasped their dolls and they moved slowly to the platform to waiting carriages or no reception party at all.

A few boys, Eddy remembered vaguely and one girl he remembered from the boat moved to the platform. Eddy picked up his bag and his bag of sweets and stepped down.

Carts and carriages waited on the sidelines. Eddy and the other unaccompanied children were pushed along and told to go to the ticket office. They looked around to see something or someone they might know but there was no one they recognized. There was silence inside the station; Eddy just wanted to go to home to his mother. He wasn't sure what he expected. All he could think was, "When do I get to see a real Injun?

The ticket agent came up to the children and offered them sandwiches and a cold glass of milk. He was young and chipper as he made small conversation with what to him were 'waifs'.

He had seen kids arrive like this with tags around their necks standing next to large trunks brought by the porters after all the other passengers had left by wagon, cart or carriage.

Soon, a farmer seated by his young wife arrived in a small cart hauled by a young black mare. He looked about and spied the little girl. "Come here; you're coming with us. Climb up beside me." Reluctant at first, she soon was seated and on her way.

She was followed by three boys all with Barnardo trunks who boarded a large wagon hauled by two high strung horses pawing the ground to get moving. "All inside? Okay, Go."

Off went the horses in a gallop which had to be halted by the farmer's whip and the farmer's bellowing, "Whoa, Whoa!"

Eddy watched all this with curiosity. He was the last person in the Station. It was 6.30; much later than expected. No one came with wagon or cart. Eddy stood alone outside with his entire world's possessions with him, his travel bag, his bag of sweets and the huge Barnardo trunk beside him. The only mark that told the world who he was, was the name Edward George Tompkins written in bold black letters on the alligator skin covered trunk and the tag around his neck.

The ticket agent kept his eyes on the road above the station looking for the family that would take Eddy home. The sun was still high in the sky in this northern town even though it was now dusk. It was still hot but for a breeze that came off the Falls below the main street.

"Come on, inside. I see your name is Edward. They should be here any time now. We were late arriving and they may have gone up town to the livery shop or they could just be talking to someone they know. Don't worry none. They will be by shortly."

Eddy didn't say a word but the young man knew he had been crying.

Just then, a little carriage pulled up with a dappled pony. Out jumped Mr. Mitchell. "You must be Edward George Tompkins. You are late and I've got chores to do. Step up boy and let's get your trunk aboard. Mrs. Mitchell has supper ready and we must'n dawdle." Eddy reached out his hand but Mr. Mitchell, just raised his whip and yelled at the pony to move.

The ride was bumpy. No words were spoken. Eddy stared ahead and thought of nothing. He couldn't even think about supper. It was just a blur to him and he didn't like Mr. Mitchell at all.

At the top of the road some miles out of town, they came to a large field. The pony pulled up and turned into a wagon path about the width of the carriage. At the end was a large brick house with a square extension projecting frontward. This contained the stairway and the entry hall and large pine doorway. On the side were two out buildings and behind the house was a large grey barn with a stone foundation. Everything was neat and tidy. Even the flower beds were laid out symmetrically. The Mitchell's had only themselves to worry about so Mrs. Mitchell had time to be fussy with her flower beds. They did not have children of their own.

As they pulled up in front of the main door, Eddy looked up to see a kindly looking lady in her early thirties. She wore an apron, her hair was pulled back into a knot and she was smiling. "Hello, Edward. Welcome. Come in and have something to eat. We'll get acquainted later."

Eddy walked up the stairs and put out his hand. With her warm hands, she shook it and welcomed him to his new life in Macaulay Township, Ontario, Canada.

Chapter 20: Trying to settle in

Mrs. Mitchell wore a bright blue cotton dress with roses woven through it. It touched her leg below her mid calf, not quite the fashion- perhaps a little daring for a farmer's wife. Over it, she wore a long dark blue kitchen apron functional for all she had to do. She led Edward into the main hall from where the stairs ascended to a square turret.

"I'll take you up to your bedroom, Eddy. Pick up your travel bag. Follow me."

The stairs were wide at first, leading to landings off of which were three large bedrooms. The early evening sun was just setting over the fields and the light was soft and gentle. At the back of the landing facing the back of the house was a door. Mrs. Mitchell beckoned Eddy to follow her through the plain wooden door and up the steep narrow stairs to the top. It wasn't an attic but rather a small room with a small window that let in just a bit of the sun.

"This is your room, Eddy"

The single bed looked cozy enough, not like the beds of the dormitory at Barnardo's or the bunks on the ship. He thought he might like it but he kept his thoughts to himself.

"Put your travel bag on the bed for now. You can wear what you have on for this evening. Tomorrow, we will go through your trunk and see what summer clothes you have. For now, we are going back downstairs to the kitchen to have a bite to eat. It's been ready for hours."

After they descended, they stood for a few minutes in the downstairs foyer. There was a large picture of King Edward on the wall and beside it was a portrait of his wife Alexandria.

The Mitchell's were loyal subjects of the crown and both had come to Canada as children with their settler parents. Their parents had worked the land of their new grants and they were proud of what they had accomplished. The Mitchells were proud too of what they had managed since getting married when they were in their early twenties. They were in their thirties now but their one disappointment was their failure to have a child.

Eddy looked up at the stern king and his wife and he remembered that there had been a similar portrait in the main hallway of that large building on Stepney Causeway where he had spent the months from January to now. It was July, 1910.

"Have you seen these pictures before?"

"Yes, Mam. They was in the place I stayed after me mom brought me there."

He noticed also a grand wardrobe made of oak. He had sometimes hid in one like that at the Home when he wanted to escape from doing chores. No one had ever caught him. The closet was for shoes and great coats but in summer, it was rarely used. They should have been packed away for the winter in the attic but Mrs. Mitchell hadn't quite got around to that. Her flower garden needed tending.

Charles Mitchell had already put on his overalls because there were still chores to be done. He had entered the house through the side door that led to the inner porch and into a large kitchen. He had taken his suit jacket off now that he was home and not out to impress anyone. He had to be smart to go to town. He couldn't be seen with his farm clothes on. He had unloaded Eddy's alligator trunk and set it near the wood burning cooking range.

"It can sit there." He mumbled. "That kid won't need any city clothes here."

The foyer led to a long hall at the back of which was the kitchen.

Opening from the hall to the left were two glass fronted doors which opened to the parlour and the dining room. They were rarely used but they were ornamental just the same.

"Come along now. Don't dawdle. You must be hungry."

Eddy followed Mrs. Mitchell to the kitchen and to a long wooden table set for three. Eddy had no time to see anything except the table and the cooking range on the other side. Mr. Mitchell was already seated. His barn boots were in the porch but Eddy could smell them. They reminded him of the horses that brought the milk and coal in London.

"Come to the table, boy. Sit down and wait for my wife."

Mrs. Mitchell tended the pot on the stove stirring nervously. Eddy fidgeted and his mouth tightened as he took his seat in the centre. The adults would be seated on opposite ends.

Mrs. Mitchell took each plate and ladled out the boiled potatoes, some mashed turnip from last season's store and a slice of pork. Serving her husband first, she made sure it was piled high. Hers was more modest and Eddy's was spare. Then she placed a basket of rolls, butter in a dish, salt and pepper and a gravy boat in the middle. The table was long and reaching across was out of the question. Eddy knew that from the Home.

"Bow your heads. Bless this food to our use and let us be truly thankful." said Mr. Mitchell.

"And please bless Eddy, our newest family member," whispered Mary Mitchell.

They sat in silence passing the condiments as needed to each other.

Mary noticed that Eddy had good manners. "He was taught well", she thought. She noticed how he ate with both a knife and a fork. She couldn't know that the use of cutlery had been drilled into the children at Dr. Barnardo's. Eddy had dreaded those lessons. He had been taught to eat correctly by his mother but many of the boys, Joseph in particular, had lived on the streets. They used their hands as forks.

"Eddy, how are you doing? Would you like more?" She glanced at her husband and then went over to the stove and beckoned Eddy to come to get a second helping.

"Thank you, Mam."

"Enjoy it, boy. Tomorrow you're going to learn how to earn your daily bread. Come and sit next to me. I have some things to say to you before you go to bed. First, you will answer to Tompkins not Eddy. I can't have any of this Eddy, Eddy, in this house.

"You'll be Eddy to me." whispered Mary to herself.

"You've come to work not dally. And first thing tomorrow morning before the sun is up, I'll be calling you to come downstairs. Your first job will be the chicken house. Then, we are going to see the barn and the fields. I'll be milking first thing and you'll be doing that very soon. So get a good night's rest. Playtime is over! Do you understand?"

He took Eddy by the shoulders and pressed a bit too hard for his liking. "You heard me boy?"

"Yes, sir." Eddy muttered. "I understand."

"That's it, for now. Time for bed. See to it, Mary. I've got more chores and I don't want the boy in my way. Time enough for that."

"I'll see to his trunk by the stove. I'll call the hired hand to take it up. It's heavy."

"No, you won't, Mary." said Charles heaving himself up by the elbows from the table.

"The old guy went home and I can lift that by myself. I want it out of the way."

Charles Mitchell was a big man, not an ounce of fat, just muscle and broad shoulders. He was as loud in voice as he was in manner. Eddy would have to learn fast and keep out of his way as often as he could. Joseph's lessons on the ship could come in handy. He better fatten himself up as well.

Mr. Mitchell picked up the trunk with both hands and heaved it up over his shoulders. He carried it through the hall, up the wide stairs, and when he opened the door to the narrow steps leading to the tiny bedroom, he hoisted it up stair by stair until he set it by the bed.

"There! That should do the boy for now. Wonder what city clothes they gave him? He won't be wantin' any of that." He wiped his brow and turned and went down the steps two by two. He continued on and left the house for the barn.

Mrs. Mitchell followed a while behind taking Eddy with her. There was still some light in the sky and it had been a long day.

Eddy wiped his forehead with his sleeve and climbed the stairs. When he got to the room, he saw the trunk that had travelled with him all the way from the dormitory of Dr. Barnardo's home, to the train for Liverpool, on the SS Sicilian, aboard the train to his destination and now it was here in this room at the top of the house.

"Alligator, you stay by me and all stay by you. I don't have any friends here- only you." Eddy whispered.

Mrs. Mitchell wiped a tear from her eyes as she watched Eddy talk to his trunk. "He must be some lonely." She thought .She put her arms around him and then pulling away she said, "I'll turn the bed down for you tonight. I want you to make it up in the morning. They told me you had been trained to do all that. Say your prayers and get up when I call you in the morning. Good night. Sleep tight."

As she closed the door and started downstairs, she tried to fight her feelings of compassion. Eddy was here to work the farm and that's what he must do. "Charles won't hear of it any other way."

Eddy liked the bed. It was pretty, more like what you'd expect of a girl's bed. He remembered that his mother had made a colourful quilt for his sister's bed out of scraps of material from the ladies' dresses she sewed every day. He searched for his night shirt in the travel bag and after putting it on, he climbed up and snuggled into the sheets and quilted top.

He looked around at his bedroom. This was first time he had ever had a room of his own but he missed the boys and the antics they got up to when the matrons and prefects were not around. The room was square and a bit like a tower with the bed facing the window. On one side was a dresser made of spruce and next to the bed was a night table with a wash basin, a pitcher and a towel, face cloth and soap and a chamber pot newly scrubbed.

He decided not to wash up. It could wait to the morning.

Chapter 21: The first day on the farm

Eddy was sound asleep. He didn't even dream so it was with a start that he heard Mrs. Mitchell call.

"Eddy, are you awake? It's time to get up."

It was still dark although there was a sliver of light in the distance.

Eddy was used to getting up early at the Home but never before the sun was up.

He didn't answer at first. He wanted to stay awhile in this cozy bed.

"Is that boy up? Woman, you said you'd look after this. Get to it before I go up and get him myself."

"It's early, Charles, and it's his first day. I'll go up right now."

Eddy could hear her footsteps on the stairs and he sat up and rubbed his eyes.

She opened the door and saw that Eddy was awake. "I've brought you some hot water to wash yourself. And here are some clothes for farm work. Breakfast is ready."

"Thank you, Mrs. Mitchell. A'll hurry."

He hoped he would get bacon and eggs as he did on the great ship that brought him to Canada hardly a month ago but it was porridge that he smelled. He washed his face and hands with the warm water that Mrs. Mitchell had put in his bowl. He had already used the chamber pot that had been put under his bed and it felt good to be relieved and clean. He reached over to the table by his bed and put on the clothes given to him. He pulled the overalls over his trousers and he was anxious to look at himself in the mirror downstairs. He scrambled down the steep narrow stairs, out through the door and then down the wider staircase to the main rooms downstairs.

"Good morning, Eddy. Sit down and eat. Say your prayers to yourself and don't be long.

Our first visit is to the hen house."

"Thank you, Mam."

Mary Mitchell could see that Eddy disliked porridge. He probably had his fill of it in the home, she thought. "You don't like porridge, do you Eddy? But, eat up because it's healthy for you and farm work takes a lot of energy."

"It's okay, Mam," said Eddy reluctantly. It didn't take Eddy long to finish the porridge. He shoved it down because he was remembering that if he didn't finish it at the Home, he would have to eat it cold for lunch. He had been spoiled on the ship with bacon or ham and egg breakfasts.

"Okay, Eddy, pick up your dish and take it to the sink for washing later."

The sun was coming up over the hills and suddenly the sound, "Cock a doodle do, Cock a doodle do" filled the kitchen as though it was coming from inside the house. Eddy jumped and tried to hide his face and cup his ears. He often did this when he was frightened as though hiding his face meant he was hidden from others.

Mrs. Mitchell laughed. "It's the rooster, Eddy. He is the master of the henhouse and he is announcing that the sun is up. He does it every day. Let's go outside and pay a visit to the master. You will get used to him."

Once outside, Mary pointed to the pole running along the outside of a wooden building. "See the rooster. He loves to sit on the top and crow. We call him Joe. He likes to be boss." The creature had red feathers and a cockade on his head. He was quite magnificent really and Eddy decided he wasn't an enemy after all.

"Now, Eddy, your first job is to clean the chicken coop and put new bedding down under the roost. Here's a pair of boots which might be a bit big and an old pair of gloves. Grab that shovel and start mucking out the droppings."

He put on the boots but they were so big that his feet felt lost in them but he had no choice if he was to walk in that filth. The chicken coop was surrounded by a large barbed fence so that the hens had ample room to roam and pick at the gravel and even small bits of glass lying around. Eddy ducked down as he went into the roost. Some hens were still roosting and others were already picking at the feed. Suddenly they set up such a racket that so terrified Eddy that he started running for his life.

"Come back, Boy." Mr. Mitchell yelled as the noise brought him out of the big barn where he had been milking. "What do you think you are doing? Damn it. Get over here."

Eddy stopped in his tracks and looked back. Mitchell was taking huge strides down the path to meet Eddy and bring him back. Already, some of the chickens had got out and were running all over the place and Eddy was covered in slime and feathers.

"What a confounded mess. Get back up to the coop and grab that shovel or I'll tan your hide with this." He held up his huge hand and Eddy ran as fast as he could up the hill. Mrs. Mitchell came running over from the garden which she was tending and hurried over to her husband.

"Charles, the boy knows nothing about animals. He grew up in London. You'll have to be patient and teach him a bit every day. The child is frightened of the animals and he is afraid of you."

"What a mess we have got ourselves into. I wasn't in favour of this, Mary, you know that."

"Now, now Charles. Get back to the milking and I'll see to the boy."

She walked up the hill and found Eddy whimpering under a tree. She tried to comfort him and slowly she convinced him to come down with her and resume the chore he was assigned. This time, he took the shovel, squinted his eyes from the ammonia of the chicken droppings, and worked the shovel into the dirt, taking it out to a pile and then coming back to do it again and again until the job was done and fresh shavings and hay were put down.

Surveying his work, Mrs. Mitchell said, "Good job, Eddy and to think this is the first time you have done anything like this. You can clean their feeding trays and water bowls now and then fill them with fresh feed and those left over veggies from last night's meal. They like cabbages and lettuce especially. And don't forget to fill their water bowls with fresh water at the tap."

The hens warmed up to him and he to them. There was no more racket and two hens were already in their nest box. Eddy rubbed his eyes and crunched up his nose. He wondered if he could get used to this and it was only the first chore of the day.

Mrs. Mitchell called him in for the real breakfast. His first food, that rather dreadful porridge was just to get him started on the early chores. All the farmers' wives did it this way. Eddy took off his muddied boots and soiled gloves and put them on the back porch steps. Then he took off his overalls and put them on a peg.

When he arrived to the table, Mr. Mitchell put out his hand and with a slight grin he said "Scared you, did they? You'll get used to it. Eat up. You earned it."

After eating eggs, corn beef hash and ham washed down with a big glass of milk and brown bread, Eddy got up, put his dishes by the sink and then waited at the table for instructions. Mrs. Mitchell washed the dishes and called to Eddy to help her with the drying.

"No. he can't do that now. We're going to the big barn. Get your overalls, boots and gloves, Tompkins. There's more to do."

Eddy wiped the sweat off his brow and gulped, "Okay, Mr. Mitchell."

As Eddy pulled on the oversized boots and struggled to pull up the overalls six sizes too big, Mr. Mitchell grimaced. "Mary, the boy needs a pair of boots, gloves that can fit him and two more pairs of coveralls. Hitch up the mare and go to town to do some shopping. We'll be through by noon and we'll be looking for lunch. After, we are heading for the fields to see if the grass is drying. We should be doing some more haying before too long. Hope the weather holds."

Eddy struggled in the boots that were too big for him and followed Mr. Mitchell past the hen house and pig sty to the grand grey barn that towered over a field of summer daisies and buttercups. It was getting hot even if it was only 8 am. Eddy stopped to take a deep breath, hike up his overalls and kick up some gravel and pebbles which he was tempted to throw.

"Don't dawdle, Tompkins."

No more was said until Mr. Mitchell opened the barn door. It disturbed the pigeons that were roosting in the loft and they flew down and settled near Mr. Mitchell's feet. He kicked the smallest one. "The filthy beasts. I should get my shotgun right now. It's about time I got rid of every last one of them."

Eddy shuddered.

"It's quiet here now, boy. We've had the cows in for milking and they're back in the field."

He pointed to a pasture up the hill. "That's goin' to be one of your jobs soon. You'll come with me at 5 when we bring them back for their evening milking. Lucy, our border collie will show you how it's done."

Mr. Mitchell walked Eddy into the main threshing area at the centre. The hay lofts were on each side and in the extension were the horse stalls. On the other side were the cow stalls. Hanging from pegs along the side were the milking pails clean and ready for the evening.

"That's another chore you will do."

Eddy was sweating not just from the putrid heat of the hay but from his own nervousness. If only he could run away.

Looking at Eddy's boots and frustrated by the fact that he now had to think about buying all these extras for this boy who was far too young to be of any help, Mitchell said "Put some of this fleece left over from the shearing and stick it in your footwear. That might help until my wife gets you new ones your size."

Mitchell waited until Eddy put the soft piece of fleece in the boots and pulled them on. "Okay now, boy. Feel a bit better on your feet?

"A bit better, sir."

Now beckoning to the gaping barn door he muttered, "Pick up your heels boy. We're going for a walk to the hay field to see how the hay is doing. We've had some rain but if today is anything to go by, she should be getting ready to harvest."

Eddy felt taller with the fleece to give him height and he could walk with less of a struggle. Reaching the hay field up the hill from the barn, Mr. Mitchell told Eddy to sit in the grass while he checked the hay. The ripened grasses smelled sweet. Mr. Mitchell picked a stalk and stuck it into the corner of his mouth. He seemed to enjoy the feel of the hay stalk and Eddy picked a stalk himself and liked it too.

"Mmm, I think it's a go for harvest. I might try tomorrow once I gather up the folks to help", Mitchell murmured to himself.

Eddy could hear him but Mitchell kept walking through the field high with mature grasses looking pleased with himself. Eddy was remembering his geography lesson back at the Home and the picture of hay wagons, horses, and men with scythes and pitchforks. This was supposed to be fun not work.

"We'll see."

Chapter 22: Haymaking

After a busy day on the farm and his introduction to the horses, Eddy sat down for supper. He was exhausted but pleased to have met the two draft horses not terribly different from the ones he had known in London. It reminded him of his real home and the family, and his little sister. He hoped the horses had been given names but if not, he planned to name them himself. He had met the brown mare and imagined himself hitching her up to the carriage or maybe riding her bare back across the field. Her name was Peggy and he liked the way she nudged up to him when he gave her some hay.

The supper was a silent time with the two Mitchells on each end of the table and he in the centre. Mrs. Mitchell deferred to her husband in all things but Eddy felt comfortable as long as she was with him. The silence was broken by Mr. Mitchell when he said, "So, how did the shopping go Mary? Did you get the boots, gloves and overalls? At the Jenkins General Store, I assume? They must have wondered why you were shopping for boys clothes."

"Yes, I was able to get everything and Eddy has tried on the boots and they fit. The right leg is a bit roomy but we can put a handkerchief in them and that should be fine. Mrs. Jenkins was curious but she knew that a number of boys and girls had come to Bracebridge on the last two trains and they were already boarded out. I told her that we had taken in a boy but I didn't give her any details. She doesn't need to know everything. Gosh only knows that she learns a lot in her business and she has a habit of spreading the news, around, and what gets passed around is a long way from the truth, sometimes. How was your day?"

"The boy has a lot to learn, what with bringing in the cows, hitching up the horses and just plain everything. You don't learn much walking the streets of the old town in the old country. At least, we came out as kids from the country over there so our learning didn't take as long. Enough said."

Eddy listened and kept eating. He hardly looked up from his plate. The meal was hearty, roast beef, and potatoes mashed with gravy. When he finished, using both his knife and fork as he had been taught, he put his utensils neatly on the plate and folded his hands.

Pleased with the boy and amazed at his good manners, Mary Mitchell got up and walked to the cupboard to get a plate of the cookies she had baked the day before. Eddy's eyes followed her with anticipation. "Could they be for me", he wondered.

"Eddy, I baked these cookies especially for you. I hope you like them."

"Just one, mind, Mary. Don't spoil the boy."

Eddy took a small bite, smiled and almost gobbled it down. "Let him have one more, Charles. He has earned it today."

Oh, all right, but just one."

Now that the chores were done, the cows back in the field after milking, the horses fed and in their stalls and the hens roosting in their loft, Mr. Mitchell moved into the day room, off the kitchen, and sat down with the evening newspaper, The Bracebridge Standard. He had his slippers on and his overalls had been put on the peg for the night. Putting his feet on the footstool, he leaned back in his comfortable chair, and took out his pipe. After stuffing it with the requisite bit of tobacco, he lit it with a match they called a Lucifer, and smoked.

Mrs. Mitchell sat opposite him in her rocking chair and took out her knitting. After a few minutes with her knitting needles she noticed how Eddy was fidgeting in the straight backed chair in the corner. "Gosh, how tired and bewildered he must be." She pondered and looking across at her husband, she nervously mumbled, "Uhuh" and then stumbled on what she wanted to say, "Eddy I have some books in our library across from the entry hall. Would you like to look at them?"

"Ya, wery much, Miss."

"We'll have to work on that accent, Eddy. But come along. I'll leave my knitting for now."

They walked together to a small room which was lined with books and papers. Mary liked to call it her library. She remembered the grand library of the mansion of the estate in Devon. She had gone there only once as a little girl before her parents decided to give up their tenant farm and strike out on their own for Canada. It was everything to own your own land and be master of it. Her parents and their parents before them going back for hundreds of years had only known working for the Lord of the Manor and carving out a simple living on a 3 to 5 acres tenant farm.

Eddy got up on his tip toes to examine a book that looked colourful but it wasn't what he thought. "I like Robinson Crusoe. Do you have it?"

"Yes, you are in luck. I have the book that my grandmother gave me many years ago."

She reached up to the top shelf and brought it down. It was a bit worn but it was full of pictures and that pleased Eddy. "Gor' blimey. Thanks."

"Now, Eddy, I am going back to my knitting. It's time for you to go to bed. There's warm water in your bowl and make sure to wash up before bedtime. You can read while it's still light and then, it's 'night, night' until I call you in the morning."

"Good night". Eddy climbed up the stairs to his loft bedroom but he was so tired that he climbed on the bed with all his clothes on and fell fast asleep. The book fell on the floor and Eddy's first real day on the farm was over.

"Eddy, Eddy, it's time to get up", Mrs. Mitchell called. Not hearing a sound, she started up the stairs herself. Reaching the room, she could see Robinson Crusoe on the floor, and the little boy sprawled across the bed, shoes still on, and fully clothed. She filled the washing bowl with warm water hoping she could get him to freshen up. "Eddy, wake up."

He moved just slightly and fell back.

"I wasn't thinking. The boy is only eight. He worked a full day in a place he does not know doing work he never knew. How do I tell Charles this? He'll never understand. He worked full days on his parent's farm since he was 6. He and his brothers never knew a day without work except maybe in the winter. "

Mrs. Mitchell and her husband had both come to Canada as children. Both families had been tenant farmers on adjacent estates. They too had been enticed to Ontario with offers of land. So, when they finally arrived, all hands had to be made to work almost as soon as they were weaned. Mary was used to work too but her father was not as hard as the elder Mitchell and he let his children play from time to time.

Mary nudged the sleeping child gently and Eddy awoke rubbing his eyes and sitting up. "You must have been sleepy. So, now wash up, get out a clean shirt from your trunk and come downstairs." Don't let me forget that we have to go through your trunk later and sort everything out. We didn't get that done yesterday because getting you farm clothes was on the top of my list. Those London clothes won't work very well here.

Eddy did as he was told and before long, he was out at the hen house repeating what he had done the day before. There wouldn't be proper breakfast until that was done. He may have had porridge the first day before chores but that was only because Mrs. Mitchell worried that he might be too weak to do anything without something in his stomach. On his second day, he would be treated the same as everyone else.

The hens didn't cackle as loud and the rooster's morning call wasn't as scary. He found himself more able to work with the shovel even if he didn't like the work one little bit. When the breakfast bell rang out, Eddy rushed towards the house, hurried to get his new boots and overalls off, and shot over to the table.

"Sit down, Eddy and meet old Harry, the hired hand. He'll be staying with us for a time. Right, Harry?"

"Ho, there, I's old Harry all right. They need me for haymaking and all that. I'll be stopping in the shed off of the barn though. It's fixed up pretty good and I don' mind it all. A good meal and a place to lie down is all I need."

Mr. Mitchell had been hard at work getting ready for haymaking. The weather was right, and the old timers had said that good weather was in the offing for the next few days. It had to be dry. Wet hay could spell disaster.

Today, they would be out with their scythes to cut and stack the hay. Not just ol' Harry but a whole array of young folk assembled in the front yard. While the men headed for the fields, the women moved to the kitchen preparing lunch for mid day. Eddy was caught up in it all and there were boys around his age in the throng all carrying buckets of water and apples to get a start on the day. Eddy walked with Harry. He carried a water bucket and some apples in his pocket.

"Hey, there, you're the new boy, ain't you", shouted a red haired boy just catching up with them.

"Yea, I guess." said Eddy.

"I'm Jack. Last name's Fowler. I live in the farm across the railway tracks down there."

"Nice to meet ya." said Eddy.

As they ran up to the hay field now filled with men and scythes, Eddy heard a train whistle. "Gor' blimey; that's a big one and it's travelling across our field going real slow. Wouldn't mind being up there in the engine. I like being on the move."

Not having a home of his own or a mother to look after him, he didn't really have anything or anyone to stop him if he got on that train and travelled to the next town. He had enjoyed the trip to Liverpool and the ocean voyage. He had a taste of freedom then and now he felt shackled with looking after those hens and whatever else the Mitchells had in store for him. He was tired of doing what he was told. He was tired of being led around by the nose.

"Ain't you coming Limy?" yelled Jack.

"Limey? I am not answering to that. My name is Eddy."

"You're goin' to hear that a lot. You all sound weird the way you say things but come on, let's have fun and join the boys up there in the top field. It's not all work. You'll see."

The sun was stronger and it was getting hot. Already, the men and boys had taken off their shirts. They were lean and brown and they looked like the pictures Eddy had seen in the geography book called, 'Canada.' The scythes were in full swing and already a lot of hay was down. The boys were stacking the hay into larger hay piles shaped like a turret which soon would be loaded on the wagons pulled by the great draft horses Mr. Mitchell considered his pride and joy.

Eddy watched Jack as he pitch forked the hay and started forming it into stacks.

"Here, let me show you, Eddy." said Jack. "Grab that pitchfork and heave like me."

Ol' Harry watched with amusement as Jack tried to show Eddy the hang of it. Harry was an expert and his hearty laugh kept Eddy in good spirits. Thoughts of the train and travel disappeared and he became part of the rhythm of men working the land.

After a while, the call came, "Lunch!!"Down went the scythes and pitch forks as the workers descended the hill towards the house. Mrs. Mitchell and her neighbours had been preparing all morning.

Long wooden tables were set up in the front garden. They were covered with bright tablecloths the women had made for these occasions. Haymaking was shared by all the farmers in the community. It was the Mitchell's turn today but tomorrow it would be the Fowlers and then the Davies', the Webster's and Gibson's. They shared wagons and horses and everyone came out to help. They brought these traditions from the countries they had left.

They made it into a festival of work and comradeship and because of it, they regarded it not as a chore but as an occasion and an excuse to get together. Farming could be lonely and back breaking but they made it possible by working together.

The women brought out plates of meat and egg sandwiches, big pots of tea, jugs of cold water and loads of cookies and strawberry rhubarb pies. The pies were Mrs. Gibson's specialty. The women chatted away.

Among them were their daughters dressed in shorter dresses and white pinafores. As they talked among themselves, one said, "I hope Ben is with the boys. He's cute."

"Hush up. How about Sidney? He's cuter."

"Come on, girls. Too much chatter. Don't put all the work on us old ones", Mrs. Gibson shouted. As well as looking after the food, she was anxious to meet her daughter's boarder who was up haying with the men.

"How is the boy doing, Mary?"

"He is doing alright, mother. He is small for his age but willing to work.

Charles hasn't taken to him at all. Of course, he's been against this from the beginning. I hope things will get better as the days go by. He is a nice little boy, really, in spite of the hard times he's been through. How's your girl doing by the way?"

"She's very shy and small for her age as well but she seems a sweet child and a hard worker from what I've seen so far. They taught them well- Dr. Barnardo's, I mean- but they must have skimped on the food. Well, I best be getting back to the kitchen. We've got a lot more to do. There's more guys than we were expecting making hay and they'll be hungry."

Mrs. Gibson beckoned to the little girl in the shiny white pinafore who was sitting by the porch waiting for instructions. Her name was Emily and she was the one being boarded by Mrs. Gibson along with three home boys. The boys were up in the field and she was learning how to do domestic chores. She was hesitant and she felt out of place. Arriving on the same train as Eddy, she, like Eddy, was finding out that life on the farm was a lot of hard work.

Suddenly, everything was buzzing. The men and boys arrived. First thing they did was go to the water pump and put their heads under to cool off. The water splashed over them and they didn't bother to use a towel. It felt cold and refreshing. Soon they took their seats at the tables and dove into the welcome food. The younger men and boys sat together. Ben and Sidney had more attention than the others. The girls waited on them hand and foot.

Eddy sat with Ol' Harry. Mrs. Mitchell and her mother came over to him. "Dig in Eddy. There's lots more."

"So, you're Eddy. I'm Mrs. Gibson, Mary Miles' mother. Nice to meet you. You can call me Grandma Gibson- they all do around here."

"Nice to meet you too," said Eddy smiling broadly as he shook her hand.

Grandma was a big woman with red cheeks and a smile that spread naturally across her broad face. Her flowered apron wrapped around an ample waist had wide pockets that were often filled with some sweet or other to give to whatever child might wonder near.

For the first time, Eddy felt comfortable. He could relax and be himself.

"Eddy you must be hungry after all that work in the hay field. Dig in. You can as much as you like and more if you want to."

She called for Emily to come over.

"Emily, this is Eddy. He came on the same train as you did back in June. He lives here with my daughter. I guess you'll be going to the same school, come Autumn.

Eddy looked up from his place and blurted, "Hello."

Emily cast her eyes down and whispered, "Hi."

After an awkward silence, Grandma Gibson said, "Emily, please get Mr. Harry and Eddy some milk"

When lunch was over, the men and boys went back to the fields and worked to sunset until all the hay was cut, stacked, loaded onto the wagons and brought down to the barn to be stored. And after everyone had gone home, Eddy sat down to his late evening meal and then went up to his room. He was tired but he kept thinking about the little girl with the blond hair, big blue eyes and shy smile. He hoped to see her again.

Chapter 23: Settling In

The days were almost always the same. Chores, mostly the hen house, followed by breakfast; then out to the barn to help with the milking and, after a light lunch, Eddy weeded the garden, mowed the lawn and picked peas and green beans.

Every afternoon, after Mrs. Mitchell lovingly tended her flower garden, she waited for the green vegetables to prepare dinner and, if Eddy picked enough, she would do some canning.

She had taught Eddy how to weed and hoe each row and how to pick the peas and beans so that there would be no waste. She didn't mind him munching on the peas but she didn't want him to endure indigestion either. Peas could play havoc with the stomach if too many raw ones were eaten in one go. Sometimes she asked him to look after the marigolds and morning glories but she wouldn't let anyone touch her dahlias. They were her pride and joy.

It was Tuesday. Her wash day being Monday and the ironing done in the morning, she set herself the task of putting up a batch of beans and she hoped to make up bottles of Lady Ashburn cucumber pickles. "I ought to call for Emily, mother's home girl, to help me, but I've left it too late today. Next time, if Charles doesn't need Eddy in the barn, I'll get him to help me instead."

She was dressed in a simple green blouse and long emerald green skirt covered with a yellow apron. She was a pretty woman, still girl like in her looks and manner and she enjoyed dressing well even for the kitchen. Her dark brown hair was pulled back in a bun with a yellow comb to hold it tight.

Eddy was happier to be with her. She was always smiling and she made Eddy feel comfortable so unlike her husband who couldn't find a kind word to say to him. "Eddy, I'd like you to help me put up these vegetables and do a batch of pickles. Go wash your hands at the pump and get a large pitcher of water." She fired up the stove and set two pots on to boil. On the table were all the bottles to be sterilized. Eddy chucked the peas while Mrs. Mitchell prepared the beans. That took most of the afternoon so the pickles would have to wait for another day.

When they were ready, she blanched the peas first and then the beans. In the meantime, the bottles were placed in the boiling water and the tops were boiled as well. She filled each jar with the peas and beans, and sealed them shut with wax.

In every household on every farm, women were getting ready for the harsh winter ahead. Each homemaker was judged by her preserves, her pickles and her jams and jellies. Mary wasn't in a competition but she wanted hers to be perfect. Mr. Mitchell was out in the barn fixing the threshing machine. He believed that idleness belonged to the devil and more than once he had yelled at Eddy,

"You are lazy, Tompkins. If I catch you one more time talking to the horses or lying in the hay, I'll thrash you. The devil seems to keep company with you and I'm going to put a stop to that."

Eddy had no interest in pleasing the man even though he knew he had no choice right now. Sometimes, he could feel red rising in his neck and face and a streak of defiance gnawing at him. He didn't cry; he couldn't cry. He kept doing what he had to do to get through the day. He was told that come October, he would be going to school. At least he could get out of work and away from his boss then.

Dinner was served at sharp 5 o'clock. There was not much small talk and the evening chores beckoned. Eddy didn't like the milking because it was hard work and he had still not got the knack of firmly holding the cows' teats and squeezing out the warm milk. But it was a lot better than cleaning the hen house or feeding the pigs although he had to admit that he liked the pigs. They had a decent enclosure to forge and Eddy liked the way the big sow snuggled up to him. But what he did like more than anything was walking the cows up to pasture after milking with Lucy, the Border Collie.

August was even hotter than July but Eddy enjoyed the cool breeze that seemed to come from the north. After leading the cows to their evening pasture, Eddy had an idea. "Why don't I go up the hill to the ridge to see what's there. No one will miss me. Come on Lucy, let's follow the breeze!"

He walked to the woodland with Lucy running beside him. It was freedom for her too. Eddy walked among the tall pines and followed a stream. He sat down, took off his shirt and slid down the bank into the water and watched the minnows swim among his toes. After trying to catch a wondering trout he scrambled up and then he lay down on the fresh needles that blanketed the forest floor. He lay there for quite a while and when he was still, two squirrels scampered by. He had been told that up in these woods wolves and wolverines still roamed and he couldn't wait to see a deer and maybe a moose.

Suddenly, he could hear his name being called from the farmhouse below "Tompkins, Tompkins. Damn you, Tompkins. Come down, this instant!"

For a moment he thought, "I won't answer" but that wouldn't do, so he called back "Up here. Heading back!" With Lucy by his side, he jumped up and ran down the hill like a greyhound and landed at the side door to the kitchen. Panting, he sat down on the stool, after putting his boots and overalls away. He hadn't been wearing his boots for his woodland adventure. He had thrown them and his overalls under the apple tree when no one was looking but he retrieved them before entering the house.

"Where have you been, Tompkins? And put a shirt on for God's sake. Look at you. Don't ever enter this house again bare-chested. Shameful, shameful. I won't have my wife all upset. You get up to your room. No evening snack for you, and with that he clouted him on the side of the head and sent him reeling.

Eddy got out of his way, rushed upstairs two steps at a time and found refuge in the book he had been reading a while ago. Right now, he wished he was Robinson Crusoe stranded on an island and just about to meet the man who would be his man Friday.

Talking to himself, he muttered, "He ain't ever goin' to hurt me. I'll get him back, I swear. Got to be a fighter like Joseph. He learned me good."

Days passed and Eddy went to the forest any time he could sneak away. He made himself a make shift cabin out of fallen branches tied with sumac vines. He piled them the way he had learned to pile straw. Inside he placed pine needles and straw he had taken up in a sack when no one was looking.

Already he had made friends with a rabbit and one evening a white tailed doe and her two fawns came out to graze. This was his kingdom and he was the King. He gave names to his forest friends and every time he ventured to his hideaway, some new creature made his acquaintance. He couldn't bring Lucy though. That was absolutely forbidden.

"I must tell Jack about my hideaway", he thought. "And, I think I should let Mrs. Mitchell know so she won't worry. But not now."

He had worked everything out. The only time he would go to his cabin was when Mr. Mitchell was at a Town Council meeting or when he was talking to a farmer friend. Every Wednesday, he was away to Town Meeting and every Friday, he would visit his parents and his brothers over in Falkenburg, the next town over. That way, he didn't get into trouble and as long as he did his chores and kept to himself, he was alright. Mr. Mitchell admired hard work and they kept the peace this way.

Chapter 24: A visitor

Eddy had worked out a way of getting through the harsh work through his imagination. As long as he could keep his woodland hideaway away from Mr. Mitchell, he could create all the stories he wanted inside his head even when he was cleaning out the hen house or feeding the pigs. The more he created, the freer he could be and the days would pass without the misery he once felt. One evening towards the end of August, a horse and buggy drove up to the door and out stepped a smartly dressed gentleman of about 40 years old. He carried a brief case and walked up the front steps.

"Who could this be?" said Mr. Mitchell, just finishing his evening meal.

"I'll go to the door and see," said his wife. "Would you put your plate at the sink, Charles, and Eddy go outside and check on the chickens." She walked to the door and was surprised to see a well dressed stranger standing with his briefcase.

"Good evening. Would you be Mrs. Mitchell? Is your husband home? My name is Mr. Parsons. I am from the Dr. Barnardo Receiving Home in Toronto. I believe you are boarding one of our former wards, Edward George Tompkins."

"Yes. Please come this way. I will call my husband."

She led him in directly to the parlour, the room that was used only on formal occasions or to lay out a loved one's body for viewing. The furniture was ornate, brought out from England as a wedding gift when her parents were married. She sat Mr. Parsons in the Victorian arm chair in the corner of the room next to the fire place. She opened the window a tiny crack and parted the curtains. "Would you care for tea?"

"Yes, that would be nice. Thank you."

She left the room and went to get her husband who had hurriedly put on a clean shirt when he heard the name Dr. Barnardo. "You'd think he could have written a letter to tell of his impending visit. I hate being surprised like this and I've still a lot of chores to finish."

After a brief pause, the Mitchell's entered the parlour together. Mr. Parsons immediately rose from his seat and with a nod, he walked over to shake the senior Mitchell's hand. A few brief words found them facing each other with Mr. Parsons in the comfortable Victorian and Mitchell upright in a straight backed chair. Mary Mitchell sat in her favourite soft cushioned chair beside her husband and folded her hands.

"If you recall, Mr. Mitchell, you were told that from time to time, there would be an inspection of your home, and the amenities afforded your ward, Edward. I am the inspector for this region, the Muskoka Lakes region, right?"

"Yes. Yes."

"I'll get right to the point. How is the boy doing? How has he settled in? Where is he, right now?"

"Outside, checking the chickens."

"Is he doing chores on the farm?"

"Yes, but just light duties of course."

They chatted away about farm work and Mr. Mitchell inquired about Toronto making small talk until Edward was summoned. While the men busied themselves with small talk, Mary had excused herself and had gone to the kitchen to prepare a pot of tea and a plateful of strawberry squares. She called Eddy in and whispered for him to go upstairs and quickly change into his church clothes. "There's a gentleman here to see you."

"I'll get ready right away but I got to get this chicken shit off me."

"Now, Eddy, that's no way to talk. Chicken leavings, please."

To Mrs. Mitchell's surprise, Eddy was downstairs in less than five minutes and looking cleaner and neater than she had ever seen him. He was ushered into the room and promptly seated in a straight backed chair next to the Inspector. Mrs. Mitchell followed with a tray full of the squares along with Royal Doulton cups and dessert plates, teapot with its embroidered tea cozy, and a milk jug and sugar bowl to match.

She asked after their preferences. "Milk first? And would you care for a square?" She poured the tea and gave each man a plate. And then looking towards Eddy she realized that she had brought nothing for him so she scurried into the kitchen to fetch him a biscuit and a glass of milk.

Mr. Parsons did not hesitate to take three squares. He had driven quite a way here and was hungry. When he had settled with his tea and dessert, he said. "Good evening Edward." My name is Mr. Parsons and I've come from Toronto to see how you are doing. I have a letter for you from a Mr. David Ryan, whom you may remember from your trip across."

Eddy's eyes lit up at the mention of the letter. He had wondered how he was and he was curious to know whether David had met up with Molly, his lady friend on the voyage. Eddy shook the Inspectors hand. "Hello, sir."

"Are you enjoying yourself here? Have you made any friends?

He looked across at Mr. Mitchell and sensing a possible rebuke later, said.

"Yes, sir. It is nice here. I like the food and I like the animals especially Lucy, the Border collie."

"You will be going to school soon. Have the Mitchells talked to you about that?"

"No, but my new friend Jack has told me we'll be goin' in October after the harvest is in"

"You're sounding more like a Canadian, Edward. You're losing your cockney accent. Just as well. It's not refined. They say that Ontarians speak the best English in the Empire. That's all for now. I'll come to see you before Christmas and you can tell me about your school days. I'll bring some picture postcards for you so that you can write to your mother and James. She has moved to a farm and she has married a Mr. Tom Redding. Be a good boy, Eddy. You may be dismissed."

Eddy almost leaped out the door but the news of his mother's marriage went right out of his head. He hardly reacted because he was clutching the letter from his dear friend and mentor Mr. Ryan and couldn't wait to go upstairs to his room to read it.

The men talked awhile and then Mr. Parsons said, "Do you wish to receive our magazine 'Ups and Downs', Mr. Mitchell?"

"What's this?"

"It's a magazine we put out twice a year. We have stories and pictures about our home children spread out across our fair Dominion."

"What's it cost?"

"$1.00 each."

"No, I don't need that. Thanks just the same."

"I'm surprised, Mr. Mitchell. Most foster parents look forward to getting the magazine sent directly by the Postal Service." Mr. Mitchell winced at the words 'foster parents' but he kept his comments to himself.

"It was good speaking to you. Please thank your good wife for her impeccable hospitality and tell her that her squares are the best I've ever tasted."

Mr. Mitchell walked him to the door. Mr. Parsons called to the driver who had actually fallen asleep. "Nice to meet you, Mr. Mitchell. I'll be in correspondence and you will receive your first check to cover the boy's expenses. I will look for monthly updates of Edward's progress and particularly his school experience."

"Have a nice evening." retorted Mitchell.

Mr. Mitchell picked up his heels and walked into the house, grabbed his pipe and settled down in his comfortable chair in the day room. Mary fluffed up the pillows, removed the tea set and the left over squares and closed the parlour door. Her day was still not over but she hummed a tune to herself and completed her chores for the night.

Eddy sat up in bed fully clothed with his shoes on. He tore open the envelope and read the letter.

"Dear Eddy,

I hope you remember me. I'm David Ryan. We were on the ship together. You must remember Miss Molly. Well, I am excited to tell you that Molly and I were married in the chapel at the home on Jarvis Street. We are moving to Saskatchewan where we will be homesteading. I hope you are doing well in your new home. Mr. Parsons will keep me posted.

By the way, I have heard from Gordon. He is happy with his great aunt and Arthur's eyes are much better. Sorry, there is no news on Joseph but they say that no news is good news. Be a good boy, Eddy.

Yours sincerely,

David Ryan."

This was the best news he had ever had. He didn't know whether to be happy or sad because he was happy that Mr. Ryan and Miss Molly were married but sad that he was so far away from them. "Someday, I'll take the train and visit them."

Chapter 25: Will Eddy ever get used to things?

Eddy was growing if not taller at least fuller. The fresh air and the good country food were doing some good. He was still nervous around Mr. Mitchell and he knew that he had to do as he was told. There was no way around it. But summer was coming to a close and there was a nip in the air. The wind coming from the north carried a note of warning that cold weather was ahead. All the farmers were busy chopping and stacking the wood they had gathered in late winter last year. That wood had been piled much as the hay was stacked and by now it had dried to the point that it would be excellent firewood for the winter stoves and fireplaces.

Eddy had learned to do the stacking of the wood in the wood shed. It was back breaking work even if he did not have to do the chopping which demanded a strong back and muscular arms. Mr. Mitchell was as strong as an ox so it came quite easy for him. Ol' Harry was too old for this work so he stayed on for the farm work and Eddy helped him. By now, Eddy worked a full day starting with the hen house and ending with barn work. Harry tended the pigs mostly but he would help with cleaning the stalls and spreading clean hay and saw dust.

In the Gibson household, it was much the same. Emily had become a good housekeeper and the boys were as busy as Eddy with the difference that there were three of them to do the work. The farm was bigger and they had more livestock but they could share the work and have some fun too.

Eddy was sure that if he told Jack about his hideout in the upland woods, they could have adventures like the Gibson boys after their chores were done. Jack ran across the field as often as he could to fetch Eddy when the chores were done. Whenever he came over, they would sit down on the front porch and play checkers but they had to have more fun than that. "Say, Jack, I have a surprise to show you. It's a lot better than checkers!"

"What could be better than checkers?

"You'll see. Follow me."

So Eddy dropped the checker board and put the checkers in the box and started up the path. Jack followed and soon they came to Eddy's twig and branch cabin in the woods.

"Wow, Eddy, this is fantastic. Do you go here often?"

"As often as I can get away," boasted Eddy, "but since it is still light, let's catch a trout with our bear hands."

Finding success, they vowed to keep this hiding place their forever secret and so from then on whenever Eddy had free time and Jack was through with his chores, they raced up to their secret place. One day in late September, the boys decided to go fishing one last time for the season. They took out their make shift fishing poles which they stored in the cabin made of hay and branches, and sat on the mossy bank. Shaded by a great pine, the water was cool and ideal for fish. "I've got one." yelled Eddy.

"He's a big one", shouted Jack. "Next time let's make a fire and cook up some for an evening snack."

"You take it home, Jack. I wouldn't dare take it down even though I think Mrs. Mitchell wouldn't mind. Wish I didn't have to sneak off to come here. If the ol' man caught me, he'd give me a whipping."

"Didn't you say he was out for his meeting?"

"Yes, but I've got to watch out just in case he comes home early."

"My dad let's me have lots of freedom." said Jack, "but I know it's not the same with you. You don't have a dad or mum, do you?"

"Yes, I do."

"Where are they, then?"

Eddy could feel his face getting hotter and hotter.

"Don't get yer dander up."

At that Eddy lurched toward him and pushed him so hard that Jack fell into the stream. Not realizing his strength, Eddy felt ashamed and bent down and grabbed his friend's hand and pulled him back.

"Sorry, old mate. I didn't mean to push you but I don't like what you said."

Jack put out his hand, "Sorry, Eddy. Let's stay friends forever."

"Yes, forever", said Eddy.

"See you in Sunday School on Sunday," said Jack.

When October came and the harvest was in, the wood stacked and the cattle brought in from the fields for the long months of cold weather ahead, Mr. Mitchell announced that Eddy would be starting school. "You're starting Monday morning. Most kids have been in class since the first of September but you, farm kids, have too many chores to do; the authorities accept that but, once there, you have got to work extra hard to catch up."

It was Thursday and the general store was having a sale on winter clothes they had preordered from Eaton's catalogue. Peggy, the mare, was outside with the carriage and Eddy was going to town with Mary Mitchell to get school clothes. He hadn't been to Bracebridge since his arrival back in July. It promised an adventure.

They drove along a dusty road on each side of which were hardwood trees now beginning to turn yellow with the change in the Season. This was North Country and summers were short. Rumbling along, they came to a wooden bridge which led them up a hill to the main street. Some new buildings of brick graced the dirt street and one, in particular, was the new Andrew Carnegie Library. Carnegie, who made his money in steel, established a foundation to provide libraries for the common man right across the country in America and the new Dominion of Canada. "When you get older, you will really enjoy the library, Eddy. They say it is wonderful and filled with all kinds of books."

After they had parked the carriage at the stable, the mare watered and given some oats, Eddy and Mrs. Mitchell stepped down and walked to the Jenkins' General Store. It was filled with all manner of items, farm equipment, axes and saws, barrels of all sorts and clothing hung from hangers inside and there were bales of cloth and large batches of wool. There were winter coats, leggings, shiny leather boots and a section for kids' clothes suitable for school and some best wear for church or picture taking at the Photography Studio.

"Hello, Mrs. Mitchell. Nice to see you. Haven't seen you for a while. I see you have your boy with you, getting sorted out for school, I dare say."

"Nice to see you too, Mrs. Jenkins. I'd like to introduce you to our foster child. His name is Edward George Tompkins."

"What do you call him?"

"I call him Eddy but he's Tompkins when he's working with my husband. Mr. Mitchell believes it's better to be formal when you're working."

Mrs. Jenkins, a particularly tall woman with a formal face and attitude bent down and taking him by the chin, she said, "So, you're the new boy then. Hello Edward. Welcome to Bracebridge."

Looking up almost to the tin ceiling, he found Mrs. Jenkins face and said. "Ello."

"So you're going to start school? Can you read and do simple sums?"

"Yea, Mam. They learnt me in my old school."

"Now, Mrs. Mitchell, I have some material to make a few pairs of britches and school shirts."

"No, I am looking for some readymade ones. I understood that you had a large order in from Eaton's catalogue."

"Oh, yes."

They looked for britches that could fit Eddy with a bit of extra room for him to grow into and cotton shirts and two pullovers for the cooler weather. Eddy tried them on and wriggled out of them when the fittings were complete. They topped it off with a plaid jacket and a wool cap and loads of socks and long underwear which felt stiff and itchy.

With that over, he looked around the shop at all the gadgets and in the corner were some wooden toys. He eyed them but didn't dare hope that he could get one for himself. Now with the shopping over, Eddy skipped outside looking longingly at the ice cream parlour up the street. Maybe, just maybe, his foster mother would take him there. "Gather up, Eddy", she said as she stepped out the door. "We're going to get you some ice cream."

"Gor' Blimey, I ain't ever had ice cream. Never." The book labeled 'Canada' he had read at Barnardo's had a big picture of children with their faces covered with ice cream some with more outside their mouths than in.

He bounded up the street with giant steps ahead of Mrs. Mitchell. He couldn't contain his excitement. For the first time in his life, Eddy could have something he always wanted. Stepping up to the counter, the young man with the white hat and apron scooped up this frothy looking concoction that looked like chocolate with flecks of strawberry and put it into a wafer cone.

Eddy took a bite and gasped. "It's cold." His second bite dug into the ice cream and covered his mouth with flavor. "Mmm. Thank you. Ma Mitchell. Thank you so much."

Chapter 26: School

He had blurted out "Ma" without thinking. She hadn't told him to call her that but today it felt right. He had to say that this was his best day ever. That was just as well because the next day, he was up early, breakfasted, dressed in his new school clothes and with slate in one hand and a bag lunch in the other, he set out for school.

"Be a good boy, Eddy", said Mary. "Have a good day."

Jack waited for him at the end of the driveway and down to the rail road tracks and along a wooded lane, they hurried off to school. Being a farmer's son, it was Jack's first day of the new Season as well.

The school was about a mile away from the Mitchell homestead. The boys from the Gibson household were running along with their slates and lunches and little Emily tried to keep up with them.

"You can come with us, Emily", said Jack. "You walk between Eddy and me. Okay?"

As they neared the school, they could see hordes of children milling around outside. Eddy had a big lump in his throat and Emily didn't say a word.

The school which sat in a big field was quite imposing and big enough for two classrooms and two teachers. The education authorities had finally prepared for an influx of children, some newly arrived on the boat, the local farm kids and these home children from England and even though they had been open since September, the bulk of the children were arriving this morning. That was the rule. Farm kids were needed on the farm first before they could attend school but the farmers had to guarantee at least 5 months off farm work at least during the day so they could go to school.

As they got closer, Eddy could see a cluster of big boys up to something. They were bent over in a kind of school boy conference. Suddenly the taller of them jumped up and yelled, "Any limey's here?"

Eddy shuddered and tried to look away to find his friends but Jack had vanished and Emily had been taken away by an older girl who felt sorry for her when she arrived in the schoolyard. She had looked so forlorn.

"Hey, boy! Yea, you with the curls. Say something!"

Eddy said nothing but he knew they meant him. Him of all the boys there that morning.

"Say Something. Damn you!"

"I, I, I don't have anytin' to say."

"There, I knew it," the tall boy slapped his hand on his thigh and yelled even louder "Say, I got a lovely bunch of coconuts. Say it now."

"No."

On hearing "No!" he grabbed Eddy by the ear and yelled, "Limey, limey. Why you over here? Go back to your home across the sea."

Before Eddy had a chance to answer back while clasping his hand over his ear, the teacher emerged with a big bell in hand and summoned the children to line up and march in.

"Saved by the bell," Eddy thought but he was so frightened he couldn't speak. They marched in two by two and lined up on the inner walls.

"Halt. I will call you each by name and in turn you will take the seat assigned to each of you new children. Stop shuffling about. Stand straight."

"Bert Gibson"

"Here"

The Gibson names were called and in turn each one took his seat.

And looking at Emily, she said, "And your name is?"

"Emily".

"And your surname?"

"I dunno, miss."

Some of the girls laughed in their sleeves and Emily started to cry. "I dunno have a surname, miss."

"That's all right, I will talk to you later. Right now you are a Gibson and you can answer to it. And I shall have none of that snickering, girls!"

The teacher continued alphabetically and eventually she came to "Edward George Tompkins'.

"Ere."

All around Eddy could hear giggles until one boy laughed out loud. The teacher glared at the boy and Eddy took note that he was the same boy who had tormented him outside. Eddy gritted his teeth and clenched his fists. "A'll fix his clock good when I get older."

"See me at recess. Hans! I will not tolerate disrespect."

Eddy was led to his seat 5 rows back from the front. Opposite him on the girls side of the room was Emily. It was their first day in school in Canada.

Walking to the big desk at the front of the room, the teacher took her place and addressed the class. She was young and pretty with long blond braids piled on her head. Her eyes were blue and there was a sparkle in them. She was dressed in a long blue skirt with a matching blouse. She wore Edwardian style laced boots. She looked over the classroom with its neat row of fastened down desks. The boys were on the left side and the girls on the right.

"Good morning. My name is Miss Patterson. Welcome to Parkland Elementary School."

Miss Patterson was new to the school when Eddy and the other home children started their education in the new Dominion. They were all in Frontier country really. So many settlers had come to this part of Ontario to try their hand at farming or work in the tannery and saw mills. Enthusiasm tempered with back breaking work was the order of the day and the children had been told to learn the three R's well because there was a future for them here.

Eddy was happy to be in her class and he was sure that she would protect him against the bully, Hans. She would protect Emily too; he was convinced of that.

They started the morning with the Lord's Prayer and the Royal Anthem, 'God Save the King' followed by 'The Maple Leaf Forever'. There were 4 grades in the primary room covering the ages of six through ten. The intermediate room comprised of Grades 5 through 8 and included children of eleven to fourteen, the age when most kids would leave and work in the trades or on the farm. The few who aspired to higher learning would be tutored to sit for an exam and if successful, they would attend a secondary school to prepare for college or university.

It was much too early for Eddy to think of anything but getting through the day and getting home before Hans and his friends could catch up with him.

The work was assigned. Sometimes the teacher combined two grades to teach a lesson in reading or writing and when one group was being instructed, the others would work on their own with work assigned on the blackboards. Often the older children would help the little ones with their reading. Eddy was called to the front with two other boys.

"Sit together and start reading the passage in this Primer Reader. I want to know what group you are in."

They each took their turn and when it came to Eddy, he read the passage about the Grizzly Bear. "The bear climbed the tree by the brook. He liked to do this because he was really a young one and loved the feel of the bark and the smell of the bals... ..balsa.."

"Balsam gum, Eddie." said Miss Patterson.

"Balsam gum" said Eddy, clearer this time.

"Thank you. Sit down. Next."

The next boy read the same passage but he hesitated on more words.

"Eddy, take your seat next to the boys and girls at the front of the class. You are assigned to the Upper Group."

The day continued with Spelling, Arithmetic and Geography. Then the lunch bell rang out. "Please put your slates away and sit down with your bag lunch. Then, you will have a short break outside and when the bell rings, you must return immediately."

They gobbled down their lunch and drank water from the pail at the back of the room. Some had to rush out to the outhouse, a three 'holer' with a bucket of lime to keep it fresh. Eddy grabbed his jacket and looked around for his friend Jack. He couldn't see him so he walked over to Emily to see if he could keep her company but the same girl who had protected her earlier, was looking after her.

Eddy stepped out into the sunlight and looked around. He didn't see his arch enemy and tried to relax. Some boys were playing football; others were kicking stones aimlessly. He sidled up to the ones playing ball and waited.

"Like to have a game with us?" one said.

"Yea", said Eddy. With a sigh of relief, he started to play with them. He had learned lots of school games at the home and he had a knack with the way he twisted his leg to connect with the ball. He got a goal right away.

"Good, oh, what's your name by the way?"

"Eddy"

"Oh, yeah, you're the new boy up at the Mitchell's. I've heard of ya."

They were just getting started it seemed when the bell rang summoning them back to class. They lined up, washed and dried their hands and sometimes their face if there was a lot of dirt and sweat on them from the playground. By the time, they were through, boys and girls separately, the wash basin looked pretty brown but they were at least freshened and prepared for the afternoon lessons.

"Take out your hymn books- the Sankey one I mean", said the teacher.

"The Sankey one? Gosh, that's in my trunk. They sent it all the way to Canada with me. I know those songs." said Eddy to himself.

Miss Patterson sat down at the old piano and sounded out the first note of "Onward Christian Soldiers." And they all joined in, mostly out of tune, but the boys especially liked the marching music. After the short hymn sing, she sat them down for a story which she would read aloud. "I am going to start a new book today because many of you are here for the first day of school. She took out the book. It was colorful and the name on the cover was The Wind in the Willows.

"Hope it isn't a girlie book", thought Eddy." I'd like some adventure."

"The Mole had been working very hard all the morning, spring-cleaning his little home."

After the first few lines, Eddy sat up and listened to every word. It reminded him of his tiny pretend cabin in the woods. It was a secret except for his friend Jack and he was sworn to secrecy.

After the first chapter, Miss Patterson put the book in the drawer of her big desk, and gave each child new chalk. "Copy the picture on the board. This is drawing lesson, number one. Can you recognize it?

"Yes, it's a chair." blurted Eddy.

"That's right, Eddy. We are going to learn how to draw starting with a simple chair which, by the way, isn't simple at all."

What a buzz of activity. Eddy could see that this was going to be a favourite. He grasped his chalk and started to copy each line until it began to take the shape of a chair he remembered from long ago.

"Well done, class. This was a good first lesson in drawing. You will become good draftsmen yet boys and artists, young ladies."

The afternoon concluded with a lesson on the harvest where each child who could, recounted their experience bringing in the grain and helping to put up vegetables for the winter.

It had been a very busy day. The bell sounded. The children gathered up their things and rushed out the door "Not so fast; Say Good afternoon Miss Patterson as you leave."

"Good afternoon. Miss Patterson. "

Eddy caught up with Jack and the Gibson home boys who were in the older class and together with Emily, they skipped, ran and walked home. The afternoon freight was climbing the hill to Bracebridge so they couldn't walk the tracks but something caught Eddy's eye and he stopped to watch. The others hurried home because they all had chores to do.

"See you tomorrow, Eddy."

"See you."

He was sure he spotted Hans and his buddies and what he couldn't believe was the shock that they were running alongside the train until the big wheels almost came to a stop. It was as if the engine had taken a rest before getting to the top of the grade. Then, Hans grabbed the rail of the fourth boxcar and pulled himself up. Another boy did the same and then the wheels began to move and the other boys stopped running. Hans and his friend pushed themselves up the steps and wriggled their upper bodies until they were sitting on top of the box car.

" Gor" Blimey. I'd like to do that."

The boys had all been warned one time or another about this new game of "Riding the rails." There were wondering men, called hoboes, all over the country riding from town to town to find work or adventure. It was a dangerous game but the railway track at the bottom of the Mitchell farm was tempting.

"I suppose Hans and his friend- I think his name is Felix- will get off at the station in town. I hope they don't get caught." Eddy picked up his heels and began running up the field to the door of the Mitchell farm house and was greeted with a rough reminder.

"Grab a glass of milk, Tompkins. You've got work to do before supper

Chapter 27: Lots to do

With the school day completed and chores to complete, Eddy was dog tired. Mrs. Mitchell sensing this said, "Now Eddy, I don't expect you to do everything. You probably have home work so after supper, Mr. Mitchell said you can do your studies and put the milking chore aside for tonight. Mind you, he expects you to get back to it tomorrow evening. We'll have to make sure you have a schedule so that you can prepare better."

So, on this night, Eddy had his supper, washed up and went upstairs to his room to do the arithmetic sums he had been given. But first, he wanted to write to his mother and brother Jim on the postcards he had been given. Mr. Parsons insisted that Eddy write at least once a year and now that he had their addresses, there was no excuse. He wanted to tell them a bit about himself and his town.

He picked out a card for Jim first. Gosh, he could barely remember what he looked like. He knew that he lived with his grandparents on a farm but that's only because Mr. Parsons had said that in a letter to the Mitchell's which he learned about because he overheard their conversation. He was pretty good at listening through the keyhole. He knew that whenever they went into the parlour with a letter from Barnardo's it had to do with him.

He picked the card that had on it a picture of Bracebridge. His penmanship had improved with practice and to make his sentences straight, he used a ruler. Using a pen, the kind that you dip in ink, he began:

> "Dear Jim,
> This is a picture of the town where I live.
> That is a bridge over the falls
> That is the wharf at the foot of the falls
> And the electric power house next to it.
> I'm fine. How are you?
> From
> George but they call me Eddy."

"I better write to mother too." He barely remembered her except for the day she didn't come back with his lollypop. But he was told to write so he picked up the second card which featured, St. Thomas English church, Bracebridge.

Using the same pen, now replenished with ink from his inkwell, he wrote,

"Dear Mother,
This the church I go to
When I go to church
Tho' Sunday school is close to it,
From,
George. They call me Eddy now."

He set the cards aside to be given to Mr. Parsons on his next visit. "Whew, I am glad that's over with. Mr. Parsons had said, 'you must write, Eddy. It's important to keep in touch.'"

But he wondered if they would ever see them. He certainly never heard from any of them and he was beginning not to care. He was anxious to read some more in Robinson Crusoe. The world in books was so much more exciting and real. He thought about his day, his walk to school, his confrontation with Hans and his mates, and his delightful day with Miss Patterson.

"I'll get used to it and I am making plans to deal with Hans, the next time he tries to bully me", he said to himself. And, anyway, Eddy had something on Hans but he would never tell- hoboes' honour-unless Hans made it impossible for him to keep a secret.

As the days went by, school work became a little easier but the chores only got worse and more tedious. He couldn't get anywhere with old man Mitchell. "He just don't like me. And I don't like him either."

On the first Saturday after his first week in class, he walked with Mrs. Mitchell to her mother's farm. Grandma Gibson was sure to have a treat; her pies were extra special and she knew Eddy especially loved pumpkin with cream on top.

It was a new experience for most of the British settlers since pumpkin and squash were regarded as vegetables and never as a sweet. Somehow, the American custom that began with the Puritans in the Boston area, of preparing pumpkin in a pie, had travelled by word of mouth to this part of Ontario. It became a delicacy and was served in October in keeping with the Harvest Festival.

"Hi Mary and welcome Eddy. I've got an extra special treat for you and Emily and the boys. Come in and sit at the kitchen table."

They sat down together and greedily devoured the pies with a fresh glass of buttermilk.

"Mmm. Thanks Grandma Gibson. Thanks a lot."

Then, while mother and daughter caught up with family and local news, Eddy slipped outside to the porch beckoning Emily to come with him. "That's real good, ain't it" said Eddy.

"I like it too", said Emily.

"Sit down with me on the swing, won't you?"

"Oh, okay, but I can't stay long 'cause I got chores to do in the kitchen."

"Say, Emily, How long have you been here."

"'Bout the same as you, Eddy. We got here the same day. I was on the train with you, don't you remember."

"I dunno. I can't remember if I saw you or not. It's all kin' of a blur."

"Do you remember the ship? I came across on the Sicil..Sicilean."

"I came on the Tunisian." said Emily.

"That was an adventure, was'n it?

"I dunno. I was sick most of the time."

"Gor'. Blimey. That ain't fair. Sowwy, Emily."

"Do you have a ma and pa?" questioned Eddy.

"I dunno. I ain't never seen them if I do." I was in the Orphanage but before that I lived in a Workhouse- I think that's what they called it. What about you?"

"I have a ma and pa. But sometin' appened and me ma took me to this home, this big house in London, and she didn' come back. I have a little sister, Beatrice. I dunno what 'appened to her? Hope she's okay."

Interrupting, Grandma Gibson said, "Emily, Emily. Where have you been? You gotta get the dishes washed and help me prepare the supper. The men have been chopping and stacking wood all day and they're plenty hungry."

"Sorry, Grandma Gibson, "said Emily as she turned to the kitchen and put on her apron.

"See you later." said Eddy but without a word Emily had vanished into a sink full of soapy water and dishes."

"I'll come by on Sunday to pick you up for church", said Mrs. Mitchell. "Maybe you can bring Emily and the boys along. They're starting Sunday School and soon they will be preparing for the Christmas pageant."

"See you on Sunday, then". With that they departed down the lane to the farm and the work that lay ahead. It was good to have a break.

When they got home, they were confronted by an angry Mr. Mitchell. "Where have you been all afternoon? And me with so much to do. You're as bad as the boy, Mary. I expected more of you. What kind of example are you setting for the boy?"

Mary Mitchell felt embarrassed and brow beaten. She hadn't bargained for any of this when her husband was courting her. There were times, she wanted to run away to the big city and find herself. She wasn't raised for a life of drudgery and toil.

Days and weeks past. School work was still interesting and Eddy was learning fast. Sunday School classes were preparing for the annual Christmas Pageant and Eddy was one of the Three Kings. Emily was an angel. Only the Canadian kids had speaking parts. The teacher didn't want to spoil it with a foreign accent and, most certainly, not a cockney accent from the east side of London. Eddy and Emily still sounded like street vagrants.

But school was a different matter. It was the custom of the Department of Education to call for an end of term concert at Christmas as well as a closing ceremony in June where all pupils were expected to do their part either in singing, recitation, public speaking or drama. Both classes participated and would present together. That could mean that the younger ones had less of a chance to be chosen.

Eddy was good at memorizing and already, he knew 'The Visit from St. Nicholas' by heart. He hoped that Miss Patterson would choose him to do a recitation. He had the voices rehearsed and he was sure to be a hit. He was convinced of that.

Hans had different ideas though. "I'm gonna stop that limey in his tracks. It's my turn to do the Christmas recitation and there's no way, he's getting in front of me."

It was Thursday, almost the end of the week and almost the end of the month. December was looming and the day of the concert was set at December 22. School closed early because a snow storm was threatened and the children hurried home, all on foot. Eddy and Jack picked up their heels knowing there was work waiting at home.

Hans had other plans. This was his day to go on the attack. He had lined up two of his mates and they hid behind the large barn at the corner of the Mitchell property.

"Say, Jack, let's take a slide down the hill. It's slippery already."

"Not so fast, buddy boy", yelled Hans as he jumped up behind Eddy grabbing him by the throat.

"You better give up on that Christmas poem or I'll have your hide good."

"Let go o' me, you bastard."

"What you call me?"

"Bastard", said Eddy defiantly.

After wriggling free of his grasp, Eddy wheeled around and with all his might, which compared to Hans, was like David to the giant, Goliath, he thrust his left fist in Han's face and knocked him over.

Jack marveled at his strength but Hans was down and crying like a baby with a bloodied nose as well. Eddy turned around and walked over to Hans who by now, like a wounded animal had got up on his feet.

"Sorry, 'ol chap, but you had it comin' and by the way, you didn't know that I saw you jump the freight the other day. Don't worry. I ain't tellin!"

Hans looked away and turned in the direction of his home. His father would not be pleased. Eddy and Jack made their way through the snow to their homes. A lot had come down in the last hour and Mrs.Fowler and Mrs. Mitchell would be wondering what happened to their boys.

Days passed and the fight was forgotten. Hans kept his distance and there was none of the bravado he had previously exhibited. Hans' friends were not as willing to huddle with him and Eddy was spared at least for a while.

Eddy had other things to occupy his mind. Eddy was chosen to recite 'The Visit from St. Nicholas' and that kept him focused and connected as nothing else had. Maybe he had inherited his father's talent as a busker. He was determined to shine.

The experience with Hans had taught him that he could stand up for himself and word got out that Eddy was fearless and brave. Some of the older boys talked to him and Mr. Jones, the intermediate school teacher who was a bit of a boxer himself, took Eddy under his wing and invited him to come to the barn where a number of young men were learning the sport of hand to hand combat. There were matches held once a month in the hall and people even paid a few pennies to watch. He kept this to himself. Mr. Mitchell would not be amused. It was all work and no play for him.

Chapter 28: Christmas Concert and the first Christmas in Canada.

It was getting close to December 22, the Day of the Christmas Concert. Regardless of that, Mr. Mitchell was even more of a task master. Eddy could hear him in his sleep. "Tompkins…….Do this. Don't do that."

Just the same, Eddy had been practicing his recitation, "Twas the night before Christmas" and he was sure that he had it down pat. He had gone over to Grandma Gibson's house and summoned Emily to listen to him and add a comment of her own. "What do you think, Emily? Do you like it?"

"I like it a lot, Eddy, and I think Miss. Patterson will be pleased."

"Can you see the reindeer? And what do you think of jolly St. Nick?"

"Oh, I can imagine them very clearly. I hope he will visit me. Will he even know where I am? He never saw me when I lived in the Workhouse. All I remember is a bit of Christmas pudding and some carolers who stood outside and tried to serenade us paupers."

"He never came to visit me either, not even when I lived in the old flat with my parents. There might have been a preacher who came by to say hello and bring us a few oranges as Christmas cheer. At the home, it was all hymns and preaching."

Grandma Gibson was listening to this and she opened the door to the drawing room and waited for a chance to speak. When Eddy and Emily saw that they were being watched, they went silent. "I was listening, children, and I could hear a bit of your poem, Eddy. How about saying it again for me?"

Eddy shyly obliged and Grandma Gibson was impressed and was sure that he would do very well at the concert.

The day of the concert came. The children dressed in their Sunday clothes filed towards the school house in the late afternoon as the sun was falling down across the snow covered fields. They came by foot and by cart and carriage; they and their parents and all entered the lantern lit school house on this very special afternoon.

The school room was decked out with Christmas lanterns and at the front stood a beautiful fir tree now adorned with candles and homemade ornaments made of paper. A make shift curtain made of bed sheets was strung from one side to the other. The children sat in the front and waited their turn to be on the stage.

Miss Patterson dressed in a blue muslin skirt and white taffeta blouse, her hair loose falling down her back sat at the piano and played "God save the King."

"Please. All stand", said the head Trustee of the Board of Education. Miss Patterson leading from her place at the piano had the audience in her hands as they belted out the Royal Anthem and when they sat down she said, "Let the concert begin!"

There was a choir of Grade 5 girls who sang "Silent Night." A group of Grade 6 boys and girls put on a short drama based on Dickens' Christmas Carol. Hans played Scrooge and Felix played Bob Cratchitt. They were perfect angels on this night and no one knew about their daring prank. Eddy had kept his word.

Eddy nervously waited his turn. He was to follow Emily who sang a solo, "Away in the manger." Eddy had only just learned from one of the boys at Grandma Gibson's home that Emily had been chosen to sing. "She has a beautiful voice. We only just found out when we heard her sing at Sunday School."

Everyone in the school room clapped when Emily stepped off the stage. She was so pretty with her white dress with green bows and she hardly seemed shy at all.

When it was his turn, Eddy dressed in a suede suit and well ironed breeches, walked up confidently, bowed his head to the audience and began:

" *Twas the night before Christmas . when all through the house, Not a creature was stirring, not even a mouse.*
The stockings were hung by the chimney with care,
In hopes that St. Nicholas soon would be there."

Mrs. Mitchell sat proudly but alone. Charles Mitchell had abstained. He wasn't having any of this tom foolery, he said.

"It's his loss", she sighed.

Someone whispered, "His cockney accent is gone. Thank Goodness for that. He sounds just like one of us."

As he continued, Eddy became more animated putting lots of dramatic action into his words,

"When what to my wondering eyes should appear,
But a miniature sleigh and eight tiny reindeer.
And he whistled and shouted and called them by name,
Now dasher, now Dancer, now Prancer and Vixen..
Now dash away, dash away, dash away all."

"What a memory the boy has!" said a lady in the back aisle.

Eddy continued not missing a word and completely absorbed until he came to the last line which he proclaimed loud and clear,

"Happy Christmas to all, and to all a good-night."

To thunderous applause, Eddy walked off and sat with the rest in the front row.

"So, ladies and gentlemen, we now end our Christmas concert. Let us all stand and sing 'We wish you a Merry Christmas.' Thank you for coming and thank you, children, for all your hard work and entertainment."

Eddy walked with the Gibson's and Mrs. Mitchell and Emily and the boys. "Will you stop for a spot of tea, Mary?"

"Yes, but only for a few minutes." Mr. Mitchell will be waiting for us. He was none too happy at being abandoned to complete all the chores himself. Of course, old Harry is with him but he's not much help these days."

Eddy felt triumphant and he would carry this feeling with him through everything he would experience in days to come. He had it in him to do big things. School closed for the holidays. Miss Patterson went home to her family in Kingston. Relatives came to visit and there was a lot of hustle and bustle in every household.

Mr. Mitchell was in correspondence with the inspector who was most anxious to learn of Eddy's progress in school. After hearing about Eddy's showing at the concert, he wrote, "Eddy is a good lad progressing well in school." This report and the one after the first visitation were forwarded to the Dr. Barnardo Home at Stepney Causeway to become part of their permanent collection on the children they sent to Canada. A file entitled, Edward George Tompkins, was begun. Another cheque for maintenance was posted to the Mitchells and as far as the Home in Toronto was concerned, Eddy was doing just fine.

There was no mention of the brutal hard work that Eddy was expected to do and no mention of how Eddy was adjusting to the cold hardness of Mr. Mitchell. Mr. Mitchell was a pillar in the community and only his wife knew how unappreciative and hostile he could be.

Christmas came to the Mitchell household and except for a Christmas card from Grandma Gibson and a hand knit pair of mittens that Mrs. Mitchell had made, that was all Eddy received. He wasn't really upset because he had not known what a loving Christmas could be. It was only after he had gone over to his friend Jack's house and seen the presents under the tree that he was hit with a sense of loss. He swallowed hard and felt the lump in his throat growing but he had to be brave and strong. He had to survive.

After the Christmas dinner and plum pudding which Grandma Gibson had spent hours preparing, Eddy went upstairs to his room. After putting his special card with the picture of the baby Jesus in the manger away, he fumbled in his trunk looking for the postcards Mr. Parsons had given him on his last visit. The picture on the card was that of sheep on a very English hillside. Draped with holly, the words in white on a red background, said, "When shepherds watched their flocks by night." Eddy knew those words by heart because they sang that Christmas carol at Sunday school.

"I suppose I should write another letter to mother. Mr. Parsons said that he would make sure it was delivered to her. She has never written to me but I want to wish her a nice Christmas just the same."

In his best penmanship, he wrote:

Dear Mother,
I wish you a very good xmas and happy new year.
I hung up my stocking.
Love,
Edward.

PS I am calling myself Eddy from now on. That's what they call me here."

He wasn't about to tell her that all that was in the stocking was a handmade pair of mittens that Grandma Gibson had made. He was grateful for that but what he wanted was a wooden toy, the one that he had seen in the store downtown.

He put the postcard on his dressing table to give to Mr. Parsons. Of course that might be well past the New Year but he tried anyway.

"Maybe, one day, it'll be different. Maybe, one day, my stocking will be full."

Eddy spent the holidays working in the barn, feeding the hens, milking the cows and harnessing the draft horses to pull the huge sled hauling tamarack for the tanning mill. It never stopped. Everyday was the same.

"I'll never be a farmer." He said.

He managed only a few breakaways with Jack when they trudged through the deep snow to his cabin now covered with snow but quite snug inside. Eddy let his imagination rule there. He named his kingdom "The Land of Plenty" and his characters were Minnie the Owl, Great Claws and Bald Eagle and John Squirrel. He made up stories which he would tell his friends and later when Emily could come up to the woods with him, they created their own magical forest which no one could ever find.

"Emily, you will be Minnie and I'll be Great Claws. Together, we will conquer the evil magician who lurks in the back woods. We will keep the forest safe for all our furry friends."

Chapter 29: Time goes by

Life went on pretty much the same day after day. Two years had passed since Eddy had arrived at the farm. He was now ten and he had become stronger but also more belligerent. The cute little boy of bygone days was replaced by a boy who felt cheated and alone even with his friends. Mrs. Mitchell tried to make up for her harsh and unyielding husband and Grandma Gibson and Miss Patterson always had a smile and a comforting word for him but just the same, he longed for a real family.

Emily and Jack remained his most faithful mates and he looked to them for companionship and a bit of fun. The inspectors from Dr. Barnardo's looked in on him from time to time and glowing reports continued to come from Mr. Mitchell who looked for his foster cheque every month.

Eddy practiced his fighting skills whenever he could get away and take lessons after school from Mr. Jones, the coach and school teacher for the upper grades. He told anyone who cared to listen that he was going to be a boxer when he grew up. His friend Jack who was more shy and retiring didn't want to engage in play fighting even if Eddy wanted to almost every time they got together at Eddy's camp in the woods.

"Want to fight, Jack." Eddy would say.

"Na, not interested. Let's play ball instead." He would answer.

And they would leave it at that.

Later on, Eddy joined a boxing group and with grown up coaches recommended by Mr. Jones, he became quite good at it. The boys would have practice fights but Eddy rarely could sneak off to join them but he practiced with imaginary opponents dancing on his feet and swinging a low punch and a swift left hander.

There was to be none of it during school hours, of course, and so with Miss Patterson, Eddy practiced his skill at reciting, preparing for the school concert at Easter. Sadly, as always after Easter, Eddy and all the farm children his age and older had to leave school to work to prepare the ground for planting, help to pull the hemlock logs out of the woods with teams of horses and do the grueling work expected on the farm.

Eddy had become fascinated with tales of Indian tribes and Hiawatha was his favourite. He had first found Longfellow's "The Song of Hiawatha" in the Carnegie Library in the town of Bracebridge. The librarian lent it to him and he took it to Miss Patterson, who listened intently as Eddy began to say the words,

"On the shores of Gitche Gumee.
Of the shining Big-Sea-Water

Stood Nokomis,the old woman,
Pointing with her finger westward."

"Miss Patterson, I am practicing this piece so I can present it at our Spring concert."

"Eddy, we haven't even started planning for it. It's only February."

"Oh, I have my heart set on it; Please let me tell you more."

"Okay, Eddy. We'll see. I'll talk to the other teacher and we'll decide. But keep practicing your lines in any case."

The days were getting longer and everyone longed for spring. Snows had come and stayed and there seemed no let up. For the settlers who had come from England, they longed to see crocuses and by early March they looked for daffodils and tulips but it would a long time coming in the north.

Mr. Mitchell kept looking for more from Eddy and Eddy had no choice but to obey. "It's about time you learned how to harness the horses and go with me to haul the hemlock out. They're looking for more logs for the tanning mill and I can't do it myself. 'Ol Harry is getting too old for this and you're old enough to help."

"Okay, Mr. Mitchell. When will that be?"

"By the end of next week while we still have snow."

Mr. Mitchell, true to his word called Eddy very early Saturday morning. Eddy was in school all week and learning his times tables and long division which was a challenge. But, he readied himself to work with the horses. He was fond of them as friends but he didn't want to use a whip or put the bridle on them. "Tompkins, time to get up. You'll breakfast later." The sun had not peered over the horizon and there was frost on the window pane and ice in the wash bucket.

Eddy came downstairs and walked to the barn to meet his master.

He was reluctant to harness these two great beasts of burden. He brushed up against them and started to speak their names.

"Come on over here!" Forget their names. You have to be their master."

Eddy barely came to their shoulders and the sledge with its two bone handles was heavy and hard to move. "Grab the bridle of the big guy. Okay, you can call him Jake ; the other's Joe, his brother. He's a bit timid, even now. Never did get broke in properly."

They were massive with broad shoulders and strong elephant like legs. Both were the colour brown and Eddy could see that they were used to working. Eddy looked up at Mr. Mitchell and waited.

"Come on, Tompkins. Get a move on. This isn't play. Show them whose boss."

After harnessing them and attaching the ropes with the master's help, Eddy led Jake and Joe out of their stalls to the crisp outdoor morning. They raised their heads and sniffed the air and snorted. Jake stamped and let out a loud "Whinny".

"Whoa, Jake. Whoa."

On cue, Jake stopped and Joe followed suit. Mr. Mitchell attached the sledge and beckoned Eddy to take the handles and guide it along. It was all he could do but he held tight and the horses, sensing that their new day master was a lot smaller than them, moved along in step.

By this time, Mrs. Mitchell was up and preparing a lunch they could take with them to the woods. She handed them both a chunk of ham, hard boiled eggs and big slices of brown bread wrapped in newspaper and two mugs of hot tea.

Eddy jumped up on the sledge with Mr. Mitchell up front on a seat right behind the horses and they started up the snow covered rutted path.

The rest of the day was spent loading logs. The horses pulled hard and in unison and Eddy was getting the hang of it. Mr. Mitchell lifted the logs that had been felled some time ago, on to the sled and Eddy helped maneuver them into place. Jake and Joe didn't seem to mind the work. They were a great team and Eddy marveled at what they could do with hardly any instruction.

"Bloody hell, what a team!" he said.

By noon, the horses and the boy were getting tired but old man Mitchell just kept going. "Blimey, why won't he stop? I'm thirsty, hungry and tired but I best say nothing", he said to himself. Jake stopped and scratched the snow with his right hoof. He did it again until the old man stopped, lifted up his head, and took the cue. "Okay, Jake. I get the message. Lunch?" He watered the horses, fed them some hay and sat on the snow pile.

"Finally", thought Eddy and he sat down too.

"Here's your lunch, Eddy. But, it's just cold water to drink. The tea's too cold. We'll have it later when we get back to the house and the missus warms it up. We don't have time to make a fire and start up the kettle." The woodsmen who worked for the big mill in Huntsville had a bunkhouse nearby but Mitchell was having none of that even though it was only a five minute walk to hot tea and probably a plate of beans.

"We've got too much to do."

Lunch over, they got back to work and only the flickering light of the setting sun slowed Mitchell down. "Okay, time to head home."

Eddy would get the hang of this soon and it wasn't long before he was the one up and harnessing the horses before dawn. When you lived on a farm and made your living this way, you didn't rest. Only the toughest survived.

Eddy was glad when Sunday came. The Mitchell's were devoted church goers and would never work on the Sabbath. They all got dressed up and drove in the carriage to their local Church of England. Mary Mitchell put on her most stylish suit and hat and her husband looking every inch, the gentleman, took the reins. Eddy, in his dark breeches, shirt and tweed jacket managed to give a good impression. That was important in this conservative Ontario town.

"My, my," the matrons would say, "the boy is a credit to the family and he's shed that dreadful accent. They might make a gentleman out of him, yet."

Others would remark, "Always a street boy, You can't get the beggar out and put a Canadian boy in."

Eddy never heard a word. He couldn't wait to see his friend Jack, his best friend from the farm next door. They could sit still in church but, as soon as they went to the building next door for junior Bible lessons or Confirmation classes, they burst into laughter and started planning their next prank.

Chapter 30: Why is Easter so long coming?"

"Why is Easter so long coming?" Eddy asked Miss Patterson on this March morning just as he arrived at school. He was early today. He'd worked hard all weekend but just being with his beautiful teacher was enough to make the day ahead hopeful.

"I've been practicing 'The Song of Hiawatha' all weekend whenever I got the chance and I want to know if you have picked the girl or boy who will do the reading for the concert yet." Eddy had practiced what to say as well. His teacher was very precise and insisted that her pupils address her politely and with correct grammar.

"Eddy, I know you really want to do this and I appreciate all you are doing but we have not made a decision yet so you'll have to be patient. We will have tryouts next Saturday."

"Oh, drats, Miss. Old man Mitchell will have me up with the horses at dawn and I'll be working all day. I won't be able to come. Please make it a school day, please, please Miss."

"Don't be saying 'Drats' and don't be calling your foster parent, 'Old Man'. That's very rude. Anyway, I'll think it over and let you know tomorrow. Now hurry out to play for a few minutes before the morning bell rings. You are ever so early, this morning."

When Eddy pushed open the door and jumped down the steps to join the other children, Miss Patterson mused about her special pupil, Eddy. He wasn't the only home child in her class. There were 3 other boys and an equal number of girls. She knew that they had come from England and were staying at farmhouses in the community. She knew that some of them were having a hard time of it and the girls were timid and slow to speak. But Eddy was different. He was a bit of a scrapper, she knew, but he had a mind of his own and he loved to recite.

She didn't know about his home life with the Mitchell's but she knew that were a highly respected couple and she had to assume that Eddy was part of the family. She had met Mr. Parsons, the Dr. Barnardo inspector twice and only glowing reports were sent to the main office in London.

When the day was over, Eddy lingered at his desk until the last child had left although Jack and Emily waited for him outside. "Miss, will you let me know tomorrow morning."

"Yes, Eddy", she said as she ushered him out and went to her desk to prepare for the next school day.

"Gosh, Eddy, what kept you so long?" said Jack.

"You'll know soon enough but am not tellin'"

Emily smiled and the three of them almost skipped all the way home. They liked the longer days and they could dream of summer. "Say, guys, let's go over to the falls before we go home. We've got time and we'll be home in time for supper," Jack said.

The snow was melting and the river was breaking up. The falls would be spectacular and the kids loved to clamour onto the rocks to watch. Of course, it was dangerous and a boy drowned last spring. They would make sure there were no adults around because they sure would spoil the fun. It wasn't much of a detour and this escapade didn't end with any mishaps so when Eddy arrived at his door, Mrs. Mitchell greeted him in the usual way,

"Take your boots off and hang up your things. How was school?"

"Much the same, Ma'am. I know my 7 times table now and the teacher said I did well on my geography quiz."

"Good boy, Eddy. Now get your old working clothes on and get to your chores. I have some important news to tell you later."

After the supper silence and the evening barn work, Eddy went upstairs and the Mitchell's settled into their usual routine of the newspaper and knitting but there was more yarn in the basket and Mrs. Mitchell's hands were hard at work on what looked like a sweater.

"You better tell him, Mary. It's going to be a big change in this household. God knows there's been too many changes this past year. But you know best, I guess."

Eddy settled in his room, took out his poem about the great Indian chief, Hiawatha, and recited the first 10 verses by heart hardly glancing at the page. He was in the forest with the tribe and Emily and Jack were Indian braves like him. He imagined the circle of Wigwams, the elders with their pipes and the dogs lying around the campfire.

"Eddy, have you finished your homework?" called Mary Mitchell.

"No, Ma'am"

"I need you downstairs. Now."

Eddy obeyed and jumped off the bed and leaped down the steps two by two. Mrs. Mitchell summoned him to the parlour and told him to take a seat.

"Do you remember the little boy over at Grandma Gibson's?

That's my sister's boy. They've been away in Toronto where they live.

Well, sometimes, things don't go right, Eddy, and sometimes, things change.

The boy is called Ethan. He's 3 years old. "

Mrs. Mitchell hesitated and took out a handkerchief. Her husband looked the other way as she tried to say what she had come to say to Eddy.

"Well, his mother got sick, very sick. It was diphtheria. She died. Her husband can't take care of the child. He's a salesman in the big Eaton Store in Toronto." She paused again wiping a tear from her eye. "He's going to live with us. He'll be like a brother to you. I know you'll be nice to him."

Eddy wasn't sure what to say. It reminded him of his brothers and his sister. He hadn't heard a word about them since Mr. Parson's first visit 2 years ago and now a strange kid was going to share the house with him. In fact, he had printed two post cards for the Dr. Barnardo Inspector to send to his mother and brother James and then he had sent one at Christmas to his mother but he hadn't heard a word and until the new boy was mentioned, he had mostly forgot about them.

"What do you think, Eddy?"

"Aw, it will be alright, I guess" Can I go back upstairs? By the way, when's he comin' here?"

"Tomorrow afternoon, I think".

"Can I go now?"

"Yes."

"Gosh, tomorrow's the day Miss Patterson is going to tell me if I've been chosen to recite a poem."

Eddy returned to his room and sat on the bed with his hands clenched. He didn't know whether to yell or cry. There was so much to keep him busy but chores and a new brother were back of the list. Hiawatha was top and that was that.

After a restless night, Eddy got up, did his henhouse duties, had breakfast, grabbed his school lunch and headed for school. The Mitchell's were too busy getting the extra bedroom ready that they hardly noticed that he was gone. Eddy ran to school skipping along the train track to get to school before everyone else. The big freight coming from Toronto had passed so it was safe.

Panting, he arrived at the school door, pushed it open and sat down. The teacher had not arrived yet and the janitor had just made up the fire in the pot bellied stove in the centre.

"What brings you here so early, boy?" he inquired.

"She's expecting me and she told me to come early."

"That's strange," he said.

Eddy sat at his desk and fumbled with his slate. His mouth was dry and his stomach hurt. Finally, Miss Patterson, so pretty in her wool coat, matching hat and warm boots, arrived with her satchel of books under her arm. As she walked up to her desk, she realized that Eddy was there already.

"Oh, my, Eddy, you are so early. Can you explain yourself? The janitor met me as I arrived at the door and he is quite worried about you."

"You told me that you would have an answer for me today. I have practiced all night to recite my chosen poem."

"Oh, my, yes. We discussed it at the Board of Trustees meeting and we have decided that you will be the pupil who gives the closing message before we close the school for the Easter holidays."

"Gosh, gee, does that mean that I can recite The Song of Hiawatha!"

"Yes, Eddy, that's right. Now settle down and try to concentrate on your school work. There's a few weeks before the concert and you can recite a few verses for the class next Friday so that you won't be nervous when it comes to the big day."

Eddy floated above the droning students as they read their reading passages and he floated all the way home hardly looking where he was going. He felt like the young Hiawatha as he sang:

"Take your bow, O Hiawatha,
Take your arrows, jasper –headed,
Take your war clubs, Puggawaugen."

As he grew closer to the house, he was jolted into reality. Outside were a coach and two horses with the driver patiently sitting waiting for the people he brought to get back in so that he could drive them home. Eddy went around to the back door, opened it just a crack and listened.

He could hear people talking quietly and as he entered, he saw that the object of their attention was a small boy with blond hair. Just as he was about to duck out of the way and creep upstairs, Mary Mitchell called out,

"Eddy, you're home, at last. Come in and meet your new brother, Ethan."

"Aren't you going to shake his hand?" said Grandma Gibson.

With a shuffle and a bit of a grunt, Eddy grabbed Ethan's hand, held it for a moment and let it go. "Hi" he said and then rushed into the kitchen. Mary Mitchell went in after him and closed the door.

"What's the matter, Eddy? Whatever is the matter?"

She put her arms around him and said, "It will be alright. You'll see."

"I'm going to recite The Song of Hiawatha at the Easter concert.

"Oh, good for you. Now, perk up and go back into the kitchen with the others."

They sat down as a family and for the first time, Mr. Mitchell talked all the way through supper and Ethan sat in a high chair made especially for him. "Let's bow our heads and thank the good Lord for his bounty and may we be truly thankful." he said.

Grandma Gibson sat awhile with Ethan, her youngest grandson, and looking over at Eddy, she said, "We'll have a birthday party for Ethan on Saturday. He really just turned 3 yesterday. I want you to come because I have something special for you too."

With a wink, she looked away, bid farewell to her daughter and son-in-law, and left with the coachman who was still waiting outside. They were paying him by the hour so he didn't mind.

Ethan was bathed downstairs and then carried up to his room next to the one with the high posted bed that the Mitchells occupied. Mary Mitchell had spent the last number of days making the room fit for a little boy. She had put up blue wallpaper with little boats and sand castles printed on it. She had placed a teddy bear on the bed. She had knit him herself and he had the most magnificent checked scarf and matching hat.

Eddy had already wondered up to his loft bedroom and he was reading 'Robinson Crusoe' when he heard the noise below. Ethan was sobbing. Eddy thought, "He must be missing his mother and father. He's lonely too."

After a few minutes with Mrs. Mitchell's soothing words, the little boy quieted down and finally fell asleep in his down covered bed. Eddy decided that he would like Ethan after all and, maybe, he could read to him tomorrow. He looked forward to the birthday party that Grandma Gibson was planning.

Chapter 31: Time passes and there is triumph ahead.

Saturday morning was shrouded with ice. Everything was covered with sheets of glass. There had been an ice storm and they would all have to wait for some of it to thaw.

"Are we still going to the party?" Eddy asked. "I can't clean out the hen house until the walkway is clear."

"You'll have to figure out how to get to the woodshed to get saw dust to put on the walk because the hens have to be looked after before any of us go to my mother's," said Mrs. Mitchell. Mr. Mitchell was in the barn and he had taken a fall on the way out even with his heavy boots but that did not deter him. Ethan was already up and having his breakfast with Mrs. Mitchell hovering over him. Eddy knew the child couldn't help it but he sure wished he was older.

Eddy gritted his teeth and grabbed his overalls and boots and headed out the door to get the saw dust and get to work. He fell as soon as he hit the walk way but he got up and with baby steps, he got to the wood shed, collected the saw dust in a pail and spread it over the walk all the way from the house to the chicken shed.

"Gotta do it. Just gotta do it" he mumbled.

A few hours passed and with the chicken coop clean and the chickens fed, he was summoned to breakfast. It had warmed up and the icicles were melting fast and it looked like they could go to the party after all.

Hitching up Peggy to the cart, they could all scramble in and head to the Gibson farm, all except Mr. Mitchell who would be in the barn all day. The world looked like a Fairy tale land with silver clad trees and buildings that looked like castles. Peggy was sure footed and before long, they were deposited at Grandma Gibson's door.

Everyone was there, even Jack, his friend and next door neighbor. Emily took their coats as they entered and they all gathered in the country kitchen. A blue frosted cake sat on the table and there were piles of cookies and pies. On another table there were gifts wrapped in red and white paper. Ethan ran to his grandmother and sat on her knee.

"Now, let the party begin", someone yelled.

The Gibson girls brought the cake to the centre and lit the three candles on top.

"Happy birthday, Happy birthday, Ethan." They all sang.

After the cake was cut and slices passed to everyone, Ethan opened his gifts. He discovered little wooden carts and a toy horse made of papier mache but only one thing caught his fancy. That was a big picture book of 'The tale of Peter Rabbit.' They were made to stand out from the page so that he could see each special character. His father had bought the book especially for his birthday and, maybe, someday, he would come and take him home.

And then Grandma Gibson called Eddy." I have something for you Eddy. Close your eyes." He barely squinted but when he opened his eyes wide, he saw his gift, 'The Wind in the Willows'. It was illustrated and on the cover was Mole and Badger. He squeezed the book to himself and jumped up and hugged Grandma.

"What a super birthday party. Thanks so much, Grandma Gibson." And with a mumble he whispered to himself, "Maybe, Ethan will change everything."

It was the first real present he had ever received and it felt good to be signaled out as special. But when they got back to the house, Mr. Mitchell was pacing the floor and the moment they stepped in, he yelled at his wife. "Here I am working myself to the bone, getting the firewood in, doing all the barn work and not even getting a bite to eat when I come in and here you go gallivanting all over as though you don't have a care in the world."

"Now, now, Charles. You knew we were going over to mother's for Ethan's third birthday. You could have come but you were too busy in the barn."

"What are you thinking, woman? Who, upon my word, is going to do all the work around here especially on a day like this?"

"Come, sit down beside me and have some cake and mother's cookies. I'll have a nice cup of tea as soon as the kettle boils."

"Well, Tompkins, you can go to the barn right now and put away that book before I take it and put it in the fire."

Mitchell sat by the stove and put his feet up on the kitchen chair.

"I'll have your tea in a minute but let me take Ethan upstairs for a nap. He's bone tired after all that excitement."

Eddy clutched his book and snuck out to take it upstairs. Then, he got dressed and went out to the barn. He could talk to Jake and Joe, his draft horse mates and give them a feed of oats.

The next day dawned bright and cheerful with a special hint of spring in the breeze. Must be coming from the South, he thought. It was Sunday and they all dressed for church. Ethan was the star the minute they arrived. The church ladies all talking at once said, "Oh, my, Mary, what's his name? He's so cute!"

"You must bring him over to meet my children. The oldest girls will love him."

"What do you think of him, Charles? Someone to help you in the barn, hey?" said the minister.

"Gonna be a while."

Eddy paid no attention because he was hatching a plan with his pal, Jack. They might go up to the cabin in the woods after church was out but they weren't sure because Emily wanted to play at her house or read a story to Ethan. So Sunday came and went. It always did and school was tomorrow.

Children seem to go with the time. They couldn't make plans or decide for themselves what would happen next. So Eddy went along with everything except for his one special desire. He wanted more than anything else to be the star of the Easter concert. He wanted his 'Song of Hiawatha' to be the best that day.

The days wouldn't go fast enough and Miss Patterson kept telling him that he would have to be patient. "You could make a costume for yourself that would make you not only sound like Hiawatha but look like him as well." He pondered this suggestion and decided to ask Grandma Gibson for help.

The day finally came for the Concert and all the people were gathered in the small school house to watch their children perform. There were songs and poems and speeches from the Chairman of the Board of Trustees and then there was a hush as the curtain parted and on walked a young Indian chief. He wore a headdress of many feathers gathered from the forest. They came from blue jays and Canada jays, robins and hawks and one glorious feather from a bald eagle.

Green and white stripes were slashed across his face and he began a war dance hooping and hollering as though prancing around a campfire. He wore a deerskin cloak and moccasins on his feet.

"Wherever did he get that get up and go," said someone in the audience but most just clapped before he could begin his recitation.

Hiawatha stepped forward and began in a gentle but powerful voice,

"On the shores of Gitche Gumee
Of the shiny Big Sea Water
Stood Nokomis, the old woman"

He paused and continued,

"Yonder dwells the great pearl-Feather
Megissogwon, the Magician
Guarded by the fiery serpents
Guarded by the Pitch Black water….."

Eddy's voice grew as he spoke these words. The audience was spell bound.
"This boy will be an actor someday."
"And to think, he isn't long out of the gutter."
Eddy continued,

"Aim your arrows, Hiawatha,
At the head of Megissowon
Strike the tuft of hair upon it….
Swift flew Hiawatha's arrow…
And Megissowon reeled and staggered forward,
Plunging like a wounded bison…

Then Eddy adding something of his own said,

"He was a good chief and divided his trophies among the people. "Shared it equally among them."

When he spoke these lines, he stopped and then bowed three times and stood tall like the chief he played.

The audience stood up and clapped and Eddy bowed again.

Mrs. Mitchell, sitting with Ethan on her knee, rose up and walked towards him,

"You have made me proud Eddy. Thank you. That was a long poem and you didn't miss a line."

The concert came to a close with 'Oh, Canada' and everyone filed out of the school house to go back to their chores and wait for Easter. School was over for the season for the farm kids but ahead was hard work and long days. Eddy was sure he could face anything now.

"I'll be a busker like my dad", he said.

After the concert was over, Miss Patterson wondered to herself what would become of Eddy. She realized that Mr. Mitchell, his foster parent had shown very little interest in the boy even though she commended Mrs. Mitchell for supporting him. If there was no real commitment to the boy's future, what would happen to his talent?

But Eddy was in the clouds. He loved the applause and the attention and he was determined to keep doing these dramatic readings forever.

Chapter 32: School's out and there is Change Coming

Miss Patterson decided that something had to be done about Edward and a meeting with the School Trustees had to be sought. Edward was out of school well before the summer holidays because farm work was first and foremost in Mitchell's mind. Indeed, in most farm families, the boys left school early for the preparation of the fields and the subsequent work ahead. The education department understood this and only required 4 months of education in these circumstances.

She had managed to obtain a copy of his Indenture Agreement from one of the Dr. Barnardo inspectors, Mr. Parsons, and she knew that the Mitchell's were obliged to send Eddy to school at least 4 months of the year. He had attended 6, 2 months before Christmas and 4 after. She feared that when he turned 11, he might be forced to stop altogether and his birthday was coming up in May. She would do her best for him but the odds were stacked against him. After all, Eddy had no family of his own and he was under contract to the Mitchell family. They had their obligations but so did he.

In the meantime, Eddy had returned home a hero after his astonishing rendition of 'The Song of Hiawatha' but Mr. Mitchell paid him no attention and insisted that he get to work.

"Get your head out of the clouds, Tompkins. Old Hiawatha is long dead and the barn needs attending. Get to it. Now!"

"Gosh, I just walked in and he's after me. I hate him," he muttered to himself but he donned his overalls, pulled on his boots and started out the door.

"Just a minute, Eddy. Here's a glass of buttermilk and a ginger cookie.

Sit here for a minute with Ethan and me", whispered Mrs. Mitchell.

"He'll be there in a minute, Sam", she called.

"Yea, so will Christmas"', he sulked back.

"Don't you let him dawdle for more than a minute or I'll be in with a stick".

Mary smiled to herself. "His words are worst than his bite, most times." she thought and turned around to be with the children.

Ethan looked at Eddy and giggled. He'd seen Eddy do his Indian chief thing and he liked the war dance a lot.

"Will you play with me, Eddy"? He asked.

"Eddy's got chores, Ethan, but maybe later before you go to bed." said Mrs. Mitchell.

Eddy grinned at the little boy but at the same time, he gulped down the smooth buttermilk and chomped at the delicious cookie before getting off the chair to head to the barn. He passed the chicken coop in a hurry but stopped to talk to the rooster who had terrified him on his first day there and before grabbing the fork to pitch hay to the horse stalls, he nudged up against Jake, his favourite draft horse.

"I'm Hiawatha. I wish we could go on the warpath and save the village below. Or maybe, we can chase down that freight coming from Toronto."

"Stop yur chatterin' boy. Get that hay and feed done fast 'cause there's the pig sty to clean out and eggs to collect. Yes, and before you get a bite to eat later, come on!" said Mitchell.

He could pitch hay faster than old Mitchell now and he didn't need any coaxing.

True to her word, Miss Patterson secured a meeting with the Trustees. Mr. Brown, the chairman, had a soft spot for the young teacher. She reminded him of his daughter, Jenny, who was studying to be a nurse in Toronto. They were about the same age.

She dressed in her best suit, plaid of the Stewart clan and bought as a present from her mother from the brand new Eaton's Store on Bloor Street in Toronto. She put her blond locks in a bun and she wore a slight bit of makeup to showcase her lovely complexion. Satchel in hand she walked to the Schoolhouse from her lodging in the village. She arrived to two buggies in the yard the horses waiting patiently to take their charges home. She walked up to the door, ascended the steps and walked in.

Mr. Brown dressed in his Sunday best met her at the door and led her to a chair placed on the side so as not to interfere with the proceedings at hand. Mr. Brown was in finance in his work life but he knew best not to wear the dark long coat he used at bank functions. This evening he sported a bright green tie.

"Good evening members of the Board and welcome Miss Patterson. The meeting is officially open. The only matter before us is one that Miss Patterson has requested. Miss Patterson, you may address the Board".

"Thank you sir."

"I've come to speak about Edward George Tompkins, presently the ward of Mr. and Mrs. Charles Mitchell. He will soon be officially indentured as a farm worker but that is such a waste of his talent. You must recall his masterly performances in his last two years with us. First was his recitation of 'The Night before Christmas' and then his dramatic portrayal of Hiawatha in that famous poem by Longfellow. The audience erupted with applause and many said he could be a Shakespearean actor or a poet in his own right."

At this, she paused and muffled a cough while straightening a loose strand of hair that had fallen over her left eye. She looked over the heads of the board members and raised her voice just a little, not strident but teacher like as when she was beginning the lesson on long division.

"I am concerned that this may be his last year with us because Mr. Mitchell has stated mostly in his absence from such performances that school is a waste of time and that the boy is needed on the farm and that he is under obligation to fulfill his duties as per the agreement with the Dr. Barnardo authorities. In the agreement, it simply says, "Mr. Mitchell promises that he will let Eddy attend school for 4 months a year but there is nowhere that it states, that he is legally obliged to do so."

She stopped for a moment and then lowering her voice she seemed to rise taller as she moved towards her final plea.

"I want assurance that school attendance will be mandatory for him and that the Mitchell's be informed that this is the desire of the Board."

Smiling and consciously making the most of her youth and admirable looks, she said, "Thank you, most esteemed gentlemen, for giving me the opportunity to speak on Edward's behalf."

"Thank you, Miss Patterson. We will deliberate and get back to you in due course."

As she picked up her satchel and began moving away from the podium, Mr. Brown approached her. He was an impressive man, a respected banker and a church trustee.

"Miss Patterson, I must commend you on your presentation and your commitment to your students. "

"Thank you, sir."

"You must come over to our home for tea, some afternoon. My wife would love to meet you and, furthermore, you remind us so much of our daughter, Jenny, who is away in Toronto."

"I would be honoured, sir."

She picked up her satchel and walked towards the door. She was glad that she had spoken on Eddy's behalf. If only she could soften Mr. Mitchell's heart.

"Good afternoon, Miss Patterson. You will be hearing from me soon."

"Good afternoon, Mr. Brown"

Chapter 33: Time passes but some things never change

Miss Patterson had impressed the Board of Trustees and after a subsequent meeting, they drafted a letter to the Mitchell family reminding them of their duty to continue to send their ward, Edward George Tompkins, to school. They added that they hoped to see Edward progress beyond primary school to the higher grades since it was clear from his performance that he was intelligent and worthy of a higher education.

Mr. Mitchell reviewed the letter a number of times. He knew most of the men on the Board and respected them but they could not know his innermost feelings. "I simply can't abide an education for a boy like Tompkins. Why, I had no education beyond Grade 5 and that didn't stop me from becoming a successful farmer and member of the town council. And I am from good English country stock. He's from the worst place in London. His mother abandoned him and if it wasn't for the Dr. Barnardo Home he would be on the street to this day."

But in spite of his emotions about this, he did accept that his ward would attend school until he was 12 but only for 5 months so he started preparing an answer. Now was the time for farming and he wouldn't think about it again until after harvest in October. Tompkins could start then along with all the farm children including Jack and Emily.

That task done, he called his wife from the kitchen where she had been fixing a lunch for the field workers, making soup for supper, tending to Ethan and chatting with Eddy. "Mary, could you come to the sitting room for moment?"

"Yes, I'll be there after I give the soup another stir."

When she entered the room her face flush with standing over a hot stove, she was curious. Sam was usually out in the barn tending to the cattle at this time.

"Got a letter I want you to see."

He had shared the letter from the Board yesterday and they had discussed Eddy's education. She felt strongly that he should attend school as often as possible. The Home Inspector had reminded both of them that Eddy's grades were good and that his teacher recommended him highly.

His letter lay open on the desk. He had used Mary's best stationery and he had used the pen only used for formal correspondence. In his neatest penmanship, he had written:

Dear esteemed members of the Board of Trustees,
I have received your letter asking that we, the Mitchell family, be attentive to Eddy's education. We agree to send him to school until he reaches the age of 12 and we agree to send him at least 4 months mostly from October to January.

Yours truly,
Mr. Sam Mitchell

He had spent most of the morning with his wife's dictionary and he had consulted her more than once about his choice of words and his spelling. In fact, Mary had corrected the words 'attentive,' 'education,' 'esteemed' and had really chosen those words for him. She was, in truth, the author of the letter but she deferred to her husband in matters like this even if she knew a lot more about composing any letter of worth.

She bent over the letter and then looked up to her husband and said,

"That is a good letter Charles. Do put it in the envelope and put it in the post tomorrow morning.

While the formalities were being handled, Eddy and Ethan sat on the floor and played with wooden blocks which Mary had bought in downtown Bracebridge in the same shop where she had bought Eddy's school clothes when he first arrived. When Mitchell returned to the kitchen, Eddy jumped up and grabbed his overalls and boots and headed for the barn. The look on his boss' face was enough to send him scurrying.

Spring was here and ploughing and seeding were first and foremost in every farmer's mind. Eddy was learning how to handle the draft horses and this was the day he was going out to plough the lower field for the first time. Mr. Mitchell was already in the barn. It had not taken him long to put away his formal letter writing self, put on his farm outfit and go outside.

"Okay, Tompkins, come with me."

They walked to Jake and Joe and after whispering to them, Eddy guided them out of the barn to be hitched to the plough with all their attendant harness and reins. He had been practicing this maneuver and he had some practice in harnessing them to the sledge when they went up to the woods to haul logs but, today, he was to lead them out to the field to haul the plough and slice through the hard ground and open up troughs for seeding.

The plough was red and shiny made of good Canadian steel and it looked brand new. "Just like the one my dad bought last month down at the hardware store," shouted Jack who had just arrived after running down the field from their farm.

"Gosh I haven't seen you since Easter. Where you been?"

"Workin'. What else is new?"

"Hey, Eddy, I'll ask old Mitchell if I can help you. I've dun it two times before and I got the hang of it. Once you get that, Eddy, it's a breeze. Well, not quite." Jack was a charmer and Mr. Mitchell knew his dad from way back and they were good friends so it didn't take much persuasion for him to agree.

"No dawdlin now. You guys have a big field to cover and I want it done today."

Today Jack was about to teach Eddy one of the most important jobs in farming. As the old timers said, "If the ground ain't broken up good, there'll be a slim harvest."

Jack did most of the hooking up of the horses to the plough while Mitchell watched from a short distance. Eddy steadied the horses. "Whoa, Jake. Whoa, Josephine." He had a couple of carrots in his pocket to give them later.

Now that they had the plough firmly hooked up to the harness, Jack took hold of the handles and started them up with a, "Go Jake. Go Jo. Steady."

Both massive draft horses began to move in a straight line towards the hedge in the distance. They knew this maneuver from way back and horses have good memories. Jack moved with the horses guiding him and balancing with his feet to keep the horses in a straight line. Then he beckoned Eddy to take the handles without stopping the horses. But Jake, the big guy was uneasy with the feel of new hands and he reared up sending Eddy flying. Jack grabbed the handles and cried, "Whoa, boys. Whoa."

They stopped, snorted and waited for their next order. These horses were smart and they knew the ropes. It was as though they could understand that Eddy was still a young boy with no experience. Eddy got up, brushed the dirt from his pants and shirt and came back to the plough.

"You can do it, Eddy. I'll walk beside you and help you balance. You gotta go with the flow, Eddy. You gotta walk with them."

Eddy took the handles again and this time with Jack by his side, he was able to walk the line to the end of the row. Turning to go back down the row was a bit more tricky but he did it with Jack right beside him. After they did two more rows, Mr. Mitchell came over and told them to take a break and he took over moving like a pro down four more rows.

Then, Eddy and Jack took over again and moved faster this time. It went on all day except for the lunch break when Mrs. Mitchell came to the field with a picnic basket loaded with sandwiches, cookies and tea. Little Ethan walked beside her and joined in the fun of planting. But he was more interested in playing in the dirt now warm from all the turning.

"You're doing a good job, Eddy, and thanks, Jack, for being such a good sport helping him get the hang of things." she said.

Mr. Mitchell sat by himself and ate the food in a hurry. "There's a lot to be done, fellas, so don't waste too much time eating."

In the distance, the Gibson's were ploughing. Eddy could barely make out the outline of a girl but he was sure it was Emily taking the picnic basket to the field. He hadn't seen her in a while and he kept thinking that when he got a chance to get away, he would beckon Jack and Emily to the woods and his Kingdom of The Land of Plenty. It was time to visit and see how the forest creatures were doing. He missed them especially John Squirrel and Minnie the Owl.

They got back to work promptly but Jack had to go home. His mother was calling from the distant field and her voice echoed against the rock that formed a cliff behind them.

"Jack….Jack…"

"Comin" he yelled. "You'll do fine, Eddy. See you later."

"Ya, when we can, let's go to the Kingdom."

"Okay. See you later."

Eddy rubbed the horses' faces and gave them both a carrot. Mr. Mitchell watched as Eddy grabbed the handles and started up. "Go, boys. Go."

They continued with Mr. Mitchell taking over every third row until the field was done.

"That looks good! If I say so myself."

He was talking to himself and hardly gave Eddy a nod. Yet, Eddy at ten years of age, had pretty well ploughed a full field.

When he got back to the house, washed up and changed, he sat down to a hearty supper. Mrs. Mitchell made sure he had an extra helping and luckily the old man was too tired to notice.

Usually, he wouldn't tolerate his ward having more food than himself but he didn't grumble or look up.

Later, when Eddy climbed the stairs to his room and picked up Robinson Crusoe, he could feel his arms tighten. The next morning, he could barely lift them but another day of ploughing lay ahead and there was no good in complaining. He just kept it all to himself but buried deep down was a growing feeling of rage and bitterness.

"One day, I'll jump the freight and head south and keep going till I get to where it is warm and you can play all day long. I'll never be a farmer. Jack, maybe but not me, Ever!"

Chapter 34: Back to School after a busy Farm Season

It was the summer of 1912 and one of the busiest farm seasons yet. The seeding done next came the planting of potatoes, turnips, carrots and beets in the garden behind the house and, after that, beans, peas, cucumbers, squash and pumpkin were planted. Tomatoes were started in the green house on the sunny side of the House. Mrs. Mitchell did most of this along with her precious perennials and especially dahlias and gladioli and Eddy was a big help when he wasn't cleaning out the hen shed and doing all the barn work. Ethan loved sitting in the dirt as she dug up the sods, raked them to the side and made rows for planting.

Mary Mitchell never stopped. If she wasn't in the garden, she was cooking, preparing pickles, making jams and jellies and putting away the fruits of her labours in late summer. No one stopped. Old Harry was getting old but his work was valued nevertheless. They couldn't do without him.

There was a rhythm to the year. After spring planting came the summer harvest and after the harvest came wood gathering and preparing for the long winter ahead. Eddy was a reluctant participant in all of this. He did his work mechanically when overseen by Mitchell but he felt joy when he worked alongside Mary Mitchell. She sang as she worked and her smile was a tonic for Eddy when he felt down hearted and broken.

"Sing with me Eddy. Ethan sings along so why don't you?

"I can't sing, Ma'am."

"Yes, you can. Let's give it a try with the mill stream song."

She loved the song "Down by the old mill stream." and Eddy joined in along with Ethan who was growing by leaps and bounds since coming to live with his aunt and uncle. They made a great trio with uneven harmonics and they enjoyed it.

Now, "Old MacDonald had a farm" was especially popular. Ethan loved that one and Mary, never neglecting her work, sang rhythmically with the task at hand. So all during the long summer, work and song were playmates away from the serious eyes of Mr. Mitchell but he rarely heard them because his world was outdoors with the machinery and the animals.

Eddy couldn't spend a lot of time with Ethan and Mary Mitchell because his days were organized, long and, often back breaking. His only reprieve came when Mitchell was in town for a meeting, mending equipment, or visiting with family and Sunday, of course.

Then, he would whistle for Jack or make an excuse to go on an errand to Grandma Gibson so he could have a piece of her pie and see Emily who was growing into a young lady. She would not be attending school in the Fall because she was now considered a full time domestic helper who had signed her Indenture agreement which tied her to this farm until she would be 21.

She was happy in the Gibson household so she didn't mind at all. She was growing taller than Eddy though the same age and she was outgrowing his Forest kingdom and the Land of Plenty.

Soon, haymaking arrived with all its work and merriment when all the young people gathered to make hay while the sun shone, as they said. But there was plenty of courting on the side to make up for it and lots of food. And after the harvest and Thanksgiving, the farm kids went back to school. Eddy was excited to be going back. He was now in the 4th grade and Miss Patterson would be his teacher again.

The gossip was that she might go to Kingston to teach at a bigger school but the Board of Trustees, particularly Mr. Brown, persuaded her to stay on with an increase in salary and a bonus for coming north in the Muskoka's for another year.

The first few weeks saw Eddy growing as a student. He was reading at an Upper School level and he devoured all the stories and narrative poems he could read. He lived to come to school. He was no longer shunned as a Limey and he had lost his London accent completely. Even Hans, his one time nemesis, spoke to him with respect. Both Hans and Eddy were anxious to get back to boxing with the teacher turned coach in the upper class and there would be time for this in the hours when Mr. Mitchell was occupied. He would have to sneak to get away but as long as the farm chores were done, he could do it.

His school studies expanded to include geography and he was thrilled to learn about maps and to learn about his continent, North America. He remembered the lessons at the Dr, Barnardo Home and he was determined to find out where Robinson Crusoe had landed. There was just so much to learn.

One day, while reading a passage in his book on North America, he came across a picture with the caption, "Loading hemp in New Orleans." This would have been March when the Muskoka was covered in snow and ice and here were men, tanned and fit, working outside. "That's where I'm going soon as I get out o' here. Away from winter and away from the old man."

In his mind, much as he loved Miss Patterson and the school, he still yearned to get away. He wasn't sure what he wanted but he knew that he hated farming and he hated being a ward of such a task master as Mitchell. Some of the homeboys were well placed and they embraced farm life but others like Eddy were exploited and used.

Although his was mixed because of the kindness of Mrs. Mitchell, his overwhelming desire was to get away. Even at ten years old, he began to see the freight train as his escape and he began thinking about jumping on and taking a ride from the tracks in his field to downtown Bracebridge where he could hide on a boxcar until the train got to the Station.

He began plotting his moves and he decided to meet some of the boys who were doing this just for fun. He didn't know if their motive was to get away or just have some excitement. "I am goi'n to give it a try after school today".

This was Friday and he knew Mitchell was going to see his parents. He had heard him talking about it to his wife over breakfast. Instead of going home, he ran along the tracks to the lower field and waited. Hans and Fritz were there but only to give him some pointers. Hans had got a real whipping from his father when he had learned of his son's perilous adventures.

"It's like this, Eddy. You watch the freight as she slows down almost to a stop as she comes around the bend. You run along beside the train as she slows even further. Then you grab on to the handle of the first boxcar that is slow enough for you. Then put your right leg up on the step and pull yourself up. Then scramble for all your worth on the steps and go to the top. Lay down on the top of the car until you get to the Station and after looking that all is clear, jump down and run for your life. You don't want the bulls (railway police) to catch you."

"Got it."

Just as he said the words, the big engine came around the bend and Eddy prepared to jump. "I'll go with you, kid, Start running." Shouted Fritz.

Fritz ran ahead and with one leap he boarded the car and got to the top. His legs were a lot longer and it seemed easy. Then, Eddy started running but his legs were too short and the train had picked up speed. At that, Fritz clamoured down the steps and jumped off tumbling in the grass until he came to a stop. Brushing himself off, he muttered through his panting,

"Next time, Eddy. You'll do it!"

Determined, he said, "Can we give it a go tomorrow? The freight comes by this way every day at the same time. It will be Saturday, and I've got chores but I can get away by 4."

"I know the schedule better than you, Eddy. We've been doing this for a while.

But sure, I'll see you tomorrow. I've got chores too and my dad is tough on me just as tough as with the home boys and the hired hands. He tells me I'll get the farm someday but I haven't the heart to tell him, I don't want it. I'd rather be an engineer and drive these big giants myself."

Eddy got up early the next day and threw himself into his work. He surprised himself and even the old man gave him a nod of approval. He waited all day for 4 o'clock to come and sure enough, Fritz and his pal Gerard, a new boy from the other side of the tracks, were down in the field to greet him. Good thing that there was a row of trees between the railway tracks and the Mitchell farm so no one could see them. This was the best place to catch a train as the train slowed to almost a walk on the upward slope from Falconberg, where it then descended to Bracebridge by Muskoka Falls.

This time, Eddy was ready. The train advanced as slow as a snail and Fritz and Gerard took to running like gazelles. Eddy was right behind them and just after they took their leap, he grabbed the handle, ran along the side for a minute and then jumped on. His heart was beating fast and his hands were sweaty but when he got to the top, he felt as though he had climbed Everest. They huddled together and Fritz did all he could to keep from shouting, "He did it."

Over on the third car from them, there were a bunch of older men sitting cross legged. They were dressed in rags and each had a knapsack probably filled with whatever possessions they had whether by work or theft. They were old timers and they knew the ropes. They waved at the boys and gave them a thumbs up.

The train slowed again after picking up speed on the downward slope to Bracebridge Station .The old tramps stayed put but lay low. The boys jumped off and ran as fast as they could before climbing down the bank to the falls. Without thinking and before they had time to catch their breath, they tore off their clothes and dove into the frothy waters beneath the falls. It was pretty warm for October and the water felt good. But they didn't stay long and soon they were scrambling up the rocks, and pulling their clothes back on.

"You did well, Eddy. Don't you tell a soul. If my Dad got word that I did this, I'd be in his jail for a month. Well, maybe not that, but he'd make it pretty rough on me if he found out."

Gerard just shrugged, "No one would miss me. My Dad is a drunk and Ma is never home."

"I best be back before they see that I am not in the pig sty chucking out the muck, said Eddy."

Chapter 35: Becoming Bolder and Outspoken

Eddy kept his train hopping adventure mostly to himself. Only Fritz and Gerard knew because they had ridden the rails with him but he did tell Jack his secret the first day they went up to Eddy's woodland kingdom now that harvest time was over and school was back in session.

"Jack, it's been a while since we came to the camp. It needs a new roof now that the fir bows have turned brown and we haven't tried to fish for forever but I've got to tell you what I've been doin' lately before I can do anything here."

"What's that?"

"I've been busting to tell you but you've got to swear never to tell anyone."

"I'll never tell but, Eddy, what's so important that it's a deep dark secret?"

"You see, Jack, I'm goin' to run away as soon as I'm old enough. It says in the geography book that down south in New Orleans, it's warm enough to make hay in March. I am going to ride all the way down there on a freight train. I've done some readin' and you can ride from here to Chicago and then keep goin' south until you hit the warm weather."

"Okay, but that's a dream, ain't it, Eddy. What would you do ridin' a train.? You have to have big bucks to do that and, anyway, you're not old enough."

"I'm goin' to ride in a box car. I tried it the other day to Bracebridge and I rode on top as far as the Station. With more practice, I could do it."

"Yes, but people get killed doin' that. Why, don't you remember last year they found an old tramp under the train, dead, and another with his leg off."

"Yea, but they were old drunks. I can do it. I know I can."

"Okay, I'll keep quiet but you be careful and don't be getting' yourself killed.

Let's get back to fixing the camp and I am dying to catch a couple of trout."

"Thanks, Jack."

Jack did keep the secret and Fritz and Gerard never breathed a word. Eddy was determined to practice every time he could from now on until he could do it, he said, with his eyes shut.

Now back at the farm and everywhere it seemed that the talk was about the new rage. Brownie cameras were being advertised in Eaton's Catalogue. Now everyone who could, would be able to buy a camera cheap and all they had to do is point and shoot and then get the film developed.

Mary Mitchell had seen it advertised in the Catalogue and had to tell her husband. "Sam, did you see that Eaton's is advertising the new Brownie camera. I'd like to order one for Christmas."

"What nonsense! You get these new fangled ideas, Mary, every time you look at that danged magazine. What would you do with a camera anyway?"

"Why, I could take pictures of the family? I could take it up to mother and take pictures there and imagine the photos we could take at Christmas?"

"Probably expensive."

"No, that's the thing. They're not expensive at all. They're only $2.00."

"That's more than we pay Old Harry for two weeks work. That's not cheap. So, for now, I don't want to hear anymore about it.

Eddy heard every word because he was in his usual place after supper, the corner of the kitchen doing his lessons. He thought hard about it and wished that he could have one for Christmas.

The months rolled by and Christmas came but there was no camera under the tree and Mrs. Mitchell said nothing to indicate her disappointment. She was used to her husband's dogmatic attitudes about anything modern although he was eyeing with envy the pictures of those new shiny automobiles that a few wealthy men had bought.

When school opened after the holidays, Eddy was glad to get back to see his friends and find out if any of them had a camera. Jack said that his father had bought one and had taken lots of pictures of the family and two or three of their new puppy.

"Do you think he'd let you borrow it? Said Eddy.

"No way. It's gold to him and he'd like to keep it that way. But, hey, did you know that Miss Patterson has one. It was on her desk this morning but I think she must have put it away in the cupboard 'cause it wasn't there when I looked again."

Eddy couldn't contain himself. He was remembering the camera man who took his picture at the Home and he remembered the time that a man with a big camera took pictures of him and his mates when they were playing on the street near his home in London. So, just as the bell rang for lunch, he walked up to Miss Patterson's desk and said, "Miss Patterson, did you get a brownie camera for Christmas?"

"What makes you ask that, Eddy?"

"Jack's' dad bought one and Mrs. Mitchell wanted one really badly but she didn't get it. I just thought you might have been given one as a gift?"

"Well, as a matter of fact, I did. But I won't use it now while in school."

"But, now that you have a brownie, Miss Patterson, you won't have to wait for the photographer to come in the spring to take a picture of the class."

"True, Eddy. We'll wait and see. Now, go out to play with the rest of the children."

Eddy let it go for now but as the weeks rolled by and spring was in the air, he got up the courage to approach Miss Patterson again. "Miss Patterson. I've been thinking. On a nice day, you could practice using a camera by taking some pictures of us outside the school. You don't have to wait for the camera man now."

"Eddy, there has to be a formal picture taken every year for the record. I am not qualified to do this."

"What I mean, Miss Patterson, is taking fun pictures of us playing outside and stuff."

"Well, I'll have to think about it. I must say you really seem to like the idea of taking pictures but class is about to start, Eddy, and you have rushed to school really early to ask me this."

"I had my picture taken on the street a long time ago and then when I arrived at Dr. Barnardo's home, the photographer took a picture of every boy dressed in the clothes they wore when they arrived. Some were really shabby but I was dressed nicely. I remember that because my mother made that outfit for me. That was before she dropped me at the home and didn't come back."

"That was two years ago, wasn't it and you still remember it even though you were only 7. Do you think about your mother, Eddy?"

"I can't see her face even though I try sometimes. She was crying a lot and things weren't very good. We hardly had any food at the last of it."

"I am so sorry. Are you happy now?"

"Well, it's like this. I like Mrs. Mitchell and I especially like Grandma Gibson 'cause she's nice to me and makes me good pies. Oh, and I like Ethan who lives with us now after his Mum died. But I hate Mr. Mitchell."

"Now, you should not say that. Why did you say it, Eddy?"

"He never says a nice word to me and all I do with him is work and it gets harder every day. He says that when I'm 12, I'll be working full time- no school, no nothin'"

"Well, Eddy, we'll see what we can do. In the meantime, go out and catch a bit of fresh air before the bell rings. And, I'll think about the camera and picture taking later. Okay?"

"Okay. Thanks, Miss Patterson."

Later that week, she was true to her word. It was a lovely day. The apple blossoms were out and the air smelled sweet. Everywhere, there were violets and dandelions. It was a perfect day for picture taking. After the school bell rang for dismissal, the children lined up to go outside. Miss Patterson had told them that she would be using her new camera to take a few pictures of the class.

"You'll be a bit late getting home today but I am sure that when we are finished you will run home as fast as you can to make up for lost time with chores or homework."

Eddy couldn't contain himself and he ran to Jack and told him that he was the one that convinced the teacher to take some pictures.

"You're some bold, Eddy. I wouldn't have the nerve. Keep it to yourself, okay?"

Miss Patterson told the children to arrange themselves the way they wanted.

"This is not a formal portrait so you can let go a bit."

The younger children naturally positioned themselves in the front with the older kids lining up on the steps. The biggest girl who was a bit bossy placed herself at the very back. Emily made herself inconspicuous but Jack stood by the wall. Fritz with his German good looks was third from the back. His brother Hans now in the upper grade wouldn't be in the picture but Eddy feeling a bit bold and brassy stood by the window with his arm against the wall.

"Smile. Say, 'Cotton Candy'.Click!"

Perhaps, well into the future, Eddy would look back on this day with pride. He had persuaded his teacher to go against tradition and be a modern young Canadian woman. What would the photographer hired to take the school portrait think? What would the parents say when they saw the picture? What would the Board of Trustees decide?

For now, the kids were excited that they were the first, maybe in all of Ontario, to be part of this and for Eddy, this was his best day but it wasn't over yet. Miss Patterson took several shots by moving around to get profiles of some of the kids and long shots for perspective. When she finished, she put her brownie camera in the carrying case and smiled saying, "Thank you, children. When I get this film developed and printed, I'll bring each of you a print to take home. Now grab your satchels and slates and off you go."

Eddy lingered and when Miss Patterson walked up the steps to go into the classroom, he followed close behind. After she entered, she walked up to her desk and put the camera case down. When she looked up, there was Eddy standing right beside her.

"Oh, you gave me a start, Eddy. What is it?"

"Do you think, Miss, that you could take a picture of just me. I want to send it back to England to my sister."

She hesitated but when she looked at Eddy's eyes and saw that he was crying she gave in.

"Okay, one picture only. Sit at your desk with your geography book.

Now look up and smile. Click!"

"Thanks, Miss Patterson. Beatrice will be so happy."

He ran out of the room, across the school yard along to the tracks as fast as his legs could carry him. He had to be home and in the barn now. In spite of that, he was proud and excited that he had become a star.

Chapter 36: World War 1

Much had happened not only in Bracebridge but throughout the Empire. The Mitchell and Gibson families were in constant correspondence with their family back in England and even though they were well established Canadians, the mother country was still home. The economy was booming but, in the newspapers, there were rumours of growing tension in Europe and since Great Britain was bound by treaties of support for various regimes, the folks back home were worried.

Eddy was growing up and he had reached his 12th birthday which meant that he might be forced to leave school and work full time on the farm. After all, an agreement had been signed between the Dr. Barnardo home and the Mitchell's that on moving to their home, Eddy would become their ward until the age of 12 when his status would change from ward to employee in the form of indenture. A certain sum of money would be paid by the Mitchell's each year and deposited in trust to the Canadian Imperial Bank of Commerce. At the conclusion of his indenture, at the age of 21, Eddy would receive the full amount owed to him. Of course, that was based on his staying with the Mitchell's until 1923.

It was 1914 and the morning paper headlines in large bold black lettering bellowed;

Canada at War

The house went silent. Mary sat beside Charles at the kitchen table and listened intently as her husband read:

'Great Britain's ultimatum to Germany to withdraw its army from Belgium expired on August 4th, 1914; Great Britain and the British Empire are now at war against the German and Austro-Hungarian empires. Canadians unite and heed the call. We shall defend with honour our motherland.'

"What does this mean, Charles? You are still in your 30's. Would you be expected to serve and if so what would we do?"

"It's only the first day. Mary. It could be over in a month. After all the Kaiser and our King are first cousins and the Czar is a cousin too. They could work this out over a scotch."

"Let's get back to business. We've got a farm to run."

"Oh, yes, and Charles, Mr. Parsons is coming over to meet us and Eddy at 3 o'clock. It's about school this autumn."

"I don't have time today, Mary. Too much farm work and I can barely do without the boy so you meet the man and tell him he can see the boy for a few minutes."

"All right."

Mary busied herself in the kitchen with Ethan on the floor playing with blocks. Mary was preparing pickles and chutney with yesterday's pickings from the garden. It had been a bountiful harvest thus far. She beckoned Old Harry from the garden, where he was picking peas. Eddy was far too busy to do this now. Eddy was out in the fields tending to the rows of potatoes in between bringing the cows in from the pasture, milking, and cleaning the barn and the horse stalls.

"Harry, I need to speak to Eddy to tell him he must be home by 2 to get cleaned up for his meeting with the inspector. Will you go and tell him right now."

"Yes, ma'am. I'll drop what I'm doing and go right away."

"Thank you, Harry."

Mary thought about what she would say to Mr. Parsons. Eddy's 12th had come and gone with no fanfare but Mary worried about what she had to say to this official from the Dr. Barnardo transition home in Toronto. She had been dreading this day since the time that they had received the letter from the Board of Trustees imploring them to keep Eddy in school. Now, with war at their doorstep, Eddy was needed on the farm more than ever. They could not spare him for school.

When Old Harry reached the potato field, Eddy was bent over hoeing up the potato rows into tidy mounds. The leaves were an emerald green but some were being nibbled by the hated Colorado beetle. There was a new product on the market which Eddy had been sprinkling on each infected plant. His hands and even his forehead were covered with a white powder. It was called Paris green. There were warnings on the packet and the word 'arsenic' was written in bold letters. No one paid any attention because this was the best stuff ever for getting rid of those beetles that devoured and shriveled the green potato leaves just as they were looking healthy and promising a good yield. No one had got sick from it although Emily at the Gibbs farm had complained of headaches after being in the potato patch.

"Eddy, Mrs. Mitchell wants you to stop now. Put away the packet of Paris green and hurry down to get dressed for Mr. Parson's visit."

Eddy looked up and at the mention of Mr. Parsons he quickly put the Paris green in a wooden tub at the end of the row. He would go back to it later. "I'll run ahead, Harry. See you tomorrow."

After he arrived at the house, Mrs. Mitchell handed him a pork sandwich and a glass of milk and told him to take it his bedroom while he got ready. She was always mindful and thought ahead for any occasion.

"Eddy, make sure you wash your hands and face well. You are covered with white powder and do that before you eat your sandwich."

"Yes, ma'am." He said as he trudged up the stairs to his bedroom in the turret.

Mary had prepared hot water, a white face cloth and a new bar of fresh smelling handmade soap. He gladly washed off the powder and the grime more because he was hungry than in anticipation of the visit. After gulping down the sandwich and flushing it down with milk, he went to the closet to get his best and only Sunday suit.

Memories came flooding in. He remembered the last day he had worn it. Mrs. Mitchell had taken him to the photography studio in downtown Bracebridge. On this day, as on most days she travelled to the town, she rode in the buggy hauled by Peggy, their brown mare. Ethan sat in front with her and Eddy sat in the back. Both boys loved the bounce and flow of the wheels as they navigated the farm roads before coming up the main street and halting in front of the studio.

They were met by the photographer's wife. "Please take a seat. My husband will be with you shortly. He is just finishing another picture of one of the Gibson home boys. We've done five in the last 5 days. One was a very pretty girl. I think her name is Emily."

"I wonder why so many, Mary?"

"Well, all I can say is, the inspector, Mr. Parsons from the Dr. Barnardo homes requested an up to date studio portrait of our foster boy. He is the inspector for all the home children up here in the Muskoka's. He probably wants pictures of all of them."

"My, that could cost them quite a bit. Studio portraits are expensive."

"Well, it's none of my doing. Oh, here's my husband now."

Eddy was summoned to the darkened room where picture taking took place. There was a long black bench with an ornate back, dark beige curtain, and a very large camera. The photographer wasted no time. He had another portrait to take before closing for the day.

"Stand there and put your hand on the arm of that chair."

The last time Eddy was before a camera in a formal studio was when he had had his picture taken before leaving for Canada. On that day, his head was shaven. He wore a cadet uniform, and he was only 7. Now, he wore a double buttoned grey tweed jacket and a pair of knee pants that matched perfectly. His shirt was white and he sported a fancy bow tie. His hair was parted close to the middle. He looked straight at the camera, his eyes mindful and his mouth slightly closed to suggest a smile.

"Click. Stay still 'cause I'm going to take another." After removing the plate and inserting another, he said, "Ready. Click. All finished. You may go."

Snapping out of his reverie, Eddy finished putting on his Sunday best. "I wonder what Mr. Parsons will say. I sure hope he reminds Mrs. Mitchell that school is important and that she should let me go."

"Eddy, what's keeping you? Mr. Parsons will be here any minute. Hurry up."

After sitting in the kitchen, he was summoned to the parlour to meet Mr. Parsons for the third time since he had been at the Mitchell's. Eddy walked over and shook the inspector's hand. Eddy had learned to be gracious with important guests. His manners were impeccable for a farm boy and Mr. Parsons was impressed.

"You're growing into a fine young man, Eddy. Please sit down beside me so we can talk. And, by the way, we were pleased to receive your studio portrait. I also liked the pictures that Miss Patterson shared with me at school as well. That was quite a day and you all looked liked typical Canadian school children, healthy and strong."

Eddy hesitated before he spoke but his first words were, "Have you seen my friend Joseph, and how are the brothers that I knew in the home who stayed back in England after all, and how is Mr. Ryan"

"Sorry, Eddy, I have not heard from Joseph or your other friends but we did hear from Mr. Ryan who is doing very well as a farmer in Manitoba." "Now, I have some news from your mother. She has written, Eddy, to tell you that she has moved and is living on a farm in Maids Morton, outside of Buckingham. That's all I know."

Eddy cast down his eyes not because his mother had finally written but because he really wanted to know about Joseph. His mother had almost completely faded from his mind. All he could remember was the sweets she had promised that never arrived. But Joseph was a true friend.

"Well, Eddy, I must get going. Thank you. Now, I have to speak with Mr. and Mrs. Mitchell."

Eddy moved quickly upstairs to change and get back to the barn. The potatoes would have to wait until tomorrow.

The whole town was buzzing with the morning headlines but none of that could possibly matter to a child.

The first thing that Mrs. Mitchell said was "What a day to stop, Mr. Parsons. Didn't you know that Great Britain and the Empire, which means all of us, are at war with Germany?"

"Oh, my god. I didn't know."

"It's shocking, but there were rumours of war so I am not surprised .But, Mrs. Mitchell, we must talk about Eddy. I do not have a lot of time and I will be visiting the Gibson family next. Mrs. Gibson is your mother, right?"

"Yes, you will be meeting Emily I dare say."

"Yes."

"Is Mr. Mitchell with you?"

"No, I regret that he cannot meet with you today. He is desperately busy with farm work and found it hard to spare Eddy this afternoon. He wishes me to speak for both of us."

"There is the matter of schooling in the fall, Mrs. Mitchell. The Board of Trustees sent you a letter, I believe, requesting that Eddy stay in school to complete his education especially given his promise as a student and orator."

"Yes, but with war declared we cannot spare him. We know he is a good student but now that he is twelve, we feel he should be working full time on the farm. He is a good, but sadly reluctant, farm hand. It is clearly not his choice but we were under the understanding that when he turned 12, he would contribute to his board by working full time. He is indentured to us now as I understood your past letter.

No, Mrs. Mitchell Eddy is not officially indentured yet even if he is working every day. You are providing him with room and board and you have a clothing allowance. His formal indenture will not begin until he is 15. It is then, after signing the formal agreement that you will begin to pay his wages. I must say that I am very disappointed that you are no longer allowing him to attend school. I am sorry that this is your choice, Mrs. Mitchell, but I know that these are trying times. May I remind you that in

April, 1917, you will be under obligation to submit the sum of $62.00 annually in payment to be sent to the Imperial Bank of Commerce?

"Yes. I know this. Please understand, Mr. Parsons, that I am very fond of Eddy but we cannot spare him. He is needed on the farm more than ever."

"Thank you, Mrs. Mitchell. I will be keeping in touch on a yearly basis. 'Course, we don't know what this war will bring."

"Good afternoon, Mr. Parsons. And let's hope it won't be long before it's over."

Chapter 37: Leaving for the homeland

The call went out for volunteers to protect the homeland and posters were put up wherever people gathered. "Enlist in a noble cause. We need you!"

Already the Gibson house hold was alight with activity. The two home boys now 17 and 18 each had enlisted and soon would be joining other young men at the station. The younger boy would be staying on to work on the farm. Many of the young men were home boys and this seemed a good way to go home and perhaps find their families but that was not on the minds of most. They saw adventure ahead, a trip on an ocean liner, joining others in a noble fight against the Huns, excitement and some money in their pockets and a neat uniform which all the girls would love.

"There's nothing more handsome than a boy in uniform." they said.

It was the first of November. Dispatches posted in the local paper already talked of German troops mounting an offensive in Belgium. At the farm, work went on as usual. Charles Mitchell had to stay put even if a part of him wanted to join up and defend the motherland. He was a farmer and his work was invaluable at home. The harvest was more vital than ever so he resigned himself to running the farm with Tompkins working alongside. When Eddy asked about school in October, he shrugged and said, "Don't bother your head about it. You've got work to do"

Eddy was determined to go to school but, for now, he just kept working. He wanted to meet up with Jack after Mitchell went to council meeting. He hadn't seen him for a while and wondered what was happening in his family.

Jack had an older brother and sister and both were over 18 and he wondered about them now that they were of age to join the army. Eddy was anxious to know the news of his other friends, even Hans and Felix, his buddies jumping the train every time they got an opportunity. Gerard had moved away somewhere. Eddy missed boxing though. He could never get away now so all he could do was shadow box up at his hideaway. Eddy was good at keeping secrets. Neither Mitchell knew anything about train hopping, boxing or his secret kingdom. He was determined to keep it that way.

After a silent dinner except for Ethan asking questions about ice-cream or such, Eddy went to the barn to finish the chores, planning to whistle for Jack and meet him in his woodland kingdom afterwards. Mrs. Mitchell was getting ready to meet the Women's Institute ladies to discuss what they could do for the war effort. The meeting was planned for 6.30 and the kitchen smelled of cookies prepared that afternoon to serve up to a discerning group of women. You were judged by your housekeeping and your baking. Best it be said that Mary Mitchell was a fine lady and an excellent cook. That news spread fast especially in women's institute circles.

Eddy knew the meeting was called for after supper so he would have a free and untrammeled evening and in September, the sun was still up until 8 at night so there would be lots of time to sneak away.

"Hoot. Hoot", Eddy blew his mouth whistle by closing his lips and taking in the right amount of air and before too long Jack was clambering up the hill to meet him.

"Ain't seen you for awhile, Jack, not since haymaking. What's going on?"

"Oh, lots."

They stood by the shelter which had lost a few boughs since the last time they'd been there.

"Let's fix it up before we sit down in it. Just over the brow, there's straw, a big pile of it they didn't pick up when haymaking was in full swing."

The boys gathered two big armfuls and wove it into the branches before getting inside. Suddenly, the bushes started moving, branches fell and it felt like a big wind storm was coming up.

"Thrash, Bang, Crash!"

"Oh, gosh, look what's in the thicket. Quick! Hide behind that oak. It's a bull moose and he is moving towards us."

They had to be brave and stay still trying not to move a muscle. The old bull rubbed his nose on the tree, sniffed and then snorted and lumbered off.

"Was that a close call or was he being friendly?"

"No, that ain't it. It's ruttin' season. Those guys go a little crazy this time of year."

With a sigh of relief, the boys went inside their woodland camp and sat down. Jack was shaking but Eddy was working on a name for their new friend. He would join Minnie the owl and John squirrel in Eddy's kingdom.

"Let's name him, Daniel Big Antlers. What do you think, Jack? Remember Daniel in the Lion's den? He was strong. And stop shivering, you make me nervous. You'll see. He'll be our champion up here in these Muskoka woods if we are careful."

"I can't be thinking of the big bull, Eddy. There's a lot I've got to tell you. All the talk in our house is the war. My brother Amos has enlisted and my sister Clara is determined to be a nurse and go overseas to look after the wounded. Mother objects but Clara won't hear anything but, 'yes.'"

"Well, Grandma Gibson's English boys, Randolph and Jonathon are going too. Mrs. Gibson worried about how they'll manage the farm without them with just her husband, the younger home boy, Roger, her daughters and Emily left. The boys are great workers and they're treated well but they wanted to go to protect Canada. I guess Emily is heartbroken because Jonathon had said that when he came back, he wanted to marry her and her just a bit younger than me. They had always liked each other but as children do when they imagine being grown up."

"How'd you know all this? I thought you said that they never included you in family discussions."

"I listen through the keyhole when they go into the parlour. They go there when they have stuff to talk about – family stuff. I mean."

"If you were old enough, Eddy, would you join?"

"No way, I don't like guns and loud noises."

"I'd go for sure", retorted Jack. "You got to defend your country. You gotta be patriotic."

"Anyway, what's your plan for tomorrow, Jack? It's Sunday and we could sneak away from Sunday school."

"Not much. Yea, let's do that. Next week, we are going down to the station to see the boys off. You'll be goin' too. Right."

"Yea, I guess so; the Mitchell's will want to wish the Gibson boys Bon Voyage."

"See you Sunday."

All the talk at church after the service was the war. So many of the boys had already enlisted. There was talk of the formation of a Muskoka Battalion but these boys couldn't wait. They had to stop the Huns before they got too far and their armies were advancing and taking more territory as each day passed.

The two German families in the community were uneasy because much as they supported their adopted country's position on the conflict, they had relatives in Germany. Hans had begged his father to let him enlist but Felix filled from childhood with tales of his fatherland as told by his Bavarian grandfather was torn between loyalty to Canada and family connections in Bavaria.

The boys were both too young to serve any army. Their parents were well liked in the community and no one thought they were anything but loyal hard working Canadians who ran successful dairy farms.

When Hans and Eddy met outside the church they exchanged glances that was a code for,

"Let's get together later."

So After Sunday School with its patriotic hymns and pep talk from the teacher, Eddy was filled with pride and a wish that he could be joining the boys. When he met Hans, all he could say was,

"Hey, are you a Hun?"

"I'm Canadian."

"No, you're not. "

"Hey, buddy, I'm just as Canadian as you are. I remember when you was a dirty Limey. And we fought over that. And, why would you want to fight anyway. They didn't treat you right and they ain't treating you right now."

"Okay, okay, Hans. Let's call a truce. We can't go anyway so why don't we just be train riders and go West."

By Saturday next, the town resonated with horses and buggies as the farm folk descended on the train station. The townspeople were out in force as well. The men were dressed in their best suits and the ladies were wearing the latest catalogue fashions trying to outdo each other with the most spectacular hats. There had never been an occasion like this before except when the Boer war was on but that seemed so long ago.

They waited in anticipation for the boys to arrive. Each family looked out for their own. Jack's people were there to see Amos off. Clara was there as well but not as a nurse. The call had not gone out for Canadian girls so she would have to wait.

The Gibson's sparing only their home boys Randolph and Jonathon, waited with the Mitchells. Emily and Eddy were there too with their Union Jacks.

As the train whistle blew and the mighty engines came to a stop, everything came to a standstill. You could only hear the church bells ringing in the square.

The young enlistees gathered at the station with the recruiting officers who would be escorting them to Training camp outside Toronto. Special carriages had been added to the train to accommodate the rookie soldiers from the whole of the Muskoka as they travelled south.

After a few words of encouragement, the boys were dismissed.

Each boy walked towards their waiting families, spoke a few words, kissed their mothers and wives, picked up their babies, waved and boarded the train. There was no time to waste.

After Amos had kissed his mother and sister, Clara, he shook Jack's hand, reminding him to help his mother and be the big brother now, and saluted his Dad, a Boer War veteran and walked towards the train.

Grandma Gibson cried as she said goodbye to her home boys.

"Remember, boys, this will always be your home. Make us proud. Be strong and brave!"

Each soldier ascended the step into the car turning to wave or throw a kiss. Each family held their union jacks high.

As the train pulled out, its monstrous wheels slowly picking up speed, a roar went up. The boys strained their necks out of the windows, the platform was a sea of red, white and blue as the flags flew, the church bells rang and everyone sang, 'God save our gracious king, Long live our gracious king.' This was followed by The Maple Leaf Forever.

Eddy looked across at Emily. "Don't cry. He'll be back. Let's go to the magic kingdom and talk to Minnie the Owl."

She looked away. How could she tell him, she was too big for all that?

Chapter 38: The Years roll by

Eddy felt strange when he got in the buggy with the Mitchell family. After saying goodbye to Amos and the Gibson boys, he felt a deep ache way down in his belly. For the first time, he felt alone. He was too young to enlist even if had said so many times, he would never go but now there was emptiness within him. There he was in the buggy sitting crunched up in the back while Ethan sat proud between his aunt and uncle. They had given Ethan their surname so now he was their adopted son. And even though Eddy was called Mitchell on the 1910 census, he was still a Tompkins and not part of the family.

"How are you doing back there, Eddy?" Mrs. Mitchell called."I haven't heard a peak out of you all afternoon."

""I'm fine. Just a bit sleepy that's all."

"Okay."

Eddy did nod off to sleep but he woke up pretty quickly when they drove into the farm yard. "Get your overalls on, Tompkins. You've got all that barn work to do before you eat. I wanted you to stay put and finish up. We didn't need you at the station. But my wife insisted."

And so it was and would be from now on. Time came for the farm kids to go back to school. It was October, the harvest was in and winter preparation well on its way to completion. They all gathered down near the tracks but Eddy was not with them. Jack looked up the hill at the Mitchell house and whistled twice for Eddy. It was their signal but Eddy did not respond.

"Where is he? I am going up to get him."

When Jack arrived at the back door out of breath from running, he was met by Mrs. Mitchell. "Sorry, Jack. Eddy won't be going back to school. You'll have to go without him."

"Why?"

"It's the way it is. Now hurry along."

With his head down and a tiny speck of water in his eye, Jack hurried off down the hill, across the tracks and along the dusty road to school. Eddy was in the hen house screaming at the rooster and throwing the straw ever way he could of think of except where it was supposed to go.

"I hate it here. I hate it. And I hate you, you old ugly rooster."

Mrs. Mitchell came out of the kitchen holding her long apron as she wove her way through the chicken litter; Eddy had just piled it in the pathway any old way. "Eddy, I can't bear to hear you yelling. I know you are angry but all hands are needed on the farm now and school is out of the question. You must understand. You have to pull your weight."

"I want to see Miss Patterson. I want to tell her what you've done." he screamed.

"Stop this at once or I'll have to call my husband."

Eddy stopped, looked away and stomped out of the chicken coop. He looked around to see if old Mitchell was nearby, and said, "I'm going down to see my teacher."

"No, you can't."

With that, he thrust his head forward and almost took a nose dive across the path towards the tracks. "No, Eddy, No. Charles, Charles" she yelled, "Come here this instant, Eddy won't mind me and he's gone to school."

Eddy tumbled down the hill and along the tracks not even looking to see if the freight was coming as it did each day at this time. He had left without breakfast still wearing his filthy overalls and soiled boots. All he wanted to do was get to school to see his teacher. As he turned the corner, he barely saw the freight moving up the slope straight towards him. He kept running with his head down. Suddenly, the train whistle blew warning signals and the wheels squealed in an attempt to stop.

As the wheels barreled towards him and the sound got louder, Eddy looked up and just in time jumped clear.

"Whew", he said as he wiped the sweat from his forehead. "That was a close call."

But it hardly fazed him because all he could think of was getting to school before classes started. Back at the farm, Charles and Mary stood on the pathway in a daze. Eddy had never defied them until today.

"He's done with school and that's that", said Mitchell.

"Are we being fair to him, Charles?'

"Fair, what do you mean, fair? I was working when I was his age. We'll be paying for his labour and no way is he going to school. There's a war, He's going to work and work hard. Don't mention school and don't ever talk to me about being fair again."

When Eddy had shaken off the gravel from his overalls, he continued on to the schoolhouse arriving before the bell. He snuck in by the side door and walked up to the front desk. Miss Patterson was sitting with her head down reading over the bible passage she had prepared for the first reading of the day.

"Good morning, Miss Patterson."

Startled, she raised her head and looked straight at the boy who smelled like a hen house and looked like a rag a muffin from the back country.

"Who are you?"

"Miss Patterson, it's me. It's Eddy."

"Oh my goodness, it is you", she said, as she looked at his face which shone bright above the worn out farm clothes and scratched up arms. "What happened?"

"They won't let me go to school. Not ever."

"Eddy, I have tried. I spoke to the Board of School Trustees and they wrote to your foster parents. They told us that you are obliged to work now. It's part of your contract. You are indentured. Sorry."

"I am not indentured yet. I want to be educated."

"I understand, Eddy, but I can't do any more."

"Why?" he cried. "My friends are here, all except Emily who is like me except she doesn't hanker after school like I do. She likes housekeeping and cooking and making quilts and, anyway, she likes Grandma Gibson a whole lot. Mrs. Mitchell is okay but she minds whatever her husband says and he won't let me go to school ever again."

"Eddy, I'll see if I can arrange some private tutoring for you but you will have to prove yourself by being the best farm hand ever. At least, we could try to get you ready for exams that could lead to secondary school but I am not making any promises, you understand."

"I want to be in the classroom, Miss Patterson."

"Now, Eddy, you'll have to go back to the Mitchell's and I have to ring the bell to start the school day."

"Okay", I'll leave by the side door. See you later."

As Eddy left, Jack peered around the corner hoping it was Eddy he heard talking in the school room. "Hi, Eddy, bad luck about school. I'll keep you up with everything. By the way, Hans and Felix are not in school either and there are the two boys up at the Garland farm who are staying on to help at home while their brother and first cousin are overseas."

"Okay. I best be gone. Old Mitchell will be mad as a hatter because I disobeyed his wife and ran off."

Eddy rushed back and when he got there, he went right into the Chicken coup to finish what he had started in anger just a few hours ago. Lifting his shovel, he bailed the old straw out and replaced it with fresh summer grasses.

Mrs. Mitchell on hearing noises of working came out to see. Eddy was back at it doing his best to straighten up the mess he had made earlier. "Good to see you are home, Eddy. Time to come in for breakfast."

Mitchell, after thinking it over made a conscious decision this time to stay away.

"I guess it didn't make any sense to the kid to be stopped from going to school."

And so, life carried on. Eddy worked from dawn to dusk getting up first in the household to make the fire up, start the kettle and go out to the barn. He hardly ever went up to his Magic Kingdom especially after being reminded at Sunday School, that "when you become a man, you put away childish things." Emily had been telling him that he was too old for fantasy and that wild animals don't have names. And Jack kept saying he was too busy to go to the hideout. So, he went up to his woodland camp and bid his fantasy friends Goodbye.

"Someday, I will have land of my own and I will build a cabin and all the animals in my kingdom will be free."

And Eddy did find a way to be self educated in a manner. Miss Patterson had arranged for a tutor who met Eddy twice a month after church to give him books and exercises in math so that he could quietly and out of Mitchell's way, prepare for his future, and he decided there and then, that he would go back to the Boxing Camp and train like Jack Dempsey who was winning prize fights in the heavy weight class all over the States. Word got out even in the far reaches of the Muskoka's.

Eddy looked up to Dempsey. He had worked as a farm hand and miner while training at their amateur boxing camp in Utah. " I'll meet him someday. I'll get on that train and head south to Virginia where Dempsey has one of the best training camps in the world."

Eddy's imagination was the one thing no one could take away from him. If he couldn't go to school, he would work to make himself strong and independent.

Chapter 39: Life continues on the farm while the battles rage in France

Every day brought the same drudgery. Mitchell managed with difficulty since there were no young men to call on to help with the harvest and the wood cutting. The haying now depended on young women, their mothers and whatever old men were left. The bulk of the workforce were fighting battles in France, dodging horrendous machine gun fire and suffocating from chlorine gas introduced by the Germans in the spring of 1915.

The two related farm families kept up with the conflict by reading the local newspaper, talking to their neighbours and occasionally receiving letters from the trenches. Grandma Gibson had received two letters from her home boy, Randolph, who talked first about his return to England, training for the front, and his failed attempt at finding a relative. Jonathon had written to Emily but she wanted it to be a secret even though she decided to tell Eddy when she saw him walking down the field from the barn.

"Eddy, Eddy, Wait," she called stopping him in his tracks.

"I'm in a hurry." Eddy called as he rounded the bend.

But running as fast as she could and clutching something in her right hand, Emily reached Eddy and begged him to sit down on the grass near the crossing. It was early May and on this day the sun had warmed the lower meadow and there were sprigs of mayflowers peaking through the grass.

"I've got to share this with you, Eddy. It's a letter from Jonathon. But, don't tell a soul. She opened the letter and began to read:

March, 1915:

My dear Emily. I really miss you. How is everyone at home? Yes, it is home. After seeing England, I am glad I live in Bracebridge. I always wondered what England would be like. But there's nothing there for me.

April 15: It's hell here. We're near Ypres, they tell me. But we're in a trench and every night we take turns shooting rats. With our shots and the endless shooting all day across no man's land, I just want to run away. But you can't. One poor fellow lost his head last night and ran over the top. The lieutenant just shot him in the bank while he was running. I think he was from Guelph, a nice boy, but so homesick, he cried for his mother every night. We couldn't say a word. It was "Just one word out of you Canucks and you are dead.

April 24: We've been attacked by chlorine gas. I just got a whiff 'cause I covered my face with a cloth soaked in urine. That's what they told us to do. I hate it here. It's hell."

April 25: I feel sick. We're going to move towards the German line tomorrow. If I don' come back, Emily, remember that I love you."

"Oh, Eddy, I am so scared. They don't say much at the house and I don't want to worry Grandma Gibson."

"Gosh, Emily, it will be alright. Jonathon is brave. He'll make it home.

I'll walk you home. I can forget boxing tonight."

When they arrived at the Gibson's, they were met by somber faces. A telegram had arrived while Emily was out walking. Grandma Gibson read it out loud,

May 1; We regret to inform you that Jonathon Beasley is missing in action."

Emily lifted her hand to her face and ran. She ran out of the house and before anyone could catch her, she was running on the tracks towards the town. Eddy ran after her. Emily kept running until she tripped on a tuft of stiff grass on the track. Eddy, not far behind, got to her and picked her up. She burst into tears. Eddy put his arms around her and comforting her said, "It will be alright, Emily. Missing in action means they can't find him but knowing Jonathon, he'll figure out a way. He's probably hiding or some kind person has taken him in."

Emily listened intently because, somehow, Eddy had often been right. Picking up her heels and putting her arm in Eddy's, she was ready to go home. On the same night, Jack came down to pay a visit and his news, not quite as grim, was still a source of worry to Mrs. Mitchell. It was about Clara. She had eventually convinced her parents that her services were needed and she had left and was sailing across to France. Dispatches talked about the menace at sea and she was especially fond of Clara

It was hard to fathom how a war so far away across the deep divide of the cold Atlantic could affect them all so much in this tiny hamlet of Macaulay Township. But they were part of the grand company of English people spread from one end of the globe to the other. There were Anzac's from Australia and New Zealand, the Canucks of Canada, the Brits from South Africa and of course the Limeys of England.

In a way, Eddy's problems with Mr. Mitchell seemed small against this backdrop but Eddy would rather have been out there on the front lines. It would be an adventure and not drudgery such as the day by day grind of farm work and his boss' hard ways. Boys like Eddy couldn't ever understand what Jonathon was saying about war; you had to be there to know.

The talk of the community was war and their boys and girls who were in the midst of the conflict. On Sunday, the minister spoke of the need to support the war effort and the ladies led by Mrs. Mitchell filled the church with gloves, socks and blankets made by the women and girls of the township. They were to be shipped abroad by the Red Cross and delivered to the troops where the need was greatest. War bonds were sold and everyone was involved in helping in whatever way they could.

Jack reported that his sister Clara was now in Belgium treating the wounded and her brother was at the front battling chlorine gas and bullets. The war had changed Jack. He now talked of becoming an engineer primarily because his teachers had noted his brilliance in mathematics and design and encouraged him to study and apply to the University of Toronto in due course. His father now encouraged him rather than pushing him into the family business- farming. There was going to be a boom in construction when the boys came home and Jack wanted to be at the forefront of helping Canada rebound after the war.

Sadly, Eddy's cleverness was wasted on cleaning the stables and milking the cows. His desperation to continue his studies had fallen on deaf ears and he grew bitter and angry. He gave up on the tutoring that Miss Patterson had arranged but he continued to box whenever he had a chance. That would be his focus from now on. The Mitchells remained in the dark as to his side activities and that's the way Eddy wanted it.

There had to come a time when Eddy would rebel. Grandma Gibson had warned her son-in-law that it wasn't healthy for Eddy to have nothing but farming on the horizon. Her home boys were in France and Emily spent her days looking after the household and knitting scarves for Jonathon and Randolph but, at least, they were loved as members of the Gibson family and not children from away.

Eddy had remained an outsider to Mr. Mitchell. His wife had begged him to be more civil and understanding. She tried as hard as she could to make up for her husband's harsh ways but she could not open his heart.

"That kid will never amount to anything. He was a street Arab when he arrived and he is still a street Arab."

"Don't say that, Charles", she would say. "He's just a boy."

"Mary, he has a dark side to him. I've known that from the start."And look at him. He is dark in complexion. I swear he is a gypsy. I've tried to knock some sense into him but he just becomes more withdrawn and insolent."

………………………………

And so, it continued. ………

Before long, it was the summer of 1918 and there was talk of a possible truce even though the killing continued. There had been no word of Jonathon but Emily was convinced that he was somewhere safe. She knew that deep down in her heart

Chapter 40: Eddy runs away

The work on the farm was becoming unbearable. Mr. Mitchell exhausted from the demands of ploughing, planting, seeding, harvesting and all the other back breaking work was becoming impossible to please. On top of this, his prime winter crop, potatoes, were dying from the incessant attacks of Colorado beetles.

"Tompkins, leave what you are doing in the stables and listen to me. That crop of potatoes you planted in July is dying. If we don't stop this beetle invasion, we will have slim pickings at the table this winter. Go up to the fields and spray every dreaded one with Paris green. You know what I mean. Drop everything and get up there."

"Mr. Mitchell, it's Sunday. Don't you stop work on the Sabbath? I had plans to meet Jack and Emily after the youth group meeting at church."

"Plans? What plans? The only damn thing you are going to do today is kill those beetles. I don't care if it takes you all day."

Eddy knew enough to just say, "Yes, sir." And he ran towards the garden shed, picked up the two cans of Paris green and hurried to the rows of potatoes in the large garden between the house and the barn. It was a tiring business this spraying with a hand pump but he was used to this every summer and he definitely did not look forward to it. He had sore eyes and a splitting headache every time after spraying the first rows and it just got worse after that. Mr. Mitchell could only say, "Get on with it."

There had been talk of a thirteen year old boy who died because he ingested Paris green. They said that it had been ruled suicide and that's an awful way to die. But everyone wondered. Did he die because he put too much of the mixture in with the water? Did he miscalculate the dose? Or was it on purpose?

Mitchell had warned Eddy about the mixture and Eddy took it seriously but how much he took in was anyone's guess. Neither Eddy nor Mitchell were chemists. Yet, they handled this deadly mixture as though they were mixing the ingredients for sour dough. All Mitchell would say was, "Don't waste a bit of this. It's expensive stuff. Remember."

There was a light mist in the air not quite rain but certainly a promise of it and it was hot. They were entering the dog days of summer and it made the days seem long and frustrating. Eddy could think of a much better way to spend an early August afternoon. He filled the spray bucket with a mixture of water and Paris green and put the lid back on the can. He had the proportions in his head and he had talked to Jack about it just a couple of days ago because they used it on their potatoes. Jack and his father always covered their mouth and nose with a cloth that looked like a thick bandage. His dad who knew everything about the latest in farming had said, "Paris green is copper acetate triarsenite. We have to be careful when we use it. Don't worry about the big words but be very careful."

Words like toxic and poison seemed scary but he was told it was safe. He knew only that it was a powdery mix that had the beautiful colour of emerald and that it killed beetles. He was also told that it was called Paris green because of its colour and the fact that it was used in the sewers of Paris to kill rodents. Eddy didn't know what that meant but he understood why you have to kill those varmints. He had seen rats on the ship coming over and he vaguely remembered rats in the refuse on London streets. Anyway, Mr. Mitchell was determined to kill all the beetles on his plants that day and he never mentioned once that Eddy should wear a protective cloth on his face.

With the spray bucket strapped to his back, he walked along each row spraying each plant until each leaf was saturated. Every potato leaf glistened like an emerald after receiving their blast of insecticide. The colour was the envy of fashionable women who desired nothing more than to be seen at a ball in a dress of emerald green. He had seen ads for the dye made from Paris green in the main store in Bracebridge. They featured a Parisian lady in a gorgeous green dress. In a funny way, it had caught his fancy then because it seemed strange that fashion and poison would go together. After all he was 16 now and girls interested him even if they seemed headstrong and rather vain.

The green can he was using bore the word Poison in bold print. It was green but it could be deadly. All afternoon, Eddy walked between the rows with the spray bucket on his back. His hands hurt and his back ached. His eyes were smarting as though he had a twig in his eye and his head felt heavy as night.

When he had finished, he sat on the grass and munched a piece of cookie left over from the day before. He was just about to put the cans away and the spray bucket in the shed when Mitchell came by for inspection. "You're finished already? That's soon, isn't it? Let me see the can. You should still have a half a can left."

He picked up the can and said, "Hey, this seems empty?" He opened it with his pocket knife, prying open the lid. No sign of Paris green powder.

Mr. Mitchell felt the red coming up over his brow, his heart started pounding and his hands were already cold with sweat. "My God, boy, what have you done? Did you use it all?"

"Yes, sir. I thought they needed a double dose 'cause the beetles were eating them poor potatoes alive. A lot of the plants had no leaves at all."

"You idiot, you damn fool idiot. You've ruined the whole crop with all that poison."

"I figured they needed more Paris green."

Mitchell could not restrain himself. "How could you? The number of times I've told you to take instruction and you always do it your way. Always."

"I, I wanted to do it right."

Mitchell raised his big burly brown hand and back handed Eddy hard across his mouth.

Eddy jumped back and raised his left fist and with a fast punch with his right hand, he struck Mitchell in the stomach.

Mitchell retaliated by throwing a punch and knocking the boy down. Eddy landed in the dirt cutting his hand on the shovel that lay on the side of the potato patch. By now Eddy's mouth was covered with blood and his hand was cut wide open. He tried to get up to throw another punch at the older man but Mitchell threw him down again this time knocking him into the shed.

Both of them, the 16 year old Eddy and the 40 year old Mitchell were panting.

Neither one was giving up.

Just then, Mrs. Mitchell came running out towards the barn. She had heard the commotion and the loud yelling. As she got to the site, she screamed out, "What's going on Charles? Have you lost your senses? The boy's so much younger and smaller than you."

Moving toward her with Eddy still on the ground, he yelled, "He defied me and he's ruined our crop. Let him lay there until he apologizes."

"Let me tend to him, Charles. I'll get some iodine, ointment and bandages."

"No, let him lay there and learn his lesson. That cut is only surface."

"But, Charles?"

"I said No. The boy has to learn to take orders. And he dared to defy me. He'll be up the minute we turn our backs."

At that, he walked towards the house muttering under his breath repeating the same words over and over, "I said it would come to no good. It's no good."

After a few minutes nursing his hurt, Eddy got up and looked around. Wiping his mouth with his sleeve, he looked around for the old man. His hand throbbed and his back felt like a washing tub wringer. "I'll get him next time. I will. I will. I'm leaving this house for good. I said I would and I am going."

Looking down towards the track, he picked himself up and tried to run but he stumbled over a rock. Determined, he lifted himself up more from sheer anger than ability and made his way towards the road that bisected the track a few yards away. Wearing the dirty overalls and the worn out boots with nothing in his stomach, he walked along the track until he got to the carriage road. "I am going to Gravenhurst", he said.

The rain had started. From the mist earlier in the day, it now came down in buckets. With no coat or rain boots, he dragged himself along hoping that someone would give him a ride. He would have liked to hitch a ride on the train but that would not happen today. The freight did not run that route on Sundays. He was out of luck so with his head down, still tasting the blood in his mouth and hurting from the cut on his hand, he trudged along until he could see the electric lights of a lumber mill. They had been electrified only last year and it sure beat gas lighting.

Eddy made a mental note of that even with the way he felt. He headed towards the lights, and went up to the door of a large brick house off to the side of the mill. The house was lit up like a Christmas tree and the large oak door had a welcome knocker, an elf with a brass cap on his head. He had no idea of the time but he could hear laughter and he could smell supper. He knocked on the door feebly at first and then he landed three loud knocks they were sure to hear.

A lady dressed in a rose covered dress came to the door and looking up at her was a raggedy boy soaking wet and dirty. With her hand to her mouth, she could barely utter, "Oh, dear me. Dear me. Come in, boy. Wait inside the door. I'll call Patty the house maid. She'll look after you. Patty, please come here."

Patty arrived dressed in her uniform. She wore a plain white cotton dress, set off with a black apron and a dainty black hat. She was no older than Eddy and she had the most delightful smile. Eddy noticed that even in the condition he was in.

"Patty, take the boy to the kitchen and give him a bite to eat. We must have lots of left over's from supper. I'll get Reginald to bring down some hand me downs. He's about the same size as the boy. Oh, but first, we've got to clean him up."

She took him into their gleaming bathroom with a sink and running water and with a clean white cloth, she cleaned off the dried blood on his face and on his hand. Having raised 5 children, she knew the cuts were superficial so she wasn't alarmed. "What is your name?"

"Eddy Tompkins, ma'am."

"What happened?"

"I got in a fight."

Eddy did not want to reveal anything to a stranger so he kept his silence on the matter for the present.

"I won't press you any further now, Eddy. You go into the kitchen and Patty will look after you.

Patty scurried about and finally brought a plate brimming with slices of beef, mashed potatoes and turnip and a glass of milk with two large slices of brown bread heaped with butter.

"Sit down at the table. What's your name anyway?"

Eddy stammering a bit sheepishly said, "Eddy."

"How come you are out on a day like this and it's pitch black outside .

Where did you come from?"

I am from Bracebridge and I came looking for work."

"Work?"

"I don' want to talk. Can't I just eat now?"

Chapter 41: Eddy in Limbo

After eating the supper that Patty served him, Eddy was called into the back room of the Mill Owner's House. He was too poorly dressed and in such a state that he would have been an embarrassment. The MacDonald's had relatives staying over and all the bedrooms were occupied. Furthermore, the pretty young women were dressed nicely and too well brought up to see a ragged boy at this time of day.

The house was a show piece for the up and coming gentry of Gravenhurst. Standing aside in its own grove of trees, the house was a grand example of early Edwardian architecture and that indicated wealth and prestige. It was not built of wood but of brick and stone, very British in tone and texture. Below but removed from site of the elegant carriage road was the family lumber mill and blazoned in large bold letters was the sign, the MacDonald/ Powell and Sons Lumber Mill. It was a fixture in the town producing shingles, laths and board lumber for the Muskoka Region. Today, it was idle because of the Sabbath but on weekdays it was alive with men and machinery.

Eddy had hoped to get work there and was about to ask Mrs. MacDonald when she brought him some clothes from her son's hand me downs. "Here's new underwear, a clean shirt, breeches, overalls, shoes and socks and a night shirt for tonight. I will have to make up a bed for you in the Office because a number of our relatives are visiting from Peterborough.

Wait here until I call you."

Eddy was feeling a bit uneasy but with his stomach full and the blood on his face and hands removed, he felt a bit better. At least he would not have to deal with Mitchell tonight and hopefully never again. Becoming more familiar with his surroundings, he opened the kitchen door and saw Patty cleaning the large heap of dishes left over from supper. "Hi, there, I just thought I might get another glass of milk. I'm awful thirsty."

Startled, Patty turned around with dish cloth in hand, her face flushed from the warmth of the huge kitchen stove and the number of dishes to dry. "You can't just barge in here like this and ask for more milk. You're a beggar and you should mind your manners."

"Sorry, miss, but I didn't think asking for a glass of milk was a bad thing."

"Anyway, here's a dish towel for you. If you're going to be here with me and if you want some milk, you'll have to work for it."

"Okay", said Eddy, "I don't mind at all."

When he was finished doing his bit in the kitchen, Patty gave him a heaping glass of milk and told him to sit down in the back room again. "Sit tight. Mrs. MacDonald will be back in no time."

So Eddy sat on the softest seat he could find in this country kitchen work room and before long he was fast asleep. When Mrs. MacDonald came in she was astonished to see the boy asleep but then it was understandable given what he had been through.

"Eddy, wake up. It's time to go to a proper bed. I've made you up a bed in the Office for tonight. We'll find you something else tomorrow."

They stepped out of the back door and walked down the hill towards the Mill. The Mill office was set to the right side of the main building. It was serviceable with an oak desk and hard backed chairs but the housekeeper had made up a bed on the floor with sheets and a thin blanket. He would not need much more in summertime but she added another warmer blanket because it was still raining. The pillows looked fluffy and comfortable.

"Sleep well, Eddy. I'll send Patty down to fetch you for breakfast in the morning."

"Thank you, Ma'am. I don't know what to say?"

"You don't need to say anything. See you in the morning."

After the Mill Owner's wife left, Eddy sat down on the bed and looked around. He was overwhelmed by everything that had happened but at least he had a bed for the night. He'd heard about runaways who had to sleep on the side of the road. He was lucky.

The sun rose over the roof of the Lumber Mill before Eddy woke up. It was Monday, and the Mill was working. There were the loud noises of machinery run by steam, the sound of carts maneuvering through the men who were lifting logs, sorting through them and moving them by large conveyer belt to be hacked and sawn inside. It was ordered and precise. Around these machines, everyone had to be on guard. Hands came off too often when a glance away spelled doom.

Eddy dressed and found the left over clothes fit perfectly. There was no mirror so he couldn't see his reflection but he was satisfied that he looked smart. Just then, Patty arrived.

"Good. You're ready. Follow me to the kitchen."

Breakfast was served to the staff in the large country kitchen. The walls were panelled with spruce wood. It complimented the appliances and furniture, an enormous stove, a huge cast iron sink and a long oak table which was used for preparation of the food and for seating the house workers.

Eddy sat down next to the cook who was a fat, red faced jolly woman. She was comfortable to be near. She smelled of cooking spices and eggs. She had prepared the breakfast for the members of the MacDonald household. They were served in the dining room in the front of the house. Now, she was ready to enjoy the meal herself. The staff picked up their plates and filled each one with bacon, sausages, scrambled eggs, fried potatoes and slices of toast which had been laid out on a side table in large copper containers. Neither Patty nor cook had the energy or time to serve their fellow workers, the house maids and the gardeners.

Eddy didn't move a muscle after sitting down. "Go get the grub, boy, like the rest of us and sit beside me," she said.

After breakfast, Mrs. MacDonald summoned him to the parlour. "Now that you have had a decent night's sleep and breakfast, we have to talk. Last night you said you had been in a fight.

What is your full name? And where do you live?"

"My name is Edward George Tompkins. I live and work at the Mitchell farm just outside the town of Bracebridge."

"What happened? You came here with blood on your hand and face. Where did you think you were going that late in the day? And, on Sunday, too!"

"Mr. Mitchell hit me and knocked me down. He was mad at me 'cause he said I messed his potato patch. I ran away and don't ever want to see him again."

"Now, Edward, I need to know more. You said you work at the Mitchell farm. You are not a Mitchell then. Are you a homeboy?"

"I don't know what I am. I just know I don't want to go back."

"How old are you?'

"Sixteen, Ma'am."

"Is there an inspector that comes to see you once in a while? Patty is a home girl and she has an inspector assigned. His name is Mr. Parsons."

"Yes, I know Mr. Parsons."

"Good."

"Mrs. MacDonald, I'd like to work in the Mill."

"I'll talk to my husband at lunchtime."

Eddy felt good at the thought of getting away from farm duties. Outside of his special friends the draft horses he wouldn't miss it at all.

Mrs. MacDonald thought over the night before. The boy had arrived without proper clothes and he had told Patty that he was looking for work. She would try to do what she could for him but first she had to talk to her husband and write to Mr. Parsons. She would wait until he returned from his office. He would be tired since it was the beginning of the week and the machinery and the men needed extra supervision after the brief Sunday break.

After supper with her family and talking to her husband, she learned that there was no millwork for the boy at the present time but that he could be employed weeding the garden and cutting the grass. Furthermore, Mr. MacDonald said he would pay him the same as the wages paid to the boys at the mill. They both felt very sorry for Eddy and since he was going to have work for wages now, they decided that he could stay with them.

"We will provide you with garden work and mill wages, Eddy, and you will have a bed in the car house until we hear from Mr. Parsons. I will write to him today and we'll see what he says."

"I don't want to go back to the farm. Please."

"Don't fret now. We'll set you up tonight but in the meantime, you can start weeding the flower garden in the front."

"Oh, Mrs. Mitchell likes her flower garden too and I have tended it many times. She is a nice lady. But her husband is mean."

Eddy started work right after his talk with the lady of the house and he settled in to the house routine quite well. Patty was very kind and even though only a bit older she treated him like a brother.

Two days passed and a letter arrived from Mr. Parsons. Mrs. MacDonald shared what he said in summary with Eddy.

"He said he was very surprised, indeed shocked to hear that you ran away from the Mitchell household and that you were doing exceedingly well when he visited you 6 weeks ago."

"Yea, he came over. I didn't say much and Mr. Mitchell wasn't even there so Mrs. Mitchell must have said that."

"He said further that he could not accept that you deserted your rightful employer and ran away unless you had very good reasons for doing so."

"Why did you run away?"

"I couldn't stand it anymore and it's not the first time that guy hit me."

"I am sorry to hear this Eddy," Mrs. MacDonald believed the boy. There was something true and sad about him and she found herself wanting to take him in permanently. Mr. Parsons' letter continued by reminding us that if they, the inspectors at the headquarters in Toronto, allowed this kind of thing from their home children, they would have children wondering all about the country making nuisances of themselves. Mrs. MacDonald hesitated for a moment before continuing. This was becoming a lot more complicated. All she wanted was to help the boy and it was clear that he was in distress.

"He says that we will have to send you back and that they would give back any money spent on the fare back to Bracebridge. But he did add that he would visit the Mitchell household as soon as you return and find out from you directly exactly what happened with a promise that if he finds that there was good reason for you to run away, he would send you back to Toronto where you lived when you first arrived in Canada in 1910."

This was just too much for Eddy to take in. He had mixed feelings because he remembered how lonely he had been in Toronto but he was afraid to go back to the farm as well. Muffling tears, Eddy asked to be excused.

"Go into the kitchen, Eddy. Patty will find you something nice to eat. This is a lot for you to handle right now. Let me figure this out and try not to worry."

So Eddy continued to work for the Mill Owners while letters were being exchanged and decisions were being made as to his welfare and future.

Back at the Mitchells there was consternation and a flurry of letters back and forth. Mr. Mitchell had not intended this to happen and couldn't understand why Eddy had run away even though when he last saw him, the boy was nursing a bloody mouth that he had given him when he discovered that Eddy had overdosed the potatoes with Paris green. He seemed to think that what he did was mete out a well deserved punishment to teach the boy a lesson.

Reading over Mr. Parsons' letter, he remarked to his wife, "I can't understand why the boy ran away. We provided for him and didn't work him too hard. No harder than I worked at his age."

"Charles, you were much too hard on him and hitting the child so hard in the height of your temper was wrong. It is no wonder that he ran away."

Chapter 42: Eddy back at the farm

Mrs. MacDonald had her hands full trying to settle Eddy and keep him at her home. Mr. Parsons had written to the Inspector at their headquarters in Toronto because Mrs. MacDonald refused to send Eddy back to the Mitchells considering his mistreatment by Mr. Mitchell. They wanted to do the right thing. From their understanding, however, Eddy was doing 'exceedingly well' in the last report filed by Mr. Parsons.

Mrs. MacDonald insisted that Eddy had arrived at their home in a destitute state and that she could not send him back to those conditions. Tired of the slow pace and lack of resolution, Mrs. MacDonald telephoned Mr. Parsons saying that she wanted to help the boy but her hands were tied.

"I will be over tomorrow afternoon."

"Thank you."

When Mr. Parsons arrived, Mrs. MacDonald was having tea with her lady auxiliary members. They met once a week to knit sweaters for the troops on the battlefield. The war was still raging after 4 long years. "Good afternoon, Mr. Parson. Do come in to the parlour. Please excuse me ladies. I must attend to some important matters."

"I'll come right to the point, Mrs. MacDonald. I have a letter from the Chief Superintendent of the Toronto headquarters of the Dr. Barnardo Charity. If you can take the time, I will read it to you."

"Yes, surely. Do please read it to me, sir."

With regard to Edward G. Tompkins

Dear Mr. Parsons,

There has been trouble with this boy, who last week absconded from Mitchell and made his way to Gravenhurst. There he found refuge with the MacDonald's of MacDonald/ Powell and Co., to whom he told his tale of woe. Mrs. MacDonald wrote suggesting keeping the boy to do odd jobs about their house. Having before me your report giving a glowing account of the boy's home with the Mitchells, I wrote Mrs. MacDonald intimating that we could not sanction his remaining and requesting that he might be returned to the Mitchells. At the same time, I wrote Mitchell informing him where the boy was and that he might expect his return. Mrs. MacDonald replied declining to return the boy on the grounds that the man had ill-treated and knocked him about. I then wrote requesting Mrs. MacDonald to return the boy to Toronto and enclosing a ticket for his transportation.

"Now, I know you mean to do everything right for Edward but we have to follow protocol. Will you send Eddy on the train to Toronto by tomorrow morning?"

Reluctantly, assuming that Toronto would be a much better place than the farm, she said,

"Yes. Thank you for all your trouble Mr. Parsons. Would you care for a cup of tea?"

"Thank you but I must decline. I have two more visits to make this afternoon and I can see that you and the ladies are very busy helping with the war effort so I must bid you, Good day."

Taking his leave, he bowed ever so slightly and walked out to his waiting carriage. Mrs. MacDonald went back with the ladies in the dining room and they continued their knitting until 4 o'clock.

In the meantime, Eddy weeded like fury and by supper time the garden looked groomed and free of unsightly weeds. Eddy was too busy to notice a car parked at the front of the house. But Patty had noticed and she burst into the parlour without knocking first "There's a man in a motor car outside. I think it's a Model T. Can you come right away?"

Looking up from her knitting while the ladies gasped at being so rudely interrupted, she called out, "Patty, go outside and ask him to wait a moment. A Model T you say? Umm? I'll be right out after I take leave of the ladies."

Patty curtsied and made her way to the car. Mrs. MacDonald hurriedly went upstairs to her bedroom to freshen up her hair and put on a more formal but practical dress. She could not be seen in her everyday attire if there was a gentleman outside waiting to see her. She couldn't call her husband because he was at the Mill overseeing the Shingle manufacture given that they had received a very large order. Just this morning. She walked down the stairs and towards the large ornate front door which she opened timidly. It was rare to see a car in front of the house.

Stepping outside, she paused and waited for the driver to open the door for the passenger. The gentleman resembled a city councillor she was sure she had met some while ago. He was dressed in a serviceable pair of trousers, a neatly pressed shirt finished off by a tweed jacket. Everything about him suggested hard work and seriousness of purpose.

He reached out his hand to the lady of the house and said, without hesitation,

"Good afternoon. My name is Mr. Mitchell. I am a farmer and city councillor in the town of Bracebridge."

"Good afternoon, sir". She said."Do come in."

She called out to Patty who was in the kitchen putting away the dishes from afternoon tea. Please make us a cup of tea and bring it to the parlour."

"Right away, Ma'am."

She led Mr. Mitchell to the parlour and offered him the Chestnut chair near the window. She sat opposite with the tea table between them.

"I will get straight to the point. I understand from the letter I received from Mr. Parsons that this is the MacDonald residence and you have living with you, our employee and ward, Edward George Tompkins."

"Yes, that is correct."

"I engaged a car to come over to collect him and take him back. I tried to call both Mr. Parsons and yourself but the operator could not make the connections."

Flushed and trying to hide her annoyance, Mrs. MacDonald answered "I have been in correspondence with Mr. Parsons and just this afternoon, he paid us a visit. I reluctantly agreed to send Eddy by train to Toronto to the Receiving home there. I must say that I was shocked at the boy's condition when he arrived quite late in the evening some while ago."

Looking relieved at the entrance of the house maid, Mr. Mitchell said, "It's a long story and I feel I was in the right and the boy had no business leaving in the pouring rain or any time for that matter."

Patty entered with a tea tray, on which stood an ornate teapot, two cups, milk, sugar and some sweets. She placed a napkin on each chair arm and quietly left the room.

"Do you take milk and sugar sir?"

"Just milk, thank you."

Mrs. MacDonald poured the tea, added the milk and handed her guest the cup along with a small plate of sweets. Taking time to utter those polite and expected words like 'Thank you', he picked up the conversation where they had left off.

"I understand your reluctance to send Edward to Toronto. However, there is no need of that now. I would like to take the boy back to our place where he has lived for the past 8 years. I admit to losing my temper and hitting him. I am troubled by this but I can assure you that it won't happen again. We are fond of the boy and Mrs. Mitchell, in particular, misses him very much."

"Mr. Mitchell, you can understand my hesitation. When Eddy arrived here he was in a terrible state and we simply had to take him in."

"I appreciate your kindness very much and I am deeply thankful to your husband as well. Considering his busy schedule, it was very kind to offer the boy work and lodging. I promise on the word of God that Eddy will not find cause to run away again."

"With that promise, Mr. Mitchell, I will agree to send Eddy back with you today but I will be in touch with Mr. Parsons to make sure that Eddy is doing much better."

"I thank you and I must take my leave soon. There are still chores to be done at the farm before sundown."

"I will call Eddy in to clean up. He has only one set of clothes and they are hand me downs from my son but surely he has a wardrobe at your home."

"Yes, of course.

Eddy was summoned from the garden, freshened up and ushered into the parlour. His face was flushed and he was visibly shaken at seeing his nemesis nursing the last sips of the welcome tea. Eddy couldn't believe his eyes when he saw his master seated in the parlour acting every inch the concerned citizen and foster parent. Standing there, he didn't know whether to be polite or rush out of the room. He shivered as he thought about Mr. Mitchell but he knew that there was nothing he could do. From the moment his mother had dropped him unceremoniously at the door of the Dr. Barnardo home in London, his life had been controlled by others and he could only do as he was told. Outside of dear Mrs. Mitchell, he could not remember a single kind word, a smile of encouragement or a thank you when the job assigned had been done well. Mr. Mitchell had never gone to a single school concert even when he knew that Eddy was reciting a poem. He had never spoken a word of praise at Eddy's school achievements and then, when Eddy turned twelve, he insisted that he leave school and devote all his time to farm work- slave work really. In the last few years with his friends at school and him at the farm, he felt abandoned and alone. Only when he ran away and found refuge and suitable work did he feel that, perhaps, he could make his own way now. At sixteen, he could find work and a place to stay. He had heard that Toronto had plenty of work for ambitious young lads and he was sure that there was adventure on the high seas. But now, his hated master had presented himself as a man of good standing and had convinced the Inspector that things would be much better in the home where Eddy had lived since the age of eight and that indeed, he would never lose his temper again.

"After all, it was only a misunderstanding over Paris green that led to this state of affairs," he had said to Mr. Parsons.

On seeing Eddy, Mr. Mitchell put down his cup and stood up. He reached out to the boy and offered his hand. Eddy shuffled towards him and tenuously offered his hand well. "It is good to see you, Eddy. Can we be friends?"

This was the first time Mitchell had ever called him Eddy. It was always Tompkins. "Maybe he had changed." Said Eddy to himself.

So, Eddy and Mr. Mitchell said their goodbyes to Mrs. MacDonald and Eddy threw a kiss at Patty and they made their way to the car. The driver who had fallen asleep while waiting suddenly lurched forward and with apologies, opened the door in the front for Mr. Mitchell and the back door for Eddy and they drove out the elegant driveway to the rough road ahead that connected the Mill in Gravenhurst to the farm in Bracebridge.

No words were exchanged except the occasional comment from Mitchell to the driver but it was mainly about directions and a bit about the weather. Eddy sat quietly in the back seat. It seemed no time at all that the car pulled into the farm yard of the Mitchell home. Eddy remembered his long walk in the rain away from this house and he was sure that would be forever. But here he was back uncomfortable and a trite embarrassed. Mrs. Mitchell was standing on the front steps and when the car pulled in, Ethan darted toward the car excited at seeing his pal Eddy back home.

Mrs. Mitchell dressed in a summer afternoon dress reached out to Eddy almost ready to embrace him but she stuck out her hand to welcome him instead. "It's good to see you home, Eddy. We missed you."

"Come and play, Eddy", said Ethan.

Eddy stepped back and looked up to his bedroom in the turret and found himself glad to be at the farm again. But Mr. Mitchell resorting to his old ways so soon said "There's a pile of chores to do, boy, but go in for some supper first."

He turned around and walked over to the driver remembering that he had not paid him. Fumbling in his pocket for some change, he completed the task and hurriedly walked into the house straight upstairs to change into his farm clothes.

Eddy walked in after him with Ethan dancing around him ready for some fun. It hadn't been the same without Eddy and he wasn't the only one who missed him. Jack and Emily had come over three times to inquire about Eddy's whereabouts always getting the same answer.

"He is visiting relatives and will be back soon."

Mrs. Mitchell could not bring herself to say what really happened. She didn't want the whole neighbourhood talking but Jack and Emily knew that Eddy had no relatives in Canada. They were sure of that. Eddy was happy to sit at the kitchen table and Mrs. Mitchell fussed over him with an ice-cream cone, his favourite, after he had chomped down a hearty bowl of soup and a beef sandwich piled high with lettuce from the garden.

"Now that you are home, Eddy, you'll need to get into your overalls since there are chores to finish before you go to bed. You don't mind, do you?"

"No, Mrs. Mitchell, I was employed weeding the garden and mowing the lawn at the MacDonald's home. They paid me mill wages too. I'll see to the chickens first. Old rooster will be glad to see me."

Chapter 43: Catching up with friends who went to war.

Eddy settled back quite surprisingly to the farm. It must have been the familiarity. The brown mare nestled up against his cheek and the draft horses seemed especially glad to see him. Even old rooster crowed louder.

Jack arrived the next day and they went up to the woods and sat in their cabin and talked over the past few days. Jack talked about his brother and sister who wrote that there was talk that the war would soon be over. Amos had been advanced to the rank of Lieutenant and was engaged in combat more times than he dared to count. Clara was stationed in a hospital somewhere in Belgium. She had fallen in love with an American army doctor not long arrived in Europe to join the war effort. She talked of an engagement and a wedding in her hometown when it was all over.

"And while we're talking about the war, Jack. How's the German boys, Hans and Felix? Since I haven't been in school, I don't get to see anyone."

"They never went back to school because they were needed on the farm. They've been keeping to themselves. There's been too much talk of the negative kind and they have just kept out of the way."

"Gosh, that's too bad. I hated Hans at first but I quite like him now. Did you know he taught me to jump up on a box car? You never know, Jack, we might meet up one of these days on freight."

"Not that again, Eddy. Get your head out of the clouds or should I say away from trains."

Somehow, Eddy and Jack were drifting apart. Their worlds were moving in different directions. How Eddy longed to be back at school and it ached when he talked to his friend Jack who was moving ahead in his life towards a goal with his family right behind him.

Eddy knew a bit more about the boys from the Gibson farm and it was worrying that Jonathon was still unaccounted for and considered 'missing in action.' There had been no word from him since April 1915 and it was now October 1918.

But the fighting continued even though both sides were bogged down in mud and carnage. People were weary back home. Waiting for word from loved ones on the front was exhausting and deeply depressing. Jack's parents were exhausted. "Mum looks tired and she's spending a lot of time in her room sometimes not getting her daily chores done and you know how we all depend on her. I shouldn't complain. I'm old enough to get my own lunch but I'm so used to Mum happy in the kitchen singing. I can't stand it when she's quiet."

After taking this break up in the makeshift cabin they had built what seemed like years ago, they started back down to the farm. Eddy had to get back to the afternoon barn work and Jack was needed back at his house. He was studying for the entrance exams at the University of Toronto and hoping to get into the Engineering Faculty.

Later that day, he walked up to Grandma Gibson's. At 16, he was given a bit more freedom especially now with Mr. Parsons looking in on him more often. And even as he walked along the road to the Gibson house his thoughts went back to the last time he had seen the inspector. In fact when Mr. Parsons had visited in early September, they had all sat down together in the parlour- Mr. and Mrs. Mitchell, Mr. Parsons and Eddy. "How are things with you, Eddy, and do speak the truth?" he had said.

He wanted to say that he was still not happy and that he hated working on the farm but he couldn't bring himself to complain in front of Mrs. Mitchell. She had been so very kind to him and it partly made up for Mitchell's continued aloofness and coldness towards him. And he didn't imagine that, at all.

Mr. Parsons had been cautioned by his immediate supervisor to assess the situation correctly. In a recent letter, he had said," *If the boy is contented and Mitchell renews his promise to abstain from any rough treatment in the future, there is no object in removing him, but you will be careful not to let him imagine himself a martyr or injured here, but let him understand that we strongly disapprove his conduct in running away, especially when you had so shortly before visited him, and, presumably, he had, an opportunity of making a complaint of the treatment he was receiving.*"

Recalling that afternoon, he had said "I am doing quite well, thank you."

"What do you mean by that, Eddy? Are you satisfied with the way things are between you and Mr. Mitchell?"

Mr. Mitchell had shuffled in his seat looking quite uncomfortable. He had looked across the room and caught Eddy's eye. Eddy began to sweat shifting in his seat and awkwardly blurted out.

"Yes, it's okay, Mr. Parsons. He does the best he can, I guess."

"What is your position, Mr. Mitchell? Is the boy living up to the expectations of his contract?"

Partly stammering, he said, "Yes, he works hard but I wouldn't say that this is what he wants to do. He'll have time to figure it out after he turns 21."

"Well, I guess I'll have to agree with you on that. So, Eddy, I expect you to be civil, work hard at the tasks assigned and try to be more content with your circumstances. You are getting room and board and a chance at a future when your time here is complete. Is there anything else you want to say?"

"Yes, I would like to go back to school and try the entrance exams for college."

"It's a bit late for that. You have not been in higher education since the age of 12 and you are now 16. We can't change that."

"I guess not." Eddy said with a certain resignation but in his heart he wanted a different future and it wasn't to be especially as long as he lived in this place.

"Thank you, Mr. and Mrs. Mitchell. I will come by in late November. Let's hope there will be some good news from the home front by then. It doesn't look good though, does it?"

"Nice to talk to you, Eddy. See you in November."

"See you then, Mr. Parsons. Goodbye."

Back from his reverie and walking up the pathway to Grandma Gibson's, he spotted Emily in the window. She was wearing her maid's outfit and with her auburn hair pulled back and tied in a neat knot; she looked prettier than he could remember. Looking up and spying Eddy, she waved wildly and beckoned him to hurry up.

Eddy skipped a beat and he practically fell into the foyer after reaching the door.

Grandma Gibson greeted him with a big hug saying, "Good to see you, Eddy. I hope you have settled back in. We missed you."

"Good to see you, Grandma Gibson. I missed you too."

"Come on into the kitchen. The cookie jar was just filled this afternoon. Emily's becoming quite a cook and she made cookies with apple filling figuring you might come by."

"I can smell them from here. Mmm."

"Take a seat. I'll call Emily. She's been busy putting up the newly washed curtains in the parlour."

Eddy helped himself to the cookie jar and found the one he was hoping for- Emily's cookie which was still warm. Emily hurried into the kitchen and sat herself down beside Eddy on the kitchen bench. She took off her apron and fussed up her hair a little but she didn't remove the bun.

"Hi Emily. Long time no see. How have you bin?"

"I'm okay. I guess."

"It's better than okay Emily." interrupted Mrs. Gibson. "We have heard from Randolph. He said 'We're putting the Germans on the run and right now we're in Bourlon Wood. That won't mean anything to you but we are mighty close to the Hindenburg line. But the most important news is that there's word on Jonathon through the Red Cross. He's in a Prisoner of War Camp and he is doing alright now after a German doctor tended to his wounds but they're not sure if they can save his leg.' Our prayers have been answered and he's alive. We are praying that his leg will heal. God willing, the war must end."

Emily put her head down trying to cover the tears that ran down her cheeks. Eddy was happy for her even though he secretly wished Emily would pay more attention to him.

As far as Emily was concerned, Eddy was her brother. She never saw him any other way even though she was sure Eddy was sweet on her. They had come from the same place. They had both been in a Dr. Barnardo home left there by a parent desperate to find them a place while they searched for answers for themselves. They had both travelled across the ocean landing in Bracebridge back in 1910. Eddy wished he were as content as she was but he had a restless spirit and wanted to travel on those big freight trains. He wanted to jump on the box cars and never look back.

 Emily wanted to be married and she dreamed of a house with flowers and a white picket fence. She was already gathering her trousseau of embroidered handkerchiefs and parlour cloths which she had embroidered herself. She learned that when she lived at the Girls Home in Essex not far from London and she kept them in her Barnardo trunk in one corner of her small bedroom in the Gibson attic. She thought about Jonathon every day and now that she knew he was in a prisoner of war camp and had been assured that the Red Cross would see to it that all Canadian prisoners would be treated humanely, she waited for his return. He had told her he wanted to marry her when she was barely a little girl.

Emily and Eddy spent the afternoon together talking away as they always did about everything but it was chore time and Eddy had to pull himself away.

"So good to see you Emily. I am sure Jonathon will be home soon. Don't you fret."

I'll see you at church, okay."

"See you then Eddy. Good bye."

Chapter 44: A crisis

Eddy had barely entered the driveway on his way home from the Gibson's when Mitchell met him with a clout across the face. "What the hell are you playing at, Tompkins? Nothin's been done and you gallivanting about the country."

Eddy turned and ran back to the dirt road shaken and embarrassed all at once.

"I swear I won't stay here but I want my wages so I'll have to grin and bear it for now", he said to himself as he wiped the dirt off his face. Picking himself up out of the despair and anger he felt, he walked back and confronted his master. "Sorry, sir, I forgot the time. I'll get to my chores right away. Sorry."

"Yes, you better, Tompkins. I've had enough. Do you hear me boy?"

And so, Eddy went to the barn, snuggled up against his horse chums, and methodically started picking up the pitchfork to clean out the stall. He could do it without thinking but his mind behind the chores was working overtime, planning how to get away for good.

Mrs.Mitchell was learning to keep her own counsel. She could see that Eddy was just going through the motions where his work was concerned. She had not been able to get through to her husband that he had a responsibility to Eddy even if only to adhere to the Indenture agreement and they had had a good meeting with Mr. Parsons back in September.

Ethan just wanted Eddy to play with him and tell him jokes and maybe take him for a walk to the woods. But Eddy kept his head down and said very little. Mealtime was always silent but there was a tension there now which made everyone uneasy.

"Can we play after supper?" asked Ethan.

"No time for that!" mumbled Mitchell glancing over at his wife.

"I best be off. May I be excused? The chickens need doing. Want to help me Ethan" suggested Eddy. They chatted the evening away with chores and that made Ethan happy and Mrs. Mitchell content.

November arrived with an early winter storm and at 4 that morning Eddy was up as usual getting the fires started, fetching the water and putting on the kettle. Mitchell was up early himself. "You've got to get out there and do some shoveling before anything can be done."

Eddy gritted his teeth and set to work to do as he was told. His winter boots were too small and they had not bought him new ones but he pushed them on and struggled with his toes pinched. The minute he got outside, he could feel the frost biting at him and he knew what frost bite was like. He tried to shovel but it was too much and he grabbed the fence post and hopped back into the kitchen.

"Hey, boy, get back out there. Do you hear me?"

"I can't. My boots are too tight."

"Okay, take mine. They are a bit big but with an extra pair of socks, they should work."

Eddy tried them on and they were far too big but he knew he could not defy his boss. His hand swipes were getting frequent and he was sick and tired of being yelled at. Out he went again but instead of shoveling, he hobbled across the field in the blinding snow to Jack's house.

On arriving, Jack's mother met him and blurted out, "Eddy, what are you doing out in the snow? You'll get your death of cold."

"I've got work to do but I need boots that fit me. Can you spare a pair of Jack's?"

"Come in and sit by the fire. I'm sure we can muster up some boots that fit."

It didn't take long to find boots that fit and two pairs of winter socks that would fit the boots perfectly. After drinking a cup of cocoa, Eddy mustered up the energy to venture out. The temperature was now above freezing sufficient for the snow to turn to rain.

"Be careful as you cross the field, Eddy. Mind you, we'll be watching you until you get there. Hope to see you soon."

"Thanks. I appreciate everything."

He picked up his heels and strode across the field arriving at the house a bit past noon. Mr. Mitchell must have been inside so Eddy picked up the shovel and shoveled off what was left of the snow. It had turned to slush and harder to lift but he managed it anyway. He crept around to the front of the house, pushed the door open and without a sound, he took off his boots and sneaked up the stairs to his room. He threw off his wet clothes and jumped into bed. The last thing he wanted this day was any confrontation with his boss. He was too tired to do another lick of work so hiding out was the best he could do.

The morning of the 6th of November dawned bright and cheerful. Even though Eddy had been up and about with his chores before light, Mr. Mitchell came thundering down from upstairs in a fit of rage. "Where the hell were you yesterday? I saw that you shoveled off the path. Then you disappeared. The wife thought you might have gone to Jack's but when she telephoned they said you had come to get some boots and then left in the rain.

I can't have this Tompkins. Either you're gonna work or you better get the hell out."

"I fell asleep."

"What? You fell asleep?"

"I was tired from shoveling all that snow and not having any boots except those awful big boots you gave me, I hiked over to Jack's to see if they could lend me a pair that fit."

"How dare you embarrass me like that?"

"I just needed boots that worked, sir."

Walking up close to the boy, Mitchell almost spat in his face when he said, "You've been nothing but trouble to me from the first day you stepped into this house."

Eddy backed away inching his way to the door and then with a slam Eddy leaped out onto the porch, grabbed his borrowed boots, coat and scarf and bolted out the yard heading he didn't know where. He ran off down the field and started walking up the tracks hoping the freight train would round the bend and slow down almost to a halt. He didn't wait long and as the freight slowed down, he ran alongside, grabbed the rail and pulled himself up. When he got to the top of the box car, he inched his way to a place where he could sit and ride along.

It was not as cold as the day before and the sun was shining bright and welcoming. He held tight and finding himself riding north, he decided he'd get off at the next town. The big engine began to slow after climbing through the rocky terrain of the Muskoka's, finally coming to a halt in Huntsville. Eddy jumped off before they got into the station and scrambling down he found his way to the town.

He was up for a new adventure except he didn't have a penny in his pocket and he didn't know a soul. After wondering the main street, he came to a small café and sat at a table near the window. The lady who served the tables came over and said "What can I do for you boy? Want a cup of tea?"

Eddy pretended to fumble in his pocket for some spare change. The lady could see that he was lost, broke and hungry. Saying nothing, she went into the kitchen bringing back a bowl of hot chicken soup, some bread and a cup of tea.

"Thanks awfully, Ma'am but I ain't got no money."

"Don't you worry about that. Jus' you dig in."

Eddy gobbled down the soup and devoured the bread and then sat wondering what to do next as he sipped his tea. Thanking the kind lady, he bowed his head and left. Up and down the street he walked looking at the store windows, sometimes going in to get warm and then leaving to walk some more. Before long it was dusk and he went back to the café. He looked for the lady in the white apron with the big smile but she was not there. Instead was a man who looked as though he owned the place. "We're closing in ten minutes. Hurry up and order, boy."

"Sorry, I ain't got no money."

"No money. What are you doing here? Where'd you come from?"

"I ain't sayin'," Eddy hesitated.

"Sit here, boy. Here's a cup of tea to warm you."

With that, he went into the back room and called the police. "I've got a vagrant here. What do you want me to do with him?"

"I'll be right over."

Next thing, there was a tall burly policeman coming in the door. Eddy sat up with a start. The owner met the village copper and brought him over to Eddy who by now was shivering in fright. "Maybe, they reported me for hoppin' on the train." he thought.

"Hey, lad, what's your name and where you from?"

"I, I ran away, sir. I got scared he was goin' to hit me again."

"Who is going to hit you?"

"My boss, Mr. Mitchell. He has a wild temper and he's been mad at me for days. I just can't do anything right."

"Now, enough of that. What's your name?"

"Eddy, sir."

"Your full name!"

"Edward George Tompkins."

"How old are you?"

"I'm 16."

"Come with me and we'll find you a place to stay for the night. And then, we'll sort this out in the morning."

The policeman wasn't new to runaways like this. He figured the boy had to be a home boy. This was about the age they rebelled and tried to get away. He knew he was indentured and under obligation to work until the term of employment agreed to be completed. He also was aware that sometimes they just couldn't stay.

They walked a few blocks until they came to a Boarding house the police used in cases such as this one. The building was made of brick and it was three stories high. It was a guest hotel for travelers from out of town but some locals stayed there receiving room and board. The policeman knocked on the door and was met by a stout woman probably in her fifties. She wore a grey wool skirt that reached to her ankles, a white blouse and a dark cardigan. Her grayish brown hair was tied in a bun and in a no nonsense voice she said, "Why, Bill, who have you brought me tonight?"

"His name is Edward, Mrs. Carson. The poor kid's been wondering around all day and except for the kind generosity of Jane at the café earlier, he hasn't eaten a thing all day."

"Come on in. We'll find him a bed for the night and I'll make him up a sandwich. He'll get breakfast first thing in the morning."

"Thanks, Mrs. Carson. I'll be by in the morning after I make a few phone calls. It's too late to reach anyone tonight."

"Be a good boy, Edward. I'll see you in the morning."

The landlady sat Eddy down in the foyer while she scrambled to find him a room. She managed one in the servant's quarters since she had a full house of boarders and travelers. After settling him and bringing him a dressing gown, she brought him a thick pork sandwich and a large glass of milk.

"Goodnight, Edward."

Eddy sat on the side of the bed and ate the sandwich and gulped down the milk. He hadn't thought much about what he was doing but he just knew he couldn't go back to the Mitchell's ever. He was too tired to think much and he hadn't a clue what was in store for him. He slumped down in bed and dreamed of trains.

Chapter 45: The end of an indenture

On the morning after placing Eddy at the Boarding House Hotel with Mrs. Carson, there was a meeting at the Police Station. The police officer who looked after the situation sat down with the Chief of Police to discuss Eddy's case.

"Now, Bill", said the Chief. "We have a difficult case here and we have to tread carefully. We will have to inform Mr. Mitchell that we have the boy here after picking him up as a vagrant and at the same time, we have to let the Dr. Barnardo Inspector know what's happened."

"We've done this before Chief Murray and there is a procedure."

"Oh, yes, but these matters are delicate especially in this case. Mr. Mitchell is a town councillor in Bracebridge and as such he commands a great deal of respect. At the same time, judging from what you say of the boy's appearance and fear of returning to the house, we have to tread carefully."

"The boy is in a bad way, chief, and I have no doubt that he has been roughly treated."

"I will call Mr. Parsons at the Toronto home right away. I'll contact Mitchell afterwards."

In the meantime down at the Hotel, Mrs. Carson woke Eddy up with a start. "Gosh, boy, it's getting late. You slept in. Come along and have some breakfast."

Rubbing his eyes and squirming in the oversized night attire, Eddy sat up with a jolt. It took him a minute to realize he wasn't in his loft bedroom at the farm and this was not Mitchell staring at him in disgust. "Uhuh, Give me a minute and I'll get dressed."

Looking at the pile of dirty clothes on the bed, Mrs. Carson was shocked to see just how badly he was dressed. "Give me a minute, boy. Eddy I mean. I've got to muster up some clothes for you. You can't go out with those on. Go ahead out to the kitchen in your night shirt. Cook will look after you there."

It wasn't the first time she had to find clothes for someone. Enough immigrants were landing in Huntsville these days with just the clothes on their back. Mind you, the boy was small for his age. Luckily, there was a shop two doors down and she knew the owner well. Indeed, he was her first cousin. She hurried to the shop, walked in, gave the particulars to the young lady at the counter and asked to speak to her cousin who was in the stock room.

A few words were all that was needed and an outfit of underwear, socks, a pair of trousers, a shirt and a sweater were quickly assembled and in no time, she had walked back to the hotel and summoned Eddy from the kitchen to try on the clothes. He had eaten a hearty breakfast and was having a chat with the cook.

Everything fitted and Eddy felt like a new boy. Even the colours were perfect for him especially the navy blue sweater and the dark pants. Mrs. Carson told him to sit in the parlour. She gave him a book of Indian Tales to read and she went about her daily routine waiting for the police officer, her friend, Bill, to come by.

Back at the Police Station, Chief Murray had reached Mr. Parsons by phone. It wasn't the first time he had spoken to him about such matters. "Good morning, Mr. Parsons. Good I could reach you. The operator took some time to make the connection but here we are. Now, I'll get right to the point. My sergeant found a boy wondering the streets yesterday."

"That's Huntsville, right?" said Mr. Parsons.

"That's right, sir. His name is Edward George Tompkins and he's run away from his foster family, The Mitchell's. He says, He's not been used right. He said, he's been beaten and he couldn't stand it no more."

"Give me a minute to look into my files, chief."

"Okay, I'll hold."

The operator came in with, "Have you finished your call?"

"No, no. Give us a minute."

"All right but you can't hold up the line indefinitely."

"I'm back, Chief. Yes, we know Edward. He ran away last summer. I'll have one of my staff located in Huntsville go to fetch him and take him back to the house."

"Do you think that's a good idea, Mr. Parsons." answered the Chief.

"We have to see what Mitchell has to say and given the circumstances, I would ask you to keep the boy with you for now. He is staying at Mrs. Carson's Boarding House. Right? We will contact her and we will pick up the cost of his stay for the time being."

"Will do, Mr. Parsons. We'll stay in touch."

Bill went immediately to the Wayfarer's Hotel to check in with Mrs. Carson. It was only a block away. As soon as he arrived, he was ushered in by the doorman, actually Mrs. Carson's husband. He performed this task during peak times and today was particularly busy.

"Why, hello, Bill. What can I do for you?"

"Hi there, old boy, I've come to see your wife who is boarding a runaway, Eddy by name."

"Sure thing, Come on in."

He was led to the parlour where he found Eddy gazing out the window.

His loud," Hi there, Eddy." startled him. Eddy quickly turned around and immediately stood at attention.

"Good morning, sir."

At that, Mrs. Carson entered the room and summoned her friend Bill to sit opposite her by the fireplace. It was a well furnished room with overstuffed chairs, a few walnut tables and the windows were adorned with burgundy velveteen drapery.

"You can sit at the table by the window, Eddy. We have some things to talk over."

"Well, how did the boy spend the night?" said the policeman.

"He slept well but come morning when I realized that he didn't have suitable clothes for this time of year, I rounded up an outfit for him at the local clothing shop, you know Cousin O'Leary's. I owe him $5.25."

"Thank you. The Inspector Mr. Parsons who is in charge of the Barnardo migrants told us this morning that he will cover all expenses, both the boy's room and board and any other expenses incurred."

"Now, an agent for the Dr. Barnardo Institute in Toronto who lives in Bracebridge will be calling on Mr. Mitchell today to discuss the boy's future so I would ask a favour of keeping him with you until further word."

"Fortunately, a better room has opened up because one of my travelers had to leave earlier than expected. So we can keep Eddy for a few more days. I'll put the boy to work doing odd jobs around the house. That way, he'll keep busy and out of mischief. Mind you, I have no cause to worry. He seems like a very polite young man. He's had some good training."

"Thanks a lot. I'll keep in touch."

"Yes, for sure. I'll see you out."

………………………………...……

Back at the Mitchell farm, Mrs. Mitchell paced the floor. She maintained her outward dignity dressing for the possibility of a visitor later in the day. It had been a very difficult day when she discovered that Eddy was missing. She thought that he was settling in and she had heard from her mother that he had had a special visit with her and Emily just a couple of days ago.

"What happened between you and Eddy, Charles? I knew that you expected more than he was prepared to give but I thought you were keeping your temper in check."

"Look, when I saw him yesterday morning acting as though nothing had happened, it got my dander up. He'd been missing all afternoon and evening with not so much as an explanation. I confronted him and he just bolted out the door. He landed in Huntsville and was found wondering the streets like a tramp ending up in a café looking for food. After the police were called by the café proprietor, the Chief of Police called me and then Mr. Parsons called right after. They're sending a visitor from Bracebridge to talk this over this afternoon. I've a mind to tell him or her that I've had enough of this and I'd sooner he was gone."

"Oh, Charles, what a pity. Eddy had such promise but I know he has been very morose lately. He keeps to himself and even avoids little Ethan."

After the police officer had left the Hotel, Mrs. Carson took Eddy into the dining room for a bit of lunch. "Eddy, you'll be staying here a bit. I've a better room for you tonight on the second floor. I'll get one of the maids to show you to your room later. In the meantime, I have a few chores for you to do. It's one way to pay your room and board. You can start in the kitchen helping with the dishes."

"Thanks Miss. I'll be glad to do some work inside."

At 3 o'clock, there was a knock on the Mitchell's door and arriving was a Mr. Johnson, bank clerk and agent of the Dr. Barnardo Institute. This was a job that he sometimes had to do- check on the circumstances in certain of the foster homes. He had been sent by Mr. Parsons to meet with the Mitchell's and to inform them of Edward's whereabouts and to meet with the family. He had not met the boy but he had been told that the boy had run away because of the harsh treatment he had received at Mitchell's hands.

Mrs. Mitchell greeted him at the door and invited him in through the foyer to the parlour. Her husband reached out to shake his hand and bid him to sit down.

"Good afternoon. My name is Mr. Johnson. I am a teller at the branch bank of the Canadian Bank of Commerce but I am also employed on a part time basis with the Dr. Barnardo Institute in Toronto. I am here to see about Edward Tompkins, a ward of yours I understand."

"Yes, he is but we've been having a lot of trouble with him lately. As you well know, he ran off yesterday."

"Yes, that's why I'm here. He's staying at the Wayfarers Hotel, under the Chief of Police's authority. He told the Chief that he ran away because he could never do anything right in your employ and that you were reprimanding him continuously."

"Look, he's in an Indenture Contract and money is set aside at the Canadian Imperial Bank of Commerce in Toronto. I pay that religiously and I expect him to work for his wages."

"Yes, but there is an expectation that he will be treated fairly."

"I do my best, sir, but the boy is insolent and lazy. Quite frankly, I'd rather be rid of him permanently."

"Under the circumstances, Mr. Mitchell, I think it best that the boy stay in Huntsville for the time being. I have taken enough of your time. I will report back to Mr. Parsons and he'll be in touch with you."

Mrs. Mitchell who had remained silent now spoke up. "We've had Eddy with us since he was 8. There's been some good times but sadly Eddy has changed. He wanted to be educated but it wasn't to be. I hope we haven't failed him."

"I understand, Mrs. Mitchell. We've had some other boys and girls who were desperate to get away and maybe search for their families back in England. There's been a lot of talk in Parliament about this migrant scheme and we're seeing some of the results right here in Muskoka. Try to rest easy. I am sure it will all work out for the best for all of you."

"I best be off. Thank you for your time."

With a bow, Mr. Johnson, a young man himself, made his way to the door. "Good afternoon. But as he left, he noticed that the boy's trunk and his bicycle were on the porch. "Looks like they are getting ready to ship him out.

Chapter 46: Leaving the farm forever

When Mr. Johnson returned to Bracebridge he immediately contacted Mr. Parsons. It was clear from his limited knowledge of the Mitchell household that Mr. Mitchell was tired of dealing with Edward and it was clear from Bill, the police officer and from Eddy himself that it was not a good idea to try and enforce his return to the home.

Mr. Johnson had further concluded that it was a sad case all around. The home was comfortable and homey and Mrs. Mitchell warm and caring. In Johnson's mind, it seemed to be a case of a boy and a man who could not see eye to eye. He wanted to give Mitchell the benefit of the doubt. He reminded himself that this was a boy taken away from his family in London, thrust in a large home for boys, sent out to the Dominion and forced to work on a farm and a case of a hard working but bitter farmer who without sons of his own was forced to rely on someone foreign and alien to him even though they were both of British stock. Mr. Mitchell was a hard man and being a staunch Calvinist he believed in the Hebrew words "Spare the rod and spoil the child." He saw no harm in his mode of discipline never for once thinking about the child's feelings. Not once did Mitchell think about the boy as a member of his family. In his eyes, Edward would always be an indentured servant.

He mused that Eddy was simply one of several thousand children who had arrived in Canada under these various schemes. Propelled by zealous believers who thought that the only solution for poor children was to remove them from their families, from the orphanages, from the workhouses or from the streets and send them to farms where they would breathe clean air and learn how to be farmers or domestics. Canada needed them and England couldn't look after them.

So, Mark Johnson sat down at his desk and picked up the phone. The operator said it might be a few minutes to get through because the lines were busy but when she did, Mr. Parsons answered and said, "Glad we could get in touch Mr. Johnson. Now, what's the news on Edward Tompkins?"

"I've been out to the house. The Police Chief did not feel we should try and force the boy to return to the Mitchell household so I went out alone. After spending a good half hour there, I have concluded that it is best that we locate another placement."

"I have come to the same conclusion. I am presently working on another client who might be willing to take Eddy into his employ. Goodness only knows that there are many applicants for farm boys but one can never be sure of a good fit and Eddy has reached the age when it's hard to teach him especially if he is sick and tired of farm chores."

"So, what do you want me to do now?"

"Ask the good lady at the hotel if she can accommodate Eddy until we either get him a place or decide to send him back to Jarvis Street where he lived when he first arrived in Canada at the age of 8. Inform her that we will take care of all expenses."

"Okay, Mr. Parsons. I will see to it. It will take another day because I'll have to take the train up to Huntsville."

"I suggest that you stay at the hotel overnight. I am sure Mrs. Carson can put you up. We'll cover your costs and give you a stipend for your efforts."

"Thank you. I'll telephone you when I arrive."

"Good old chap. Thanks."

Meanwhile back at the hotel, Eddy had been put to work cleaning off the sidewalk in front of the premises with a promise of a good supper in the dining room afterwards. Eddy was tasting freedom for the first time in his life. He had broken free of his shackles, so he said, and he could only see bright days ahead in spite of having no money.

His chore finished, he wondered up the street and peered through the shop windows. He wished he had taken his bike so he could really explore. That bike was new to him. It's one that the old farm hand had given him. "I can't use it anymore. You might as well have it", he said.

Returning to the hotel, he was met by the senior maid who promptly took him to his new room on the second floor. It had a little sink where he could freshen up. He quickly changed from his old clothes to the new ones he had been given this morning. "Supper will be served shortly. You'll hear the dinner bell and come down quickly when you hear it. The grub goes fast when there are a lot of mouths to feed."

Eddy was hungry and he hardly waited for Grace to be said before he dug in. He enjoyed sitting with the other guests at the hotel. It was a far cry from the Mitchell table where hardly a word was said. Everyone talked and every once in a while someone would look Eddy's way and inquire after him. It didn't amount to much more than, "What's up?" or "Where do you come from- I detect a bit of an accent." Eddy answered in brief sentences and continued eating.

Two days passed and Eddy was put to work sweeping the floors, washing dishes with Cook or helping the maids carry wood for the wood stoves. He was content to do it. Mrs. Carson was friendly and the maids especially the younger of them were not only pretty but kind as well.

Time did not hang over him. Life was timeless. He was still not sure what he was doing or what would happen to him but he knew that he would never be under anyone's thumb ever again. He even liked getting up early to help cook prepare breakfast. He was the toast maker this morning using a special rack that he laid on the stove. When the bread was browned on both sides, he plastered each slice with farm fresh butter and piled them on a large platter before putting them in the warming oven before the guests arrived.

It was 7 o'clock when an announcement cut into the daily programme on the Radio. This announcement is coming to you from London.

"The *War is Over! The armistice has been signed. It was signed at 5 o'clock am, Paris time, and hostility will cease at 11 o'clock this morning, Paris time.*"

It was 7 o'clock in Huntsville. Cook jumped up and down with the ladle in her hand that she was using to scoop out the porridge in a large bowl. "The war is over. It's finally over. Praise be to God."

Over breakfast, the talk was all about the War. Everybody had someone overseas. All Eddy could think of were Jack's brother Amos and his sister, Clara and Jonathon and Randolph, Grandma Gibson's home boys. Emily must be dancing with joy and Jack's family must be so excited. They would all be coming home whole except for Jonathon who had lost his right leg.

Church bells were ringing all over town and out in Eddy's church too. Shop keepers were already putting up Union Jacks and there was talk of a town gathering in the Square. Canada's soldiers and Canada's nurses would be arriving soon, they said and what a celebration they would have on the day the train carrying their heroes arrived.

Of all things, this was the day that Mr. Johnson arrived at the hotel after taking the train from Bracebridge. Mr. Carson met him at the door and led him to the Reception Area. The celebration brandy had gone to his head.

"My good lady wife will attend to the details and I'll ask the Cook to make you a cup of tea or would you rather a shot of whiskey, Ha. Ha!"

Mrs. Carson walked into the Foyer to greet him. She was the only one who could walk without giggling. "Please sign the book, Mr. Johnson. From your call earlier, I see that you are here on Edward Tompkins' behalf at the request of Mr. Parsons, the superintendent of the Barnardo children in the Muskoka Region. How long do you wish to stay?'

Oh, just overnight but I will ask that you pack up Edward's belongings such as they are, since we are travelling to Toronto on the late morning train tomorrow. "Oh, that's rather sudden. We were getting rather fond of the boy. He has an infectious smile and my husband has really taken to him. Oh, well, it's for the best I suppose. By the way, have you had your dinner?"

"No, I'm afraid I have not."

"Very well. Dinner will be served at 5 o'clock but let me show you your room first. Of course, you will want to meet Edward this afternoon."

"Yes".

So Mr. Johnson went to his room, freshened up and then returned to the parlour where Eddy was waiting for him having been summoned by the Landlady. Eddy sat very still with his back straight and his arms folded. He wore the new clothes again. He knew this might be an important meeting.

Mark Johnson walked towards him and thrust out his hand. "Hello. You must be Edward. I'm Mark Johnson. You can call me Mark."

"Hi."

"Now, I'll get right to the point Edward. I've been talking to the Mitchell's. Mr. Mitchell is quite fed up with you. It's the second time, you have run away. He says he thought things were going well since the Summer but that you have been less willing to work and more difficult. Is this so?"

"I hate it there except for Mrs. Mitchell and Ethan. Mitchell always finds fault with me. I can never suit him and he yells all the time."

"Has he ever hit you?"

"Oh, yea, many times. He's got big hands and it hurts when he gives me a back hand across my face. I never know when it's coming. It's like an exclamation mark."

"I'm sorry to hear that, Edward."

"I don't ever want to go back. Ever, please?"

"You won't have to. Tomorrow, we are boarding the train for Toronto. You will be returning to the Barnardo home on Jarvis Street where you stayed when you first came to Canada. We tried to get you another placement in Roxboro but it didn't work out. The farmer withdrew his application for a farm boy at the last minute so we had to change our plans. Your trunk and your belongings are being shipped on the train and should arrive at the same time as we do. Do you remember Toronto?

"Kind of but not much."

"So, it's settled then. Let's go to dinner."

They walked in together, Mark in his business suit and Eddy dressed in well ironed trousers and navy blue sweater to join their fellow lodgers. The other guests were seated at a circular oak table covered with a crisp white tablecloth. The senior maid took pride in her ironing. They were served a roast beef supper with all the trimmings followed by apple pie with assorted cheeses.

Mrs. Carson fussed over her guests and attended to each and every need. She was the best hostess in town. No wonder her hotel was always full to capacity. She took special care of Eddy making sure he had more milk and more pie than anyone else. Eddy was the centre of attention after Mark told the group that Eddy was going to the big city tomorrow. Eddy was sure to find the pot of gold on Spadina Avenue, they said.

Now, back at the Mitchell's, they were seated at the kitchen table when Charles Mitchell took out the letter he had received from Mr. Parsons in the afternoon mail. He had been reluctant to share the news with his wife, Mary. "Mary, take Ethan to the library. I don't want him hearing this."

"Come along Ethan. Let's get Robinson Crusoe down from the shelf. Do you remember how Eddy loved to read that to you?"

When she returned, she moved over to be close to the kitchen stove. The room was cold and the temperature outside close to freezing. Her husband joined her in the straight backed chair. She sat on the Windsor chair to face him.

"Well, here it is......

Toronto, November 12, 1918
To: Mr. Charles Mitchell
Re: Edward George Tompkins

Dear Sir:

I have duly received your letter, and about the same time a communication from the Chief of Police in Huntsville informing us that this boy was under his charge having been found wandering about. It is *evidently useless our attempting to force his return to you and he has been brought down by one of our agents and is here at the present time. I am afraid the only thing now remaining is to make a settlement with you for the time he has been in your employ and to ask you to send down, with the least possible delay, the trunk and belongings that I presume he left behind him. I note that in accordance with the agreement. the sum of $51.25 is due from you and this amount you will kindly remit to our Bankers here, making use of the printed form and addressed envelope that you will find enclosed herewith. Yours faithfully,*

    Mr. Parsons

Charles looked up from the letter to find his wife's face awash in tears. "I guess that's the end of that, Mary, and we'll be better without the fuss."

She stood up and walked away.

Chapter 47: In Toronto again

It was the morning after the announcement that the war was over. The celebrations went on until the wee hours. The townspeople had waited so long for this. Many families waited with anticipation for their sons to come home but others wept because their boys and 2 nurses from the town who had gone overseas would not be coming back. They would be forever somewhere in France or Belgium.

Mrs. Carson woke Eddy up earlier than usual. He had a long day ahead of him and she wanted to make sure he had a bountiful breakfast and a good send off.

"Eddy, it's time to get up."

Stretching and yawning, Eddy sat up in bed and moaned, "Ugh, uha" and turning to sit at the edge of the bed, he sighed, "Wish I could stay here, Mrs. Carson. I was getting to like it a lot."

"It will be alright, Eddy. Toronto is a big city and soon you'll be able to go downtown and see for yourself. It sure is different from the country with all the comings and goings, trams and buggies and model T's. Anyway, get yourself dressed in that new outfit I bought yesterday. This time you have a dark brown cardigan to wear with brown trousers. My cousin says it's a gift because of the way you helped him get the banners up on the shop yesterday instead of skipping out and joining the festivities."

"Gosh, Thanks, Mrs. Carson and please thank your cousin for me."

Eddy dressed quickly and he liked what he saw in the mirror. His dark hair was full and curly and he seemed to have got taller. He was pleased with himself and when he joined everyone in the dining room, he was met with, "Looking dapper, Eddy. "

"Good show, boy" piped up the English gentleman just arrived from London to tour the region. Eddy beamed and sat down to breakfast opposite Mark Johnson, his escort to Toronto.

Afterwards, Mrs. Carson called Eddy aside. She whispered, "Take care of yourself, Eddy, and here's a little something to tide you over. Slipping a $5.00 bill in his pocket, she continued, "Now, don't forget to write me after you settle in."

Eddy reached up and put his arms around her, "Thanks so much, so very much, Mrs. Carson."

"Now, you better get going and get your things. Your bag is packed. My husband had an extra suitcase so it's now yours."

She then went to the Foyer to settle the bill with Mr. Johnson bringing with her a sizeable picnic lunch for himself and Eddy which Cook had prepared. They could buy tea on the train. Mr. Johnson gave her a letter from Mr. Parsons saying that all expenses would be paid by the Dr. Barnardo Institute and that she could expect the cheque covering Eddy's board, his overnight stay and the cost of the clothing and other incidentals in the next week.

Eddy joined them, suitcase in hand. He looked very much a young man in his new winter coat and wool hat also purchased from the shop next door.

Satisfied with the arrangement and pleased that she could accommodate Eddy and Mr. Johnson she bid them both goodbye.

"Thanks for everything, Mrs. Carson", said Mr. Johnson.

"It was a pleasure. Have a good day and a pleasant ride to the big city."

The hired cab was waiting outside to take them to the Station and in no time, they were aboard the big train and in the passenger compartment. Eddy looked around at the plush seats.

"It sure beats a box car" he sighed.

With a lurch, the big engine moved forward and soon it was moving along the tracks with a rhythm that Eddy set to music in his head. He loved the sound, the whistle blowing as they reached Bracebridge and beyond. Through the craggy boulders, past blue lakes and down towards the city, the big engine roared. He thought he caught a glimpse now and then of something he remembered the last time he rode on this great Canadian train. Those thoughts became a dream whereupon, he was sitting in a pub with his parents long ago. His dad was reciting a long poem about a highwayman and the diners around him joined in the refrain.

"The Highwayman came riding, riding, and riding, up to the old inn door" In his dream, he was reciting the poem before a large audience.

The chugging up the steep grade woke him out of his reverie but he soon settled into sleep before the train came to a stop in some station down the tracks. Suddenly awakened but still in a dream state, he remembered the time when he had recited "Hiawatha" and Miss Patterson had been so proud. Where was Miss Patterson now? He had heard that she had returned to her home and was getting married to a young Anglican minister.

Now fully awake, he said, "Why are we stopping?"

"They have to change the engine. We'll be on our way again in no time."

How about some lunch? We've got some goodies here. You wait here and I'll go to the dining car to order some tea. The steward will bring it along in no time."

"I'll go, Mark. I love the way the train moves especially when you go from car to car. You sit there with the newspaper and I'll bring back the tea. I'll tell the steward so he doesn't have to."

The dining car was way in the front so it was quite a journey getting there. He thought of the few times he'd ridden on top. He was glad to be in a cozy car in November but he was sure he would be riding the rails again. He had plans and he wasn't telling anyone. When he got back balancing the tray with the teapot, two cups and the bowl of sugar and the little pitcher of milk, he was amazed that he hardly spilled a drop.

Mark was engrossed in the Morning News. Every page had details about the last battles of the war, the reviews of the Armistice and the sad stories of the boys who died on the last day of fighting. He didn't notice Eddy until Eddy spoke,

"Got our tea. That did some doing but here we are."

Mark took out the picnic lunch packaged in a red and blue quilted bag. There were four sandwiches and oatmeal cookies which Cook had prepared especially. After the first bite, Eddy sputtered, "Great grub."

Mr. Johnson happy to be called Mark for the time being was worried about Eddy. After all, when a boy ran away from his indentured service he was considered a fugitive. He could be put behind bars and yet he was treating this boy as a fellow traveler. He and Parsons had talked it out and they had convinced themselves that he had cause to run away yet they wondered if they were making the right decision. It was the Chief of Police that had put the final stamp on it. And, in truth, they were comfortable with their decision. Mind you Mr. Johnson was worried about what was in store for the boy when he got to Toronto.

Mark and Eddy settled into a bit of small talk and both nodded off to sleep. They had been travelling since 11 o'clock and it was now 4 in the afternoon. The steam engine had picked up speed on its last lap and with a loud whistle, they came into the outskirts of the city.

"We're getting close", said Mark.

Suddenly, Eddy felt scared. He slumped over and tried to suppress tears he knew he couldn't let anyone see. The train slowed down to a crawl and soon they were inside the massive Union Station which people said was like Paddington Station in London but not as big. The glass roof was supported by iron girders and through the grand dome, you could see daylight but it looked cold and uninviting. They could have been in a gigantic cave with stalagmites glistening beneath an opening. Sounds echoed back and forth and people seemed to vanish in the crowds.

They both reached up to grab their suitcases. Putting on their warm coats, they moved to the door and climbed down to the platform. It was a scramble to move through the crowds of women and children, men in business coats and hats, baggage handlers and noisy workers. Before long, pushed along by military police, they finally came out into the late afternoon light now dim with the approach of winter.

They hailed a cab and soon found themselves rocking along the cobbled streets to Jarvis Street and the Toronto home for receiving migrants from the Dr. Barnardo Home in London. Eddy recognized the massive grey house and terror gripped him. He grabbed his throat with his gloved hands and let out a gasp.

"Whatever is wrong, Edward." Mark said, somewhat startled by the boy's reaction.

"Been here before. Hated it."

"I think it will be a short stay. They are looking for another placement for you now that the farmer in Raeburn withdrew his application."

Eddy said nothing in reply. He could only think of escape from this dreaded place and he had no intention of ever farming again.

They were met by the Superintendent and after the rudimentary greetings and assignment to rooms, they entered the dining room for their evening meal. Mark Johnson went separately to a smaller room where the masters were sitting and Eddy was seated in a large hall filled with young boys speaking a foreign tongue which he barely recognized as the Cockney speech he spoke when he first came to Canada.

After the meal, Eddy was taken into the Superintendent's office and there he took his leave of Mark who would be leaving for Bracebridge in the morning. Mark had family a few streets away so he would be staying the night there. Reaching out his hand to Eddy, he said, "Good luck, Edward. I am sure it will all work out for the best. Goodbye."

"Goodbye, Mr. Johnson. We had a good train ride down. Thanks for that."

Eddy turned his back and was about to leave the office when a gruff voice bellowed, "Not so soon, boy. We have some things to talk about. Sit down."

Eddy fidgeted with his thumbs and his knees knocked as he sat waiting for the man to look up from the papers in front of him. The man's name was Dr. Townsend. He was skinny and his face was drawn up in what seemed like a permanent frown. "Uh, huh Mmm," he mumbled as he flipped through the papers and then he spoke in a voice that seemed to come from way down inside him.

"I have before me much that is unsatisfactory. You have been a problem to us for the past 6 months. Mr. Parsons has spent untold hours on your case and now you are with us. Do you understand, Tompkins that you could be sitting in a jail in Huntsville if it weren't for the intervention of the good Mr. Parsons and the Chief of Police who took pity on you?"

"What do you have to say for yourself, boy?"

Eddy's face was red with rage but he dared not show it. "I have nothing to say, sir."

"What do you mean nothing to say?"

"Well, I have plenty to say. You have run away from your obligations on two occasions and you have caused us to spend a great deal of time, personnel and money on you. So, while you are with us, you will work for your keep. Secondly, we intend to place you in another situation as soon as a placement comes available. Thirdly, we expect you to adhere to house rules and make amends. Do you understand?"

Eddy stammered "Yes."

At this, the doctor summoned the housekeeper and she, in turn, took Eddy to the dormitory.

There, beside the bed in the furthest corner stood his alligator trunk.

Chapter 48: Finding his way

After a fitful night kept awake by coughing and stifled whimpers, Eddy sat up in an unfamiliar bed surrounded by boys of varied ages waking up to their new reality too.

Next to him was a boy of about 8. He had reddish brown hair and a face full of freckles and dried tears. Eddy leaned over and whispered, "How's it going, old chap?"

"They sent me back. The farmer I was with said I was stupid and lazy and he didn't want me no more."

"It will be alright. What can I call you?

"Jeremy Powell" he said.

"Get dressed Jeremy. We'll go down to the dining room together. We'll get some grub there."

Herded along by the matron, they filed their way to the morning meal. It wasn't much but it would fill their bellies anyway. He sat Jeremy down with some boys his age, and then wondered off to find some boys he could sit with. "Can I sit with you guys?" said Eddy

"Sure. Hey, you look as if you live here with the way you talk."

"Nah, it's just temporary. They haven't figured out what to do with me yet."

His mind wondered back to his days in this house and remembered how confused and lonely he felt. It seemed he was the only 'old boy' here. All the boys now here must have been sent back because it didn't work out for them on the farms to which they were indentured or boarded out. The ships had stopped shipping migrant children during the War. They would start up again in late May and this place would be packed again. Why worry about it, he thought. It's a waste of time. He had to start figuring out how to get out of this place.

After breakfast, he was assigned his tasks, mopping down the floors, gathering up the slop and rubbish from the kitchen and carrying wood for the parlour stoves used to heat this drafty place. He moved about strategically. Before too long, Eddy had struck up a conversation with the rubbish collector. He was a scruffy old man with a fellow about the same age as himself as his helper. They sat in a crude cart with a bench up front to sit on when they were driving the draft horse who looked as old as his master.

"Hello, there, I'm Eddy and I'm the new boy."

"So, what, just throw that garbage in the cart and the slop in that barrel there", he bellowed.

"Okay, okay, I get it."

Eddy figured that he could get some valuable information out of them because they knew the ropes. Rubbish collectors get around and some people's trash was someone else's treasure so they might have a little business on the side. "How's things?"

"Pickin's never good at this place and, anyways, since the war, it's been almost empty 'cept for the rejects they send back. You must be one o' them. Down town at Eaton's is where the treasures is."

In London, Eddy remembered their chant, "Any old bottles or bones."

After loading the trash, Eddy said, "do you guys come by every day?'

"Course we do, idiot.. You got trash every day so every day, we're coming by. The rats have a feast if we miss a day."

After going back into the building, Eddy took up mopping. Joining him was a plump but cute girl whom he surmised to be about 18.She walked as though she was dancing and she laughed a lot. He wasn't sure if she was one of the maids, kitchen helper or a home girl. "Maybe she ran away too. Course not", he said to himself. "There are no girls here except the maids and the staff."

He stood holding the mop by his side looking the girl up and down. "She's got nice legs", he thought. "I'll start at this end and meet you in the middle." he said.

"Don't be daft. I do this every day and you do as I say."

Sidling up to her, he smiled. "Have it your way then. I'm not fussy."

They soon established a rhythm with the girl punctuating each mop swirl with the beat of a song familiar to Eddy as well, "Daisy, daisy, give me your answer do. I'm half crazy over the likes of you."

Soon, he was singing too. "I'll call you Daisy."

"Honest to God, you dummy, that is my name. My dad says they named the song after me."

The days melted into weeks and soon spring was in the air. He was getting to know Daisy really well even sneaking a kiss here and there. "Come on, Daisy, give us a kiss", he'd say.

"I don' wan a kiss."

"Just one." he'd say.

"I'm not getting caught with the likes of you", she'd say but she enjoyed sneaking around the corner when Matron was busy talking to the milkman.

Eddy was learning about the goings on in the hotels the rubbish collectors frequented. There were a lot of vagabonds about and heaps of travelers and immigrants of all sorts. Roland, the garbage guy's helper seemed to know everything.

"Say, Roland, you wouldn't ask around if there any jobs. I want to get out o' here."

Sure enough after a few days, Roland called Eddy over as he was loading the last bit of Sunday trash into the cart. "Listen up. Gladstone Hotel downtown is looking for dishwashers. They're not fussy. Want me to ask if they might need a guy like you."

"Gor' Blimey. Yea. Ask for me."

"I've got to know some nice girls who work there and they'll show you the ropes. I'll let you know tomorrow."

So later, mop in hand, he confided to Daisy. "I've got an idea. Swear you won't say nothing."

He told her his plans if he got the job and she swore silence. "Maybe I can get a job there too."

"If it works out, Daisy, we'll get out 'o here together."

Eddy was excited about adventure ahead but he couldn't help but worry about little Jeremy who reminded him of himself when he was first here in this cold mansion. "What's up today, old pal?"

"Nothin'," he said taking his thumb out of his mouth.

"Did you read the book I got you?"

"Not yet."

"I thought you liked reading."

"I like it better when you read to me."

"Okay, tonight before lights out, I'll read another chapter."

Eddy kept working waiting for the day when Roland would have some news.

It came sooner than he thought it would. It was Tuesday, a week after he first heard about the job when Roland grabbed him by the arm, "You've got the job. It's on the quiet. They don't pay much and they don't ask questions but if you work hard, they'll keep you and put you up in the garret on the top floor with all the others. Now, this is the plan. This Friday put your belongings in the trash barrel and load it on the cart. And when no one's about, we'll pile you in and put an old sack over you. And away you go."

"What about Daisy? You said you might get her a job too."

"Not so fast, buddy boy. We'll work on that bye and bye."

"Okay, Friday it is. I'll be ready."

Eddy didn't say a word, even to Daisy and Jeremy. A part of him thought he should stay put and do things right when out of the blue and half way to the appointed day, The Governor called him to his office.

"Good morning, Edward."

Standing stiff with his hands behind him Eddy blurted, "Good morning sir."

"I have some news. A farmer and his wife from Cornwall are interested in having you work for them. Of their two sons who fought in France, only one will be returning. The other died at Ypres. The one expected home this summer lost an arm so they are in desperate need of a strong young man like yourself. We would like you to be ready by Friday to take the train to Cornwall. They will meet you at the station."

"I, I wasn't expecting this so soon, sir."

"Well, where there is a need, we must oblige. You surely understood that it was just a matter of the right time and the right situation, Edward. Be up sharp at 7, get your breakfast and meet me in my office by 8 o'clock. You can get back to your chores now."

Eddy slumped out of the office with his mind in a blur.

"7 o'clock sharp? Roland won't be here until 8." He mused. Fast action was necessary. Fortunately, he had 2 days to organize himself so the next morning taking Roland aside he said, "You have got to get here Friday morning at 7. I'll skip breakfast. They hardly ever check attendance then."

"Fair enough. We'll roll up at 7 and have everything ready, do you hear?"

Eddy made sure to behave as normal except for his bundle of clothes which he hid in the slop closet by the back entrance. Friday came and before anyone had finished breakfast and chapel afterwards, Eddy had snuck out, loading the trash, the slop and his bundle of clothes on to the cart. Then with Roland's help, he climbed in and covered himself with a canvas cloth.

With his head well covered until they were safely on Yonge Street, they clattered along the cobblestone street, past the big shops finally arriving at the back entrance of Gladstone hotel.

"We're here, Eddy. Sit up as though it's been like this all along. Scurry in and ask to see Johnnie. They all know him and tell him that I sent you."

When Eddy got out from under the canvas, he jumped down, gave Roland a hand shake and hurried in through the doorway. The workers were busy putting food stuff on the shelves and on seeing someone strange suddenly in their midst, one yelled out,

"Hey, what are you doing here?

"I. I'm looking for Johnnie. Roland sent me."

"What's your name?"

"Just say I'm the new dishwasher."

"Okay. Come with me."

Sitting on a stool outside the kitchen was a man with a huge belly smoking a pipe.

"Hey, Johnnie, I've got someone to see you. He said Roland sent him."

"Jolly good, thank Roland and tell him I'll see him tomorrow."

"So, your name is Eddy. You got away. Good."

"Leave your bundle over there. Let's get you started."

The sinks were in an extension off the massive kitchen. Three girls were hard at work bringing dishes in, piling them by the sink and deftly clearing off the left over food into a barrel. There was one dishwasher and he looked as if he hadn't slept in a week. His hands were in suds piled high.

"Hey, got a minute, Frank. I've got you a helper. He can do the rinsing and the drying. We got to move this stuff a lot faster. Management isn't happy and with the hotel full, we got to get a move on."

Frank looked up through the steam, mumbled a few words and got back to work. Johnnie picked up an oilcloth apron off the hook and gave it to Eddy. "You can get to work right now." Eddy hesitated and then thinking the better of it, plunged into the business of rinsing the dishes Frank handed him and after placing each one in the drying rack, he repeated the motion until the first lot were finished and he could pick up the dish towel and begin drying them.

"I can help you with that" piped up the scullery maid whose job it was to give a hand when the dishes piled up. Eddy was glad of the help and he rather liked having a girl in a blue dress and white apron by his side.

"This ain't at all bad", he thought.

After his shift was over, he was led into the staff room where he enjoyed supper and then, he was escorted to his sleeping quarters on the fifth floor. He was told that the girls' bedrooms were on the other side with a wall separating them from the boys.

His roommates greeted him with, "Good to have you with this, Eddy. If you don't cause us trouble, we won't bother you. Want to join us in cards."

"I just want to hit the sack, if it's alright with you. That was rough work doing those dishes."

So, bidding his new mates, "Goodnight", Eddy fell into a deep sleep. He dreamed of the Jarvis Street home and he could hear the astonished Superintendent pace the floor when he realized that Edward George Tompkins had somehow got away.

Chapter 49: Heading out

Waking up in his new surroundings threw Eddy into a spin. For a moment, he forgot that he was sharing a room with fellow workers in a hotel in downtown Toronto. He was back at the Mitchell farm remembering that he must get up to start the fire when one of his roommates called out, "Your shift's already started Eddy. Better get going."

In a blur, he wiped his eyes on his night shirt and sat up. "Do I get a bite to eat first?"

"You're a bit too late for that but don't worry, one of us will get you a piece of toast and a mug of tea. You can grab something later."

He hurried to dress giving his face a wash over with cold water to wake him out of his bad start and he leaped the stairs two by two until he reached the sinks. There was no one except him to do his shift. The hotel guests were still eating so he had a few minutes to fill one sink with soapy hot water and fill the other with clear water.

He plunged his hands into the suds and it felt good warming his body in the process. The girls were just beginning to bring the dishes when Johnnie arrived in a huff. "It's about time."

Eddy soon got into the flow and he made sure he was on the job ten minutes before his turn from then on. There was lots to do in this town after his shift was through and the boys made sure to introduce him to some of the hang out joints down the street. The railway station across the street was a hive of activity and there were plenty of customers needing a room for the night, a meal in a fancy spot or a rendez vous with an old friend.

"Have a cigarette, Eddy."

"Try this beer."

He tried the stuff, laughed a little and kept his thoughts to himself.

After the first month and now it was Christmas time, Eddy got his first pay packet. Johnnie handed him a brown envelope just big enough to fit into his shirt pocket. He waited until he was in his room upstairs to open it. "$4.50. Wow!"

He clasped the 4 crisp dollar bills and put them in his top drawer. The change he put in his pocket. He'd live off the hotel food and save every penny he could.

New Years came and went with its hotel parties and this meant heavy work, soapy hands and a sore back but Eddy liked the people and Johnnie was a good boss. And while at work the first week into the New Year, 1919, he thought he heard a familiar voice.

"Hi there, Eddy."

"Daisy, it can't be you. I thought you'd never get away from Jarvis Street and Dr. Townsend."

"Well, I wasn't beholdin' to him anymore. I had served out my time with a farm couple in Barrie and they arranged a job in Toronto for me. I was meeting up with Roland regularly and as soon as he told me there was a job at Gladstone as a kitchen helper, I jumped at the chance. Townsend was none too happy but he bid me good luck and here I am."

"Johnnie helped you too then?"

"Well, he does well with the rubbish guys. He picks up stuff that people leave behind and Roland and the old guy find customers so it works for both and, anyway, Johnnie is Roland's uncle and the old driver, Weston by name, is Johnnie's brother in law. He looks older than he really is. It's all in the family, like."

"Oh, I get it", said Eddy picking his hands out of the suds.

"Okay, Daisy, enough chat" shouted Johnnie "Go in and meet the cook. You'll be working short order with him. No chef worth his pay cuts up his own vegetables. That will be your job once you get used to the knives." She glanced away from the thought of kitchen weapons and spoke to Eddy

"I need to tell you somethin' later, Eddy," she whispered.

"Maybe, we'll have our break at the same time. We can talk then."

"Okay"

Eddy didn't see Daisy until the following day at breakfast and bursting for news he said, "What's up? I'm dying to know."

She sat as close to him as the table would allow and leaned into his face. "I heard something at the home you might like to know but it could be hearsay. The talk was all about you after you got away and the kitchen helpers couldn't help but pick up snippets here and there when they served Dr. Townsend and the staff at table. It seems like there was a letter come for you from your mother."

"My mother? I ain't heard from her for years."

"From what they said, she wants you to come back to England to help on their farm."

"I don'wanna ever work on a farm again. But, I'd like to see my little sister. She'd be 15 now and it would be good to see my brothers again. It's been a long time. I've got a lot to think about."

That got the wheels turning in Eddy's head. Now, if he were to go to England, he'd have to save up his money and get to the port of Montreal. The ice on the St. Lawrence wouldn't be out completely until June and maybe he could get a job on a freighter then. Up until now, getting away was all he cared about but now an adventure loomed.

Daisy fitted in easily and soon she was too busy going shopping on her day off with her girl friends or happy trying new hairdos and make up to bother with Eddy. And he was busy working hard, occasionally going out about town with his mates or looking at maps in the small library off the entrance way. It was for the guests but in after hours when he dressed up with a shirt and tie, no one noticed him – no one who cared anyway.

Time passed and soon Eddy had put enough money aside to afford the third class fare to Montreal and a room near the Port.

It was June. The uniformed man at the ticket counter of the Station just across the street had told Eddy that the Port of Montreal was open and ships would be arriving from England and the Continent loaded down with soldiers returning home. They'd be filling the holds with lumber or wheat and other Canadian goods for the trip back.

"Do you think they'll be hiring."

"I should think so. Why? Are you thinking of shipping out?'

"I'd like to. My folks live over there."

Eddy talked it over with Johnnie who said he would give him a letter of reference and if he came back, there would be a job for him. In no time, his bag was packed, his money rolled up in a paper bag and slid between the bottom and the inner lining of his suitcase and he was on his way.

"Have a good time, Eddy. I'll miss you." Daisy said.

"See you." And with a wink and a wave, he was off.

He bought his ticket and picking up his bag and a rolled map he had taken from the library, he boarded the train. It didn't take long to reach Montreal. The miles just whizzed by. When he arrived, he walked straight to the Visitor's Counter. It was run by a benevolent group of ladies who were there to help passengers in distress or just help with directions.

"How can I help you, young man?"

"Where can a fellow get a room for a few nights?"

The older of the two ladies smiled and started searching in her pamphlets for an answer. She pulled out a brand new leaflet, looked it over carefully and said. "I think I have found you the perfect place. It's the brand new YMCA in downtown Montreal. I'll give you directions and you can catch a trolley outside the station. The driver will let you off there."

"Thanks, Mam. I'll go outside and watch for the next trolley to arrive."

Eddy could hardly contain his excitement. He liked the look of Montreal. The streets were wider, the shops fancier and he noticed the fashionable men and women in elegant dresses and fancy hats. He had developed a liking for expensive clothes even if he couldn't afford them. He climbed into the trolley marked Centre Ville and asked the man standing behind him in the queue where he could find the trolley that would take him to the YMCA.

"This one is okay"

"Thanks."

He boarded the trolley and sat on a hard seat towards the back. Before long, the conveyance stopped in front of a 5 story building with a Mansard roof. The entrance was imposing and the sign above it even more so. It read, ' YMCA Montreal. The first YMCA in North America.' Eddy gave the driver 20 cents and bid him goodbye.

Stepping down, he felt a bit nervous. He had not called to book a room. He hoped he would be in luck. It was 4 o'clock in the afternoon. He had to figure that he was early enough.

Putting a bold face on and picking up his heels, he entered the wide foyer and walked up to the counter which stretched right across the room. Above the counter, it read in bold black letters on a copper background, 'Dedicated to helping young men in mind, in spirit and in body.'

"Hello, Bon jour. How can I help you?" asked a young man dressed impeccably in grey trousers, a white shirt, blue tie and dark blue blazer. It had the crest of the Y on the left side.

"I, I need a room for a few days."

"I need to know more than that. What's the purpose of your visit to Montreal, young man?"

"I'm going to look for a job on a freighter."

"Did you say, 'Look for a job.' You mean you have not procured one as yet."

"No, I'm new here. I'm trying to get back to England to see my family."

"We like to know your plans before letting you a room but I can see that you are trying to secure passage to England by working your way across. That is commendable. What is your name?"

"Edward George Tompkins"

"I will rent you a room for 5 nights and then we'll see how you fare, job wise. If you need an extension, we'll decide then. Please write your name and home address here in this ledger."

Eddy wrote his name and he put as his home address, Bracebridge, Ontario, care of Mr. Mitchell. "They surely won't check that." he thought.

The young attendant led Eddy up 3 flights of stairs to a serviceable room with a sink. The single bed was next to the window and on the opposite end was a bureau. Eddy could see that the mattress was thin but the bed had two wool Hudson Bay blankets so that should keep him warm.

"Supper will be served at 6 so you have time to eat this evening and breakfast is at 7 sharp. There is a 10 cent fee for each meal."

"Thanks"

Eddy walked over to the bed and sat down. He jumped up and down to see how it felt. The springs seemed solid enough and, anyway, this wasn't the Ritz Carlton. He looked out the window at the city and in the distance, he could see the port with at least 4 ships berthed at the pier. He could see Mount Royal in the centre of the city and he remembered his history lesson about Jacques Cartier discovering the island in the great river.

He remembered the big river which had brought him and his fellow travelers as far as Quebec City and now he was down river about 100 miles ready to reverse his journey back to England, his country of birth.

"Tomorrow morning, I'll be out on the dock looking for work. I better be at my best," he mused.

His stomach rumbled a bit deeper than usual. He hadn't eaten since his lunch on the train. It was time to see about dinner. On reaching the cafeteria, he pulled out his wallet and placed 10 cents in the container, picked up a tray and walked along the long counters behind which were the various supper items. There were beans and mashed potatoes, ground meat with gravy and carrots and peas. A young man also wearing the YMCA crest on his apron served up Eddy's choices on a plate and handed it to him. At the end of the counter were hot tea and coffee, cocoa and bread and butter. Choosing tea with bread and butter, Eddy walked with his full tray to a table on the far wall. Then he realized that he had not picked up dessert so he put down the tray and hurried back to retrieve an apple pie and the napkin he forgot. Sitting down, it dawned on him that he had made his own choices for food and not just eaten what was put in front of him. That was new and exciting.

Chapter 50: Exciting to meet an old friend from the past

After supper, Eddy was taken on a tour of the Y's facilities. It had the latest in gym equipment for the young men who either stayed at the hostel or for the countless Y clubs being formed to ensure for their members 'a sound mind in a sound body'. Eddy was led to the Reading Room which was filled with books; he learned about the educational courses being offered and he was enthralled with the boxing ring and all the equipment to train.

Eddy hadn't been to the Gym in Bracebridge since last August after returning from the Mill and he never was able to reveal his interest in boxing to the Mitchell family. It remained a passion but one he had to put aside during those last months at the Mitchell household. And now, this Y had everything a young man could possibly want. He could even borrow the appropriate gym clothing. Tomorrow would be his first day in the gym and he could even practice weight lifting again. He could hardly wait until morning.

After breakfast on his first full day, he went downstairs to the gymnasium, borrowed gym clothes and hastily put on a pair of blue shorts and a blue top. On his feet, he wore sneakers, a super rubber soled shoe introduced to the mass market in 1917. As he looked in the full length mirror in the locker room, he could see his hero, Jack Dempsey staring back at him.

"Hey, that's me", he said.

As he emerged and walked over to the weight room, he noticed a tall blond fellow on the bench. Sweating and wiping his forehead with a towel, Eddy sensed a familiarity. There was something about the way he lifted his hand to his head that reminded him of someone he knew.

Walking closer but not wishing to make himself a nuisance, he ambled over to the lightest weights and organized himself to get ready for his first lifts. The tall boy stood up and looked over in the direction of the weights while raising his hands over his eyes as if to look into a distant view.

"Hey, there, don't I know you from somewhere?" he yelled.

"Seems to me, I know you too but from where?" replied Eddy.

Eddy put down the weights he was about to lift and walked over to the bench.

"By God, you wouldn't be Eddy? Would you?"

"It's me, Joseph. The last time I saw you was on the train heading for Ontario."

Eddy couldn't help but leap towards him and yell, "Joseph, it's so great to see you. I never thought I'd see you again."

They sat down on the gym mat, cross legged. The years vanished and they were back on the SS Sicilian and Joseph was teaching him how to box so he could protect himself from bullies. Eddy and his friend, Gordon, were just little guys and Joseph was their coach and protector in that strange world of guards and supervisors.

"It's so good to catch up, Eddy. I wondered how you made out."

"Well, it was okay I guess until the last couple of years. My boss Mitchell was tough on me and I ran away and here I am. What about you?"

"It was hard but we came to an understanding of sorts. I finished my contract out and I am getting ready to sail back to England if I can get a job on a ship."

"It seems I remember that you had no family so who will you visit when you get there, if you do get there, of course?"

"Hey, let's get back to the weights and maybe we can try a bit of sparring in the ring. I know the ropes. Been here for a month. I'll fill you in on England over lunch. But now let's do what we came down here for."

"Fair enough", said Eddy.

"I'll need a refresher, Joseph. Haven't been weight lifting for a while and haven't been at a punching bag in dog's years."

It wasn't like the old days. Joseph was 21 years old to Eddy's 17 but they could be equal mates now and there was so much to catch up on. During the lunch of soup and biscuits, Joseph began to tell his story.

"You see, Eddy, I was living on the street when the Barnardo people found me. Actually, it was the geography teacher who came to the place where we were hiding. We were living in an abandoned warehouse living off whatever we could scrounge, beg or steal. When I first saw you, I was nasty and I bullied you. I hate that I did that. But we became friends especially on the ship going over to Canada. You were such a little kid pretty wet behind the ears as they say.

After leaving you for Peterborough and the farm, I was able to keep in contact with the geography teacher, Mr. Jones, through the inspector, Mr. Peterson. Mr. Jones was finally able to track down who I was. I didn't have a surname and I could only vaguely remember a sweet lady who sang songs to me and then it was over and I was wandering the streets. I grew up on the street, Eddy."

"Gosh, that was hard. How did you survive?"

"You do. You get used to it. I had my mates and we scrounged food wherever we could. Dr. Barnardo saved me from all that and it wasn't so bad working on a farm. I went to school right up to Grade 11 and I was doing okay but they needed me too much during planting and haying season so I had to give it up. Anyway, I know a bit about myself and my family now. Turns out, I'm Scottish from Glasgow. My name is Stewart. My mother had me when she was 16. She died when I was barely 4 and no one cared enough to take me in. But, and here's the great part. My mother had an uncle who went to Australia. He came back to England after making money in the gold rush and he set up a printing business. On inquiring about his favourite niece, the daughter of his departed sister, he learned that she had had a little boy whom she named Joseph after himself but when he checked further, he learned that she had died. Not willing to leave a stone unturned, he finally learned that I had been sent to Dr. Barnardo's Home on Stepney Causeway and subsequently shipped to Canada. Through correspondence with the Jarvis street home in Toronto, he learned that I was working on a farm. He's offered me an apprenticeship so that's why I am going back. He said he could pay my passage but I want to earn my way across. So here I am. And to think that I had no idea who I was or who my parents were. I lived in no man's land and it's sure great to have a family."

"That's so good to know, Joseph."

"What about you, Eddy?

"I am going to give England a try but I don't want to work on a farm. After my mother dropped me off at the Stepney Causeway door, she went back to Buckingham to her parents. By then she had dumped all of us somewhere except for my youngest brother. She married a farmer and it's only now after all these years that she's told the Barnardo's that she would like me back to help her husband run the farm in Maids Morton. I would not have known except for Daisy at the Jarvis Street home who overheard this story. Heck, it might be just hearsay but it's an excuse for an ocean cruise. Ha. Ha."

At the end of this exchange, the boys headed to the gym to weight lift, take on the punching bags and spar a little in the ring. Then they showered, dressed and headed for the docks.

It was a hot day, so they slung their jackets over their shoulders and practically raced down the streets to the port. Lined up were ocean going freighters with two to three funnels. There were men and horses piled almost on top of each other loading grain from the West. At least 2 ocean liners had arrived and passengers streamed down the gang planks. They carried their lives on their backs. Children clamoured around and the stevedores hollered at them to get out of the way. Joseph and Eddy were lost in the crowds and had to maneuver their way to the loading sheds.

Joseph got up the nerve to walk up to an officer and say, "Any jobs on the ship? There are two of us. We're able bodied. I'm 21 and my mate is 17. We want to work our way back home."

"You'll have to come back tomorrow. When you do, go to that building to your left. They can let you know what's up."

"Nothing going today, Eddy. Let's take the trolley downtown and get a bite to eat in one of them French cafes."

The next day after a hearty breakfast, Joseph and Eddy walked down to the port. Most of the ships there the day before had left but new ones had arrived. They were impressed with the RMS Adriatic with its massive funnels and impressive prow. It carried both freight and passengers. Sometimes they took on crew at the last minute if they were short and after talking to crew members at the French café the night before, they learned that there might be a place on it.

"The best thing to do," whispered one strapping bearded stoker with a bit too much drink in his belly "is come down on Tuesday morning when she is due to sail. Just wait at the jetty, and if they need you, they'll beckon you on. I'll keep my ears and eyes open."

It was the first of the week and believing that they had a chance to get on the ship, Joseph and Eddy rounded up their things, enjoyed the gym facilities, and then set to work to spend the afternoon in the library catching up with the news and writing letters.

Eddy had been feeling remorseful about leaving his friends and turning his back on Mr. Parsons who had been reasonable with him especially after he ran away to Huntsville. He did have reason to be bitter with Mr. Mitchell but there were good friends that he had left behind. The only address he had was that of Mr. Parsons so he decided to write a letter and leave it with the clerk at the front desk to mail.

After purchasing some note paper, an envelope, a pen and a stamp. Eddy sat at the desk with an ink well and blotting paper. Situated by the window, he could look out over Mount Royal and muster his thoughts. He began with 'Dear Inspector Parsons' but he struck that out and started again. He decided not to name the place where he was. It was important to be vague. And he had to be sure to have the job before sending it on. After all, he had not completed his contract and he could still face jail even if he had good reason to leave as he did. On second thought, he would not give the letter to the clerk but mail it from the dock instead.

Dear Mr. Parsons,

I am writing to you from Montreal. First of all, I am sorry for all the trouble I caused you and for leaving Jarvis Street the way I did. Thank you for all that you did for me. Now when you are in Bracebridge, could you kindly relay my good wishes to Mrs. Mitchell and Ethan and when you visit the Gibson's could you ask Mrs. Gibson to give my best regards to my friends, Jack and Emily and her home boys, Jonathon and Randolph. Oh, and could you call on Miss Patterson and tell her how much I appreciate all that she did for me. Sorry, I don't know her married name.

Again, thank you.

Sincerely,

Edward George Tompkins

After using the blotting paper to ensure that there were no smudges, Eddy folded the letter and placed it inside the envelope. Addressing it and placing the stamp strategically on the upper right side, he sat with his hands folded, pleased with what he had done. Tears ran down his cheeks which he quickly brushed away. "How are you doing, Joseph?" he said.

Joseph didn't look up from his desk. He had more letters to write.

Chapter 51: Heading home.

Tuesday arrived with the sun coming up over Mount Royal. The church spire echoed the colours of the dawn and even from their bedrooms, Joseph and Eddy could hear church bells.

After a hurried breakfast, they rushed down to the dock where the RMS Adriatic was tied. Men with their shirt sleeves rolled up and the top buttons unfastened pushed carts, loaded bails as their bosses yelled orders and horses snorted at the loads being piled in the carts.

Joseph was the first to venture up the gang plank. He didn't wait for a call; he had to take the first step.

"Halt there matey. Wher'dya think yar goin?"

"We were told to come down here today. They are looking for more crew."

"Just a minute. I'll get the Officer who does the last minute hiring."

Joseph nervously fiddled with his thumbs while Eddy paced the dock looking up every minute he could without tripping over wagons and bales. It seemed like hours before a young man dressed in Merchant Navy Uniform walked over to Joseph.

"So, you and your mate are looking for work. Well, you're in luck. We have more freight than passengers on our return run to Liverpool and we have a need for a hefty guy like you to help stoke the engines and we could do with an extra cabin boy who is energetic and quick on his feet.

"Well me and my mate are just what you're looking for. We've been working on farms in Northern Ontario for the past 9 years and we've done everything from hauling and splitting logs, to working the horses in ploughing season to every bit of heavy labour you can imagine. Eddy, there, down at the dock is a few years younger than me but he knows how to work too. And, me, well, I know how to lift heavy hay bales and drive a team of draft horses."

At that, the Officer called Eddy to come on up. The three met in the purser's office for a quick interview where the work on board was explained. They filled in some papers and were told to gather their things and be ready to sail by 6.30 PM.

"Thank you, sir, and Thank you very much", they both said as they all but jumped down three wobbly steps at a time to the water's edge. Joseph sprinted ahead back to the Y and Eddy followed in a skip and a jump.

In his head, he could imagine the journey. He skipped over the work part and just thought about seeing icebergs and whales and maybe even an albatross although he knew there were no albatrosses in the North Atlantic but he got intrigued by the fact that they spent most of their lives at sea travelling across the vast Southern Ocean.

On reaching the Y, they went immediately to the reception desk and told the clerk that they were checking out. After talking a bit and sharing their hopes for the high seas, they went to the Cafeteria for a lunch of ham sandwiches and corn chowder.

"Say, what da yah think Eddy." said Joseph as he slurped down the hot soup.

"It's too good to be true. And so fast too. They must really need extra men. I wonder what a cabin boy does. I guess I'll learn pretty fast."

"You'll be a deck hand, Eddy, doing just about everything from helping the cook in the ship's kitchen to carrying food down to the forecastle to sometimes doing errands for the Captain."

"How do you know, Joseph?"

"I read a lot and I have been interested in stories about pirates who lots of times started out as cabin boys before becoming privateers."

"You're goin' to work as a stoker, Joseph. That'll be tough, won't it?"

"It sure will be working down way below deck stoking the big boilers that keep the ship going. They say the heat is awful but I figure I can do it for a week or two just to get over to the old country to meet my uncle. Anyway, let's get our suitcases, sign out and head for the ship."

"I must make sure I get my letter posted down at the dock." Eddy muttered.

"I'll get the desk clerk to post my letters. I don't have anything to hide." answered Joseph.

After goodbyes were said to the YMCA desk clerks, Eddy and Joseph lifted their heads high and walked slowly towards the great ship moored at the dock below. Eddy found a post office box and shoved his letter inside giving the box a kick and a kiss as he said goodbye to everything he had known for the past 9 years. He was just glad to get away. Maybe, there would be a welcome for him back in England but then he kept thinking that they had given him away when he was just a boy of 7. Why would they welcome him now?

Joseph and Eddy pushed their way through the crowds and with their new ship's papers received just that morning, they boarded the RMS Adriatic. The purser pushed them briskly towards the First Mate who showed them their sleeping quarter's way below deck in a dark hollow filled with hammocks and bunk beds.

"Grab a bed and put your stuff on it for now. I'll show you to your work stations but you won't start until tomorrow morning sharp at 5 o'clock. Go get some grub with the others."

It was getting close to 6.30, the time of departure. The engines were being fired up. The deck was awash with workers getting the ship ready and the paying passengers were out on deck looking down at friends and family who had just said their last goodbyes. Muscled men pulled up the anchor and the last moorings were unleashed and with a lurch, the ship began to move. Smoke arose from the funnels and the horn blasted three bursts of sound which almost knocked Eddy over.

Shouts went up from the passengers as they waved and yelled their last goodbyes and the people below waved handkerchiefs and arms straining their eyes as the ship slowly moved out into the great St. Lawrence.

On each side of this river discovered by Champlain two centuries ago were the farms of those who had settled the land for the French king. In the distance to the left were the Laurentian Mountains still snow capped even in June.

By this time, after grabbing some slim pickings in the galley, Eddy and Joseph stood on the deck. They didn't have to start work until the morning so they leaned over the side and watched the seagulls that followed them relentlessly as they sailed towards Quebec City and beyond.

"Say, it's a mighty ship, ain't it."

"Yea." answered Eddy but his mouth was dry.

He wasn't sure what he had got himself into. He didn't regret running away but he was going to cross a big ocean and he was shaking at the thought of what he would say to his mother. He wasn't sure he wanted to see her. After that day when she dropped him off saying she would return with his favourite sweet, he had never heard from her. There was never a birthday card, a Christmas present or anything that showed she cared.

"A penny for your thoughts, Eddy?" said Joseph.

"They're not worth a penny. Let's leave it at that."

"Let's make ourselves scarce and go below. We're goin' to have to get used to this hulk so let's look around."

They walked to the decks below finding their way into steerage. This place had been filled with immigrants from Russia, Romania, Italy and Ireland but on the return voyage, it was mostly empty. One family huddled together speaking a language neither boy had ever heard. Eddy and Joseph wondered why they were going back and later they learned that they had not passed inspection from the Customs and Immigration officials and were being deported to their homeland.

As they sailed past Quebec into more open waters, the boys bedded down. They closed their eyes only to be awakened sharply at 5 AM. Before reporting for duty, they went up on deck. Eddy opening his eyes wide to catch the first glimmer of light leaned over to Joseph.

"Gosh, it's hardly dawn and we are a long ways out on the St. Lawrence." he said.

Afterword

My father sailed to England at the end of the First World War on a ship he had boarded in Montreal. He worked his way across as a cabin boy. He was 17 years of age. He finally met up with the mother who had abandoned him as a little boy. It was not a happy reunion. He stayed awhile there and spent time getting to know his older brother James Tompkins who had been raised by his maternal grandparents, his younger brother Arthur Stopps who had been given the surname of his mother's new husband and his sister Beatrice Tompkins who later married and became an Ackford because, as she put it, she wanted a name that bore no taint. His mother Ellen Tompkins had lived with a married man, Edward George Reynolds and she bore him 6 children, 2 of whom died. It was this sham marriage and subsequent abandonment that forced her to make the decision that led to my father's unceremonious dumping at the Dr. Barnardo Home for destitute children. Dad was the only one in the family sent to the Colonies, as they called Canada and other places in the British Empire. His brothers stayed near her in Buckingham and his sister was sent to a foster home.

On his return, he stayed only a few months earning the name of Red the Indian from Canada. He tanned a deep brown in the summer while his siblings were light skinned and very British. He couldn't wait to leave and return to Bracebridge to the place of his indenture. He boarded the SS Metegama and arrived in Saint John in January 1920.

After his return to help with the haying season, he rode the rails out West to work the harvest and finally headed south riding on the top of a box car until he reached Richmond, Virginia and Jack Dempsey's boxing camp. He stayed awhile sparring with would be prize fighters and then went on to Asheville, North Carolina. He married there and had 2 sons Paul and Ross. He gave them the name Reynolds, his father's name. Sadly the marriage ended and he finally married again, raised a family of 4 and left for New Brunswick in 1947.

Bibliography

Bagnell, Kenneth. The Little Immigrants The Dundurn Group, Toronto, Oxford

Bean, Phillip, Joy, Melville. Lost Children of the Empire

Corbett, Gail. Nation Builders, Barnardo Children in Canada, Dundurn Press, 2002

Denniss, Gary. Macaulay Township, In Days Gone By, Herald Gazette Press, Bracebridge, 1970

Humphreys, Margaret. Empty Cradles, Doubleday

Roberts-Pichette. Great Canadians Expectations, Global Heritage Press

Printed in Great Britain
by Amazon